W9-BTP-380

ST. MARTIN'S

MINOTAUR
MYSTERIES

GET A CLUE!

Be the first to hear the latest mystery book news...

With the St. Martin's Minotaur monthly newsletter,
you'll learn about the hottest new Minotaur books,
receive advance excerpts from newly published works,
read exclusive original material from featured mystery
writers, and be able to enter to win free books!

Sign up on the Minotaur Web site at:
www.minotaurbooks.com

ST. MARTIN'S PAPERBACKS TITLES
BY RANDY WAYNE WHITE

Sanibel Flats

The Heat Islands

The Man Who Invented Florida

THE MAN WHO INVENTED FLORIDA

RANDY WAYNE WHITE

St. Martin's Paperbacks

*This book is for Hervey, Jon, and Casey Yarbrough,
Steve Wise, Jim Lavender, Peter Matthiessen, Dr. Dan
White, Lee and Rogan White, Bob Fizer, Gene Lamont,
Co. Don Randell, Dr. Tom Gillaspie, Roberts Wells, and
Dr. Harold Westervelt—allies who have, during many
travels and trials, proven steadfast in their friendship
and unfailing in their support.*

THE MAN WHO INVENTED FLORIDA

Copyright © 1993 by Randy Wayne White.

All rights reserved.

For information address St. Martin's Press, 175 Fifth Avenue, New York,
NY 10010.

Acknowledgments:
For permission to reprint the words and music of "Orange Blossom
Special," by Ervin T. Rouse, copyright © 1938, 1957, 1965 by MCA
Music, a Division of MCA Inc., New York, N.Y. 10019. Copyright
renewed. Used by permission. All rights reserved.

Library of Congress Catalog Card Number: 93-29099

ISBN: 0-312-95398-4
EAN: 80312-95398-0

Printed in the United States of America

St. Martin's Press hardcover edition / December 1993
St. Martin's Paperbacks edition / March 1997

St. Martin's Paperbacks are published by St. Martin's Press, 175 Fifth
Avenue, New York, NY 10010.

20 19 18 17 16 15

AUTHOR'S NOTE

❦

This book is a work of fiction. Names, characters, places, and incidents are either the product of the author's imagination or have been used fictitiously. An example: the town of Mango on the outskirts of Tampa should not be confused with the Everglades fishing village of Mango found only in this book. Another example: the late Ervin T. Rouse did exist, and the genesis of the "Orange Blossom Special" is put down as he related it. However, he was the author's friend, not Tucker Gatrell's. Mr. Rouse, the author believes, would have embraced the exigencies of fiction as warmly as he once embraced his fiddle at the old Gator Hook Bar and Grill. Otherwise, in this novel, any resemblance to events, locales, or actual persons, living or dead, is entirely coincidental.

The author also wishes to thank those who patiently provided information on genetic testing and on the marine sciences. Particularly generous with their time were: Dr. William Hauswirth of the University of Florida; Dr. Noreen Tuross of the Smithsonian Institution's Conservation Analytical Laboratory; Dr. Roy Crabtree and Dr. Paul Carlson, both with the Florida Marine Research Institute. For information on water turbidity and the procedures with biofouling sea mobiles, Marion Ford drew heavily from the work of Dr. Brian Lapointe. Michael D. Calinski of Marine Habitat Foundation, Inc., also provided an excellent demonstration on the filtering abilities of the units. It should be stressed that all errors, exaggerations, misunderstandings, and misstatements of fact are entirely the fault of the author.

*Here is land, tranquil in its beauty, serving
not as the source of water but as the last
receiver of it.*
—Harry S. Truman (Address at dedication
of Everglades National Park)

*Oh, goddamn it, we forgot the
silent prayer!*
—Dwight D. Eisenhower (at a cabinet meeting)

PROLOGUE

❦

The northern latitudinal line known as the 26th parallel bisects cities and countryside and rolling open ocean. It parallels the Tropic of Cancer in the Atlantic; it touches the Midway Islands of the Pacific. It joins unsuspecting villages such as the mangrove hamlet of Mango on Florida's west coast with uncaring cities such as the concrete tumult of Miami on Florida's east coast. The 26th parallel loops the earth, binding all sorts of things, linking the familiar with the exotic. As the earth spins, west to east, the line tracks the sun, creating a heat channel along the equator, so it is always hot and bright somewhere along its band.

The 26th parallel is no more important than any of the other latitudinal lines created by navigators, but it was of particular interest to meteorologists that autumn because of a strange thing that occurred in one of the parallel's regions, the Sahara Desert of North Africa. In September, a great wind began to blow over the desert. The wind was created by tropical air drawn to North Africa that sank, absorbed moisture, then shot skyward—a phenomena known as a Sahara High. A Sahara High is not unusual, but one that blows for more than a month is. The wind blew hot over Egypt, Libya, Algeria, and Morocco, gathering strength. It gusted, swirled, and grew into a withering gale that lifted sand—thousands of tons of sand—into the air. When the superheated wind, saturated with sand, collided with cooler air over the Canary Islands, there was a sustained explosion. The sand was blasted through the stratosphere into the mesosphere and was suspended there, fifty miles above the earth's surface. There, the sand granules attracted fugitive traces of vapor, creating noctilucent clouds—luminous formations that drifted seaward.

This glowing cloud mass, created by the great Sahara sandstorm, was visible to people in the unsuspecting villages and uncaring cities for thousands of miles along the western cusp of the 26th parallel. It was visible in Cairo and Casablanca and

Las Palmas. It was visible to people living in the Azores, the Abacos, and on the peninsula of Florida, too; fragile land breaks immersed in the sea, and thus more intimately connected with the wider world. At sunrise, the sun burned through a glowing curtain of peach and rust. At sunset, the sand-laced eastern sky caught the light and reflected desert gold. At night, the clouds smoldered in the wind and throbbed with dull flame.

The extraordinary thing, though, was that only a small percentage of people living along the 26th parallel noticed. In North Africa, there were wars to consider, and there was also the damage caused by the sandstorm itself. In the Azores and Abacos, spectacular sunsets were nothing new, but satellite television reception was. Sunsets could not compete. The same was true in Florida, but on a richer scale. There was television, Nintendo, tourist traffic, air-conditioned malls, lottery tickets, Epcot, condo association meetings, greyhound races, cool, dark bars, and water beds. October in Florida is hot. People don't get out to look at the sky much.

A few did.

On a Thursday morning that October, in the Gulf Coast village of Mango, Tucker Gatrell stepped off the porch of his ranch shack and considered the sky. It was dawn and the eastern horizon was the smoky, iridescent color of a hot camp fire. "Holy Lordy," he said, touching his old horse, Roscoe, on the muzzle, "I ain't never seen nothing like that." Then he stood and looked for a while before saying, "Either the Everglades is on fire or they gone and blowed up Miami. Probably killed millions." When Roscoe shook his head and popped the ground with his hoof, Tucker said, "Me, too. I'm pulling it's Miami."

On that same morning, on the Loop Road in the belly of the Everglades, Ervin T. Rouse noticed the sky for the first time, and he went inside to get his fiddle. More than forty years before, Rouse had written a song titled "The Orange Blossom Special" and he sold all rights to a New York publisher for three hundred dollars. The song became world-famous; Rouse did not. But he still liked to play and write, and, man oh man, that sky deserved a song.

Thirty miles north, looking through a second-floor window of the Everglades Township Rest Home, Joseph Egret blinked his eyes when he saw the boiling crimson sky and sat down quickly on his bed. *Them fat nurses,* he thought to himself. *Them fat nurses is giving me weird drugs. I gotta get out of this goddamn rest home.*

Up and down Florida's west coast, people living on boats noticed the sky because people on boats don't have much else to do. A man named Tomlinson, who lived on a sailboat in Dinkin's Bay, Sanibel Island, saw the sky, and the beauty of it was like a sweet, sad weight that brought tears to his eyes. He sat on the bow of his boat in full lotus position, face to the sunrise, and began his morning meditation: *This earth, this earth, so magic and so tragic. Magic and tragic . . .*

On another sailboat, anchored out in the same bay, Sally Carmel was holding a mug of coffee, staring. The strange clouds, the bizarre fluorescence—it was so lovely, but what could cause such a thing? Along with a lifelong interest in birds, Sally had a minor in interior design, a master's degree in photojournalism, and she knew a great photographic opportunity when she saw one, so she hurried below to get her camera gear. She would skip her morning swim.

Living on a house on stilts in Dinkin's Bay, a man named Ford, who ran a small marine-specimen supply company, noticed the sky and puzzled over it. He moved around the boardwalk that fringed his house and looked again. He checked his watch, for he was a punctual man and eighteen petri dishes, already prepared with saline solution, waited for him in his lab. But this phenomenon—this flaming orange sky—invited thought, and Ford could not resist. From the bookcase beside the reading chair, he selected three books and began to read. Ten minutes later, he put two of the books away, still puzzled. He stood and went to the world globe in the corner and, from a book on meteorology, matched the wind-stream currents to the 26th parallel on the globe. It took him a while to assemble the possibilities, but then he smiled to himself and closed the book. "Sandstorm over the Sahara," he said aloud.

Then Ford put the book away and began his work in the lab.

ONE

❦

Seen from a mile away, the sailboat was a solitary white husk suspended on space. Each day at sunset, a lone female figure appeared on the boat's deck, striped off T-shirt or bikini with a careless gesture, and dived into Sanibel Island's Dinkin's Bay.

It was something hard not to watch. But Marion Ford, who lived in a house built on stilts in the same bay, refused to watch. Not that he didn't want to. Oh, he wanted to, yet wouldn't allow himself—not since the first time when he stumbled upon the woman's ritual, scanning the bay with the Celestron telescope mounted on a tripod near his reading chair by the north window.

He'd seen the woman materialize out of the boat's companionway, watched her stand at the taffrail with her back to him, peeling the shirt over her head—a woman he had never seen before on a boat he did not recognize. Ford had held his breath, eye to the telescope, some atavistic sense hoping, perversely, that she would not be as attractive as her hair and shoulders promised. Then his breath caught as she turned slowly, shaking amber hair down onto tanned shoulders, good strong face, long, long runner's legs, and the late sun glazing muscle cordage, rich body, and body hair in honey-shaded light.

Ford had let his breath out slowly, watching. *Whew-w-w-w.* Feeling a pain akin to loss because, shimmering on the radius of the telescope's lense, the woman seemed as remote and unapproachable as a far small planet.

That first time, Ford had stayed near the telescope, watching her swim, waiting for her to climb up the stern pulpit so he could get another look. And he was at the scope the next afternoon, too . . . which is when he caught himself. . . .

Acting like some damn Peeping Tom.

And the reality of what he was doing, imposing on a stranger's privacy, set him back a little, offended his own sense of self, and that was it. No more telescope. Not at sunset, anyway, no matter how badly he wanted to look.

Ford found nothing wrong with using the scope to sweep past the boat at other times of the day, though. He had used the telescope before the sailboat arrived, and he convinced himself that it was a breach of his own private habits to give it up. So in the week since the sailboat had showed up, he had assembled a personal portrait of a woman he had never met but who, at sunset, drew his eyes like a magnet, standing on the stern of the small white vessel, a lean silhouette on the blue distance.

Island woman, with her long legs and long hair, skin glowing. Living out there alone, wearing floppy hats, taking photographs of wading birds and pelicans, up and out at dawn on her dinghy to use the stark morning light. Rowing the boat like she knew what she was doing. Bicycle lashed on the cabin roof, sack of oranges hanging from the stanchion along with the wash-bright cotton skirts, towels, and blouses—and a steering vane, so Ford knew she was rigged for a long trip, probably touring the coast.

He liked that. Independent woman out making her own way, designing her own life. At least, that's the way he imagined her, him sitting there alone in his cabin, reading or listening to his shortwave or working in his lab at night. Taking the unknowns and building them into a person of his own creation, seeing the woman he wanted to see, one that matched her beauty, and it gave him something to think about when the late wind freshened through the clattering mangrove leaves and night seeped through the cracks of his old house.

So why didn't she come out to look when he puttered by in his twenty-four-foot flat-bottomed trawl boat? Or idled by in his flats skiff, acting as if he was looking for waking fish but actually hoping for an opening to hear her voice, her name? And why did she never come into the marina?

Sunset was not an easy time for Ford. He busied himself in his lab or gave himself small jobs and hoped visitors would come by. He spent even more time working out—running, calisthenics, swimming in the bay—than normal, and, for the first time in his life, he began to read newspapers. Newspapers were great blotters of idle time, an effective antidote to introspection.

Ford avoided the telescope. . . .

FISHING CELEBRITY MISSING IN GLADES
THIRD DISAPPEARANCE IN
FOUR WEEKS

Television fishing celebrity William Bambridge was reported missing yesterday, according to a spokeswoman for Everglades County Sheriff's Dept. The host of the popular fishing show "Tight Lines!" Bambridge was reported missing by the show's producer, James Lawrence Jennings.

According to Jennings, Bambridge left Barron Creek Marina, five miles south of the village of Mango, alone in his 17-foot boat two days ago, Oct. 13, to scout the area in preparation for the next day's shooting. "He didn't come back that night," according to Jennings's statement to the department, "so we just figured he'd broken down. Since our sponsor manufactures the motor Willy uses, we weren't too eager for publicity. But we've looked and looked. We just can't find him."

Bambridge's disappearance was the third report of a missing person the department has received in the last four weeks.

On Oct. 1, Chuck Fleet was reported overdue, then missing, while working in the remote island region north of Everglades National Park boundaries. Fleet was working alone, and neither he nor his boat have yet been found. Fleet is a surveyor.

On Oct. 5, Charles Herbott, an environmental consultant contracted by the state, was reported overdue, then missing, while working in the same area.

The region is one of the largest uninhabited areas in the United States. It is known as the Ten Thousand Islands because of the complex network of islands in the area.

According to a network promotional release, "Tight Lines!" is a fishing show geared to upper-economic-income-range sportspeople. The release describes William Bambridge as "not just an ex-

cellent fly fisherman. He is also a college literature professor, and viewers love Big Bill's poetry
reading at the end of each show."

Bambridge is known as "Big Bill" because he is
said to weigh in excess of 300 pounds. He is author
of the book *To an Unknown Tarpon, With
Love.* . . .

Just before sunset on Thursday, October 15, Tomlinson took advantage of Ford's invitation to stop by the stilt house for supper.
Tomlinson, the late sixties hipster who wore his shoulder-length
blond hair and dark beard like tattered flags; a gentle-hearted soul
who power-pounded beer and grinned like a stray dog. Tomlinson,
who lived on his sailboat, a sun-battered Morgan moored a few
hundred yards off the mangrove bank and just across the channel
from Ford's stilt house. Lived there alone with his books on history and philosophy, his Moody Blues and Grateful Dead tapes,
the cabin smelling of oiled teak, diesel, sandalwood incense, and
the Japanese reed tatami mat upon which he sat to meditate each
sunrise and each sunset while his boat, *No Mas*, swung on its
mooring line like a weather vane.

Ford liked Tomlinson; liked the man's intellect, his kicked-
back quality; was amused by his outlandish hippie politics. He
had watched him earlier, sitting cross-legged on the bow of his
boat, burning incense: a bony silhouette as motionless as a wading
bird. Saw him stretch, disappear into the cabin, and return
dressed, hauling his dinghy in hand over hand, so Ford knew it
was time to finish up work in the lab.

Now Tomlinson sat in the chair beside the telescope at the
north window, wearing a long-billed fishing cap, a baggy tropical
shirt, and flip-flops, leg draped over one arm of the chair, holding a
beer. Miller beer in a clear bottle, and he was looking at Ford
through the bottle, saying, "Man a' man, you look weird. A real
strange shape and color 'cause of the glass."

Which Ford didn't understand at first, but then he got it: The
bottle was distorting his image.

"Uh-huh. Just don't spill anything. I scrubbed the floor yesterday, got down on my hands and knees."

"You know the transporter room on 'Star Trek'? An energized

body getting beamed down—that's the way you look. Or that crazy sky this morning. Fizzy molecular dispersement."

"Right." Not paying much attention, Ford was concentrating on his old shortwave radio, a Zenith Trans Oceanic. Beside the radio, on the table, was curled a black cat, Crunch & Des. The cat had been named after two famous fishing guides by the fishing guide friend who owned him. Ford said, "I cleaned out my main fish tank, too. Changed the sub sand filter, checked the salinity, the pH. The whole business. I had a squid die last week, always a sure sign of trouble. They're so delicate."

Tomlinson said, "Wouldn't you hate getting ordered on a landing party with Kirk and Spock?"

"Huh?"

"The television show. Being sent down with those guys."

"Spock? I don't think I know . . . Dr. Spock, the baby guy?"

Tomlinson was still viewing the world through the bottle: a huge blue eye. "Just about certain death for a common crewman, getting beamed down with Kirk and Spock. They don't last even one commercial. I'd crap my pants right there on the command deck, tell Kirk I'd gotten some bad Romulan prunes or something." He lowered the bottle, resting it on his leg as something on the table caught his attention. "Hey," he said. "You aware of that? Your phone, it's off the hook."

Ford said, "I know."

"You want it off?"

"That's right."

"Because you were working in the lab and didn't want to be bothered, huh?"

Ford, who tried to make a living from his small biological supply business, said, "I was doing a procedure. Making up starfish embryology plates. The whole business has to be timed just right, and there are eighteen stages. From the germinal vesicle right through fertilization. Zygote, blastula, gastrula, the entire chain of development. I couldn't be interrupted."

"You started yesterday?"

"Nope. Got the order two days ago and I collected yesterday. I took Crunch & Des with me. He's a pretty nice cat."

Tomlinson was still staring at the phone. "But you're done now."

8

"For the day, yeah." Ford looked up from the radio. "Why? You want to use the phone."

"No—"

"Then you're expecting a call. You told someone to call you here." Being logical.

Tomlinson said, "Nope. I heard Jeth was trying to get in touch. I went into the marina this morning to get ice and Mack told me. He said Jeth tried to call you all day yesterday, only couldn't get through. It was busy—your phone. And you hadn't been into the marina for a couple of days."

Mack was manager of Dinkin's Bay Marina, which was just through the mangroves, three hundred yards down the shoreline. Jeth was Jeth Nicholes, the marina fishing guide who had taken off to travel to Palo Alto, California, but had ended up in São Paulo, South America, due to a miscommunication with an airline clerk who'd had no experience with Jeth's bad stutter.

The cat was Jeth's, and Ford was keeping him while he was away.

Tomlinson said, "So your phone was off the hook yesterday," showing Ford that he could be logical, too.

Ford said, "Maybe it was."

"Even though you weren't working in the lab."

"Guess so."

Tomlinson was smiling, tugging at the brim of his fishing cap, trying to draw the guy out and enjoying it. "You don't want to talk to Jeth?"

"Of course I want to talk to Jeth. It's not that."

"Ah. Some women hounding you. I've toured that course, amigo."

"Good Lord, no." Ford was growing impatient. But then he said, "Well, there're a few who call, but they don't exactly hound me. In fact, I wish a couple of them would."

Tomlinson said, "Then what? You want to be a hermit, just take the phone out. I can relate to it, man. Solitude. Nothing like it. Be a perfect way to go—if you knew how to brew beer and had a female hermit living down the road. Nice young one with blond hair, maybe. That would be a good spiritual way to live. Seriously."

Ford was kneeling before the radio, touching the fine-tune dial as carefully as the tumbler of a safe, trying to lock in Radio Romania. He had a brief mental flash of the red-haired woman out on her sailboat. Beyond the window was the orange windscape of clouds at sunset. It was swim time, and the woman would be out there on the stern of her boat. Probably taking her clothes off right now, standing with the moist air of the bay on her.

Ford made a point of ignoring the telescope as his head swung toward Tomlinson. He said, "I've got the phone off because this old guy I know, lives down the coast, he's been calling me a lot, and I got tired of it."

"Oh. So it's not Jeth."

"No, it's not Jeth. It's this old guy."

"Why don't you want to talk to him?"

"The old guy? Because he's crazy, that's why. Or probably just senile." Correcting himself because he preferred precise language. "He's about seventy-one, seventy-two. Senile dementia. Or alcohol poisoning. Both, maybe, the way he drinks."

"So why's he bothering you?"

Thinking, When Tomlinson hasn't had food, the beer affects him and he asks too many questions. Ford said, "Because I used to know him. I mean, I do know him." Which wasn't enough for Tomlinson; Ford could read it in his expression, so he added, "He's my uncle." And knew instantly that was a mistake.

Tomlinson said, "You mean you're not taking calls from your own uncle?" Packing a lot of disapproval into his tone.

Pious old hipster. . . . As if he didn't have the ethics of a goat. Standing, suddenly eager to get supper going, Ford said, "That's right, I'm not taking his calls," already surveying things in the little kitchen: propane stove, countertop, sink with spigot that piped in rainwater from the wooden cistern outside, braced at roof level. Nice grouper fillet soaking in lime juice for him; green tomato slices with sweet Florida onion he'd fry for Tomlinson if Tomlinson would just let the damn issue drop.

But Tomlinson wouldn't. "That's not the uncle who raised you, is it? The old guy who played Triple-A baseball with Preacher Roe? Way back?"

"He didn't raise me. I lived with him for three years. Well, two—it just seemed like three."

"Then it is him. On that little ranch. You told me about it. Mango? The name of the town where you lived."

"Mango isn't a town; it's not even much of a . . . well, it's an old fish camp about thirty miles south, where the coast turns in, just above the Ten Thousand Islands. It used to be a little cattle port, too, back when they shipped cattle to Cuba. And I think I've talked about this all I want."

"This old guy raises you, your uncle, and this is the way you repay the kindness." Tomlinson was shaking his head, genuinely disappointed. "I don't want to get heavy about this, Doc, but, karmically speaking, you're pissing all over your own aura. Black mood ring stuff, man. The vibes"—Tomlinson put his nose in the air, as if sniffing for rain—"the vibes here are definitely out of whack."

Ford was cracking eggs into a bowl, then he poured in Italian dressing and added six dashes of Louisiana Bull hot sauce. "Look, Tomlinson, I don't pry into your private affairs, and I'd appreciate the same consideration." Talking as he used the whisk, blending the batter as carefully as he would his lab chemicals.

"Hey, don't get chilly on me, man. Don't put the shields up. You're not under attack here." His mind drifting back into 'Star Trek' mode, but looking at Ford earnestly, his palms held out in supplication. "Who's your buddy? Come on, give us a smile."

Ford said, "Geeze!" but smiled a little, anyway.

"So you don't mind if I put the phone back on, just in case? For Jeth, I mean."

"No, go ahead. I don't care what you do."

Tomlinson stood, replaced the phone, and, while he was at it, crouched in front of the little ship's refrigerator and reappeared with another bottle of beer. "I shouldn't be telling Jeth's story, but Mack says he's become some kind of hero down there in Central America."

Ford looked up from the bowl. "Jeth's in South America. Brazil. I've been getting cards from him."

"Yeah, but a month ago he started working his way back to Florida, and he got to this little island republic off Honduras a couple days before they had a hell of an earthquake. Somehow, Jeth saved the life of the president's mother. Or his aunt, maybe. Now the president wants to reward him by making him a citizen and ambassador to someplace. France, I think."

"He's joking. Or Mack's joking. That can't be—"

"Mack was dead serious. Said Jeth was, too. Jeth wants your advice. Mack was pretty sure it was an ambassadorship."

Ford said, "With his stutter, Jeth probably said they were giving him an Ambassador fishing reel and . . . France? He probably said a new pair of pants. That's just crazy."

"This guy, the president, his mother was having tea on the presidential yacht when the earthquake hit. Or maybe his aunt. Some important woman, and the tidal surge swept her overboard. Everybody in the whole town is panicking, and Jeth looks out and thinks he sees a dog drowning. You know Jeth and animals. He swims out, but instead of a dog, he finds a drowning woman. He told Mack she looked like a Pomeranian. Now he's a hero."

Ford was laughing; couldn't help himself. Picturing Jeth down there in Central America, the hero of some island republic where he probably couldn't even speak the language. Being hosted at dinners, getting his name in the papers and considering an ambassador's post—though that couldn't be true. Not that Jeth wasn't smart, he was. But ambassador to France? Tomlinson and Ford played with the idea while dinner sputtered in the cast-iron skillet; exchanged different scenarios as gray dusk absorbed orange sunset, then faded to darkness, with stars sparkling beyond the stilt house's windows. They were still talking about it, just finishing dinner, when the telephone rang.

Ford said, "Boy oh boy oh boy."

Tomlinson was already up, headed for the phone. "Probably Jeth's social secretary. Doing phone gigs while someone feeds Jeth grapes." But when Tomlinson picked up the phone, he said, "Nope, this isn't Duke. There's no Duke— Oh! Hey, wait a minute—" Tomlinson put his hand over the mouthpiece, looking at Ford. "Does your uncle call you Duke? It's an old guy—"

Ford said, "I knew it."

Into the phone, Tomlinson said, "You want Doc Ford? Hah! You call 'em Duke?" To Ford, Tomlinson said, "Tucker Gatrell. It's your uncle, right? Why's he call you that?"

Ford thought, Because he's crazy as a loon, that's why. He was standing, taking his time while Tomlinson said, "Sir, you don't mind me asking, why do you call him Duke?"

As Ford took the phone, Tomlinson was laughing, repeating what he'd heard: "Said because you sit on your butt all the time, read books, and act like an asshole!"

Ford said, "Good to talk to you, too, Tuck. But don't call me Duke," talking into the phone but giving Tomlinson an evil look.

Ford listened, then he said, "Some drugged-out old hippie who hits me up for free meals. Uh-huh, probably a draft dodger. Commie drug fiend, yep, no doubt. Yeah, that's him laughing. Kind of a hyena sound. Uh-huh. Firing squad, you bet, they probably shoulda. Machine-gunned the whole bunch."

Ford was listening, still looking at Tomlinson. Then he said, "I know, I know, you already said . . . great discovery, amazing stuff. Why wouldn't I believe something like that?" He was silent for a time, then said, "Your horse, Roscoe, right. Sounds like quite an animal. But I'm a biologist, not a vet. Besides, I don't have the facilities to test water. Not the kind of tests you're talking about."

Ford listened a while longer, and Tomlinson's eyebrows raised a little when Ford said, "But I'm not the guy for the job. You need a real scientist for that. Cellular regeneration, fascinating stuff, but way out of my league. I just don't carry that kind of weight—"

Tomlinson waited patiently, moving dishes to the sink, listening, until Ford hung up the phone. Then Tomlinson said, "That's the crazy old man? He sounded full of vinegar to me. What's he want?"

Ford swung down into his chair, turning his attention to the shortwave radio. "I don't know what he wants. Tuck never comes out and says what he wants." Being uncommunicative again.

"Ah, come on, he was telling you stuff—"

"He didn't tell me anything."

"Sound carries in a room this size. Cellular regeneration. I heard that."

Ford said, "He likes to steer people. Like his cows. Turn them this way and that. A Florida cowboy, that's what he was. A fisherman and a cow hunter. Tuck never comes right out and says what's really on his mind. He wants to use me somehow. It was bad enough when he wasn't crazy. I mean, senile."

Tomlinson said, "I like the guy and I never even met him."

From the old radio's speaker, a voice said through the static: "You are listening to the Voice of Romania." Still looking at the radio, Ford said, "Here's an example. What Tuck told me was. . . ."

"What? Come on."

Ford said, "He says his horse found an artesian well way back in the mangroves, and his testicles grew back. The horse, because he was drinking the water. He'd been gelded."

13

"Yeah?" Tomlinson sat beside Ford, noticing the radio for the first time, thinking, Romania? That's some powerful rock station. To Ford, he said, "Uh-huh? The water healed the horse. So what's the weird part?"

TWO

When Tucker Gatrell hung up the telephone, he thought, That nephew of mine. I shoulda whacked his pants back when I had the chance.

He needed to get Marion Ford involved in things; needed an outside helping hand with a little respectability up there in the county seat. Not that Marion hung out with those shitheel politicians, but at least he was a scientist—or so Tucker had heard—and them dim bulbs who always got themselves elected might pay attention to a scientist. Give him a little time, at least. Which was something they wouldn't do for an old person who had no money to speak of. When politicians looked at old people, all they saw was saggy skin wrapped around a voting finger.

Tucker stood tapping his big worn fists together, then he pulled out his pocket watch and checked the time. Little after seven, so what the hell? Why not just go ahead and keep things moving? Lord knows, he'd spent enough time talking to his attorney, old Lemar Flowers. And reading all that little bitty print in all them books and papers. Then flying all over creation with his buddy Ervin T. Rouse; 'bout froze his butt off in that ratty little plane. Now he had to start putting the rest of his ducks in a row, so to speak, find himself a helper, and he knew just the man—well, knew just the Indian, anyway. Joseph Egret, if he hadn't gone wacky up there in that rest home. Get Joseph and a few others; hell, start having some fun for a change. He still had—what?— nearly four weeks before that meeting old Lemar had finagled for him.

Yeah, about that. Three weeks and a few days till the state park people came down and tried to take his land.

So there was plenty of other stuff to keep him busy while Marion came around. Marion would, too. Say what you want about that nerdy kid, he was dependable. Good man in a fight; always was—at least until the navy people sent him off to college and made an egghead out of him. Goddamn navy. Marines, now there was an outfit. Not that the marines weren't shortsighted at times—like not drafting him during the big war because of his age. But he'd joined up anyway just to have the chance to meet those hula girls down there in the South Pacific.

Tucker rambled across the plank floor of his little ranch house, into the room that had once been Marion's, back when Marion was in high school. Cramped room with a window. Tuck kept his own clothes there now. In a pile on the cedar chest or on the floor, where they were easy to get to. There was still plenty of time to make the thirty-mile trip into town, but he wanted to look presentable. Find some clothes that weren't wrinkled or didn't smell like his horse, Roscoe.

Sorting through the clothes, Tucker was thinking, It's about nigh damn time I start looking respectable and make something of myself.

He'd been moping around that damn ranch, dirt-poor and lonely long enough. Yep, get off his ass and make a last-ditch effort to get the upper hand on those wormy bastards trying to run him off his own land. And that's just about exactly what he was going to do.

He stopped for a moment and looked beyond the window glare outside. He could see the silhouette of his barn—that needed fixing!—and the silhouette of Roscoe standing beneath a gumbo-limbo tree, probably asleep. A little ways farther was the jumbled form of his junk pile: boxes, car parts, a busted refrigerator, trash . . . and the rotting fly bridge of an old boat.

I hate seeing that damned old boat, so why the hell have I kept it around so long?

Talking to himself, Tucker answered his own question. "Because I'm a screwup, that's why."

It was true enough. He'd been screwing up his whole life; that's the way he felt. No wife, no children, no accomplishments, unless he wanted to count a bunch of inventions and other schemes that never worked out. Which he didn't. Didn't count any of them. They didn't deserve credence, he'd messed them up so bad.

Nope. Not a single accomplishment. He'd spent his entire life casting around like a pointer dog in search of anything that smelled even faintly of adventure. And what had it gotten him? Broad shoulders and bowed legs. Scars. Open real estate where his front teeth should have been. The stub of a right ear—the rest of which had been bitten off by a Nicaraguan lady in a moment of high spirit. A case of jungle epidermosis that lighted gasoline might cure, but nothing else would.

He had spent his life as a fisherman and a Florida cowboy, which was the same as saying he had pissed it away. He'd done everything there was to do on the water—and had invented some stuff no one had ever done before. He'd worked cattle in Cuba and Central America, spending his nights getting drunk by a camp fire or in some rat-hole bar, and his mornings fighting low blood pressure depression and hoping he hadn't promised to marry the stranger who slept beside him.

Tucker picked up a shirt, held it to his nose, and said aloud, "Whew-whee!" and tossed it aside. Well, one of his dreams had always been to be rich enough to have somebody to do his laundry. A big ranch house, too, with flush toilets. Yeah, and a cook who didn't give him any lip. Somebody who could cook Chinese and make tomato gravy. Maybe a couple thousand acres of land, too, with no fences and a string of good horses and, perhaps, one of those new pickup trucks with the great big tires. He could buy some bumper stickers for it.

Yeah, and a couple kids would have been nice, too, though Marion had come pretty close to being like that; a son, for a couple years at least. Only he never could quite figure out Marion. What the hell kinda boy was it that would hate the nickname "Duke"? Or spend his spare time catching bugs and fish and looking at them under a microscope?

Tuck had sniffed his way through the whole pile of clothes, then was about to go through them a second time when he figured, What the hell, he didn't mind smelling like a horse. Not Roscoe, anyway. Big rangy Appaloosa, white with charcoal spots on his rump, and he didn't smell half bad. Kinda sweet, really. Not like that fifteen head of cattle out there in the pasture beneath the coconut palms. Snot hanging from their muzzles, dropping pies all over the place. Made him not want to eat meat, and he wouldn't if he didn't like steak so much. Dumb cows.

But Roscoe wasn't cow-dumb; he was smart. Roscoe was so smart, he was kinda like a buddy. Hell, back in the old days, he'da ridden Roscoe into town. Did that plenty of times. But now there was too much car traffic, which Tuck didn't mind, but Roscoe didn't like it. Not that Roscoe was skittish, he just couldn't stand being passed. Made the horse real sour dealing with things faster than himself.

Tucker Gatrell dressed himself in jeans, boots, a blue guayabera shirt to match his eyes, then set his best triple-X cowboy hat on his head, a stained white Justin. From the icebox—he stilled used an icebox—he took out a bottle filled with silty black water, swampy-looking water he'd gotten that afternoon. He took a little drink, smacking his lips at the muddy, sulphur taste of it, and spit it out. "Man, that's rank!" Then he sealed the bottle and put it into a paper sack.

Goin' into town. Tucker thought, hit diggity damn. Getting that old Saturday-night feeling even though it was only Thursday. Carrying my ticket to fortune, fame, and maybe my own cook.

Then he pushed open the screen door, patted his old pit bull, Gator, on the head, and climbed into his Chevy pickup truck, roaring off into the October night, about to pay his first visit to Everglades Township Rest Home; find his old partner Joseph Egret.

No one lived at Everglades Township Rest Home by choice. Joseph Egret, age mid-seventies, certainly didn't. Elderly residents lived there because they were homeless or because the local courts had deemed them dangerous—an unattractive situation that the local media condemned at least once a year, then promptly forgot.

Joseph had not spent the last eleven months of his life at Everglades Township because he was homeless.

Tucker Gatrell knew nothing about any of this because he didn't read newspapers or watch television and, furthermore, he hated old people. More specifically, he hated old age. The fact that he was no spring chicken had no mollifying effect on his prejudice; if anything, it was sharpened. As a boy, his hatred of aging had been seeded by his own grandfather, who took strange joy in stealing sips from Tucker's drinks, then washing back nasty specks of cracker or tobacco. It would have made most boys queasy, but not Tuck. It just pissed him off. And Tucker Gatrell was never the sort to forgive and forget.

The lobby of Everglades Township Rest Home was empty when Tucker walked in—empty except for a woman in a nurse's uniform sitting in front of the television. Fat woman on a folding chair. Huge breasts and wide hips draped in surgical white, spreading over the seat like rising bread dough. Tucker stopped behind her and cleared his throat loudly. The nurse seemed not to notice. So he went to the desk and signed his name into the visitor's book, thinking that's what she was waiting for. But nope, she was still hypnotized by the television. On the screen were two actors in fancy clothes, their hair fluffed as if they'd stepped into a wind tunnel, then plunged their heads into hair spray. "Dear God," the woman actor was saying, "it's true—you are prejudiced! You beast!"

Tucker cleared his throat again, and the nurse spoke for the first time, lifting her head briefly. "Stop making that noise—please."

Tucker took his hat off, trying to appear sociable and respectable. "It's visiting hours, ma'am. Says so right there on the door. I got a person I need to visit."

The nurse made no reply until a commercial came on. She looked up then, as irritable as if Tucker were a six-year-old asking for a glass of water. "What are you doing out of your room? And where did you get those awful clothes?"

Tucker said, "Huh?"

"And that bag—you better not be trying to sneak liquor in here!"

Tuck was in a good mood, and he really was trying to be polite, but he wasn't made of stone. After all, these were his best clothes.

"I ain't outta my room, 'cause I don't live here," he said with some heat. "And it's none of your goddamn business how I dress. Just tell me where my old partner Joe Egret is and I'll leave you be."

The nurse leaned her face toward him. "That kind of garbage-mouth language won't be—hey, just who do you think you are?" She lifted her bulk out of the chair. "If you don't get back to your room right now, I'll call the orderlies!"

Well, hell, enough was enough. . . .

Tucker took two quick steps and kicked the television off its stand, really putting his leg into it. The television landed on the linoleum with a crack, and the screen went fuzzy, flickering and throbbing.

Tucker grinned at the new expression on the nurse's face. He had her attention now, by God! He spoke before she could get a word out. "Now you listen here, missy, you tell me that room

19

number—or my boot's bound for hemorrhoid highway. Comprendo? As in your backside."

The nurse's face had paled. "My God—you're terrible."

Tucker still had his smile. "Yes ma'am. I heard that before. Now where's my partner?"

"Our television set!"

"That's right."

"You . . . bastard!"

"You kiss your mama with that mouth?"

"Get out of here right now!"

Tucker took a step toward the woman. "I ain't gonna say it again."

The nurse took a quick step back. "The Indian? Egret, you said?"

"Yep, the Indian. A great big one." Tucker held his hand over his head. "About so high."

The woman's legs appeared wobbly. "I was watching my favorite show!"

"Just tell me where the old fool is, you can keep on watching."

"What I'm going to do is call the . . ." Then she paused, looking at the television. "Hey," she said, "it's working again."

"Not for long if you don't—"

"Oh, for God's sake! He's up the stairs. One of the rooms toward the end of the hall. Find it yourself."

Tuck started to walk away but then stopped. "I know what's going on in that mind a yours, ma'am. You're thinkin' the moment I head up the stairs, you're gonna call the law. Or them whatever you call it—orderlies? But I'll tell you what: You give me ten minutes with my old partner Joe, I'll leave real quiet like. You don't, you can kiss that television of yours good-bye."

The woman flinched, some of her anger returning. "I won't tolerate threats against our television set! It's our only recreation."

Tuck was smiling. "Then you best not risk it. Ten minutes. Understand?"

The television screen faced the ceiling. The actors with the sprayed hair were tangled in an embrace, whispering to each other. The nurse said, "You leave me alone till this show's over, I don't give a damn what you do." She glared at him once more, then didn't look at him again.

* * *

The rest home's second floor was a catacomb of narrow bed pens, and Tuck pushed open one door after another until he saw Joseph Egret. Joseph stood at the far end of the room, by the window. He wore a hospital gown that tied at the back; black hair hung to his shoulders; his head and his hands shook with a slight pathological tremor as he held his fingertips to the glass, as if trying to reach through to the outside.

Tucker stood at the doorway, looking in. Except for the window, the room was dark, and his eyes were having trouble adjusting. He was also trying to adjust to the room's odor. The stink hit him when he opened the door; caused him to snort and cover his nose. The smell seemed to come from the beds, only one of which was occupied: A shrunken figure lay connected by tubes to a sack of clear liquid suspended from a stand. The smell was a potent mixture of urine and some other odor that, had Tuck been younger, he would have recognized as the malodor of age and dying. He was standing with his hand over his nose when a quivering voice said, "It's that damn Indian. The stink. He farts continually and smells like a wet dog." The figure in the bed was talking, an old man with tiny bright eyes.

Tucker said, "Well, you don't smell like no box of Valentine candy yourself, buster," and pushed his way through the stench. He reached up to tap Joseph on the shoulder, saying, "Hey, you old fool—you gone deaf or something?"

Joseph turned to face him for the first time, and Tucker had to step back a bit—that's how surprised he was at the way Joseph had changed . . . had changed more in a year than Tucker would have thought possible. The great wedge of a nose was the same; the same high Indian cheeks, too. But now Joseph's beamy shoulders swooped like folded wings, and the sharp, dark, humorous eyes Tuck remembered were a syrupy glaze. He didn't seem nearly so big, either. Once Joseph had been six and a half feet tall, weighed probably 250. What the hell had happened?

"Gawldamn, Joe," Tucker said gently, not wanting to hurt his old friend's feelings, "these vultures stick a pin in you and let the air out? I've seen road kill looked healthier than you."

Joseph looked down, blinking at him, as Tucker added quickly, "Course, I don't mean that in a bad way."

There was no reason to get Joe mad; they'd been friends too long for that. Friends for more than fifty years, ever since they were teenagers, a few years after the completion of the Tamiami Trail, which crossed the Everglades and connected Miami with the west coast of Florida. In those days, he and Joe had developed a mutual bond that ensured honesty, affection, and scrupulous concern for the other—that bond being a massive white liquor still that either would have shot the other for. That still had produced forty gallons of liquor week in, week out, with little labor or upkeep on their part, and earned for them enough money to buy most of the villages on Florida's west coast. Had they wanted to buy villages. Which they didn't.

It had taken the two of them the best chunk of a month in Havana to piss all that money away, but they had managed. And they had been secretly proud of the inventive methods required to do it.

After government men destroyed the still, Tuck and Joseph had joined talents in a variety of enterprises over the years, which included running rum, smuggling in Orientals from Mexico, smuggling in Mexicans from the Bahamas, and running guns to Castro's revolutionaries, for which they received absolutely nothing and were, in fact, just happy to escape with their lives.

In recent years, they had spent a few evenings each month together. Sometimes, they'd poach a gator or two, knowing full well there was no longer anyplace in America to sell an illegal hide. Or shoot a few white ibis—curlew, Tuck called them—and fry them up with rice and tomato gravy. Some nights, Tucker would let some of his cattle escape, blame the neighbors, and contact Joseph with a desperate plea for roundup help. Actually, it was just an excuse to ride and drink as they once had, and the bulk of their sentences began, "Remember that time . . . ?"

Mostly, the two men drifted apart. All friendships begin on a chance first meeting and usually end on an equally unexpected last encounter. Friendship is more closely related to alchemy than to chemistry, so it is always a little bit of a surprise that the laws of mortality still apply. Joseph Egret retreated to a cypress strand a few miles north of the Tamiami Trail, where he lived in a shack with a thatched palmetto roof and a 1971 *Playboy* calendar on the wall. Tuck retired to his scrub cattle and mullet skiff in Mango.

The last thing Tuck had heard about Joseph was from a bartender at the Rod & Gun Club in Everglades City. The bartender told him that Joseph had been found, sick and near death, in his shack by some hunters, who had contacted the county welfare people. One of the welfare people had approached the sleeping Joseph with a rectal thermometer. Joseph had rallied sufficiently from his surprise to throw the welfare worker through the wall. The welfare worker contacted the Sheriff's Department, got a judge to sign the right papers, and now, the bartender told Tucker, Joseph was paying his dept at Everglades Township Rest Home.

"Serves 'im right," Tucker had said at the time. "Teach 'im not to throw white people around like that."

But that was before Tucker had descended into the despair of his own loneliness; before his horse Roscoe had discovered that sulphur spring; before Tuck had realized the spring's wonderful potential; before the state, those bastards, had tried to pin him to the wall.

Tucker was thinking about all of this when he touched the shoulder of his old and beloved friend. Well, he was thinking about it a little bit. Thinking that once he had been nothing more than a cow hunter with evil ways, but now he was elevating himself, coming to this nasty damn place to rescue an old friend.

"Joe, you okay?" Tucker asked. "Can you hear me?"

Joseph looked at Tucker, and his eyes seemed to focus for a moment. "Lordy God," he said, "I hope somebody locked up my wallet."

Tucker took the big man's arms and shook him slightly. "Hey, Joe, it's Tuck. Me, your best friend!" He'd expected a warmer reunion.

Joseph studied the face before him. His mind was a gauzy shambles of reality and dreams, and his eyes were milky. "I know who you are. We got another whiskey run to make? I want to count the money this time, you cheatin' bastard—"

Tucker was still shaking him gently. "Joe! Listen to me. We ain't run no liquor in fifty years."

"I don't care if it was a hundred. You shortchanged me on that run to LaBelle. Don't think I ain't got ways of finding out."

"How in the hell . . . I mean, damn it, Joe, you're talking nonsense."

"Say, Tuck," Joseph continued vacantly, "how 'bout we go jacklightin' tonight. Kill some gators. They're giving Indians four bucks a hide over to Miami. Seven bucks to white men, so I guess you better handle the sellin', but goddamn it, I want to count the money before it hits your pocket—"

From the bed, a querulous voice interrupted: "Why waste your time trying to reason with that stupid Seminole? He talks gibberish. Nothing but gibberish. And I need my rest!"

Joseph shook away from Tuck and lumbered toward the shrunken figure in the bed. "*I* told you about that," he said.

To Tucker, the dim figure yelled, "Make him leave me alone!" Then to Joseph: "Go away, you red devil, or I'll buzz the nurses' station and have the orderlies tie you down again!"

Joseph found the plastic tube running from the sack into the old man and pinched off the flow. "Take it back. Say I ain't a Seminole."

Bright Eyes moaned, "Are you trying to kill me?"

Tucker was right there beside Joseph, and he whispered, "Hey Joe—will that really kill him?"

Joseph shrugged. "If it don't, I can choke him," he said.

Tucker turned to the figure and directed hastily, "Say he ain't a Seminole. Say it real nice like." He didn't particular care about the old man, but for Joseph to get mixed up in a murder trial now would completely screw up his plans.

"Okay, okay," hollered the man, "you are not a Seminole." His gaze swung to Tucker. "Now please get this stinking Indian away from me!"

Joseph released the tube, saying, "That's better." Bending over the man, he added, "I won't stand for disrespect." Then he turned and tottered back toward the window, which is when he noticed the sack Tucker was carrying. "Hey," he said, "you bring me a present? Nice can of snuff, maybe?"

Tucker pulled out the plastic bottle and held it up to the window. "Better than that. I got something here that's gonna fix you right up."

"Hum," said Joseph, clicking his tongue softly. "White liquor, maybe? Only, hey—this looks kinda yella. You ain't playin' no trick on me. It better not be—"

"It ain't whiskey, and I ain't playing no trick, you old fool." Tucker put his hand on Joseph's shoulder and began to whisper. "I got a favor to ask, Joe. Big favor that could do a lot of good for us both. Say—I bet they make you take a lot of drugs and stuff here, huh."

Joseph's mind drifted away, then drifted back again. "Nothin' any fun. I just take pills. All kinds a colors a pills. The fat nurse brings them."

"From now on, I don't want you to take another pill. Not a one."

"But it's my medicine."

"Hell, you don't look sick to me. You feel poorly?"

"Dang right I feel poorly. I'm old."

"I'd do it for you, Joe. I truly would. You wanted me to stop taking my pills, I do it in a second. Just 'cause we're friends."

Joseph said, "Sure, you can say that. But they stick 'em up your butt, you don't take them. They got about six or seven orderlies here, and I ain't as young as I used to be."

Tucker was shaking his head, a pained expression on his face. "Just pretend to take 'em. Gawldamn, you're stupid! No wonder you ended up in this shit hole, without me around to do your thinking."

Joseph gave him a flat look of warning. "I ain't that old, Tucker."

Tucker Gatrell said, "Okay, okay, okay," and began to whisper some more. After a few minutes, Joseph said, "Roscoe's nuts growed back? So what?" Tucker whispered again, and then Joseph said, "I'm the one they got locked up, but you're the crazy one."

Tucker said, "There ain't nothing in the world crazy about it. This water's got vitamins in it . . . minerals. Something. You know what they got now? Hell, they got whole stores now that sell nothing but vitamins. And you go to a grocery store, they got shelves and shelves of water. People actually pay money for it! This here's like two things wrapped up in one."

Joseph's mind drifted away for a moment, and he said, "My granddaddy, he used to tell me about that."

Tucker said, "Damn right!" But then he said, "Tell you about what?"

Joseph reached for the bottle. "Let me have a taste. I'll tell you if it makes me feel any healthier."

"Well, you ain't gonna notice it right off, ya idiot. Takes time." Tucker jabbed a finger at the side of his head. "I was drinking the water for only about a month when this here ear I lost in a fight started to grow back."

"You didn't lose that ear in a fight," Joseph said dubiously. "Some whore chewed it off down when we was in Caracas."

25

"Nicaragua," Tuck corrected. "And it was so a fight—sort of. But that ain't the point. The point is, it's growing back."

Joseph studied the pink stub of ear. It didn't look as if it had been growing. He tried to remember what Tuck had looked like the year before, but all that came to his mind was they way he had looked when they were young men.

"My granddaddy, old Chekika's Son, told me," said Joseph. "Water where the sick people could go and get better."

Tucker was nodding, sensing that he was winning Joseph over. Getting a little excited, too. If he could convince someone as stubborn as Joseph in only a few minutes, it wouldn't be hard at all to convince a couple of million normal people in the weeks he had left. He said, "Hell, I'll help bust you out of this place now if you want. Damn—wish I'd brought my gun." Tuck was patting his sides, just in case he had remembered.

Joseph said, "Nope. If I start feeling good enough to break out, I'll do it when I'm ready."

"But no more of them damn pills. I've been reading about that. Just drink the water."

"I'll see how it goes. I don't trust you, Tuck."

Tucker motioned to the walls, the ceiling. "I suppose you like living in this honey bucket."

Joseph looked at Tuck. "When I'm ready"—meaning it was not to be discussed anymore.

Tuck left, but Joseph kept the bottle of water.

In a rare lucid moment, Joseph Egret wrapped the bottle in his dirty underwear and hid it beneath his bed. The rest home's staff never looked under the beds, perhaps because to look was to acknowledge the existence of bedpans. They couldn't empty what they didn't see.

Joseph hid the bottle with the few valuables not already stolen by the staff (all they had left him was his deerskin boots and his old black Wyoming cattle roper's hat), and so the bottle was there every morning and evening when he wanted a drink from it.

He also followed Tuck's advice about the dozen or so pills he was supposed to take each day. Medications, the nurses called them, bringing the bright plastic capsules around on a cart in rows of tiny paper cups. Had he refused to take the pills, the orderlies would have been called—he'd already tried that. So what he did was toss his head back as if he was swallowing the pills, but he really transferred them into his big hands, to be thrown into the toilet later. The nurses didn't pay a lot of attention. They were busy making check marks on their charts so they could hurry and get back to their television programs downstairs.

On the third day, Joseph awoke, realizing that the numbness that had long deadened the left side of his body had disappeared. Like an arm that falls asleep and then slowly awakens, there was a strange residual itch, but it was not unpleasant. And the numbness was certainly gone. He also began to experience a growing restlessness, a sort of psychic itch—which *was* unpleasant. He had spent the bulk of his eleven months at Everglades Township Rest Home in a drug-induced reverie, never really coherent enough to realize or wonder how his life had degenerated to the point where he now carried a catheter bag on his hip as comfortably as he had once carried a .38-caliber Smith & Wesson. This new itch filled him with a black depression that caused him to be feisty by rest home standards. He broke the tiny mirror in his room because he did not like the gaunt reflection that stared back at him. That did not assuage his despair, so he went from room to room breaking every mirror he could find. Joseph also discovered that he was desperately hungry, so he sneaked to the kitchen, threatened the head dietitian with a knife, and rummaged through cans of government surplus food until he found two pounds of hamburger, which he ate raw. On the way back to his room, he yanked out his own catheter tube, went to the bathroom, and, after enduring an initial burst of pain, found he didn't need the damn thing.

The orderlies had had more than their share of trouble with Joseph, and when they found him, they knew what to do. They tied his hands and feet with plastic tie wraps and threw him facedown on his bed. Four hours later, when he was released, old Bright Eyes in the next bed made an observation about Indians that Joseph found offensive. In his dark mood, there seemed only one honorable thing to do—beat the little bastard to death. He would have done it, too, if one of the fat nurses hadn't banged into the room, looking for the individual she referred to as "the perverted son of a bitch who stole our *TV Guide.*"

The orderlies tied his hands and feet again; left him bound all night.

On the morning of the fifth day after Tuck's visit, Joseph awoke, finding a mature but attractive rest home volunteer standing over him. The woman had a sponge in her hand and a name tag that read MARJORIE. Joseph rubbed his eyes clear and saw that she was staring at him, a vexed expression on her face. Which puzzled Joseph until he noticed that the sheet over his hips peaked with the abrupt contours of a two-man mountain tent. He peeked under the sheet to see what created the tent, then returned from beneath the covers, surprised and pleased.

"Mr. Egret," the woman said, "I hope you're not hiding something under that blanket." She said it primly, but kindly, too. Her hair was gray-blond, she had nice brown eyes, and the pink volunteer's uniform brought out the color of her face. He had never seen this woman before; they rarely got volunteers.

"Please," the woman said, "I'm giving you a chance."

Joseph combed his fingers through his hair, hoping he looked as good as he felt.

"I'm scheduled to give you a sponge bath, but if that's a liquor bottle under the covers, I'll . . . well, I won't report you—just as long as you take it to the bathroom right now and dispose of it."

Joseph settled himself, folded his hands behind his head, and smiled rakishly.

"Please, Mr. Egret. If you don't cooperate, I'll have to notify the nurses, and you will be in a great deal of trouble." The woman tried to sound stern, but sounded nervous instead. Maybe it was her first day as a volunteer. Maybe it was her first sponge bath. Joseph wagged his eyebrows and said nothing.

The woman took a deep breath, reached up, and pulled the privacy curtain around his bed, then threw back the sheet that covered Joseph's hips.

The woman was astonished. Joseph would have known that from the expression on her face, even if she had not sputtered, "Goodness gracious!" Surprised and maybe a little bit pleased, too, for Joseph was guilty of hiding neither a wine nor a whiskey bottle. He was only in a romantic mood. "Why . . . I'm very sorry!" The woman's face was red, and she was smiling but trying not to, and he hoped he recognized a flicker of interest in her eyes.

Joseph didn't mean it, but he said, "I sure am sorry about this, too, ma'am. But a woman pretty as you, I just can't help myself." Testing the sincerity of her interest, watching her face.

"You don't have to apologize. . . . I should have been more . . . then I was just so surprised. . . . I mean, it's not like I haven't . . . I mean, I have a gentleman friend, but we don't . . . then to see *that . . .*"

She was stammering so badly, Joseph reached out and took the woman's hand. Then he held her when she made a unenthusiastic effort to pull away. Joseph was no bully, but it had been his experience that a woman came to a man's bed only for one reason.

"Please, Mr. Egret, I'm working."

He was pulling her closer, closer, then he pressed a friendly kiss to her mouth, tasting the lipstick.

"You can't do this, Mr. Egret. . . . We can't . . . I don't even know you: I'm not well; I'm not. I have this heart condition . . . please!"

Joseph interrupted modestly, "Aw ma'am, I'm pretty sure your heart's outta my range."

But the woman would not consent, and so she sat and talked to him for nearly an hour. He told her stories. He made her laugh. He knew white people liked to hear the old stories about what it was like to be an Indian in the Everglades. A few of his stories were even true.

She gave him a hug and a little kiss before she left, and Joseph had the feeling she might be back. He was right. Long after dark, she leaned over his bed as if to see whether he was awake, and Joseph kissed her. The volunteer whispered, "Hi there yourself!" and immediately assumed the sexual offensive, attacking him with a vigor that startled Joseph and made him feel almost meek.

Later, she gave him a sponge bath and rubbed his back. The next day, when she was supposed to be at her gentleman friend's country club selling baked goods for the greenskeepers' fund, Marjorie returned instead to the rest home with a tin of Copenhagen snuff and a brand of chocolates that Joseph Egret said he loved.

THREE

❦

Late Monday morning, October 19, Ford was standing over a half dozen five-gallon buckets, all of them filled with seawater. Along with the seawater, each bucket held odd-looking mobiles made of wood and rope. From each of the five wooden crosspieces hung nine short lengths of rope knotted into another wooden crosspiece on the bottom. And each strand of rope was alive—or so it seemed to Ford. Each was a solitary host to a small world of living, siphoning jelly masses and sea growth: sponges, soft corals, tunicates, sea squirts, barnacles, oysters, and tiny skittering crabs.

"Biofouling assemblies," the books called the strange mobiles. Ford had made these himself, then set them out in the bay beneath buoys to attract sea life. One month later, this was the result.

Ford bent over the buckets and looked into them. A few of the crabs had jettisoned from the hanging mass and now crawled around the bottom. He wanted to weigh each assembly so that he could calculate how much growth the units might be expected to attract on a week-to-week basis. Later, after they had spent more days and nights floating in the bay, he wanted to be able to arrive at the optimum growth potential for each assembly. Set up a cubic-inch ratio.

For the research paper he wanted to do, such bits of datum would be important.

He stared at the buckets, hefted the weight of the sea mobiles experimentally, then gently returned them to the water. He scratched his nose, then hefted another.

I'm wasting time, he thought.

His notebook and pencil were at his right on the stainless-steel dissecting table. But the screened window was on the left—a window through which, if he bent just a little, he could see the lone sailboat out there near the mouth of Dinkin's Bay. So his mind kept wandering; kept thinking about the woman. Not consciously thinking of her—not much, anyway—but a steady undercurrent of musing and projecting going on in the cerebral layers that should have been considering the biofouling assemblies.

Not that he wasn't interested in his creations. He was. It was a new hobby, a fresh little project. Ford always had a short list of new projects and a long list of old ones. He was compulsive about it, as if he didn't want a free moment in which his mind might be allowed to wander. It was always one species or phenomena after another: bull sharks or tarpon or redfish or red tide. Filling notebooks with diagrams and observations in his tiny fine print. Dissecting or photographing or collecting and cataloging. Spending orderly hours in an orderly day interrupted only by his nightly timed runs (from Dinkin's Bay Marina to Sanibel Island Elementary and back), calisthenics, and a swim in the bay.

But Ford's mind was wandering now. Taking the lithe brown shape he'd seen through the telescope and giving the woman a more detailed face; supplying her with a cool, sure personality. Putting himself on the boat with her, relaxed and lost in interesting conversation. She'd be intelligent, of course. Many sailors were, though their egos too often were proportional to their intellect, which was a sign of immaturity. But that wasn't an absolute; no proof that she would be that way. And sailing a boat single-handedly along this shallow-water coast implied a rogue spirit that he liked. And to strip off her clothes like that and dive into murky water where lesser, prissier people worried about sharks and stingrays . . .

Ford threw down the pencil he was holding. "Concentrate, damn it!" Talking to himself, trying to get his mind back on the project at hand. "You're acting like some moon-eyed adolescent. Get to work!"

He pulled a yellow legal pad to him and wrote: *"Reversing the Effects of Turbidity and Nutrient Pollution on Brackish Water Littoral Zones."*

There, he was started.

He wanted to demonstrate the impact of murky water on seagrass beds and, hopefully, find out for himself just what effect the siphoning animals—sponges, sea squirts, and tunicates—had on murky water. That's why he had built the sea mobiles. That's why he had set them out in the bay to attract the kind of growth that boaters and dock builders despised.

He touched the pencil to his tongue, then wrote:

It is generally accepted that there has been a decrease in the population of finny fishes in the coastal waters of Florida. It is also generally accepted that the growing pressure of commercial fishing and sportfishing have had an injurious impact on the fishery. In Florida, for instance, more than 40,000 commercial fishermen and more than 5 million sportfishermen access the resource annually.

Ford stopped and reread what he had written. He would have to footnote the statistics, but the sources were from his own library and he could look them up later. And he didn't like the word *injurious*—to him it implied a sentimental, or at least a sympathetic, interpretation of an observation. He struck a line through it, replaced it with *adverse*, then continued:

However, it is the purpose of this paper to demonstrate that gradual changes in the water quality— i.e., increased turbidity from loss of ground root structure, and the increase of nutrient pollution from sources generally thought to be benign—i.e., the fertilization of lawns and golf courses—play an equal, if not greater, role in the reduction of the population of finny fishes in shallow water zones.

He stopped again. Jesus, he was beating around the bush. What he wanted to say was that Florida's coastal regions had lost more than half of their sea-grass beds because of fouled water. Hundreds of thousands of acres of sea meadow gone because there was too much phosphate and fertilizer from too many mine pits and developments draining daily into the estuaries. The fertilizer caused phytoplankton to bloom wildly. Saturated with the microscopic algae, the once-clear bays turned a murky, milky green. The murkier the water got, the more grass beds that died because sunlight couldn't get through the murk. No sunlight, no grass. That simple. When the grass died, the shrimps and crabs disappeared. So did the fish. So did the sponges, the tunicates, and the sea squirts that filtered the water and had once ensured that it would remain clear.

There were other factors, of course. Fluctuating salinity—many saltwater fish couldn't tolerate that. By building the Tamiami Trail, by digging the Buttonwood Canal through to Florida Bay, by dyking Lake Okeechobee, just to name a few, the state and federal governments had inexorably altered the flow of water through the Everglades. Then the state biologists, who were notoriously short-sighted, brought in an exotic tree called the melaleuca because it was a fiend for water and they felt it would help drain breeding areas for mosquitoes. But melaleuca trees were also fiends for re-production, and even fire wouldn't destroy them. Now the melaleuca—just as the exotic kudzu had in Georgia—was taking over the Everglades. Out of control, it competed with other exotics like Brazilian pepper and casuarina trees to sap the land dry.

Oh, there were many other factors. But Ford had settled upon the question of turbidity because it was so seldom considered.

In his paper, he wanted to demonstrate that it was a terrible, destructive cycle. No, not a cycle, because that implied a return to course. It was more like a cancer. It just kept getting worse and worse. In the meantime, the sportfishermen blamed the commercial fishermen. The commercial fishermen blamed the sportfish-ermen. A passionate argument requires that issues be black and white, a straight path of cause and effect. Too few would look beyond the logged weight of fish corpses to see what the real problem was. Even fewer wanted to understand, because to acknowl-edge the real problem was also to acknowledge that banning cottage-industry netting was not a solution, only a delay. And the water just kept getting murkier, suffering gradual and insidious changes not only in turbidity but salinity, as well.

It all came down to water. . . .

Ford began to write again, but his pencil tip broke. He spent five minutes sharpening it, using a lab scalpel to get it just right. When the point broke again, he stood and threw the pencil across the room.

"You're not getting any work done at all!" Reprimanding him-self, but unaware that he had spoken aloud, just as he was not aware that he sometimes spoke aloud to the fish in his big tank. "You're farting around, wasting time."

Yeah, and that troubled him. Ford hated interruptions in his workday. Now he was the interruption—his imagination, any-way. Which was frustrating as hell, frustrating to the point where he felt like banging into the wall a few times, like the horseshoe crabs he kept out in his big tank. Maybe that might clear his head a little bit.

It's her, that's the problem. The woman out there on her boat.

Finally, he gave up. He put his notebook and pencil away, then carried the buckets outside so he could return the sea mobiles to the bay. As he lugged the buckets, he thought to himself: By definition, she's your neighbor, and neighbors are supposed to be friendly. So just go out there and introduce yourself.

Oh sure. Had he gone out and introduced himself to Ralph and Esperanza Woodring, who lived out on the point? Nope. It had taken him a year to meet them. Had he gone over and introduced himself to Tomlinson, who was anchored just across the channel? Nope. They'd finally met at the marina, both in to buy cold quarts of beer.

"You're not only acting like an adolescent, Ford, now you're lying to yourself." Talking again as he returned to his cabin and began to change into a fresh knit shirt and khaki sailcloth shorts. Thinking, What's happened is, you've created a fictional personality for a woman. You want to meet that woman because you hope she might be just a little bit like you want her to be. But you're afraid, too, because she may be a disappointment, plus you might make an ass of yourself, going out there uninvited.

Ford sat on his cot and began to put on clean socks. You pride yourself on honesty, so at least try to be honest with yourself. You have no interest in welcoming a new neighbor. You're lonely. Hell yes, admit it—you're lonely living out here by yourself.

He was putting on talcum powder, thinking about it all. At least trying to put on talcum powder—he couldn't find the damn stuff. Ford was hunting around, moving things on tables. He found a box of baking soda. Well, maybe he didn't have any talcum powder. So he looked for cologne, but all he could find was a bottle of vanilla extract that he used in eggnog at Christmas.

"Goddamn it, what the hell kind of bachelor am I? No talcum powder, no cologne. No wonder I live alone."

Might as well be a hermit, like Tomlinson said. Hesitating over the box of baking soda, he poured a little into his palm, sprinkled in a few dashes of vanilla extract, and mixed it between his palms. I used to get invited places. Key West for Hemingway Days. To Greek Epiphany Day at Tarpon Springs: the sponge diver thing.

The Gasparilla Festival at Tampa. All sorts of places, and I always said no.

He patted the baking soda beneath his shirt and around. Home-made talcum powder. Pathetic!

Going out the door, he stopped to pet Crunch & Des, thinking, About time I started getting out and meeting people. Unless I want to end up all by myself, crazy as Tucker Gatrell. Which was a connection he preferred not to ponder: the genetic nexus; the cellular linkage between himself and his wild relatives, disorderly people of balmy humor and mad blue eyes. Antecedents from which he'd been trying to distance himself all his professional life.

Stepping down into his flats skiff and starting the big outboard motor, he thought, Show a little courage. Go out and meet her. Then you can get some work done, get back to the routine. As he threw off the lines and idled toward the sailboat at the mouth of the bay, Ford said aloud, "Next thing you know, I'll be talking to myself."

Every day for a week, Sally Carmel returned to her sailboat around noon to clean and store her camera gear, then pack the day's film, carefully dated and catalogued, in the cool plastic lock box she always carried. The light was bad from late morning to early afternoon. Way too bright in Florida, it burned great shards of shadow into the film, so it was a good time to get organized—to soup the film when she was shooting black and white, or to do the daily back-cracking, knuckle-barking maintenance work all salt-water boats required. There was always something to scrape or polish or sew or paint, and she'd been having problems with the engine, too, a normally dependable little Atomic 4 inboard that lately had been having fuel-line problems. Or fuel-filter problems; it was difficult to tell on a diesel. What that meant was, after the engine sat idle for a time, she had to tap all the lines, bleed them, then reprime them—a hell of a job that she normally would have hated but now, oddly, enjoyed.

Well, not so odd, really. Working on the engine focused her attention, blotting out all other worries or personal hurts, so it was a pleasant thing to do while recovering from a divorce. A tough divorce, though not violent. Just cold and disappointing and empty, like her two-year marriage to Geoff. Geoff, who had grown up rich and made a show of living simply, though part of his charm was money. She could admit that to herself now. Money was a part of the reason she had married him, that and the chance to be a part of the things he wanted to build. That's what he was, partner in a firm of consulting contractors and architects—builders who specialized in the big, mirrored high rises and modern malls. Creators of beautiful places with indoor gardens and fountains, and she had convinced herself that she could be a part of that by marrying him. After all, she had minored in design and interior decoration in college.

But Geoff had also been funny and serious and shrewd, a modern-day hero, or so she had thought. Which appealed to a small-town girl like her. And it wasn't until they were married that she began to see him for what he really was: a spoiled little boy who'd had his own way his whole life and who would not tolerate a partner with independent ideas and her own way of doing things. So he had bullied and denigrated and tried to undermine her confidence, taking her apart piece by piece. Which worked the first year, because she loved him—she truly did—but didn't work at all in the final year. Or at least that's the way she saw it. She could be a headstrong bully herself. A ball breaker, that's what Geoff had called her. That and a lot of other things. And he was probably right in some ways.

She had sorted out a lot on this sailing trip; had had some startling insights and revelations while she gave Geoff the month she'd promised to get his stuff out of their little house and find a new place to live. Her house, really. She'd inherited it from her mother and they'd redone the whole house together. Yet even though they'd been separated for more than a year, he was just now getting around to hiring movers to crate his things—the television, some of the furniture. That was fine with her. Lazy child, that's what he was. Lazy but shrewd, and he scared her a little bit. She could admit that now, too.

Which was why she was on this trip—to give him time to get his stuff out. She'd been cruising for more than a month, clear up Florida's west coast to Panama City, now nearly all the way back home, taking photographs for an assignment she'd received from the Audubon Society. Making a photographic record of the progress of immature pelicans on seventeen island rookeries along the coast where ornithologists had counted nests and eggs ten months before. Actually, sixteen rookeries that had been counted, and this seventeenth in Sanibel Island's Dinkin's Bay, which her crazy old neighbor had told her about. Except he called it Tarpon Bay, which was how the old-timers knew it. He had told her it was one of the prettiest little mangrove bays in Florida, and he was right, plus there were five tiny island rookeries in the middle of the bay, trees sagging with pelicans and cormorants and great blue herons. So she'd stayed here nearly a week, taking photographs, working on the boat, and swimming each day at sunset. Swimming nude because she liked the feel of the water on her body; the skin and marrow intimacy of being naked in dark water. Swam nude until, one morning, sitting with her powerful binoculars watching birds, she noticed that pervert who lived in the stilt shack futzing with a telescope. Saw him steering the barrel toward her boat, and she'd ducked out of sight just in time. If he watched her in the morning, he probably watched her at sunset, too, so that was the end of the nude swimming. The creep. A couple of times, he'd come puttering around in his boat, pretending that he was fishing. Didn't even have the courage to pull up and introduce himself.

But there would be no swimming today. Today she was packing, getting things squared away because she was leaving. Would pull the anchor about noon and catch the outgoing tide, headed home. Probably have to anchor off Marco Island for the night, find a lee shore in the Ten Thousand Islands, then motor on in through the islands to the long dock near her little house. Not her dock, but it was her house; now it was. It was Tucker Gatrell's dock. Her crazy old neighbor. Down there in Mango, where she'd grown up.

By noon, Sally Carmel had everything packed and lashed and stowed, but she couldn't get the engine started. It had fired perfectly that morning; she'd started it and let it run. But then, with the tide just right, the motor had gulped, spit, and quit. So now she was wedged into the stern pulpit, half her body in the engine hold, upside down and hair dangling. Up to her shoulders in grease and diesel fuel, bleeding air out of the fuel filters.

She had a 7/16-inch wrench in her hand, trying to loosen the purge nut. To do it, she had to put her left hand in the bilge to balance herself, which made it tough to put any torque on the bolt. Now she mounted the wrench on the nut, took a deep breath . . . applied pressure . . . but the wrench slipped and her fist smashed into the exhaust manifold.

"Ouch!"

Sally righted herself. Oil was dripping off her from some-where—darn it, from her hair. It must have swung down into the bilge when she slipped. Oil was trickling down her face. Her arms were already a slick black mess, and now her hand was bleeding. She studied the white crease on her knuckle; could see blood beading from the tiny capillaries.

She put her knuckle to her lips and sucked. Feeling frustrated and thinking, I ought just to sail this thing out. Which she would have done, but she had to run the narrow channel out of the bay, then take the Intracoastal beneath the Sanibel Causeway in a running tide. She pictured her pretty twenty-seven-foot Erickson smacking into the cement pilings. Pictured the keel plowing into a turtle-grass bank on this falling tide. Nope. She had to get the air out of the lines and get the engine going.

She couldn't work with this goop all over her. She rose to get a towel, which was when she noticed the green flats boat flying toward her. Coming out the marina channel, dolphining across the water-slick bay until the guy standing at the wheel got it trimmed out.

Oh no, the pervert from the stilt house.

That's all she needed now. Him plowing around gawking at her.

Well, she would ignore him. Pretend as if he just wasn't there. She cleaned off her face, toweled off the wrench, and leaned into the engine hold again, turning her attention to the purge nut. But she could hear the boat getting closer and closer; heard the pelicans in the nearby mangroves drop down off the limbs, laboring to flight on creaking wings. Could hear the boat slowing to idle, could feel her own boat rise and roll in the skiff's wake, then heard the skiff's motor shut down.

The bastard was stopping.

Then she heard, "Hello the boat. Anyone home?"

She blew through her lips, a fluttering noise of irritation, and sat up.

"I'm home. What do you want?" Which sounded even sterner than she'd planned, but what the hell. She didn't have time, and this guy had ruined her sunset swims.

There he was, standing at the wheel, drifting along in his boat, and she could see that her tone had taken him aback. Could hear it in his stammer when he answered, "Uh—I thought— Well, I just stopped . . . stopped to say hello. Being neighborly. I live in the stilt house." He motioned with his head. "Off the south mangrove bank—"

Sally interrupted. "I know, I know. By the marina—" But then she stopped herself. What in the world was wrong with this man's face? Splotches of white on it, like clown makeup. Or like he'd been baking and sneezed into the flour. She didn't want to stare, but gad.

He said, "You need some help working on your engine?" He smiled a little. "Looks like you're up to your elbows in it," meaning the grease.

Kind of an interesting-looking guy, really—healthy, with muscles and wire glasses, but he had that gook on his cheeks. Maybe he had poison ivy or something. But then she thought about him looking at her through the telescope and got mad again.

"You think you know more about my own engine than I do?"

"Not at all, I—"

"You think women can't work on engines?"

It took a moment, but his smile disappeared. On the skiff, Ford was thinking, Her face isn't as pretty as I thought. Eyes too sunken, cheeks too narrow. What is that, grease in her hair? as he said, "I think you're overreacting just a tad to a—"

"Or maybe you were studying my engine. Back there in your little house with the telescope." She made an airy gesture with a black hand. "Maybe you weren't peeping at me."

The man said, "Ahem," as if he'd been stuck with a needle but didn't want to show it.

Sally said, "That's right. And I don't have much time for sneaky people."

The man said, "You assume too much," in a flat way that surprised her a little. She expected him to be defensive. She sat looking at him as he started his skiff and touched it into gear, idling away. Then over his shoulder, he said, "If you need help with the engine, give me a call on the radio."

Not wanting to let him off so easy, Sally answered with heat, "I won't. Don't you worry."

The man leaned on the throttle of his fast skiff. He didn't look back.

It was late afternoon before Sally Carmel got her own boat running properly. And she didn't raise Mango until late afternoon the next day.

FOUR

❦

By Wednesday, October 21, Joseph Egret felt good enough to make his escape. His joints didn't ache as badly, and he didn't feel medicine-crazy anymore. He thought about trying to contact Tuck, maybe ask him to come up and keep the orderlies busy while he sneaked out. But that wasn't smart because Tuck always had to do things his own way. Had to do it with a lot of style and tricks just to let people know just how fancy-minded he could be.

Naw, he'd escape by himself. Be a lot quieter that way. Hell, if he was real quiet, the nurses might not even notice and, after a week or two, they'd forget he was ever there.

That's what he'd do. Be real-l-l-l sneaky quiet like them TV Indians. Maybe lift a few scalps on the way out. That made Joseph smile, lying in his bed, looking at the ceiling. Lift the television set, more like it. Be nice to have down there in the Glades. Be nicer if he had electricity, too, but who could say he wouldn't stumble upon a nice little generator some day? And it was best to be prepared. Besides, Tuck had electricity at his place, and that's where he'd be living. Tuck hadn't invited him, but they both knew that's what was going to happen if Joseph made it out.

Joseph snuck into the room across the hall to watch another eerie sunset—he'd never seen the sky so strange, and he was convinced it was one of those earth signs his grandfather had told him about. Maybe the sky was telling him not to linger. The fiery clouds could mean it was getting late. Or maybe it was telling him to take that television set. Hard to say. Joseph returned to his bed to wait for darkness, but he drifted off to sleep. He would probably have slept right through if it wasn't for a dream he had, a strange dream in a world of burning sky and white celestial light in which his grandfather smiled at him, sitting behind the wheel of a shiny convertible, maybe a Cadillac. Which made no sense—his grandfather had preferred Chevys. What made less sense was that the passenger door was open, as if he expected Joseph to get in with him.

You telling me to go ahead and die, Grandpa?

Nope. Tellin' you to get in the damn car. You already dead.

Joseph sat up with a start, breathing heavily in the darkness. He'd had a dream . . . then he couldn't quite remember what had happened in the dream. Something about dying, and there had been a lot of white light. There was a nice car in the dream, too. But then Joseph remembered he planned to escape that night, and he didn't think about the dream anymore. He swung out of bed.

He got down on his hands and knees and found the bottle of water Tuck had given him, and he emptied it with a long drink.

Tastes good, he thought. Sulphury, like a bay smells.

He also found his deerskin boats and black roper's hat. He put them on, feeling the soft leather, grinning at the weight of his old hat. But that was all he had to wear. They'd taken his clothes, and now he wished he'd asked that nice aide, Marjorie, for clothes rather than snuff and chocolate. Should have asked her to bring a pair of her gentleman friend's golfing trousers and one of those sweaters with baggy arms like Arnold Palmer wore. That woulda been nice, but it was too late now. And he couldn't hitchhike to Mango wearing a damn gown that flopped open and showed his butt.

Joseph stood in the darkness, thinking. Then suddenly it came to him. He knew where to find clothes. Well, sort of. The orderlies had locked him in the rest home's big storage locker once, and he knew just where to go. He slid out into the hall, looking this way and that, moving quietly through the shadows. He could hear lone voices coming from some of the rooms, crazy babbling. Could hear the television turned up loud downstairs, which meant the fat nurse was probably sitting there eating candy. Could also hear the *bong-bong* that meant someone had pressed their call button, wanting help from the orderlies. Which was bad. Joseph swung around and saw the light flashing over the door of his own room—that damn little bright-eyed bastard trying to get him in trouble again. He considered going back; maybe wrap the IV tube around the little jerk's throat. But no, he didn't have time. He had to hurry.

Joseph shuffled along, almost running. The storage room was behind the double doors at the end of the hall, and he pulled them open. Inside were boxes of all sorts of stuff, Christmas decorations and mops and a box of donated Halloween costumes, kept for the party they had each year so the television people could take pictures and prove how happy everybody at the rest home was. Joseph started opening boxes, throwing Christmas stockings and plastic pumpkins onto the floor. There was a suit in there somewhere. He'd seen it—a gray suit. Then he found the jacket and tried to pull it on over his shoulders, but it was way too small. Couldn't even get it over his arms. He found a dress, a red one with frills, big as a tent.

I'd hitchhike back to Mango buck-naked first.

He threw the dress on the floor with the suit coat. He kept pawing through the box, holding costumes up to his chest, then tossing them over his shoulder.

People get to this place, the crummy food must make 'em shrink.

He held a black costume up, almost threw it into the heap, but then reconsidered. It was bigger than the rest, so he ripped off his gown and tried it on.

"Hum . . ." Looking down at himself: black costume with a black hood and white bars across the chest and a single white band down the front of each leg.

White stork costume maybe? No-o-o . . .

Joseph thought for a moment. Nope, it was a skeleton costume. That's what he was wearing, a skeleton suit, only his boots and calves stuck way out of it, and so did his wrists. But that didn't matter. He liked the way it felt, nice and soft, plus black was a good color for him. Set off his eyes—a woman had told him that once.

Joseph put his hat on and turned to the door . . . then stopped, listening: footsteps coming down the hall, squeaking along on the linoleum. Quickly, Joseph flipped off the lights and stepped back against the wall just as the storage room doors were pulled open. One of the orderlies stood there, looking right at Joseph, it seemed, blinking into the darkness. The thick orderly with the chubby face and the tattoo on his wrist. The one who'd whacked him with surgical tubing that time, then tied him up. Joseph pulled his fists to his sides and was just about to leap on the man when the orderly turned on his heels and let the doors swing shut, calling out, "The Injun ain't in here, Hank!"

42

Joseph relaxed and waited. Amazing. How could the orderly have missed him? It was a good omen—Joseph knew that. A very good sign for a pursuer to look right at him but not see him.

Joseph crouched a little, listening. He could hear the rubber-shoe noises of the two orderlies going room to room. When he could no longer hear them, he peeked his head out and took a look. All clear, so he shuffled past the elevator to the stairs and clomped on down. The fire door at the first floor had no window, so he had to crack it open to look, and there sat the fat nurse and the two orderlies, backs to him, watching television. That quick, they'd given up the search. Maybe a dozen old people beyond the staff, sitting at tables playing cards. An old woman yelling, "Play me a spade, goddamn it! Either bid or get off the can!" Her thin voice rising over the noise of the television.

So how was he going to get past them? He thought about maybe pulling the upstairs fire alarm, sneaking out in the panic. But no, that'd bring the police, and he didn't want the cops after him. He was thinking about it, standing there in the stairwell, when, unexpectedly, the doorknob was pulled from his hand, the door was yanked wide open, and an old man tottered past him without saying a word.

Joseph didn't hesitate. He stood in plain view of the whole room, and there was no other option. He tipped his hat to the orderlies and the nurse, as if he was going for an evening stroll, then walked right out through the front doors.

The nurse and the orderlies never budged. Never said a word.

It was almost as if he were invisible.

As Joseph moved along the night streets, he began to assemble a plan in his head. It was about thirty miles to Mango, where Tuck lived—thirty miles of busy streets and fast traffic. And the orderlies might come looking for him, once their TV show was over. Which meant he couldn't stay out in the open; couldn't risk hitch-hiking because, if they caught him, they might put him jail. A boat was the best way to go, run right down the coast and cut in through the Ten Thousand Islands. But he didn't have a boat. Didn't have a dime to call Tuck, either. Or maybe it cost more now. It'd been a long time since Joseph had used a pay phone.

I could steal a car. . . .

That was an idea. Joseph was not a thief by nature, but if someone left their keys in their car, they deserved to be reminded that it was a dangerous world. But that would mean the police. And Joseph didn't like or trust the police. It was a natural distrust, one built up over long years of living just outside the law. As Tuck was fond of saying, "A cop and an undertaker got a lot in common. Neither one of them buggers wants to talk to a man when things is going smooth."

No, Joseph decided, he would not steal a car. But if he found some coins on the floor of an unlocked car, that was another story. Then he could call Tuck and get a ride. Until then, he'd have to walk. Find a way to head south and stay out of sight in case the orderlies came cruising for him.

Joseph hurried away from the rest home, keeping the three-story concrete hulk at his back. He walked past car lots and Burger Kings, then turned into the first residential section he came to. But damn, there was traffic here, too—Florida had become one big car lot. Then he saw a car coming that looked official—had lights on top—so he began to cut across back portions of lawn, ducking under clotheslines and skirting bright windows. For the first time, he began to relax. He traveled quietly, enjoying his new freedom and the scent of the October night. He hummed a little tune, too—a tune he remembered as an old Indian song, the birth song, perhaps, but that was actually the big band hit "Tangerine."

"Tangerine makes a lady da-dum. Tangerine da-dah-de-dum . . ."

As he walked, he was constantly testing himself, exploring joints and appendages for the various discomforts he had suffered. But there were none. Well, the pain wasn't as bad, anyway. That water . . . Tuck had been right about that vitamin water. Joseph had known the man for fifty years, and it was the first time Tuck had ever been right about anything.

For once, one of my grandfather's stories has come true. . . .

Thinking that, believing it, produced an odd feeling in Joseph—a strange, floating sense of intoxication, as if he were outside his body, looking down from above. Made him dizzy—that's how strong the feeling was—and he stopped in the shadows of a ficus tree to gather himself.

This is just great. My body's gotten better, but my mind's turned soft. What the hell's going on here?

He stood in the shadows, hoping the feeling would pass.

People who did not know Joseph well considered him a simple man of few needs and fewer thoughts. In truth, he was as intelligent as he was sensitive, and, like most sensitive people, harbored an innate mistrust of his own intellect. Added to this burden was a lifetime of wrestling with his own Indian heritage. His grandfather—called Chekika's Son—had been the great-grandson of Chekika, the giant Indian who had been shot, then hung, accused of killing settlers in the Florida Keys. Chekika, his grandfather had told Joseph many times, was the last of west Florida's native race. In him flowed the blood of the warrior Calusa, a sea people who had built high shell mounds that could still be found on the islands; built them long before the straggler Seminole and Miccosukee had wandered onto the peninsula.

Growing up in the Everglades, Joseph's grandfather had told him the Calusa stories; shared the Calusa legends as if they were great truths: On the full moon of the autumnal equinox, owls could speak as humans do; that the souls of brave men soared like eagles, seeking revenge long after they had died; that there was a great plan, a great order to the earth, and that their people, the ancient ones, would one day regain the coast they had once ruled.

But, one by one, as he grew older, Joseph saw the legends collapse beneath the weight of his own worldliness. He realized, in time, his grandfather was just another Indian drunk destined to die in an Immokalee flophouse, an empty wine bottle at his side. He learned that most people, no matter what color, stopped fighting long before their last heartbeat. Finally, he came to understand that the land called Florida would be inherited by those who cared least about it: the concrete merchants and tourists and out-of-state rich people. His loss of faith had long been an emptiness in him, but Joseph was also well grounded in the vagaries of existence: Life was scary enough to make a sled dog shiver, and a man had to get along as best he could.

But now one of the legends had come true: the story of the living water—a spring once sought by the Indian sick to heal themselves. Did he really believe that? *Yes . . . no! . . . maybe.*

Tuck was a con man; about that, there was no doubt. So why, Joseph wondered, did his own mind feel so much clearer after drinking the water? Why did his body feel so much better? He stood in the shadows, leaning against the tree, considering. Before him were expensive ranch-style homes, concrete and stucco, with

45

neat lawns and palm trees potted on little cement islands. In the eastern sky, clouds throbbed with eerie light, as if a bright wind was trapped within, probing for escape. Ghostly looking shapes up there in the night sky, so strange and unfamiliar that a disconcerting sense of doom flitted through Joseph's mind . . . which was when he remembered the dream he'd had.

You telling me to go ahead and die, Grandpa?

Nope. Tellin' you to get in the damn car. You already dead.

It all came back to him, the whole strange dream. Not a happy realization, either, because Joseph knew the dream for what it was.

Damn death dreams. Always come when a man's got other stuff to worry about.

Yes, no doubt about it. He had had a death dream.

"Some joke, Grandpa!"

Joseph sagged against the tree. He was going to die. Dreams like that didn't beat around the bush. Came right out and said what they meant. Hey . . . wait a minute. Joseph straightened as a new thought entered his head. In his mind, he tallied the feelings he had experienced in the last hour: unexpected freedom, absence of pain, soaring intoxication. Plus, that orderly had looked right at him without seeing him, as if he were invisible. Same with the fat nurse. Didn't even notice him.

Maybe I'm already dead!

"Oh shit," Joseph whispered.

Maybe he hadn't left the rest home, after all. Maybe this was all just a hallucination. Maybe, just maybe, he really had died and now his spirit was soaring.

Joseph bounced up and down on the ground a little. *Don't feel like I'm soaring.*

He thought about one of the few movies he had ever seen. In that film, a man got hit by a car. When he awoke, he was standing in line to board a train. His name was on the passenger list, but the man couldn't remember why he was there. But he found out. That man was on his way to heaven! Then another thought struck Joseph: If a train took you to heaven, maybe you had to walk to hell.

Quickly, he pinched himself. *Ouch.* It hurt, but was that proof?

No. Hadn't the man in that movie kicked over a trash can and hurt his foot? Maybe they let you keep all your physical feelings— except the sinful ones, of course.

There, that was an idea.

Joseph made a cursory check through his brain for dirty thoughts.

Nope, they were still there.

That did it; told him all he needed to know. He wasn't bound for heaven; he was on a one-way trip to hell.

Just about exactly what you deserve, you dirty man. . . .

The back door of the house near which he stood opened, startling him. He heard a voice say, "You stay in the yard now, Dracula!"

Joseph stiffened. "Jesus Christ," he whispered, "Dracula?"

But it wasn't the one he had imagined. This Dracula was a big black dog with pointed ears and skinny hips. It loped across the yard, then froze when it sensed Joseph.

This will be a good test. If the dog barks, I'm alive. If it doesn't . . . well, I've got problems.

Suddenly, the dog gave a low growl and charged right at him. Joseph grinned—he must still be alive, because that mean dog wanted to bite him! But then the animal banked sharply to the right and disappeared, howling, into the shrubbery. Joseph was thrown into such an instant state of emotional turmoil that he didn't even notice the cat streaking off ahead of the dog.

"Can it be I'm really dead?" Joseph wailed—out loud, for he was certain that no one could hear him. "Am I really a goddamn ghost?"

Then he heard a train whistle from the far distance. "Shit—now I've gone and missed the train to boot!"

He felt wretched. He remembered all the things he had left undone in his life. He punished himself with myriad regrets and accused himself of a thousand stupidities. He groaned and moaned bitterly until the door of the house flew open again and a man stepped out. "Get outta this yard, you damn cat!" Then the man at the door watched in shock as a huge figure dressed in a cowboy hat and skeleton costume went moping across to the next lot, then out of sight.

But soon Joseph Egret, who in his entire life had never allowed regrets to linger, began to recover from the shock of being dead. If he were a ghost, his new form might offer certain opportunities that his old living form had not. He studied the possibilities as he walked past more nice houses. He could steal money most probably. Take from the rich and give to his friends. That would be nice. And he might make a ghostly visit to the women's shower room at the local college. He had always dreamed of a chance to do that. Maybe being a ghost wouldn't be so bad, after all. He'd become a phantom Robin Hood—with hobbies.

By now, Joseph was feeling better. Death would have its advantages—if he was left to his own devices. He didn't want heaven; he just wanted to be left alone. He would visit his old friends and scare the hell out of them. And no adult better harm a child while he was around! Joseph grinned maliciously. Those fat nurses back at the rest home better be on their toes the next time they reached for a tampon. As for Tucker Gatrell's claims that he had found the living water . . . well, that just made no sense. But then, Tucker rarely did make sense.

Joseph was on what seemed to be a vast rolling lawn now. Houses surrounded him. He walked up a hill and came to a patch of soft grass with a flag in the middle: Thus he knew he was on a golf course. Joseph had never been on a golf course before. It smelled good. Down the rolling fairway, beyond the tar-slick pond, he could see the clubhouse. It was lighted as if for a party. People mingled outside beneath Japanese lanterns and the swimming pool was Jell-O green. Joseph remembered that Marjorie had said something about a bake sale at the country club. That had been days ago, but maybe they had some food left over. Joseph loved rhubarb pie and he was fond of peach cobbler. He decided to have a look.

As he got nearer, he could smell something cooking on a grill: steaks. Joseph liked steak even better than cobbler. He peeked through a bush and saw a chubby man in a chief's apron turning slabs of meat in a long row. The smell of the meat made Joseph's stomach growl, and he thought, If I'm a ghost, then I'm a hungry goddamn ghost. And if I'm not a ghost, I'll swipe a couple of them steaks, anyway.

Joseph kept a high copse between himself and the party. He watched the people laughing, talking, carrying drinks around. People with money, he could tell that by their clothes. People who knew one another but who seemed tense about something, nervous. Joseph could sense that, too. Then some of the people moved, clearing his view, and he could see why. Beyond the pool a man and a woman were arguing. The man was tall but slumped with gray hair. He had a drink glass in his hand and he was talking loudly, slurring his words. Saying mean things.

I'll be damned—

The woman was Marjorie.

Joseph watched this outrage for a time. Marjorie tried to walk away from the man, but he caught her arm and jerked her back. She began to cry, covering her face with her hands. The man pulled her hands apart, then hurried after her as she ran toward the clubhouse. She got to the clubhouse first, and the man stopped short, furious. The door that swung closed behind her read LADIES' LOCKER ROOM.

Joseph did not hesitate. If ever there were a job for a phantom, this was it. That the partygoers did not seem to notice as he sauntered toward the dressing room reassured Joseph. And when the man who had been harassing Marjorie let him pass through the door without question, he felt positively bold.

Being a ghost is gonna be fun, Joseph thought.

Tuck was frying his supper and humming a tune written by his old flying buddy, Ervin T. Rouse, when he heard a car slide to a halt outside. He looked through the window. Big bloated car—Tuck couldn't tell the makes anymore—and Joseph Egret was climbing out. The Indian waved a farewell as the car tore off, throwing dust.

Joseph came into the house, grinning broadly. He carried a heavy grocery sack and there was a swelling beneath his eye.

Neither men were the type for social preamble or reunion niceties. Tuck went back to the stove, saying, " 'Bout time you got the *cojones* to leave that rat-hole rest home."

Joseph placed the grocery sack on the table. "Got steaks in here—some of them already cooked. Steaks and beer."

Tucker turned the chicken he was frying and got another pan for the steaks. "Stole 'em I suppose." Looking meaningfully at Joseph's swollen eye.

"This?" Joseph touched his face. "There was a lady friend of mine in trouble. This guy got upset when I followed her into the shower room. I woulda ducked, but I thought I was a . . ." It seemed rather silly now, thinking he was a ghost. "Anyway, I didn't think he could see me. After I knocked him and two or three others in the pool, things got kinda crazy. There was a lady

49

screaming around with no clothes and a fire got started. But they didn't see me take these steaks. If they did, nobody said nothing."

Tuck decided not to pursue it. Later, around a campfire perhaps, it would be a good story to hear. Find out why Joseph was dressed like a skeleton, too. Had to be an interesting story behind that. But now, if the police came . . . well, it would be refreshing to be able to tell them the truth—that he didn't know anything about it.

The two men ate the chicken and steaks in silence, then Tucker leaned back in his chair, patted his stomach, and said, "Still takin' good care of myself, Joe. Left just enough room for a six-pack." He stood, found a foil packet of chewing tobacco and paper cups. Pushed a cup, then the foil packet across the table to Joseph, saying, "That woman who brung you, she's not coming back?"

"Women love me," Joseph explained sagely, "but they love to leave me, too." He had had two wives and more romances than Tuck, and he knew it was true. "But she said she might come see me someday. Said her gentleman friend was just drunk and hardly ever like that, but she'd see." Joseph said all this sadly, but Tucker recognized the thread of relief in his voice.

"Know exactly what you mean," he said, addressing the undertone rather than the words. "I had to pay a man cash money to take his woman back. Had to do it in secret so's she wouldn't find out. Hardest part was actin' heartbroke. That woman thought she was the best chili cook in the world. Had the windows open for a month after she left, just to air the place out."

Joseph nodded, comfortable in the understanding of an old friend. He had his nose to the foil pouch of tobacco, smiling at the sweetness of it, smiling at being out, alone, and on the loose again. "You going to the porch?"

Tucker had stood. "Yeah, but you ain't goin' nowhere till you put on a shirt and a pair of my jeans. Take off that stupid suit. After that I'll take you on a little walk, say good evening to Roscoe."

When he'd changed, Joseph followed Tuck outside, across the porch to the sand yard. Stars were pale blue in the black sky and thunderheads flickered in the high darkness, east over the Everglades, drawing wind from the mangrove thicket beyond the pasture. The village of Mango, what was left of it, was on a weak curvature of mud flat that created a harbor, and the harbor curved away toward the charcoal haze of the Ten Thousand Islands.

The islands separated Florida's mangrove coast from the Gulf of Mexico.

"Sally Carmel's back," Tucker said. He could see her sailboat moored off the end of the long dock. The halyard was flapping in the breeze, tapping against the mast, and Tucker thought, Whew, what a lonely sound.

"Who?"

Tuck said, "That little girl used to play around here. That tomboy kinda girl that liked birds. I know you remember her mother, Loretta."

Joseph made a soft whistling sound. "You bet I remember Loretta. Ran the fish house. Real tough business woman, and that body of hers . . ." He let the sentence trail off, picturing Loretta with her blond hair and the way she'd looked in a shirt with buttons.

Tucker had stopped at the shed, rummaging around until he found a Coleman lantern, saying, "I know, I know, but Loretta's in her grave now, so stop thinkin' what you're thinkin'."

"Just admiring her memory, that's all."

"Uh-huh." He fired the lantern. "Sally moved back a couple years ago, fixed up her mom's old shack"—Tucker motioned toward a white cottage with lighted windows—"fixed it up nice. Had some guy living with her a while, a husband, but then she kicked him out. Snooty kind of guy, thought he was smart."

"Good for her."

Tucker opened the pasture gate, and the two men walked along side by side, going slow, talking. Joseph knew where they were headed without having to ask—to the source of the water. As they walked, Tucker talked about the fish company closing down, about people moving away from Mango so they could make a living. "I still got them five shacks I used to rent. Down there off the mud flat? But they're all falling in. Can't get anybody to rent them 'cause they're such a mess." Then he talked about the state people planning to take the land so they could add it to the national park that extended down the west coast to the Florida Keys. Most of which Joseph already knew, but he let Tucker talk, anyway. Was used to the noise the man had to make; kind of enjoyed it, in fact, because it required so little effort on his part.

Tucker said, "So only a couple of us even bother living here anymore. The Hummels still live where they lived, and there's old

Rigaberto with those idiot chickens of his. Them gawldamn birds—now I like a rooster that makes noise in the morning, but the bastards he's got go at it all day. Bunch of little banties, and you know how mean they are. I had a couple nice cats, but the damn chickens run 'em off, stole their damn food out of the bowls. And we got a new woman up the road who raises a garden with pink flamingo statues in it. She gives me collards, and her husband's a hell of a nice guy. And there's a retired church organist lives in that trailer. Come a windy night, she'll wait till 'bout midnight and start banging out 'The Old Rugged Cross' full bore. But sometimes she calls me and I do her heavy lifting, then she has me over for breakfast."

"I like a good breakfast," Joseph said.

"Hell, then tonight when she's asleep, we'll go roll that organ a hers out the door again. Give her a reason to invite us."

"Again?"

Tuck cleared his throat. "Well, somebody give her the idea that, the way the earth spins, things can roll around at night."

Joseph didn't say anything, and Tucker replied to his silence: "A man's gotta eat, don't he?"

The scrawny cattle in the pasture shied at the approach of the men, then calmed, chewing, when they saw it was only Tucker. Roscoe came trotting out, big white horse nodding his head, pawing. Tuck said, "You don't believe me about the vitamin water, look at this." He put his hand on the horse's flank and put the lantern on the ground. "There they are, plain as rain. Roscoe's nuts."

Joseph squatted and looked. "I don't remember you having him gelded."

"Sure did. Vet had him twitched and drugged, and Roscoe still tried to take him apart." Tucker scratched the horse's neck. "Didn't you, boy? Ha! Living out here with no mare, he was starting to act weird, but I see now it was them damn heifers leading him on. Won't happen again, old boy!" Tuck took something from his pocket—a carrot—and the horse followed behind as the two men cut across the pasture, through the low myrtle and palmetto thickets. Mangrove trees at the edge of the bay formed a natural fence at the back end of the pasture, and Tuck held the lantern high, looking for something. "It's around here someplace," he said. "Little opening in the mangroves." He swore softly when he stepped in a fresh cow pie, then tripped and almost fell as he tried to clean his boot.

"Hum . . ." said Joseph, starring. "What's that thing you kicked?" He picked up something and held it to the light. "Stick with a ribbon on it."

Tucker was still cleaning his boot. "That? Oh, that. Doesn't seem to be much of anything. Golf flag for midgets? Ha-ha."

"Looks like a survey stake to me."

"Yeah, well—you named it." Tucker dropped the stick he had been using, picked up the lantern, and resumed the search. "Florida state flag, that's what it is. I can't fool you, never could, so I might just as well come out and say it plain."

Joseph said, "That'll be the day."

"Naw, I mean it. I was going to tell you, but not tonight. Didn't want to spoil your homecoming. Hell, you know how sentimental I am."

"Uh-huh."

Tucker said, "Here it is!" meaning the path. Then to the horse: "Stay here, Roscoe. I don't want you dropping pies in the water." Tucker stepped over a little arch of mangrove roots, snaking his way through the low trees. Mosquitoes found them—a swirling veil of silver in the lantern light—and Tucker continued to talk as they twisted along the trail, ducking low. "What's going on, Joseph, I used to own 'bout a hundred and twenty-five acres. Owned that whole stretch along the bay, them docks, the shacks—well, hell, you know what I owned."

Joseph knew. Tucker had once tried to get him to buy half of it.

"I was what us businessmen call land-poor. Wasn't making much money on cattle, but the damn commissioners kept raising my taxes 'cause it was waterfront. See"—he stopped to look around at Joseph, emphasizing the point—"that's the way they run all us old fishermen out. Rich people want to live by the water, so they tax waterfront property like it's all owned by rich people. If I was to tell you what I was paying every month in taxes—" Tucker started walking again. "So I had to sell off a big chunk of it just to pay the bills."

"You sell it to the government?"

"Hell no, you think I'm nuts?" Tucker spit. "Sold it to a big company. To a land trust, it's called. Sold a hundred acres and kept twenty-five. My place, the shacks, and the docks."

"Never pictured you selling your land."

"Yeah, but things was tight. Plus, the state was going to take it, anyway. That's what I figured. Them bastards. But I've been fighting 'em. Showin' them they're not messing with some kid. Lemar Flowers, he's been helping me right along. You remember—"

"The judge? Judge Flowers, sure I remember him. He's tricky."

Tucker smiled. "That's the man. Only he ain't a judge no more, just a lawyer. He got into some kinda scrape with a neighbor. The neighbor tried to nudge the boundary lines over by building a toolshed that crossed the line. And old Lemar—I can picture him doing this. Old Lemar, he climbs up on a bulldozer and just runs the toolshed down. Flattens it. He had to stop being a judge after that, that and the way he loves his liquids. But I knew the moment I heard that story, Lemar was just the lawyer for me. The one who could help me fight these state buzzards, keep them outta Mango."

Joseph said, "Mean, keep them from taking your twenty-five acres."

"My twenty-five? Hell, no. Keep them from taking any of it."

"But the rest of it ain't your land no more, so I don't see how it matters who owns it."

Tucker cleared his throat—the sound of a patient man. "See, that's the difference 'tween you and me, Joe. You don't use your brain."

"Yeah," Joseph cut in, "and you're like one of them lizards you grab but the tail comes off in your hand. Being different from you is what I like."

"I'm just saying you don't have my knack for seeing how things work. Don't mean nothing bad by it. But use your head. The state comes in here and makes a park, why, hell, it'd be like livin' in a prison. Them people in uniforms walking around, giving everybody orders. Paintin' everything gray or green. Gad! Galls me just thinking about it. My land! And they're just so dang sneaky about things. The ones in the uniforms, they act high and mighty enough. But them state guys who wear the suits, they're the worst. They come down here trying to shake my hand, smiling at me in that snooty kinda way. You know, like a school principal kinda smile? Like they got all the power in the world. They can squash me like a bug if they want, but they want to be professional doin' it. Bastards ain't never had to make a payroll in their life,

54

ain't never had to bust their balls to pay for a prime chunk of land, but they can stroll around here like they own the place, tell me what I've been doing wrong."

Joseph tried once more. "But if you sold it. If it ain't your land—"

Tucker made an odd noise, a little chortling sound. "That there's where it gets complicated. Yes indeed! Just trust me, Joe. I ain't a man to be taken lightly. You know that."

Joseph nodded. Tuck could have been lying all night, but that much was true. He was not a man to be taken lightly.

Tucker said, "Me and Lemar Flowers, we got it all worked out. Well . . . parts of it. Me, I'm working out the rest. You know how them state people, they're so sneaky? They come down here trying to push the whole thing down my throat. Tryin' to do it real fast, just wham-bam, thank you, ma'am. Wantin' to do their tests and surveys for all their fancy permits? Well, Lemar, he sets them down and makes 'em agree to hold a meeting. A public hearing, you know, right here at my place before their board or commission or whatever the hell it is condemns my land. Hell, you shoulda heard them scream about that. Those hearings, they always hold up to Tallahaoooo. But Lemar fixes it so they can't come on my land to do their tests unless they agreed. November ninth, that's the day. A Monday. Plenty of time." Tucker made the chortling sound again. "All I had to do was slow them down a little."

Tucker kept on talking, but he was getting repetitive, so Joseph tuned him out. Tuck was saying a lot, but he wasn't saying everything—he never did—but the whole story would gradually reveal itself, and Tuck's schemes were often interesting. They almost never worked, but they were interesting. Tucker was manipulating him, but Joseph didn't mind. It was like buying a ticket to get into a movie theater. Being manipulated was the price.

Joseph said, "Yeah, yeah, uh-huh," walking along, enjoying the freedom of being out in darkness. It had been a long time since he'd been in a mangrove swamp, and he liked it; liked the way the muck sucked at his boots, sending up a sulphur bloom with every footstep. A bruised kind of smell, like walking on something alive. Then they came onto higher ground and a little clearing— not a clearing, actually, but a hollow walled by trees and roofed with limbs. In the center was an abrupt hill of sand and shell.

Joseph could hear the shells crunching as he followed Tuck up the incline.

"Indian mound," Joseph said.

"Yep," Tucker said softly. "Little one." He turned the lantern's knob, and the light faded with a gaseous hiss. "Didn't even know it was here. Roscoe found it, not me."

Joseph stood, feeling easy. He'd been on many Indian mounds—his people, the Calusa, had built them all along the west coast of Florida. Built them out of shells of all sizes; left pottery shards a thousand years old or more, but little else. Because the mounds were the only high ground around, early settlers had homesteaded them, farmed them, raised their children on them, moving inland only when cars replaced boats as the common means of conveyance. Joseph had spent most of his childhood on one mound or another, but he'd never seen one like this. At the top of the mound was a little circular spring. The spring was lined with rock. Some of the rock had fallen in, and water bubbled out of the rocks. Tucker had turned out the lantern for a reason: The water sparkled with turquoise light, like little fireflies being swirled in the current.

Impressed, Joseph said, "Sure looks like it's got vitamins in it."

"You bet it does."

"Almost looks . . . alive. Like salt water on a dark night when you stir it around. And I thought you was lying."

"Lying, hah! Not me, Joe." Tuck stood with his hands on his hips, staring at the water, before he said, "Lot of these islands got artesian springs, but I ain't never seen none like this. Has to be some kinda natural piping to get the water up this high. Probably just like your grandpa described it, huh?"

"Nope. He always said it was a river. The legend, you mean? That was supposed to be a river. This ain't no river."

"No, but she perks right along."

"Besides, they already dug out all the rivers. Straightened 'em for boats. If it was real, that river, she's gone now."

"God amighty, it sound's like you're complaining. This'll just have to do."

Joseph got down on his stomach. He dipped his hands in the water and watched it drip from his fingers. He wiped the water over his face, then drank from the spring. He looked up at Tucker.

"This close to the bay, you'd think it'd taste salty. But it don't. It tastes . . . it tastes like . . ."

Tucker said, "I know. A little salty, but more like sulphur. But that ain't no big problem. Maybe we can work out some kinda filter system. Or put cherry flavor in it. People like a good cherry drink."

Joseph said, "Naw, I didn't mean—" He was staring into the spring, but then he looked up at Tucker. "Filter? Filter this water? You crazy? Wait a minute—" He stood, wiping his hands, face-to-face with Tuck. "I'll be damned. You don't even believe it yourself, do you?"

"Believe what?"

"You know what I'm talking about. Believe about this water, what it does—"

"Now that's a helluva thing to say, Joe! I'm only the man who discovered it. Well, Roscoe."

"That's the way you always do it, actin' so innocent."

"How the hell you want me to act when I am? I'm tryin' to tell you about what happened. The old bastard kept disappearing, and it took me about a week to track him here. Once I saw Roscoe's personal gear'd growed back, it didn't take me long to put two and two together." Tucker jutted his jaw out. "And tell me this—what's the first thing I did? Go ahead and become a millionaire? Nope. I went and rescued my old buddy from the rest home. Now this is the thanks I get. Calling me a liar."

"You don't got to lie, Tuck. All I'm saying, why run it through a filter if you believe it's got vitamins in it?"

"What the hell do you care if I'm lying or not? Made you feel better, didn't it?" Tucker still had his chin out, a serious expression on his face. "Now, after all we've been through, you saying you don't trust me?"

"I never did trust you. I'm talking about this little spring."

"Why would I make up a story about it?"

"That's what I'm askin'."

"Joe, if I was gonna make up a story about vitamin water, why'd I need you? Think about it a minute."

"Well . . . I can't figure you. Never pretended I could."

"There ain't a reason in the world, that's why. You're my oldest and best friend, so I got you in on it. Hated to think about you rustin' away in that damn rest home while I'm down here getting spunkier every day, just full of the old Nick like when I was young. You saying that jug a water didn't make you feel pretty good?"

"Yeah, but maybe it's just in my mind."

Tucker hooted. "No offense, Joe, but you ain't got the imagination. You think you imagined your back not hurtin', your joints not hurtin'?"

"Well . . . they still hurt, just not so bad."

"Gawldamn it, don't you ever get tired of complainin'?"

"I'm just telling you, that's all."

"Then what about that fight you was in tonight? You imagine that?"

Joseph began to nod his head slowly. "Now that's true. That's true enough." Then he offered, "And I was with a woman only a few days after you brought me the jug."

Tuck studied Joseph a moment. "You was with a woman? You mean you—"

"Yep. Sure did."

"Naw."

"Three times."

"I'll be—" Tucker found his footing and crunched his way up to the spring, then got on his belly. "No way. Not three times?" Joseph was nodding his head as Tuck scooped water into his hands and took a tentative drink, listening as Joseph told him, "Not counting the next morning. Five or six times in all. I kinda lost track."

Tucker made a face at the rotten-egg taste of the water, wiped his mouth with the back of his hand, then put his whole face in the spring. He came up shaking his head. "Whew! I can't get enough of this. Probably a regular soup of all sorts of healthy stuff."

"Yeah," said Joseph, "that's why you can't filter it."

"Huh?" Tuck was standing, wiping his hands on his jeans. "Filter it? Hell no, we can't filter it. I meant *change* the taste of it, that's all. Get it sweetened up a little so people will buy it. Did I say *filter?*" He leaned forward to make his point. "Joe, this little spring is gonna open all kinds of doors for us. You know what they sell now? Little green bottles of water from France. I got a couple at the house. Damn stuff's got *bubbles* in it, and they still get a buck a bottle. You know how much we can sell this stuff for? About twenty bucks a jar, if it's worked right."

"Sell it in jars," Joseph said. He was shaking his head.

"Right. Which brings us to the heart of that little problem I was telling you about."

Joseph said, "Huh?"

Tucker cleared his throat and said, "Them survey stakes I brought to your attention. There's a small matter of me not owning this property no more."

FIVE

❧

An investigator from Florida's Department of Criminal Law arrived at Dinkin's Bay Marina on a late Thursday afternoon, just after the fishing guides got in and just before Ford left in his twenty-four-foot trawl boat—the cedar-plank netter he'd bought used in Chokoloskee more than a year ago and had chugged up the inland waterway past Mango and Naples and Fort Myers Beach, so he could drag the shallows off Sanibel, collect specimens for his marine supply business.

The investigator's name was Walker, Agent Angela Walker, out of the St. Pete office, sent down by the governor's office in Tallahassee. She could have signed out one of the department's white four-door Chryslers, but she drove her own new Acura Legend LS instead, plum red, with brown leather interior, slowing at the highest span of the Sanibel Causeway to get a better look at the bay below, the Gulf glittering toward the western horizon, the long green island with its white beach borders, mansion-sized homes showing through the trees, and the black cowling of a lighthouse sticking up above the palms and casuarinas.

My, my, my, she thought. Look at all the money. . . .

At the stop sign, Angela Walker turned right on Periwinkle Way, stopped at Bailey's General Store for directions, then followed Tarpon Bay Road through the mangroves and into the shell parking lot, trying to find some shade beside the Dinkin's Bay Marina sign—BEER, BAIT, FISHING GUIDES.

Stepping out of the Acura, with its tinted windows and CD player, was like leaving a small, cool fortress; like stepping into a kiln, the whole place silenced by the heat, the parking lot nearly empty, a sleepy little clearing on the water with docks and boats that was a blur of searing white until she got her sunglasses on and her eyes adjusted.

October in Florida is too damn hot. Shoulda taken the job in San Diego. . . .

She was wearing a linen skirt and a sleeveless silk blouse, both from Dillards, oyster-shell white over navy, and she considered leaving the linen jacket in the car but decided it wouldn't look professional. Be like going off without her ID, badge, and .38 snub-nosed S&W with the checkered grip, all department issue, all kept in her purse unless she was on a hot call. Then the ID was pinned outside the jacket, the .38 S & W kept under the jacket in the Jensen quick-draw holster. Not that she had ever been on a hot call. No. She'd been with the department less than a year, recruited out of New York University right after graduation, master's in criminal science, lured to Florida through the state's minorities hiring program—not that that was ever mentioned to her. But she knew. She also knew that with her 3.5 GPA she could have gone anywhere she wanted.

In the jacket, in that heat, Agent Walker was already sweating by the time she got to the marina office and asked the man behind the glass counter where she could find a Mr. Marion Ford.

"You're looking for Doc?" The man behind the counter had an accent, Australian . . . no, New Zealand. She could tell by the upward lilt when he said, "Just once, it would be nice if a pretty woman came in and asked for me."

Walker said, "You're very kind," and waited.

"Doc lives down the shore there—you can see just the corner of his place through the mangroves. See? The little gray house on piles." The man was leaning, looking out the window. "I'd call for you, but he's been keeping his phone off lately. Rather a private man."

"Yes, I've tried his phone."

"You might walk on down. Just follow the path from the parking lot, and if he's not there, you can leave a message. Or I'll pass a message along—"

The woman said, "Thank you very much. I'll check at his house."

In the parking lot, she let her eyes linger on her new car, finding that some of the delight in it had already faded. She'd had it only two weeks, and the payments were going to be a strain. A Japanese car, at that—they were notorious racists—but it was such a beautiful car, machined like a fine watch, sleek and solid, and she'd fallen in love with the damn thing. She trailed a long brown finger over the fender, noting the patina of dust. From now on, maybe she'd drive one of the pool cars. Save washings, and this salt air couldn't be good for the finish.

"Hello . . . hello? Anyone home?"

A gray boardwalk wobbled out to the house, and Agent Walker stood with one foot on it, calling. Quiet-looking place with its tin roof and wash hung out on the line. All men's clothes, khaki and whites, nothing feminine about the place at all except a kind of measured neatness.

"Hello?"

She could see movement at the far side of the house, someone on the dock below, and she walked on out, glad she'd worn plain flats, because the spaces in the dock would be a hell of a place to catch a heel. Fall off the dock and she'd go right into the muck, no water at all, like the tide was out.

A man's head poked up over the dock. "Yeah?" Man with wire glasses, hair salt-streaked, blond, his expression none too friendly. But she walked on out anyway, taking her ID from her purse as she went, ducked around some pilings, and stepped down onto the lowest dock, where she could see the man was standing in a funny-looking boat—wide wooden thing with poles and nets. Beside it was tied a sleek fiberglass boat, turquoise green, with a big black engine. Fast, probably cost a lot. She wondered what it would be like to try skiing.

"Are you Marion Ford?"

"That's right."

Walker introduced herself. The man made no effort to shake hands, but he did take her ID wallet. He studied it, his eyes swinging from the laminated photograph to her face. "Florida Department of Criminal Law," he said. "You've had your hair cut shorter."

She gave him her professional, congenial smile. Had to be friendly with them if you wanted them to talk. "Florida is a lot hotter than I thought it would be."

"Not like New York, huh?"

"Well, it can be hot there, too." She stopped talking, her expression puzzled.

The man said, "Your accent."

She replaced the smile. "I keep forgetting—I'm the one who talks funny down here."

The man held the ID wallet for her to take, then turned his attention to the boat, messing with ropes and nets, not looking at her.

"I was wondering if you might have time to answer a few questions."

Instead of saying, "About what?"—that was almost always the first thing they asked—he said, "I'm just getting ready to go out. I have to catch the low tide."

"It wouldn't take long. We're trying to get some background information on a relative of yours. Strictly routine. A man named Tucker Gatrell."

Instead of asking, "Is he in some kind of trouble?"—they almost always asked that if the questions were about a friend or a relative—the man in the boat said, "Then why don't you talk with Tucker Gatrell?"

"I've already spoken with him."

"He suggested you talk with me?"

"No. But for our background files—"

"The tide's waiting, Ms. Walker. I've got to start the engine and get going."

She tried a different approach. "Mr. Ford, I've driven all the way from St. Petersburg. I haven't been with the FDCL long, and they've given me this assignment, more than thirty people to interview, and if you could just give me a few minutes . . ." Playing on his sympathy, something she hated to do.

The man stooped, pressed a button, and the boat's engine clattered—*Pop-apop-POP-POP-POP*. She had to talk over the noise. "Maybe I could go out in the boat with you?"

For the first time, he smiled a little. "You'd get your clothes wet. Shoes all messy. I'll be dragging the nets." He had an irritating confidence, sure she would refuse.

"That's all?" Agent Walker swung down onto the boat, not giving him a chance to reply. "It'll be a good place for us to talk, out on the water."

Ford was thinking, Exactly what I deserve, giving her an opening like that. She set me up. He was standing at the wooden ship's wheel, one of the old ones made of fitted mahogany, steering across the shallows of Dinkin's Bay. The woman stood beside him, looking out the windshield, small black purse on the control console between the compass and the throttle lever, not saying much. Long-bodied woman, maybe twenty-four or twenty-five, had the practiced professional aloofness that more and more females were affecting when dealing with men—so determined to deflect any male assumptions about their competence that they also voided any chance of personal interaction, upon which acceptance and judgments of equality were based. Wore perfume. Nails glossed, but not long, and she had the gaunt facial bone structure and coloring Ford associated with people of the western Sahara.

First the sandstorm, now her.

"Is this what you do for a living, net fish?" In the little wheelhouse, Walker didn't have to talk as loudly to make herself heard over the engine.

"That isn't on the printout they gave you? My occupation?"

"It said 'Sanibel Biological Supply.' That's all. Well, that you're a marine biologist."

Ford said, "Uh-huh," steering the boat past the fish-house ruins off Green Point, then back into the main channel, past Jack Thomas's house and Esperanza Woodring's place, where chickens scratched beneath palm trees by the dock. He turned west into narrow Tarpon Bay cut, then angled north onto the grass flats before throttling down, stopping the boat. Pine Island Sound spread away northwest to southeast, a gray water field of flux and flow that showed the swirls of rising bars and the contours of grass bottom smooth as a golf course. Low tide, late afternoon, and not many boats were out. But having the woman along neutralized the delight Ford would have felt being alone on a spring low, watching water drain away until the sea bottom showed itself.

He unlashed the net booms and cranked the outriggers down, listening as the woman said, "Maybe I should tell you why I've been assigned this interview." She was still standing by the wheel, trying to stay out of the way.

"Why you're interested in Tuck Gatrell," Ford said.

"He is your uncle."

"He's my uncle."

"But we're not interested just in him. We're interested in everyone who lives in that little village, Mango. And other places along the boundaries of Everglades National Park, too. We're trying to build our files."

Ford eased the boat into gear and threw the nets out, watching to make sure they didn't swing out tangled. He said, "Oh?"

Walker hoped he would say more; hoped his tone would suggest the approach she should take. So far, the man didn't fall into the textbook categories of friendly witness or hostile witness. It was as if he was standing back, watching from the gallery, not even there. She had a sheath of data sheets on all the work-ups—people she was supposed to interview—but Marion Ford's was only two paragraphs on a single page. The biology business, navy, and ten years with the NSA, National Security Agency, which implied all sorts of interesting possibilities, and why she'd jumped onto the boat instead of just setting up a phone interview. See what the guy was like for herself.

She said, "Part of that area—around Mango, most of the village—is being annexed for a state park project. A sort of add-on to Everglades National Park, and we're doing backgrounds on landowners to see who might be hostile to the project. A kind of survey."

She watched his face to see whether he believed that. He said, "That explains it," though she could tell he didn't buy it at all, something in his tone. Way too passive. So she added, "Of course that's not the only reason."

Ford was at the throttle, looking back at the nets, checking his watch. He wanted to do a short drag, seven minutes tops. Didn't want to crush any of the unwanted specimens in the accumulation of tidal grass and sea hydroid. Easing back on the throttle, he smiled at the woman and said, "You mean there's more?"

"You've probably heard that three men disappeared in that area within the last few weeks."

Ford said, "I don't think so. Where?"

Walker studied him for a moment, thinking that he might be lying. "Three men in separate boats on separate days," she told him. "You haven't heard anything about it? It was just south of Mango, on the park boundary."

Ford said, "And you suspect Tucker Gatrell?"

"No, not at all. I'm—we are—just trying to assemble a picture of the people in the area, trying to get background. Two of the men had been hired by the state to complete an environmental survey project. A census, they call it. And we're trying to come up with a list of people who might have a reason to . . . ah, object to the survey." She smiled, watching him. "People think law enforcement is all guns and car chases, but it's not. Not at the FDCL. It's mostly research. Interviews, like I'm doing now."

"Must be a long list."

"Of people to interview? They gave me only thirty names; maybe that's not all of them. The third man was a fishing celebrity. He had his own television show."

Ford said, "Were they similar? The three boats. That could be a key."

"No. I mean, I'm not sure. Three boats couldn't all be alike. That would be too much of a coincidence." The question had thrown her. He'd been way back on the fringe of the conversation, then suddenly he was at the heart of it. "The key to what? You mean they could have been faulty boats and sunk?"

He said, "But you're just doing the interviews. Someone else is doing the investigation."

"Well . . . yes and no . . . but back to the three boats—"

"What did Gatrell tell you?"

"He didn't say anything about the boats."

"About anything else, I mean."

"I know, but—"

"Did you go down there, talk to him in person?"

"No. I talked to him on the phone, a preinterview, trying to set up an appointment. He didn't tell me much."

Ford said, "I never found a way to make Tuck shut up." Already, he was dropping back from the topic. In and out, Walker thought, like a mongoose.

Walker said, "Oh, he talked. But not about what I wanted. He just rambled. He's . . . kind of charming in an odd sort of way. He talked about himself, the way old people like to do. Perhaps exaggerating a little—not that I minded."

Ford said, "Only a little?"

"He told me he had invented some kind of fishing—stone crabbing?"

Ford said, "That's true. Back in the fifties, he and his partner— an Indian named Joseph Egret—experimented until they found an effective trap. They supplied a Miami restaurant called Stone Crab Joe's."

"He told me that he had discovered shrimp fishing, too."

"At night, that's what he meant. He was one of the first to figure out that shrimp came out of their burrows at night. Shrimpers have fished at night ever since. He wasn't lying there."

Agent Walker was beginning to sense a small rapport growing, built around questions about Tucker Gatrell. She said, "He told me he'd poached those pretty birds, egrets, and alligators. That one night he'd shot and skinned more than three hundred—"

"Only Tuck would brag about that."

"And that he was part of the reason so many Cubans had migrated to Miami. He'd supplied Castro with guns."

Ford said, "He ran guns."

"And rum."

"From Cuba and Nassau. All true. During Prohibition back when he was in his teens."

"And that he'd worked for the man who built the road across the Everglades, but it was a failure because the equipment kept sinking in the mud, and it was his idea to use a—what did he call it?"

"I don't know what he called it, but it was a floating dredge. A dredge on a barge that dug its own canal and floated along behind. The fill created the roadbed. Tuck was a boy, a water boy for a man named Barron Collier, and supposedly he said—"

Walker said, "Yeah, it was something funny—"

"Tuck says a lot of funny things."

The woman finished the story for him. "He said, 'Jesus Christ, Barron, man only makes two things that float, shit and boats. And you can hire yourself another boy if you think I'm walking through shit clear to Miami.'"

Ford said nothing, listening to her. The woman had a nice low laugh, let a little bit of the girl show through, but Ford could see what she was doing, trying to build a working intimacy. Pretty good at it, too.

Behind them, on the slick water, was a roiled trail, like a brown comet's tail, showing the path of the nets. He shut down the engine, cranked the outriggers up, swung the nets over the culling table, and spilled the contents. A whole world of sea life gushed out: filefish, pinfish, sea horses, parrot fish, tunicates, grasses, comb jellies, spider crabs, blue crabs, a calico crab, a couple of horseshoe crabs, and flopping rays. For a moment, sorting the specimens, he forgot that the woman was there, but then she said,

"He told me this other story, too, about how Disney World got started up there in Orlando."

"Tuck's not shy about taking credit—"

"But it wasn't Walt Disney, or anybody like that, it was this other man—"

Ford said, "Dick Pope. That's Tuck's Dick Pope story, about how he was the one who got theme parks started in Florida. Tuck used to take Mr. Pope fishing, the guy who started Cypress Gardens—it was always Beautiful Cypress Gardens in the newsreels, the ones with Esther Williams and the old movie stars—and Tuck says he's the one talked him into it. Then the Disney people came along and a lot of others. Reptile World. Sea World. A lot of them."

Agent Walker said, "Truly an amazing man."

"Tuck always kept moving," Ford said.

"And that he was President Truman's favorite fishing guide, the one who decided they should make the Everglades a park."

"No . . . well, yeah, but he's stretching it. It's not as big a deal as it sounds. The old-time Florida guides—there weren't many of them, only a handful—took out a lot of people like that, famous. Presidents and athletes and movie people. Forty, fifty years ago, west Florida was still wilderness. Sparsely settled. Tuck was one of only two or three guides in the whole region, so he got his share."

"And Thomas Edison—"

"It was a big wild area with just a few small-town access points—"

"That Edison put him, Mr. Gatrell, in one of the first moving pictures, them fishing for some kind of fish."

Ford said, "That's what he says. But I'm not sure I believe Tuck's Edison stories. Edison died in, what? The early thirties. Tuck was pretty busy running liquor then."

"It sounds like he's done everything."

"Seventy-some years in a young state, it adds up."

"And that he's the last Florida cowboy . . . only he didn't call it that. It was something else—"

Ford said, "See? The guy exaggerates. There're a lot of cattle people left in Florida. Florida's one of the biggest cattle producers in the country. He's always been like that."

"Being his nephew, you've probably heard a lot of them."

Ford turned from the culling table to look at her. "I've heard my share of Tuck's stories. But why don't we go straight to the questions you want to ask, save us both some time."

Walker thought, Just when I thought he was softening up. . . . She said, "There're no set questions, just background stuff. I'm trying to—"

Ford cut her off. "You're trying to establish who in the area has a history of violence. You have a profile built, and you want me to supply a few pieces of Tuck, see if they fit. Who would kidnap or kill three men? Who knows those islands well enough to get away with it? I imagine the county law-enforcement people did air searches until they got frustrated, then called you in. Your department. And if you had suspects, you'd be talking to them, not doing deep background."

Walker had been looking at all the flopping, crawling, oozing creatures on the table, watching the man sort it so quickly, putting most of the mess back in the water. She was thinking, I'll never go swimming in the ocean again. She said, "That's right." She looked at Ford, who was shaking the nets out, getting ready to head back. "You know him. Is he prone to violence?"

"You've checked his priors. You know he is. But not in that way."

"He knows the region. I mean, there are thousands of islands, like a jungle—"

"He guided in the Everglades, I already confirmed that. Tuck grew up in the islands. He knows them."

"Considering all he's done in his life, he's certainly shrewd enough. Maybe even brilliant."

Ford said, "I wouldn't say that."

Walker said, "Do you think he fits the profile? I'm only asking for his own good."

"How would I know anything about the profile of a kidnapper or killer?" Ford started the boat, smiling at her. "I'm a biologist. Isn't that what it says on the data sheet they gave you?"

"Yes . . . from what they gave me—"

Ford kept talking. "Tucker Gatrell can be irritating as hell, and he has a temper, but he's not the guy you're after. He's an old man, for God's sake. He should probably be in a home or something."

Agent Walker said, "I'd love to meet him. Maybe I'll drive down there tomorrow," using her tone to tell Ford she'd be the judge.

Ford said, "You do that. See for yourself."

* * *

Ford sorted the specimens, putting sea horses and horseshoe crabs into the big saltwater tank on the deck, watching the sea horses right themselves in the aerator stream of raw water, finding tailholds on blades of turtle grass, while the horseshoe crabs plowed along the bottom. Ford's eyes lingered there, the cool haven of salt water, then looked to see whether Agent Walker's car was gone from the parking lot. It was. No strange cars, anyway. Jeth's four-by-four—he'd left it there while he was traveling—and MacKinley's Lincoln, Ford's own old blue Chevy pickup, then the cars that belonged to the live-aboards.

He checked his lab to make sure everything was orderly, the stainless-steel dissecting table sponged clean, all the specimen and chemical jars in their places. Then he stripped naked and stood beneath the rainwater cistern, showering the sweat away before changing into fresh shorts and a blue stone-washed chambray shirt off the clothesline.

It was sunset, the pearly after time, and the sky over Sanibel Island was wind-streaked with cantaloupe orange, purple swirls of cloud. Beyond the docks, mangroves settled charcoal black, blurring into smoky hedges as light drained from the bay. The lights of the marina bloomed on, and out of the closing darkness came the squawk of night herons hunting crabs on the mud flats and the mountain stream sound of tidal current dragging past the pilings of Ford's house.

He stepped out onto the porch and looked at Tomlinson's sailboat. It was a dark buoy on the copper-glazed water, and he could see Tomlinson's silhouette, lean as a bird, straggly-haired, sitting on the bow of the boat. Meditation time. The man was out there every dawn, every dusk, even in storms, as if the sun might drift off station if not for his shepherding. Communing with nature, or maybe talking with God. No telling with Tomlinson. Or maybe thinking about his baby daughter, Nichola, with her mother up there in Boston, where Tomlinson had flown at least once every two weeks since the baby had been born—until recently, suggesting to Ford that things weren't going too well between Tomlinson and the child's mother.

Even mystics have their problems. . . .

Ford hated to interrupt him, but he didn't relish the idea of driving to Mango and seeing Tuck one-on-one. Tomlinson would be just the right buffer. Give the crazy old fool someone to hound while Ford stayed on the periphery and tried to decipher just what kind of scheme he was cooking up now.

Three men missing . . . well, he'd wondered about it since the first time he saw it in the paper. Christ . . . Tuck couldn't be involved. . . . But then Ford thought, The hell he couldn't.

He stepped down to the dock and started his flats boat—a skiff with low freeboard and a poling platform over the outboard motor—and idled toward the west side of the bay. At the channel opening to the marina, he heard a hoot and looked over, to see JoAnn Smallwood and Rhonda Lister sitting on the stern of their old Chris-Craft, waving to him. Holding something in their hands for him to see—margaritas, probably, inviting him over for social hour. Maybe they'd broken up with their boyfriends. Or maybe their boyfriends were out of town. Two good-looking working women—one tall with short hair, one small with a body—who lived aboard at the marina, so Ford had not allowed himself to get physically involved. Didn't want to risk emotional discord in the small marina community. But now, knowing he had to go see Tuck, he found them more tempting than ever.

No wonder I don't have any social life.

At the sailboat, Tomlinson said, "Hey, you bet man. Love to meet the old dude, your uncle. But maybe I should change clothes."

Ford said, "Well, yeah . . . I don't think a sarong's the thing to wear." He could smell incense burning in the cabin below, sandalwood or rosewood, something musky.

Tomlinson said, "Sarongs are nice and cool, though. Perfectly sensible when you think about it. But we're slaves to fashion in this country. You ought to see the looks I get when I wear this thing to town. And it's the best, top of the line, pure silk I bought in Jakarta. The Pierre Cardin of Indonesia, but people just don't appreciate that kind of quality here."

Ford said, "I think I'll run my boat back. I'll wait in the truck for you."

"Hell, I ought to give you a sarong for your birthday, Doc. 'Bout time you wore something that didn't come from Cabelia's catalog. Just the thing for you, out there wading the flats. Except you get kinda weird tan lines."

Ford started the boat. "You could wear a shirt, too. People are old-fashioned down there in Mango."

They drove across the causeway off the island, then turned south onto Highway 41, the coastal highway that linked Tampa and Naples before crossing the Everglades to Miami—the road that pioneered South Florida's development. Built with a floating dredge, it was also known as the Tamiami Trail.

The Tamiami Trail had become the region's trunk line of growth, a stoplight artery of shopping malls, 7-Elevens, Kentucky Frieds, and shoe outlets, with access roads that led to planned country club communities with their guarded security gates, Bermuda grass vistas, and dredged lakes. Spring Meadow, Royal Hawaiian, Coral Reef—names invented by advertising agencies that had no linkage to reality, to the makeup of the land, but the logos looked great, and sanctuary from the crush of Florida-bound humanity sold big. They scraped the land bare, trucked in the sod, the prefab house frames, the PVC, and plasterboard. Then they built the boundary walls high.

Ford drove along at a steady fifty-five, windows down, taking in the night scenery and smells, listening to Tomlinson, slowing through Estero and Bonita Springs, then took the Naples bypass south and almost missed the narrow road that angled west into Mango. It had been so long, perhaps fifteen years, that he didn't recognize it. But he remembered the twisting mud-flat route well enough. The tide came right up to the road and crossed it in some places. Then the road curved sharply beneath palm trees. Mango Bay rose out of the mangroves to the right and the village was on the left: moon-globe streetlamps and a few old houses on a low ridge of Indian mounds that looked over the water. Tuck's ranch was at the end of the road on the highest mound, a low gray shack with a tin roof and a sand yard cloaked by trees. Lights from the windows glimmered through the leaves.

Tomlinson said, "Does it look smaller? When you go home, the place is supposed to look smaller."

Ford said, "It never seemed that big to begin with."

He turned down the drive and parked beneath a tree beside Tuck's pickup, saying, "Tuck's usually got at least one or two mean dogs around. He always did. So watch your step."

He stepped out into high weeds, walked to the porch, and rapped on the door. No answer. He could hear cattle behind the house, the occasional bawl, as he peeked through the window. Dishes were piled in the sink. Some kind of grease had slopped down the stove, coagulating in midstream. Beer cans and spit cups marched across the kitchen table like figures in some crazy chess game. The house was just as Ford remembered it: comfortable chaos beneath a layer of dirt. Just seeing it irritated him. The mess. The disorderliness of Tuck, his life, the whole damn backwoods Florida lifestyle.

Then he turned a little, not wanting to look, but he looked, anyway. There was Tucker's junk pile out beyond the barn. The rusting, rotting spore of a long and sloppy life. All the random shapes smothered over with vines, and there was the cloaked shape of an old boat's fly bridge, as if the boat were growing out of the ground.

Within him, Ford felt a fluttering hollowness, a bone-deep sense of loss. The fly bridge might have been a tombstone, hunched there in the weeds. Then Ford felt anger.

That pathetic old son of a bitch . . .

Tomlinson broke into his thoughts, saying, "He couldn't have gone far. His truck's here."

Ford cleared his throat and kicked at a shell. "He's got a horse, so the truck doesn't mean anything. He could be anywhere—Marco Island, Miami. When the mood's on him, he just saddles up and goes."

"You want to wait?"

"No. But I will. I've got to talk to him."

Tomlinson was fanning his hands in front of his face, smacking at his bare legs. "Geeze—mosquitoes! I'm getting eaten up. No wonder this place hasn't been developed yet."

Ford said, "That's the only reason, you're right. But then your body becomes immune to the blood thinner they inject and they don't bother you so much." He was standing with his hands on his hips, trying to see out into the pasture, looking along the water's edge. "I want to get this over as quickly as I can."

"Don't blame you, man. I'm being drained dry."

"Maybe you can take a walk around, check with a couple of the neighbors, ask if they've seen him. I'll stay here in the bugs in case he comes back."

But Tomlinson said he'd rather wait, if Ford didn't mind him standing down by the dock where there was a breeze. So Ford walked down the road and tapped at the door of the first place, a trailer with flower boxes in the windows. He could hear organ music coming from within the trailer, so he banged louder until an elderly woman in a pink housecoat answered. She told Ford, no, she hadn't seen Tucker since that morning when she made him and his big friend breakfast.

Ford said, "Big friend?"

The woman said, "The man who doesn't talk much, the one with long hair. Tuck's partner."

Ford said, "That big friend," thinking, So Joseph's still around. That made him feel better at least. He'd always liked Joseph.

The woman said, "He's such a sweet man, that Tucker. All the problems we've had around here with our things sliding all over the place. One night to the next, I never know which way my furniture is going to roll. I think it's earthquakes. And Tucker's always right there to help. Checks on me a lot better than my son ever did."

Ford said, "Uh . . . yes ma'am. Things can sure slide around," and hurried on to the next house, a pretty white clapboard cottage with yellow shutters and a Spanish tile roof, a place that he vaguely remembered, only he didn't remember it being so neat. Someone had put a lot of paint and time into renovating the house, getting the yard just right, hanging baskets on the porch, like something out of *House & Garden*, with louvered blinds and a little bit of light showing through. Ford pushed the bell, and when the door opened, he was already saying, "I'm very sorry to bother you, but I'm trying to find—" before he realized he recognized the woman who stood looking through the screen door at him: sizable woman, lean, in T-shirt and running shorts, with copper hair pulled back in some kind of braid, holding a book in one hand. Ford said, "Hey—" because he was surprised. It was the woman from the sailboat, the one photographing birds in Dinkin's Bay.

When she opened the door, there was a nice expression on her face, pleasant, expectant, but the expression faded and her mouth dropped open a little. "It's . . . you!"

Ford said, "Wait just a second here—"

"How did you . . . what do you mean by—"

Ford said, "I know this looks bad, but you don't understand."

"You followed me!"

"No, I didn't even know it was you. I mean, your house." He

74

raised his hands, a gesture of innocence, which the woman misinterpreted. She jumped to lock the screen door.

She said, "I'm calling the police! And if I ever see you around here again—" She slammed the wooden door.

Ford could hear her working the lock inside, and he raised his voice. "My uncle lives down the road. I'm trying to find him, Tucker Gatrell."

There was a silence. Then the door cracked against the chain lock, and Ford could see a wedge of hair and one pale eye, probably blue, though it was hard to tell in the porch light. The woman said, "You're lying."

"No, I'm not. Tucker Gatrell's my uncle."

"I don't believe that nice old man could be related to a pervert like you."

"Hey, watch it there."

"Now you're following me around!"

Ford started to say something, then just shook his head. "Believe what you want." He turned to leave, but then he stopped, thinking. He tapped at the door again. "Hey," he said. "Hey, one more thing. Are you listening?"

The door was closed. He waited in silence—maybe she was at the telephone dialing 911—but then her voice said, "Now what do you want?"

"I'm curious about something. How did you happen to anchor in my bay? Dinkin's Bay, I mean."

"I don't see how that—"

"Did Tuck suggest you go there? Maybe he planted the idea somehow—"

"I was on my own schedule, doing my own work . . ." But the way she paused told Ford she was thinking about it.

He said, "He did, didn't he?"

"No!"

"Are you sure?"

"He told me there were some nice rookeries there, that's all."

Ford said, "That old bastard tried to set me up."

The door cracked open again. "How dare you call him that!" Now she was mad again. "Did Mr. Gatrell make you spy on me through your telescope! That's a crappy thing to do!"

"I wasn't spying. Well, just once, but then I—"

Bang. The door slammed again.

* * *

Ford jammed his hands into his pockets and walked back along the road, not looking at anything, fuming. No more searching for Tucker. No more trying to help. Let the woman from the Florida Department of Criminal Law show up unexpectedly and hold his feet to the fire—he didn't care. Let them implicate Tuck in the kidnappings and send him off to Raiford Prison. Even if he didn't kidnap anyone, the world would be a safer place with Tucker Gatrell behind bars. Someone should have locked him away twenty years ago, him and his schemes.

Ford stopped walking, his ears alert to an odd noise. He had passed through the gate onto Tuck's property and was standing in the middle of the shell drive, headed up the mound to Tuck's shack, his brain scanning to define the soft *swish-swish* sound getting louder, closer, perhaps—like someone slapping a scythe through tall grass, plus a rumbling vibration almost like a growl—

"Gezzus!"

It was a dog charging him, hunkered low and running through the tree shadows, teeth bared, not barking until Ford reacted by taking three panicked steps and diving toward the limb of a gumbo-limbo tree, swinging up.

"Good dog, nice dog—get away, damn you!"

The dog was leaping at him, throwing itself into the air, mouth wide: a big-shouldered dog, brindle-striped, with a head the size of an anvil. Some kind of pit bull, or a crossbred catch dog. Yeah, that was it. One of his uncle's cattle dogs, used to take cattle down; grabbed rogue cows by the nose and held tight.

"Tomlinson!"

No answer.

"Tomlinson, you okay?"

Silence.

The damn dog had probably already gotten to Tomlinson; probably ate him up on the spot. Clinging to the tree, Ford had the fleeting vision of Tomlinson rationalizing some kind of karmic intent while being chomped to pieces, perhaps even finding a moment of peace as he was reconstituted and introduced into the food chain.

"Hey, Duke, that you boy?"

It was his uncle's voice.

"Tuck? Tuck, you call this animal off!"

"Don't worry, he won't bite."

"The hell he won't!"

Tuck's voice was getting closer, sounding as if there was no need to hurry, saying, "No reason to get huffy about it. Sounds like somebody got out on the wrong side of the bed this morning." Ford could see him walking down the drive in no big rush, big bandy-legged man in jeans and scoop-brimmed hat, two men coming along behind. Tomlinson and probably Joseph. At least they were hurrying.

"Gator, hoo dog! That ain't no coon you got treed! Back off!"

Tomlinson had caught up to Tuck and he was first to the dog, grabbing his chain collar, cooing, "Now, now, Gator boy, we sort of lost control there, didn't we?" Which sent the dog into convolutions of gratitude, wagging his tail, slopping Tomlinson with kisses, rolling on his back to get his belly scratched. "O-o-o-o, you act so mean, but you're really just a sweety pie. We're just a big scar-faced baby, yeah . . . yes we are. . . ." Rubbing the dog's ears.

Ford dropped down out of the tree. He'd lost a sandal, and he flapped around looking for it in the darkness, too angry to speak. He heard Tuck's voice. "Looka that, Joe, don't it make you want to kick that damn dog? Goes all fish-eyed over a hippie but trics to bite my own flesh and blood."

Tomlinson said, "Animals love me. I can communicate telepathically."

Tuck said, "Well, there ain't been no telegraph in Mango for forty years, so don't get no fancy ideas about my livestock. You ever heard something so crazy, Joe?"

Tomlinson said, "I mean silent communication, mind to mind. The indigenous peoples know about it, isn't that right, Mr. Egret?"

Joseph said, "I don't think I know them people." Then he asked Tuck, "What's he talking about?"

Ford found his sandal about ten feet from the gumbo-limbo tree—he'd made an amazing leap, getting away from the dog. He turned full-faced to his uncle for the first time as Tucker Gatrell said, "Duke, it's my opinion they shoulda gassed your whole generation except for you and Oliver North and maybe about twenty others."

The sandal was broken, damn it—his favorites, which he'd bought in Guatemala, handmade just for him up in the mountains near Chichicastenago. He'd done some work there during the revolution and had had them all those years. Ford picked up the sandal. The leather thong had snapped. He begin to limp up the drive. "Tuck," he said, "for the last time, don't call me Duke."

Christ, Tuck had his photograph hanging on the wall, right where it'd always been, covering the plaster hole above the couch—the bullet hole from the pearl-handled revolver Tuck used to carry like a gunfighter on cattle drives and that had gone off unexpectedly while being cleaned. Or so Tuck said. He'd been drinking whiskey at the time; white liquor, he called it, though it wasn't. He'd bought it at the store, just like anybody else. Jim Beam.

Tomlinson said, "Hey, Doc, you were about the straightest-looking kid I ever saw." He was looking at the photograph: Ford in high school, head and shoulders, crewneck football jersey, green numerals showing. "Man, you had hair like one of those guys who used to go around punching us at the demonstrations. Seriously cold-looking eyes, man. The vibes still jump right out."

Tuck was getting something out of the icebox, bent into it with the door open, so his voice had an echo. "So you're hanging out with hippies now." It was his "so it's come to this" tone. He stood up, holding a six-pack of Old Milwaukee, red-and-white cans. "You boys thirsty? Don't got no illegal drugs, we shoot the bastards down this way."

Tomlinson smiled. "Brewskis! I could use a couple of those."

Ford said, "We're not staying. I want to talk with you about something. It won't take long."

"You bet, Duke."

"Tucker, my name—"

"I mean Marion. Gawldamn, why my sister ever named you that—"

"Then call me Ford."

"That don't sound right, neither. You're a lot more Gatrell than Ford. Just like your mama." Now he was talking to Tomlinson. "My sister was real prissy neat, too. The boy here would get so pissed off if I left my boots out or spit on the floor. Even when he was ten, he acted like he was an old man. Couldn't hardly get him to smile. Going around collecting things, bugs and fish, like he was trying to tidy up the world. Looking through those glasses of his."

Tomlinson was nodding, taking it in. "You two even look a lot alike. I can see it now."

Ford had his hand up, rubbing his forehead. "Oh man oh man. . . ." He hadn't wanted to come; had avoided it for precisely this reason. All the years he'd worked to break free, now here he was right back where he'd started, knee-deep in it.

Tuck said, "Tell you what we'll do, Marion. Let's walk out to the pasture and I'll show you boys that little spring we found, the one's gonna make us rich."

"I don't want a beer, I don't want to see the spring. I want to talk with you in private, then I'm leaving."

"It's up this pretty little Indian mound."

"Indian mound?" Tomlinson's attention vectored. "I'd like to see it. Count me in right now. That's one of my main areas of interest, you know. Did Doc tell you?" Then he said, "You got any bug spray I could wear? You got the worst mosquitoes I've ever seen. Some Jungle Off, maybe? Or Cutter's?"

To Joseph, Tucker said, "When he gets to gasoline, let him have all he wants."

Tomlinson reached out and put his hands on Joseph's shoulders and said in a slightly louder voice, *"Atsi-na-hufa o pay-hay-okee!"*

Joseph stood motionless.

Tomlinson said, "You understand? I bet you do." He turned to Tuck. "I was asking him if he was from Big Cypress or the Everglades. I can only speak a little Creek, which I know is distantly related to the Miccosukee tongue."

"Yeah, yeah, ask him all about being a Seminole." Tuck was grinning at the possibilities, nodding his head. "You hear what he called you, Joe? Why don't you take him on out, show him the spring, and explain things to him. Take your time."

Tomlinson was talking right along. "I can speak quite a bit of Lakota though. Some of those AIM people—the American Indian Movement?—they're like my brothers. You know, from back in the old days. You and me"—Tomlinson held up a clenched fist—"we've got a lot to talk about, Joseph. No, seriously. They even gave me a name, the brothers. It's Tenskawatawa. Means the prophet."

Joseph's big face was troubled, flustered. "I can't understand nothing when he talks, Tuck. I don't want to show him around."

Tuck said, "Me and Marion got to have a little private talk. You two go on now."

Tuck was sitting across the table from him, already on his second beer. Ford hadn't had any. In just a little bit, he'd have to get in the truck and drive. Plus, he never drank more than three beers a day and he didn't want to waste those three down here with Tuck. When he got home, then maybe he'd sit on the deck, over the water, and pound them one by one. After all this craziness, it might help him sleep.

Tuck kept talking about the spring he'd found, about his horse, Roscoe, about Joseph's miraculous recovery—the point being Ford should help out by testing the water, give the stuff some credibility—and every few minutes he'd look at Ford and say, "You're looking good, boy. By gad, it's good to see you. Back here where you belong!"

Ford didn't feel as if it was where he belonged, and Tuck didn't look so good to him. He looked old, as if he'd shrunk down smaller after so many years of rough use. Bowlegged old man with skin stretched tight over a bony face, as if it had been soaked in salt water, then sun-dried until just before it split. What hadn't changed was Tuck's eyes; politician's eyes, robin's egg blue, always set on wide focus, taking in everything, picking out angles and calculating approaches. Ford could sense him calculating now and wanted to beat him to the punch; keep him from getting started so he could say what he had to say, then get out.

"I'm going to make this quick," he said.

"Hell, boy, you just got here!"

"A woman stopped to see me today—"

"Bet she was a good-lookin' thing. Hah!"

"A woman agent from the Florida Department of Criminal Law."

"Oh. You ain't in some kind of trouble?"

"She was asking questions about you. You heard the name Angela Walker? Agent Walker?"

"Can't say as I . . . Wait a minute, now—"

"Woman asking questions about the three men who disappeared down this way."

80

Tuck had his cowboy hat off, wiping his hands over his hair. On top, there were only a few wisps of thread, almost bald, but the sides were still sun-bleached, not much gray. He put the hat on the table. "Now that you mention it, seems I did talk to a woman like that, only I got to telling stories and she didn't say much about nobody disappearing. It was on the phone."

"She will tomorrow. She told me she was coming to see you."

"Always good to get company, specially female. Is she a looker?"

Ford said, "She's a cop, and you better not forget that. Now here's what I want to ask you." He leaned forward, trying to get his uncle to pay attention. "Those men, did you have anything to do with it?"

"The men that disappeared?"

"Damn it, you know that's what I'm talking about! A surveyor and an environmental consultant; had something to do with connecting Mango with the national park. Is the state trying to condemn your property?"

"Condemn my property?" Tuck appeared offended. "This house is solid as a dollar. Why'd they condemn it?"

Ford stood up so fast, his chair fell backward. "Don't pull this act on me! Your dumb and innocent act, Christ. I don't have time for it, and my guess is you don't, either. You know exactly what I'm talking about."

"Okay, okay, sit yourself down—"

"For once in your life, try being straight."

"You're right, you're right. Hell, Marion, you're always right. Always were. Never seen such a boy for being right all the time. Used to drive me nuts, the way you was always right. And here I am acting like the original shitheel."

Ford had righted the chair and was sitting down, adjusting it to the table. "Okay then. The three men."

Tuck said, "The three what disappeared, yep. I heard about them. I got a radio, don't I? I listen to the country station WHEW, the Country Giant, and they talked about it. The surveyor. And something they call a state ecologist. Environmentalist? Something like that. The one man was, and third was that fat television fisherman. They all got lost down in the islands and never made it back. But what you're askin' me is, did I make them disappear? Answer to that is no damn way."

"You never saw them?"

"I didn't say that." Tuck had the foil pouch of Red Man out, then got up to rinse his Styrofoam spit cup in the sink. He wadded a paper towel and put it in the cup, saying, "The surveyor and the ecologist man, they came here. Boy named Charles and a boy named . . . something else, I don't know. Hell, my memory. But they was here, but not at the same time. The one named Charles, he did the ecology stuff. He called it an environmental survey, only it wasn't really surveying. He just took little samples of this and that across my property. Looked at the birds and wrote things on a paper.

"Now, most surveyors, they're okay. Boys who like to get outside and found a way to get paid doing it. But this Charles was a asshole, got right up on his high horse just 'cause Gator tried to take a chunk outta him. But, hoo—you know about that!" Laughing, thinking about Ford up the tree.

Tuck said, "I'd a run him off, but me and Lemar Flowers—did you ever know Lemar? Well, me and Lemar worked out a kinda deal where I had to let them do their damn tests, taking water samples and looking at the birds. That sorta thing. I had to let 'em, or they'd put my butt in jail. And I been to jail. So he come down and looked at the water, took little bottles of it, and then this other man come and put down a bunch of stakes with little flags, and that was that. As far as the fat fisherman, I seen him on the television down at the Rod & Gun; they got a TV in the bar. Catch a fish, and he'd read poetry. Least he said it was poetry, but it didn't even rhyme. Great big fat boy with a pink face. Way I see it, good riddance. One television fisherman down, only about three hundred more to go."

"If the state took water samples, why do you want me to test it?"

Tucker said, "Because them state boys might be liars. I want my own tests." He winked. "You want a level playin' field, it's best you do your own rakin'. Besides, that Charles man, he's one of the ones disappeared. Him that took the water samples."

Ford said, "The lady cop, Agent Walker, she's trying to find people who'd have a motive."

"Anybody with a TV's got motive to kill a TV fisherman. Hell, there ought to be a bounty."

"Did you ever see them in their boats? If I knew what the boats looked like—"

"Never saw the state boys in boats. The TV guy, they was always boats too small for a boy his size. But them disappearing, hell, people been disappearing in the islands my whole life, Marion."

"Well, yeah. But not three."

"Uh-huh, uh-huh, I hear what you're saying, but listen to me." Tucker sat up straight and leaned across the table to make his point. "To them, it looks real safe sitting home, drinking tea with their pinkies out, studying the charts. But then they get out there in a boat by themselves, everything looks the same, 'bout a million islands. The water's black, not blue, and the bars will rip a motor right off the transom. Maybe about twenty or thirty of those islands, people used to live on and farm, raised their babies and buried their dead. Gravestones still out there, growed wild with weeds, like Fakahatchee. 'Cause they had a few Indian mounds on them. High land. The rest of the islands, which means about nine thousand nine hundred, nobody's ever even been on 'cause it's all mangrove swamp and the skeeters is so bad, you suck them down your lungs." Tuck sat back, held the cup to his lips, spit, then took a drink of beer. "That's how I growed up, Marion. Joseph, too. Hell—your mama, she told you what it was like, making a living down in these islands. And she came along way late, the youngest of the litter, never had to go around dipping stump water outta air plants for something to drink, never had to sleep out in the mangroves, huntin' enough skinny birds to feed a family. Every day of our lives, we had to scrape and scratch to live, and that's no bullshit. These modern timers, they'd cry like babies if they had to spend one night out there. You'd think they'd give us a little credit, let us be. We're the ones who toughed it out and settled this place." Tuck was getting angry.

Ford didn't like the man mentioning his mother. Didn't want to hear any more of it. He said, "Agent Walker doesn't care about how tough you had it. Nobody else does, either."

Tuck said, "If she thinks I give a good goddamn about three pussy-assed outsiders went and got themselves lost, I'll set her straight right off. Come down here waving their college dee-plomas around, think they can take our land away—" Starting to lose a little bit of his control. Ford watched him, thinking, If he's

83

not a suspect now, he'll be a suspect when Walker gets done with him.

Tuck said, "That's the hell of it. They can take my land, do whatever they want, 'cause they got the law on their side. Or what passes for law. Come down here high and mighty, snot-nosed kids working for the government, bossing us old-timers around, the ones gutted out the pioneer days, and, mister man, that's not exactly what Harry had in mind when he talked to me about making the Everglades into a park."

Ford thought, Harry—Harry Truman. Tuck sitting there talking like he and the President were best buddies, used to toss back beers together. Well, maybe they had. There was a black-and-white photo Tuck used to keep in his wallet, him and Truman with about thirty snook and redfish strung on a bamboo pole, each of them holding an end. Truman with those wire glasses glinting beneath the brown fedora, Bess smiling in the background in a flowered dress. Taking out the photo, Tuck would always say, "Here's Harry and me when I got back from fighting Japs in the Pacific. My way of thanking him for dropping the·bomb."

Now Ford said to Tuck, "You lose your temper with Agent Walker, she puts you on the list of suspects, they'll take you in for questioning. That means getting a lawyer, sitting in a room—"

Tuck said, "I already got the best lawyer around. And you don't tell me about sweet-talking cops. If she asks my address when we're done, it'll be to send me a Christmas card."

"What she's going to ask is where you were October first, October fifth, and last Wednesday, the days the men disappeared."

Tucker started to say something, but then the phone rang and he got up, saying, "I'll try to make up something good." Grinning, with teeth missing, back under control again. Into the phone, he said, "Big Sky Ranch."

Ford had forgotten he called the place that. Thirty-some feet above the bay, house and barn built on shell mounds, made it one of the highest points in the southern part of the state. Tuck's little joke.

Tuck said, "Hey, it's you. . . ." He listened, then said, "Yeah, I got a nephew—hell, you know him. Right, yeah . . . that's the one. It is, too. I wouldn't lie. . . . Naw, he didn't. Peeked at you through a telescope? I can't believe he'd do something so low. . . ." It went that way for a while, Ford fidgeting in his chair, then before hanging up, Tuck said, "Come on down and tell him yourself." He turned and looked at Ford, tilting his head and smirking. "You've been bad, Marion. Got my neighbor all riled."

Ford took the offensive. "That's another thing. Tricking that woman into anchoring in Dinkin's Bay, hoping we'd get together and I'd have a reason to come to Mango. Just so you could get me involved in your little scheme. Geeze!"

"Tell me true now"—Tuck was taking his chair, rocking back—"what's she look like in the all together? I been tempted myself, but I known her so long, it'd be like peekin' at my own daughter. A telescope—hoo, that's fancy!"

"Where the hell's Tomlinson? I've got to go."

"I got to walk you back and see the spring first. You ain't give me a chance to tell you what's goin' on, what they tryin' to do to this place."

Ford was at the screen door, cleaning his glasses with his shirttail. He said, "You want me to stay so I can meet your neighbor," as he cupped his hands around his mouth and yelled, "Hey—Tomlinson! Let's go!" He could see two dim shapes, Tomlinson and Joseph, coming back through the pasture.

Ford heard the chair screech on the wood-slat floor, heard Tuck's boots and knew he was standing right behind him. "Meet her? Hell, boy, you already know her. You known Sally Carmel most your life. You didn't know that's who it was?"

"That's not . . . wait a minute—" He paused, considering the hazy memory of a strawberry-haired child in jeans, skinny-legged, teeth missing, following him around asking lots of questions. What kinda bug is that? Why do you keep those fish in jars if you're not gonna eat 'em? Ford said, "My God, that's her?" Feeling Tuck's hand on his shoulder as he said it, then heard Tuck's voice: "Been a long time since you come home boy. I was beginning to wonder if I'd ever get you back to Mango again—"

Ford cut him off. "Tucker, I'm not back. I'm just delivering a message."

"You say that like a man who still holds a grudge."

"Can you think of a single reason why I shouldn't?"

"I can think of about twenty. Twenty years, that's a long time."

Ford turned to look into the man's face. "Yes. Yes it is. Twenty years is a lifetime to some." Then he called, "Hey, Tomlinson! Let's get going."

Tomlinson's voice: "Sure, man. But you got to see the spring, taste that water. I got a jar of it, Joseph gave me." Tomlinson bouncing along behind the bigger silhouette of Joseph Egret, the mean dog, Gator, trotting out front.

As Ford started his truck, Tuck came hurrying up to the window, his cowboy boots clomping in the shell drive. He thrust in a brown envelope, papers inside. Ford could tell by the feel. "You get some time, read this. It'll help you get started on your research."

As Ford's truck backed down the mound, Tuck called, "Next time, don't let it be so long between visits. Hear?"

SIX

❦

William Bambridge, Ph.D.—tenured professor of American literature at Oberlin College in Ohio, author of *To an Unknown Tarpon, With Love,* and host of the popular television fishing show "Tight Lines!"—sat in a shell pit looking at his blistered hands, his bare legs crisscrossed with cuts from hacking sugarcane on this godforsaken island, too physically spent, too emotionally exhausted to swat at the haze of mosquitoes that drifted around his face. His gray Tarpon Wear shorts were soaked from the muck floor; two of the buttons had popped off his green Tarpon Wear shirt, so that his belly protruded. A week of working like a slave, sleeping on the ground in the pit, had turned his clothes to rags. Even his leather Top-Siders were ripping at the sides from being wet all the time. Sitting there like a mud-smeared Buddha, Bambridge inhaled deeply—choked, spit, gagged, spit; could feel mosquitoes burning his pharynx and the back of his throat.

"Ah-h-hhg!" He slumped over, retching.

"Goddamn it, Bambridge, if you start crying again, I'll give you a reason to cry!" One of the Chucks talking. Charles Herbott, the environmentalist, and Chuck Fleet, the surveyor, were sitting on the shell floor with him, the pit so small that they couldn't move, couldn't even sit without touching one another.

The other Chuck, Chuck Fleet, said, "If he wasn't so damn . . . big, we'd have room to lie down at least, maybe get some decent sleep. I slept okay before he got here."

"You mean fat—just say it!"

"Ah, Christ . . ."

Bambridge began to sob, covering his face with his hands. "I don't want to be here any more than you do! It's not my fault I got lost, then came looking for help when my engine quit—"

"Quit crying!"

"Broke down, just like you two—"

"None of us likes it, Bambridge. We just have to hang on until they find us. They will. You've heard the planes."

"He'll work me to death first. I'm not like you two. You're used to the outdoors. I can't take it anymore. The bugs and the heat—I just can't! I'm an educator, for God's sake!"

One of the Chucks, Charles Herbott, said, "Every morning, it's the same thing, him bawling and whining. I can't listen to much more of his crybaby bullshit, I'm warning you both right now!" Furious, threatening violence with the intensity of his voice.

Charles Herbott did that a lot, lost his temper.

Fleet said, "The old man'll be coming for us pretty soon. We ought to rest instead of argue. Hey—" He was ignoring Bambridge. The two Chucks had made a point of ignoring him since the evening of the first day he'd arrived. His first night in the pit, he'd broken down so totally that his hysteria had become contagious, a kind of emotional electrical current that had zapped them both and pushed them close to panic. Now, when he cried, they acted as if he didn't exist. Fleet said, "Hey, you know, I was thinking—"

"That and slap mosquitoes, what the hell else is there to do?"

"Naw, the old man, I was thinking about him." Fleet had a couple of shells in his palm, bouncing them like coins. "He may not be as crazy as we think."

"He's . . . just look at him—insane. Look at his eyes."

"Yeah, but listen. I was thinking, why is it he waits till late afternoon to make us work? 'Cause of the storms, that's why. See?"

"It's because of the heat. We've already talked about that. He works us in the full heat, he's worried we'll die and won't get his cane in. Son of a bitch is a slave driver, and him a—"

"Maybe, maybe, but look: The search planes only come in the morning. That's why. See? The storms build up every afternoon this time of year, so the old man knows it's the only safe time to have us out. Works us then."

"Yeah . . . ?"

"So the planes won't see us."

"I see that, but I don't get—"

"I'm just saying if he's crazy, at least he's smart crazy. Too smart to kill us."

"That's what he's going to do! You know it is! Him and that gun!" Bambridge blubbering again.

Charles Herbott said, "Maybe . . . I don't know. He keeps saying he's going to let us go. And if he does, I'll tell you this, I ever get my hands on that old asshole—" Making a twisting motion with his hands. Herbott, the environmental consultant, was a little man with tight weight-lifter muscles, the kind made in a gym, doing reps in front of a mirror.

"But see, if he's rational, rational in his own way"—Chuck Fleet was thinking and talking—"then maybe all this really does make sense to him. Our boats break down—"

"They didn't just break down. I knock the prop off my engine, you tear the foot off yours, and him right there to help saying no use to call on the radio, the hand-held VHFs wouldn't reach—"

"See? He was right about that. I tried. We're out of range down here. The radio wouldn't reach."

"But that he'd tow us back to the shack, make sure we got help. He was lying about that, just tricking us."

Bambridge broke in. "There's the difference. He wanted you two. Me, my engine stopped, then I dropped my radio over and I had to paddle and paddle. He should let me go!"

Charles Herbott said, "Bambridge, I hear that story one more time, I'm going to kill you myself."

Chuck Fleet said, "If you two would just listen. Understand what I'm getting at? Us broken down—run aground, he sees it— then he really did have a right to salvage our boats. The instant we got out, anyway. In his own mind, he had a right, I'm saying. Not that any normal person would do that. But he's old, old Florida, understand? From the days of the salvage industry: old maritime law said it was legal to take an abandoned boat, and the owners had to pay a percentage of the manifest. That was the law. Hell, it might *still* be the law, for all I know. That's what he means when he says we got to work off our debt."

"But my boat hit something that shouldn't a been there. He laid a trap—"

"Maybe he did. Like the old-time wreckers. They'd move the channel lights, run boats onto the reef. Same thing."

Charles Herbott stood and put his hands against the shell wall of the pit. His first day there, Fleet had told him, don't try to climb out, he'd already tried. The shell was so loose, the walls could come down on top of them. But Herbott had tried anyway, and, sure enough, it was like trying to climb through a landslide. The idea of being covered with shell and suffocating—

Fleet said, "He's rational. That's what I'm saying. In his own way. I think he's going to make us work off our debt and let us go."

"He's a killer, and we all know it!" Bambridge again. "He pointed his gun at my head!"

"No, he's never done that, never pointed his gun at any of us. Never come right out and threatened to shoot any of us, when you think back."

"He's sure as hell implied it!"

"Think what you want, I'm just trying to look at it from another point of view."

Herbott said, "So he doesn't think he's doing anything illegal."

"That's what I'm saying."

"And he has no reason to kill us? Doesn't matter. If he ever gives me the chance, I'm going to shoot the old scumbag myself, or beat him to death with my bare hands." That was Charles Herbott's favorite topic, how he was going to take the old man apart.

Chuck Fleet said, "The point is, he thinks things out. That's why he works us in the afternoons, when the storms blow through. No planes."

The two Chucks talked about that, passing time. They'd talked about everything, mostly how to get away. But when they weren't in the pit, they were working those thick cane patches planted in among the gumbo-limbo trees, or turning the cane press by hand like mules. And the old man stood within shooting range with his double-barreled 12-gauge, but never close enough for them to jump him.

"I've got to get out of here or I'll go insane!"

The two Chucks ignored him; they always did. William Bambridge put his face in his hands, waiting for more tears, but he was all cried out. He could feel the blisters on his palms, spongy against his cheeks. The mosquitoes were all over him; he could feel their needle touch on his legs, could hear them whining in his ears, could feel their wings feathering the hair on his arms. The old man had said the pit was the only place they could sleep and still be out of the bugs, plus he'd built a thatched roof over it to keep out the rain. "Skeeters and sand flies," he called them. But the bugs were nearly as bad below as they were above. Worse, the maddening things were more attracted to him than to the other two men—of that Bambridge was certain. He'd read that somewhere, that mosquitoes preferred certain body chemistries to others. Where had he read that?

Thinking about it reminded him of his nice library in his nice little house back home—the library with all the books on chess and literature, a whole small section on the culinary arts, even a few books on fishing, including a dozen copies left of his own, *To an Unknown Tarpon, With Love.* Bambridge had spent a vacation week at Rio Colorado Tarpon Lodge in Costa Rica—never did land one of the damn fish—then spent two years writing the book because he had a federal grant, and if he didn't work on it for twenty-four months, he wouldn't get his quarterly checks, and what else was he going to write about? His dull life in Ohio? Then, wonder of wonders, the book won the UPLA—University Professor's Literary Award—which, in turn, had prompted *The New York Times* to invite him to contribute the occasional fishing column. And that had prompted several of the television news magazines to use him as an on-camera fishing expert. Which was probably why *People* magazine had referred to him as the "Dean of the American Outdoors" in the two-paragraph story about his book selling to the movies. Which had prompted the national television syndicate to contact him about doing the fishing show.

The show had done pretty well, too; got picked up by quite a few markets, and the numbers were pretty good. The sponsors came through with money and a lot of product, so he'd requested the sabbatical from teaching. Not that it would have mattered had the college refused. He had tenure—he could do what he damn well pleased. So he took the fall quarter off to take the show on the road, get the hell away from those tiresome shows on walleye techniques on Lake Erie. Brought it down here to Florida to check the place out, thinking maybe it was about time he moved from teaching into a full-time television career. . . .

Only to stumble into this nightmare. Held captive in a hole with two strangers—one of them, Herbott, a violent bully—defecating in a bucket, surviving on nothing but water and some kind of greasy fish. Even the two Chucks didn't know what it was. Being worked to the point of nausea and beyond, waiting to die or go mad.

This is hell, this is hell, this is hell. . . . Sitting there repeating it in his mind like a mantra.

It couldn't be happening, yet it was.

Bambridge stirred and swiped the mosquitoes off his arm, then smacked at his legs. Then he began to slap at his whole body in a growing frenzy, not unlike a drunk slapping snakes in the grips of delirium.

"Get them off me! It's not fair; it's not fair. . . ."

"Knock it off, Bambridge. You're kicking me!"

"Hey—shut up, you two. He's coming, the old man."

"He's nuts! You kick me again, I'll beat the living shit out of you, Bambridge. I mean it!"

"Quiet!"

William Bambridge stilled himself abruptly; sat there trembling, knowing only that this horror couldn't go on. He had to end it, somehow, someway. He couldn't abide another day working in the heat, living with the insects. He sat looking toward the opening of the pit, like looking out of a well, and saw the silhouette of the old man appear, bent at the hips, peering down. The old man's raspy nasal twang: "You boys got so much juice, I'll put you to work early," which Bambridge heard as, "Yew baws gah so-o-o moch jews, ah'll putchew tah whark airr-ly."

Bambridge got to his feet, dusting the shells off his wet butt, watching the silhouette stoop over something—the long wooden ladder he lowered each day.

"Sir? Sir? I have to tell you something." Bambridge had his hands cupped around his mouth, trying to sound pleasant but authoritative. "I'm ill—sick. Very sick. I can't work today. I simply can't."

The old man was futzing with the ladder, talking to himself.

"Sir? Sir? Captain!" Which was what one of the Chucks called him—Fleet—like a chain-gang worker in a movie about the Deep South. "I'm trying to discuss something with you here, get something settled—"

The ladder began to slide down into the pit. The old man said, "Onliest thing you got to settle is the man's day's work you owe me."

"I can't! Don't you hear me?" And the tears came again. "I'm sick, I tell you. I can't work in the fields today. If you try to make me, I'll . . . I'll run away. I mean it!"

The old man's voice: "You do, you'll never make it off this island. I mean that."

"You'll shoot me? That's what you mean, isn't it!"

"I mean a fat 'un like you ain't got the gumption to make it. Now quit your talkin'."

"Then why don't you shoot me? I wish you would! Shoot me now, for God's sake." Bambridge had his back to the shell wall, and he slowly rode it to the ground, collapsing in sobs. He didn't look up when he heard one of the Chucks, Fleet, say, "Captain, he's telling the truth. He's either sick or he's lost his mind. Either way, we wish you'd get him out of here."

"Me, too, old man. Do us all a favor." Herbott's surly voice.

The old man said, "You boys jes take it into your minds you don't want to work; you think that's the way things is."

"No sir, Captain. We'll do our work, all we owe you. It's him we're talking about."

There was a long silence, the old man muttering. Then: "You there!" The old man was talking to him; Bambridge could sense the focus of his attention. "Climb up outta that there hole, Fat'un."

"I'm not going to the fields." Bambridge said it flatly. The exhaustion had been replaced by a rock-bottom resolve. He didn't care anymore what the old bastard did, what the two Chucks thought. "Nothing matters," he said. "Go ahead. Shoot."

"Didn't say nothing about no fields. You owe me work—"

"I already said I'll pay you! Pay you anything you want if you get me back—"

"One of them there checks, no thanks. I had my money in a bank oncest and lost it."

"Then cash, for Christ's sake!"

"But you don't got it on you." The old man made a whoofing noise, cynical. "I tow you back now, I'll never see you or yer boats again."

"You will, too! We've told you a hundred times, we don't have the cash on us—"

The old man said, "Then you owe me work, and you'll by God do it. You can't do man's work, maybe you can do woman's work. Can you cook?"

"I'm not work—" Bambridge stopped, realizing what he was being asked. He looked up at the silhouette. "Yes . . . yes, I can cook. I like to . . . I'm a very good cook."

"Can you sweep and scrub and wash?"

93

"Inside your home, you mean?" Bambridge had never been inside it, a bamboo thatched hut beneath trees, but at least it had walls to keep the bugs out. "I can do that, yes. Scrub, cook, anything. And stay there, out of the bugs?"

The old man was holding the shotgun now. Bambridge could see it as he squinted up at the bright Florida sky. "Get yo' big butt up the ladder, then."

Just like old times . . . That's what Tucker Gatrell was thinking. Sitting on the porch with Joseph Egret, the wooden chairs kicked back and their feet propped on the porch railing, swatting mosquitoes and spitting chewing tobacco.

Could be forty years ago . . . could be ten years . . . hell, could all be a dream. . . . That's what he was thinking.

Mango Bay spread out before them, and the tin roofs of the abandoned fish shacks caught the morning sun like mirrors and flung the light obliquely, in dusty yellow rays, back onto the little curve of fishing village. In the strange light, coconut palms leaning in feathered strands were isolated along the road, set apart from the mud beach upon which they grew. They seemed fragile and singular, gold and gray, as if shaped by a hurricane wind, then marooned in stillness. Small portions of Mango caught the light and were elevated from the mundane because of it: wedges of cypress planking, a lone piling, the bow of a sunken mullet skiff, the rust streaks beneath the COKE sign hanging outside the deserted store, Homer's Gas and Sundries.

There was a sweetness in the air, too. Tuck sniffed, sitting on the porch. The cloying perfume of jasmine mixed with the sulphur and protein odor of the bay. He lowered the paper in his hand—there was a whole box of papers and folders beside his chair—and inhaled deeply. "Smells good, don't it?"

Joseph nodded his agreement. "That's bacon frying. Maybe down at the organ lady's house, Miz Taylor's."

Tuck turned his nose upward expertly. "No-o-o-o, don't think so."

"Next place down, then. Sally Carmel's?"

Tuck said lazily, "More likely. Wouldn't hurt for us to walk down and check up on her. That Sally, she's the independent sort, but I can tell she misses having a man around. Always something to lift or move for a woman living alone. I worry about that girl."

"Yeah," Joseph said, "and she might be cooking hotcakes, too."

The two men were quiet for a time, languid in the fresh morning heat. Then Tucker said, "I tried to fix Duke up with her, had it all arranged just right. But he messed it up. Peeked at her through a telescope when she didn't have no clothes on. She's mad. Oh, she's real mad."

Joseph said, "A telescope, huh? I'd a never thunk of that."

"Yeah, Duke's smart, no denying it. He got the Gatrell brain"—Tucker glanced at Joseph out of the corner of his eye to see how that was accepted—"but he never got my gift for dealin' with people. You know how people just naturally love me."

Joseph turned and spat.

"But Duke, he's always been kinda a cold fish. Say, you remember why he moved out on me?"

Joseph hesitated for a moment. Did Tuck mean the real reason Marion had moved out? Or did he mean one of the excuses Tuck had given? After a moment, Joseph said, "Sure, I remember. Marion had to do all the work around the place while you sat around drinkin' beer. I don't blame him."

"Naw, that's all wrong. Well, it wasn't just that. You don't know the reason?"

Joseph knew. He waited, wondering whether Tuck would talk about it.

But Tucker said, "I come home one day after being off someplace. Okeechobee?" Tuck was trying to remember. "Naw, it was forty-mile bend, down on the Trail, 'cause that was the year the gators came up the creeks thick. Anyway . . ." He scratched his head. "What was I talkin' about? Oh—I come home one day and the whole kitchen table was covered with bugs. All kinda bugs laid out on this cottony sort of material. Hell, palmetto bugs big as my fist, so I throw'd the whole mess out—"

It wasn't the real reason, but Joseph was nodding his head, playing along. "That's right, you threw out his bug collection."

"Packed his bag, stormed out, and moved up to the islands off Fort Myers. Him just sixteen years old, rented his own place, made his own money, and still found time to play ball. Only seen him about a dozen times since. He was off with the government, doing some kind of work. Going to college. I'm going to have a hell of a time getting him back down here."

Joseph said, "Sometimes a place has bad memories. After living

95

two months with my first wife, I never wanted to see Miami again."

Out on the water, a little bay shrimper headed out Wilson Cut. Its outriggers were folded like the wings of some bony pterodactyl and smoke spurted from the exhaust stack, out of synch with the delayed *pop-poppa-pop* that reached them across the water.

"That's little Jim Bob James growed up," Tuck observed. "No smarter than his daddy, trying to shrimp during the day. Oh, I tried to tell 'im."

Joseph sat and listened, hoping Tuck wouldn't get started on how he had discovered that shrimp came out at night, because that would lead him into the first stone-crab trap they had built—well, actually Joseph had figured out the trap and about the shrimp, too, but Tuck always took credit—and that would lead to all the things Tuck'd done first, before anybody else in Florida caught on, which would lead to his long, sad wondering why they'd ended up so poor when everyone else had gotten rich. Joseph didn't care anything about money—he never had—but he hated to see Tuck depressed, because that caused him to talk even more than usual. Joseph had his mind on that bacon frying down at Sally Carmel's place.

Instead, Tucker said, "You know old man James was mad at me till the day he died just 'cause Duke tossed that cherry bomb into their privy."

Joseph said, "It was you that threw it, not Marion. Did Mrs. James ever recover?"

"Oh, hell yes. She was always a little deaf, anyway. Course, they blamed it all on Duke, that and some kinda constipation they said required hypnotics or hydraulics or some damn thing. How was I supposed to know she was in there? Most folks have a sign, but not them Jameses. I never did like that woman, anyway. Too dull."

"Not so dull in some ways as you might think," Joseph defended mildly.

Tucker sat up, interested. "You mean you and Mrs. James . . . you two?"

Joseph shrugged. "Lavinia was a lonely woman. She'd leave the porch light on for me sometimes when old man James was out in the boat. Said he smelled of fish."

Tucker shook his head in amazement. "If I had any respect for womanhood at all, I'd left you right where you was, dying in that rest home."

"Women like me," Joseph said simply.

"Hey now, Joe"—Tucker leaned toward him—"tell me true about something. Would you've ever tried to thimble my wife?"

"You never had no wife."

"I know that. I'm just asking, would you of messed with her? If I'd gotten married."

"But you never did. You never did get married. Almost did—that Cuban girl, the one with the little blue sea horse on her hand, a tattoo—"

"Jesus H. Christ, Joe! I'm just askin' a simple question. Would you've thimbled my wife? Gawldamn dense Indian—"

Joseph considered the question for a time. He rolled his chew from side to side and slapped at a mosquito. "I guess so—if she had nice skin."

Tucker's face described contempt. "I'll be go to hell. And after all I've done for you."

"I like nice skin," Joseph said. "You want me to lie?"

"That woulda been the polite thing to do! Friends is supposed to do things for each other." Tucker simmered for a moment before he sighed and added, "Know what's sad? I couldn't be trusted with your wife, neither. Not if she was in a loving mood." Tuck caught the sharp look Joseph gave him, so he added hastily, "Which she never was. Either of them."

Joseph said, "That the truth?"

"God honest, my right hand on the Book."

"Hum-m-m-m. Your timing musta been off then, 'cause the second one run off with that bird-watcher from Long Island. Skinny man that wore things around his neck. 'Noculars? Or maybe he had somethin' you didn't."

Tucker started to react to the implications of that, then decided to drop it. He ruffled the paper he was holding, then picked up the box of papers and put it in his lap.

The shrimp boat was out of sight now, behind the scattering of mangrove islands that was the first green gate to the maze of the Ten Thousand Islands southward.

"You know something," Tucker said, his voice sounding tired, "we're both just a couple of low-life sons a bitches."

Joseph nodded his agreement. There was a big bluebottle fly

buzzing around, and he was waiting to get a shot in with his load of tobacco juice.

Tucker said, "Pitiful, that's what we are. Makes me want to get down on my knees and pray for forgiveness, all the bad things we done." He looked over briefly at the bigger man. "Least you're an Indian. You got an excuse."

Joseph was listening but not giving it his full attention. He had his eye on the fly, watching it like a cat.

Tucker said, "Me, I got no excuses. I lived a bad life and I admit it." He raised his voice, looking up. "Hear me God? I admit I ain't been worth a deuce all my life. Coulda done good. Instead, I done bad." His voice became reflective. "Course . . . some might say it was a little stupid to send me down here with a trigger finger and a tallywhacker if You didn't expect me to use 'em." He paused and looked toward the sky again. "But I ain't the kind to second-guess, Lord!"

The fly was buzzing, soaring, descending, its circles getting smaller and smaller. Joseph waited.

"It's the damn truth. I been a sinner my whole life. I've lied, cheated, messed with married women, drank liquor, and, God forgive me, even killed a man, shot him dead—"

The fly landed on the railing, and Joseph spat, a real zinger, which hit the fly—but also Tuck's foot.

Tucker lifted his boot, studying the slime with disgust. "Jesus Christ, Joe, I been bad, but that don't give you the right to spit on me!"

"Wasn't spittin' at you. There was a fly."

"Well, you hit my good boot! Gad—"

Joseph pointed at the struggling fly. "That look like I missed? Besides, you never shot no man."

"Did, too. Shot lots of Japanese. What ya think us marines was doing over there in Hawaii?"

"That was the war. It don't count. I meant you never shot no one else."

"Hell I didn't—That one-eyed fish buyer down in Campeche."

"You didn't shoot him; you shot at him. I was there. You missed. You never could shoot."

"That's right, I shot at him. Out there on the docks that night, it was cold as hell, and he jumped in the water. He got pneumonia and I heard he got complications and died only about a year later.

Same thing as me holding the gun to his head." Tuck folded his hands and looked out over the water. "That good-for-nothing beaner haunts me to this day."

Joseph stood and stretched.

"Hey," Tucker said, "where you going?"

"That bacon smells done. I was gonna go down to that girl's, see about breakfast."

"Sit yourself down. I'm talking about something here."

"If I always waited till you stopped talking, I'd starve."

"I'm talking about what to do with this here discovery of mine—the vitamin water. I'm saying we got a chance to do something good for a change. I got a plan."

Joseph said, "You always got a plan. But ain't none of 'em ever worked."

"And do you know why that is, Joe? Have you put any thought at all into why it is that all the things I discovered, all the smart ideas I had, that they all just kinda floated away from us and made somebody else rich?"

Joseph thought for a moment. " 'Cause you're a fuckup?"

"No!" Tuck made a face, genuinely offended. "No, the only difference is advertising. The whole kit-n-caboodle right there. I never advertised my ideas—I just gave 'em away. And you want to know why?"

Joseph didn't want to know, but he didn't say it. Tuck was going to tell him, anyway.

"The reason I give the ideas away was 'cause I never took 'em seriously enough. Never realized how important they was at the time. When I had Dick Pope out fishing, I said, 'You like to tow people on boards behind boats, just fence the place in, charge admission. Like a circus that doesn't move. Maybe even a restaurant.' He says, 'Cap'n, I like that—a circus that doesn't move. Call it Beautiful Cypress Gardens' Ski Show.' Joe, that's just what I told him." Tuck snapped his fingers. "Next time I turn around, he's making thousands on Cypress Gardens and he's showing what's his name, Mr. Disney, around, saying he should do the same. My idea, Joe. Same with the shrimp and the stone crabs. And when I told Mr. Collier to build a boat around his dredge, it just didn't seem important at the time. Hell—" Tuck's face had softened, his smile a little dreamy—"you know how it was. Florida was so big and wild, there didn't seem no need to grab hold of any particular piece of it. There was plenty for everybody. But now they got her carved down into just a little bitty thing. 'Bout got the juice all sucked out of her. That's why I come up with this plan. Thought Florida would last forever, but she didn't. Been thinking the same thing 'bout my life, tell you the truth. Water or no water, we ain't getting any younger."

Which cut right into Joseph's thoughts: thinking about his grandfather, Chekika's Son, holding the door of the Cadillac open.

You telling me to go ahead and die, Grandpa?

Nope. Tellin' you to get in the damn car. You already dead.

Joseph hesitated . . . sighed . . . said, "Okay, okay, I'll listen to your plan. But couldn't you tell it over breakfast?"

Tomlinson was telling Ford, "The old dude's been spending some time at the library . . . the courthouse, too. You look at this stuff?" He was sitting in Ford's lab, on the steel stool near the stainless-steel dissecting table, while Ford hunched over the dissecting scope. Tomlinson had the contents of the envelope Tuck had given them spread out on the table.

Ford said, "If he was at the library, it was the first time. More likely, he had someone else do it for him."

On the transparent base plate of the microscope, Ford had mounted a cross section of a piece of loggerhead sponge he had taken from one of his sea mobiles. Ford could see the spongin fibers of the sponge's osculum magnified by the scope—its excurrent water opening—as well as the opening vascular wall of the spongocel, where food and oxygen were filtered from the constant flow of seawater. And there was a curling flagellum, the hairlike structure that pulled the water in. Most striking, though, was the cross-thatched symmetry of the animal's silicate skeleton. The skeleton was an intricate pattern of fluted ramps on a curving honeycombed infrastructure. Enlarged a thousand times, what Ford saw might have been an extraordinarily modernistic painting. Enlarged a billion times, a single filament might have been a stairway designed by Dalí.

Sponges consisted of a cooperating community of different cells, and Ford was remembering something he had read. A biologist had done a census on a loggerhead sponge, counting more than sixteen thousand animals, most of them snapping shrimp and crabs, living in the canal system of that single sponge.

He looked up from the microscope and readjusted his wire glasses. "I don't suppose you could bring the pitcher of iced tea in here? It's so damn hot for October."

"No lie, October's always hot. Just as soon as I finish sorting these papers."

Ford was nodding his head. Hot, hot, hot. Through the window, the noon sky was a white haze, the bay greasy flat. The marina baked at the water's edge, the boats immobile in their slips, gray and blue and fiberglass red. Except for Mack sitting on his chair in the office and one of the live-aboards standing on the dock hosing the deck of his boat, there wasn't much movement. Everybody off at work, or maybe sipping beer at the Lazy Flamingo, trying to stay cool. Ford said, "I don't know, maybe I should get air conditioning. I keep thinking about it."

"You've got the ceiling fans, and you get the nice breeze off the water. Air conditioning's not natural, man. We've raised a whole generation of canned-air zombies. My daughter, Nichola, that's not going to happen to her. You know the type: Give me Freon or give me death. It goons up the brain cells. I know about that stuff." Tomlinson had separated the papers into little piles, patted them, then went out the screen door.

Ford heard the volume on his Maxima marine stereo system kick up, Jimmy Buffett singing "Cowboy in the Jungle," which flashed Tuck Gatrell into his mind. Wiry man with great big brown wrists and wild blue eyes . . . he looked so damn much older than Ford had expected.

Tomlinson came back with the iced tea and a can of beer for himself. He picked up a packet of papers to show Ford. "These are all newspaper stories. You look at them?"

Ford said, "Nope," returning his attention to the dissection scope, the Wolfe Zoom binocular system. He loved the feel of it, the finely machined parts and the superb objective system, solid beneath his cheek and big right hand.

Tomlinson said, "These stories are all about miraculous cures, about healing waters and mineral springs. Some of these stories are from the . . . yeah, from the *National Enquirer*. Then some other newspapers—"

"Are they all Xeroxed?"

Tomlinson said, "Let's see . . . yeah, all but a couple. How'd you know that?"

Ford said, "Because I know Tuck."

Tomlinson was reading, not aloud, but making a noise with his mouth, skimming the stories one by one. He said, "There's a well near Lourdes, in the south of France, where people go to be healed by drinking . . . hey, I know that place. It's where Saint Bernadette saw the Virgin." Tomlinson grinned. "Chalk one up for parochial schooling, huh?" He was reading again. "Here's another about a pond in Quintana Roo—that's Mexico, right? Cured a bunch of people with yellow fever. A river off the Zambezi, a stream in County Galway, Ireland . . . here's one about a lake in Mongolia where people bathe and live to be two hundred years old. All these places, like local treasures. That's what this one's about—"

Ford said, "Uh-huh," using surgical scissors to clip open another tiny section of the sponge. The sponge was air-light, almost hollow. The animal seemed to be all fiber and air. What kept it alive?

Tomlinson said, "Now here's a couple of stories about the state planning to acquire land around Mango to create a park that adjoins Everglades National Park."

Ford said, "They're originals, not copies."

"Right! You did look at this stuff. Let's see"—he was leafing through the piles—"and here's a plat map of your uncle's property. He had . . . one hundred twenty-seven acres—'more or less,' it says—and he sold off all but twenty-five to a company called . . . It was right here, the copy of a letter on legal stationery."

"Who's the attorney?"

"Wait a minute . . . he sold it all to a company called Development Unlimited, which it says is part of some kind of enterprise—Kamikaze? Geeze, that's what it says. Sounds Japanese."

Ford said, "I wouldn't think they'd name a company that."

"Why not? *Kamikaze* means 'divine wind.' You know, I speak quite a bit of Japanese—oh, here's the attorney. Lemar Flowers, that's the man's name, the guy who handled the deal for your uncle. Sounds like your uncle sold off his property, but now he's found this spring, he wants it back."

Ford was removing the slide from the microscope, thinking that if he transferred more sponges and tunicates into his big tank, he might not need such an elaborate filtering system. They were perfect cleaning systems, perfectly designed. He said, "What's the date on the newspaper story about the state planning to acquire the land?"

Tomlinson picked up the papers again. "December of last year."

"And when did he sell his property?"

"Ah . . . February this year. Three months later."

"Are there any dates on the copies about those places, the different springs around the world? Not on the stories, but on the photocopies themselves?"

Tomlinson said, "No-o-o, but he had to start collecting them after he sold his land. If he'd known about the spring and believed he could make a lot of money on it, why would he have sold?"

Ford said, "Yeah. Why would he?"

A few minutes before Angela Walker pulled into the drive, Tuck and Joseph were walking homeward along the bay road after eating a late breakfast at Sally Carmel's. Tuck's dog, Gator, and his old Appaloosa, Roscoe, followed along behind, and every few yards the horse would nose up and butt Tucker in the back.

Finally, Tuck turned and said, "Dang it, Roscoe, if I'd wanted to ride, I'd a brung a saddle!"

The horse shook its head, mane flying. To Joseph, Tucker said, "The old fool's been acting like a colt ever since his *cojone-e-es* growed back." Like he was complaining, but smiling because he was pleased. "Wants to head out on the trail, see if he can find a friend."

Joseph recognized the manipulative tone; knew this was not just some innocent comment, and he replied to the declaration it was. "I ain't got a horse. I can't go on no saddle trip—and I ain't riding double with you."

Tuck began to protest but then dropped the pretense. Joseph was too suspicious for it to be any fun. He said, "I can get you a horse. They got a bunch of them up to Cypress Gate Acres."

Joseph thought for a moment, couldn't place the name—Cypress Gate Acres—then remembered the big development they'd built in the north part of Everglades County with all the houses and canals and even a nice shopping center with a store where Joseph had once stopped to buy beer. He asked, "They sell horses up there, too?"

"A few of them people keep horses. I reckon one of them's bound to be overstocked. Little five-acre ranches with corrals where they teach the horses to jump. Jumping horse, that'd be nice to ride, huh?"

"If I had enough money for a horse," Joseph said, "I wouldn't 'a been at that county rest home. I'd a been at the other place, that Sunset Retirement place, the one that plays church bells every night. I heard they got a sauna bath there."

"First time I ever heard you worry about money."

Joseph knew what that meant. "Uh-oh," he said.

"Uh-oh what? What's that supposed to mean?"

"You plan to steal it. The horse. That's what it means."

"Not steal, just borrow it. Take it for a test drive, then pay when we're flush. I'm no horse thief."

"Just long as it's not some kid's. I'm not gonna make some kid cry by stealing his horse."

Tucker said, "We'll find one with a fat owner. Do the horse a favor. Besides, we used to graze cattle up that way and I don't remember giving anyone permission to build a dang city. 'Bout time we got a little payback."

Joseph was thinking about the last horse he'd owned, a tall chestnut gelding, seventeen hands high, worked cattle on free rein and would hold until dawn. Buster, that was the horse's name. But then Joseph had gotten married the second time, moved to Miami with the woman who sold real estate and who apparently liked bird-watchers, and Buster had jumped the fence at the place he was being boarded and got hit by a cement truck. That was . . . twenty-five years ago?

Tuck was talking about the trip, taking horses and bedrolls, saying how they'd ride right across the Everglades, pick up Ervin T. Rouse, Tucker's fiddle-playing friend, bring him back to live in Mango. That was part of his plan. Find about a half dozen of their old friends, get them to drinking the water. Then when the government people said the water was a fake, Tuck would say, "Look at these old-timers. They don't look spry to you?" Make enough money to buy his land back that way. Only why the state would want to give up its park idea, Joseph didn't know. Not that it mattered. Joining up with Tuck was better than going back to his chikee hut in the Glades, staring at the old *Playboy* calendar on the wall.

Tuck had been naming names, people he wanted to see again. Then he said, "The only one we can't take horses to is Henry

Short. That little mulatto bastard's still alive. Must be ninety-five. I hear he's squatting down in the islands again, that patch of mound. Hell, it's so far back in, I doubt you even know it. No Name Mound, that's what I used to call it when I was fish guiding."

Joseph asked, "The mound back in from Lostman's River or the one north, closer to Loser's Creek?" When Joseph was little, in the years before his grandfather died drunk in Immokalee, the old man had taken him to all the mounds to camp and fish. All told, it took the whole summer. But the one near Lostman's was so jungled up, they hadn't stayed more than a night, and his grandfather had refused even to stop at the other mound—it was a "power place," his grandfather had said—whatever the hell that meant. "Indians, we never stay here. Too many spirits. And the mosquitoes are bad, too."

"The Loser's Creek mound?" Joseph said. That would be just like Henry Short, staying on a bad mound.

"That's the one. The water's so thin, you can't even use a motor. Hell, maybe we *could* ride the horses!"

Joseph was thinking about Henry Short, wondering whether he really was alive. Sometimes Tuck talked just to talk, making up things, but it was interesting to hear Henry's name after so many years. A long time ago, a bad man by the name of Ed Watson had lived in the islands. Henry Short was supposedly the man who shot him. Shot him first anyway, before the whole island of Chokoloskee joined in, shooting the corpse so they could all say they did it. Watson had supposedly murdered a lot of people—shot Belle Starr out west before running south—but then he ran into Henry. As a boy, Joseph had seen Henry once, a small, creamy-skinned man with funny-looking eyes, like his body was there but his mind was off living someplace else. Him carrying a shotgun in the crook of his arm, standing there beside the Smallwood General store in Chokoloskee, quiet among the white people, and scary-looking because of it. At least he had scared Joseph.

Joseph started to say something about Henry Short, ask whether Tuck was joking, but instead he said something else, figuring Tuck wouldn't tell him the truth, anyway.

"Tuck?"

"You keep interruptin', Joe, how you gonna learn anything?" Tucker had stopped at the shell drive to his ranch house, studying the small white car there sitting in the shade and the woman in the nice clothes standing beside it.

"Tuck, when I get my horse, I think I'm gonna call him Buster."

"Well now, that ought to bring us some luck." Tuck was walking again, fixing a friendly expression on his face. "Ought to attract every cement truck for a thousand miles." Then he said, "Keep your mouth shut and let me do the talking." Meaning the woman.

As if Joseph wouldn't have done that, anyway.

Tucker was on his best behavior—Joseph could see that. Smiling at the woman policeman, saying, "Yes, ma'am," "No, ma'am," "Wish I knew, ma'am," to almost every question, looking at the ground, his thumbs over his belt, his face shaded by the brim of his cowboy hat. The two of them standing, leaning against the porch railing after the woman said she'd been sitting for two hours, the long drive down, so she didn't feel like taking that chair on the porch. To which Tuck had said, "Ma'am, I hate to see a young woman pretty as you out in the heat. So why don't we move to the shade and I'll bring you a nice glass of sweet tea."

Oh, he could be charming . . . and the way he acted even older and more hobbled-up than he was. Grandfatherly—that was it, the way he was behaving. Which made Joseph think the old bastard knew more than he was saying, the woman asking him about three men she said had come to the islands and disappeared.

Tuck hadn't mentioned that before. Some famous fisherman and two men hired by the state, sent down to check out Tuck's land, or what was once his land, so they could present the information at some meeting so the government could get its permits and do whatever it had to do. That hearing Tuck had told him about, only now the state was having to hustle around, do a lot of retesting because nobody could find the men who had done the original testing.

"There's an element of law called the chain of custody," the woman, Agent Walker, said, looking right at Tuck. "There's a strict procedure for taking samples and having them tested. The bottles, the envelopes—whatever—they have to go straight from one person's hands to another person's hands, everything sealed, labeled, and signed for. Now those men have disappeared, the chain of custody has been broken because some of those samples—I don't know what, soil and water, maybe?—they disappeared with them."

Tucker looked real serious and concerned. "Makes you want to move to Canada, don't it?" he said.

"Something else," Walker said. "I understand the state is having trouble finding the principals who purchased your land. What was it, some kind of blind land trust when you sold it? The hundred acres. So legally, I guess there's no way they can find out for sure who owns it. At least not yet."

"You know, ma'am, I think I heard somethin' about that."

The woman waited for Tuck to say something else, but when he didn't, all she said was, "I'm sure you have."

"Word gets around. Even in these parts."

Joseph felt the woman about to say, "I'm counting on it," but she didn't. Looking around, she said, "This little place is so pretty . . . those old streetlights, the little houses . . . so pretty I wouldn't blame anyone for trying to come up with a way to stop the park."

Tuck was right with her. "Stop it, ma'am? Who the heck would want to stop it—forgive my language."

"You mean you like the idea?"

"I think it'll be da . . . dar . . . awful nice when they get that park built. Maybe they'll kill off these skeeters so they can put out their picnic tables and camping places for trailers. Be nice to have some folks from Michigan and O-hi-ho runnin' around. You think they'll be a swimming pool?" He slapped a mosquito on his arm and flicked it off with his finger.

The woman said, "I wouldn't know about that, Mr. Gatrell. I'm trying to find out what happened to those men."

Tucker started walking toward the woman's car, saying, "Just wish I coulda been more help," handling her so easily that Joseph had to admire him. Tuck had his talents, there was no denying.

But getting into the car, Walker said, "Oh—there was something I forgot to ask."

"You name it, ma'am."

"Are you familiar with Barron Creek Marina just south of here?"

"I should say I am. Used to work for Barron Collier when I was just a sprout. You ever wonder how they figured to build a road right across the saw grass—"

"Yes, you told me that story, Mr. Gatrell. The floating dredge. When I called you on the telephone last week."

"I did?" He chuckled as if befuddled. "I gotta tell you, old age is 'bout the most unexpected thing ever happened to me. Now my brain's gotten leaky—"

"What I wanted to ask was, were you at that marina on Thursday, October first, and Monday, October fifth? The Barron Creek Marina?"

Tucker had his hand on his jaw, thinking. "Is this October we're in now?"

"You know Larry Baker, don't you?"

"Larry runs the marina, ma'am. He's a regular peach. I knew his daddy—"

"Mr. Baker told me that you were at the marina those days. The morning, both times. He said he saw Chuck Fleet and Charles Herbott talking with you, going over a map. Nautical chart, I mean. He said you might have been giving them directions."

"Now those two names don't ring a bell. Those men, the two you mentioned, are they from around here?"

"Herbott is an environmental consultant and Fleet is the surveyor you said you met working in your pasture—"

"That's why the names sounded familiar!"

"You talked with each of them the day they disappeared. That's what Larry Baker told me."

Joseph was thinking, Look who's handling who now, watching Tuck smile as if he was a confused old man. Tuck said, "Ma'am, I was a fishing guide in these parts prob'ly before your daddy was borned, so I can't go near a marina without people hauling out their charts, askin' me this or that. Where the snook? Where the tar-pawn? How you get to so and so? Don't want to brag on myself, but I'm kinda famous in these parts as a waterman."

"I realize that, Mr. Gatrell."

"You ever wonder why President Truman come to these islands to fish? He come to see me."

"Last week, on the phone, that was one of your most fascinating stories. But what I need to know now is, what did Charles Herbott and Chuck Fleet ask you?"

"Wish I knew, ma'am. Like I said, there's always so many. But if Larry Baker said I talked to 'em, you can bet it's the truth. If he wasn't drunk."

"Do you remember anyone asking you the shortest route to the boundary of Everglades National Park? What is that, about twenty miles from the marina?"

"When people ask that, I always send 'em to the outside, down the coast in open water. They get back in those islands, it's awful tricky and dangerous, ma'am."

"I guess Mr. Fleet and Mr. Herbott found that out." The woman started her car, adding through the open window, "You try to remember, Mr. Gatrell. I'll be talking to you soon. Or perhaps someone from the local Sheriff's Department."

Tucker was waving, smiling. "Look forward to it. Company's better'n cold beer at my age."

As the car pulled away, already going fast along the bay road, Joseph said, "If it was you who messed with those men, I hope you tried to shoot 'em. That way, I'd know they're still alive."

Tucker said, "Joe, sometimes you remind me of a lost ball in tall grass."

"That woman'll be coming back—I ain't lost about that. She sees something in you. Did you do it?"

"Hell no. You think I'd a been seen in public with men I was about to kill?" Then walking up the steps to the porch, Tuck said, "Better get your gear together. We go horse shopping tonight."

SEVEN

❦

Along with the typical Friday-night procession of telephone complaints about loud drunks, loud parties, domestic squabbles, and burglaries, the Sheriff's Department's Cypress Gate substation, located in a cinder-block annex beside the Toys "Я" Us shopping center, also received two unusual calls from one of its solid citizens, Mr. Pendergast, owner of the community's three McDonald's restaurants.

At slightly after 9:00 P.M., Mr. Pendergast notified the department that he had received an anonymous inquiry that had left him uneasy. "A man just called saying he had heard great things about my son's favorite horse and said he was interested in buying it," Mr. Pendergast told the dispatcher.

"What's odd about that?" the dispatcher wanted to know.

"I don't have a son," Mr. Pendergast said. "Then the man who called me said, 'Well, maybe it was your daughter's horse I heard about.' "

The dispatcher said, "And you don't have a daughter?"

"Right," Mr. Pendergast said. "The caller, he sounded like an old man, or I would have hung up on him right then and there. All the cranks out around these days. But he sounded nice. Very polite in a southern sort of way, and I happened to mention that my wife would be very happy if I sold all my horses—horses are a hobby of mine, you see."

"And?" the dispatcher said.

"And then the man said something very strange. He asked me if I was a bird-watcher."

"A bird-watcher?"

Mr. Pendergast said, "Does it sound to you like he might be ah . . . unbalanced? I've been sitting here worrying."

The dispatcher said, "You have no idea who the man was? You didn't recognize the voice?"

"Not at all. Old man, as I've said, southern accent. I have no dea how he knew I had horses or how he knew my name and number. That's what worries me. He asked me if I was a bird-watcher, and when I said no, he thanked me and hung up."

The dispatcher asked, "Do you have your name on your mail-box, Mr. Pendergast?"

"Uh . . . yes."

"And your name's listed in the phone book?"

"Oh right, I see how he could have gotten the number now," Mr. Pendergast said. "That makes sense. But why would anyone ask such strange questions?"

The dispatcher said, "If the old man calls again, I'd try to find out."

At 11:35 P.M., Mr. Pendergast telephoned the Sheriff's Department substation a second time, but this time the call came in through the 911 system, which flashed onto the computer screen the name and address of Donald H. Pendergast, 1861 Old Naples Road. The dispatcher recognized the name, but Mr. Pendergast's voice sounded different because the man was clearly near panic.

"I've called to report there are chickens in my stables!"

"Could you say that again."

"Chickens, for Christ's sake. In my stable!"

"Mr. Pendergast, you need to calm down if I'm to under-stand—"

"Chickens! Do you understand me now? Someone put chickens in the stalls with my horses. Chickens everywhere! There must be twenty, thirty of them."

The dispatcher had picked up the VHF microphone with his free hand to put on-duty deputies and emergency medical services on alert. But now the dispatcher was beginning to wonder whether Mr. Pendergast, the solid citizen, might also be a little drunk. "Let me get this straight, Mr. Pendergast. You say chickens are harass-ing your horses?"

"Yes! I mean, no—not harassing, but they were in the stalls and my horses were terrified, trying to kick the place down. I went out to see what all the noise was about, and that's when I found the chickens."

"Your chickens escaped and got in with your horses?" The dis-patcher was thinking, Man, I'm glad we've got this one on tape. C liff will love it.

"No, the chickens didn't escape; my horses did!"

"But I thought you said the chickens were in the stalls. I mean your horses were in the stalls with the chickens—"

"Would you just shut up and listen, for Christ's sake?" Mr. Pendergast was shouting now, thinking about all the taxes he paid and the disrespect he heard in the dispatcher's voice. He had to fight the urge to say, "I pay your salary!" Instead, he said, "About twenty minutes ago, I heard a terrible racket out in the stables. I went outside to take a look. I thought there might be a fire, my horses were so hysterical. I went straight to Wildfire's stall, and that's when I saw them."

"A horse?"

"No—chickens, goddamn it!"

"I mean Wildfire, that's a horse?"

"Of course it's a . . . Listen you—Wildfire is a ten-thousand dollar jumper. You'd better start paying attention."

"A jumper's a horse? I really am trying to understand here, Mr. Pendergast—"

"Of course it's a horse. I mean it is . . . I mean he is, Wildfire. There were chickens in his stall. All the stalls. That's what was making my horses terrified."

"So your chickens did escape and got in with your horses."

"No . . . look, this is the only time I'm going to say this— DON'T OWN ANY CHICKENS!"

"So where did they come from?"

"That's what I'm trying to tell you. Someone snuck in here and put chickens in the stalls. Horses that aren't used to chickens go nuts when that happens. They were kicking down the doors. That's why I had to let them out."

"I think you did the reasonable thing. So now the chickens are free—"

"The horses! I let the horses out! Seven purebred jumpers. Now they're running loose around the countryside because whoever brought the chickens left the pasture gate open."

"Mr. Pendergast, you're calling nine-one-one to report you've been sabotaged by chickens—"

"Listen, you goddamn dolt, I'm calling to tell you to get some squad cars over here right away to help me catch forty thousand dollars' worth of horses!"

The dispatcher, raising his voice to match Mr. Pendergast's, said, "Hey, buddy, I don't have to put up with the name-calling."

"The hell you don't," Donald Pendergast yelled. "I pay your salary! And if we don't find all those horses by dawn, it'll be your ass!"

Joseph Egret had ridden all kinds of horses in his life, but he'd never been on one so smooth-gaited as this. Big-withered stallion, so black that he looked glossy blue when the light was just right, and man could he fly. The scrawny little cattle ponies he and Tuck had ridden in all the far-off range places, Cuba, Nicaragua, the Pacific coast of Guatemala and Costa Rica, they were knot-hard and knew the business, but they would have looked like terrier dogs compared to this animal. The night before, Friday night, Tuck had stopped at Rigaberto's place, the neighbor who kept the loud chickens, and bought twenty of them, little brown banties. Paid cash and put them in cages.

"If I didn't hate these little bastards so much," Tuck had said, "I coulda never forced myself to eat as many as I did. Now they're finally gonna do something besides stick in my teeth."

Three hours later, about an hour before midnight, they sat in Tuck's old truck with a horse trailer hitched to the back, pulled off on the side of Old Naples Road, and Tuck said, "Looka there at all the horses coming. Running down the road like scared rabbits."

Joseph had said, "We gonna steal all of 'em?"

"Steal?" Tuck snorted "We ain't stealin' nothing. I give away some chickens for free, and now we've found a bunch of horses running wild. This used to be free range, remember. My advice to you is, pick out one of those mustangs and see if you can break it before morning. That's when we saddle up and head east."

Only they hadn't pulled out that morning because Tuck had said he'd thought of some stuff he had to do, mostly contact more television and newspaper people. "Advertising," Tuck kept saying. "Not advertising is the only reason I ain't rich right now." But Joseph guessed Tuck had postponed because he was so tired, the way he looked after being up most of the night catching the tall horse, then getting him into the trailer, then getting him into the same barn with Roscoe without anyone getting kicked or horse-bit.

Tuck didn't look good. Looked like some of the air had seeped out of him, he was so worn down.

So now it was Saturday afternoon, late, with thunderstorms building over the Everglades, purple clouds the size of castles drifting toward Mango and the Gulf, which was one of Joseph's favorite times of day if he didn't have to be on the water. Nice breeze and it smelled good, too. The bay smelled salty, like oysters, and there was the lemony smell of key lime trees growing on the shell ridge that crossed the pasture. And the horse—there was that smell; a little lathered up because they'd been riding for about two hours, along the bay road clear to the Tamiami Trail with its fast traffic, then through the melaleuca and oak flats to where the saw grass began.

Joseph liked the saw grass. Clear to the horizon, it didn't stop the wind. But the wind made designs in the grass, drifting pale streaks and swirls on yellow fields that spread away to cypress hummocks in the distance: dark domes of shade in so much sunlight that it hurt the eyes. Joseph had missed the saw grass.

"Good Buster, nice Buster. How you like this, Buster?" Joseph kept talking to the horse, getting acquainted. "See that slough there? I kilt a deer there once. See that little creek there? Used to be a prime place for otters. Goddamn, Buster, you got to canter the whole way? I'm an old man—couldn't you walk a bit?"

But no, the horse had a sweet quartering gait, bouncing along as if the earth were a trampoline, smooth as a rocking chair. Unless they came to a fence, then the horse wanted to go; wanted to open the throttle, and Joseph had to lean back on the reins to hold him. "Them ain't no breakaway fences like the horse show's, Buster, them's the real McCoys. You're in the real world now."

Finally, though, Joseph decided to call the horse's bluff; let him go just to see what would happen and, God almighty, that horse went from a dead stop to a full run in about two strides—or so Joseph would tell Tucker later—headed straight for a five-strand barbed-wire fence. The next thing Joseph knew, he was airborne, arching over the fence with Buster beneath him.

"Lordy, Buster, you must got wings!"

After that, no fence stood in their way or altered their route. Buster didn't know a thing about cattle—Joseph had tried to work him a little on the way out, using a couple of Tuck's half-wild Brahma crossbreds. The horse had shied, fighting him the whole way, stopping only to lift his tail and splat a load. Buster didn't give a damn for cattle. But he could jump.

Joseph considered riding clear to his old chikee shack, but it was way back in, about ten miles off the Trail, along a natural lane of high ground that drifted in and out of the saw grass—Pay-hay-okee, his grandfather had called the region. Joseph had headed that way automatically, not really considering the distance, but when he got to the weed-choked ridge, he turned the horse abruptly. There were all kinds of trails and byways in the Glades—people didn't know about them anymore, but they were there. Joseph had been traveling them since childhood, so why should he waste his time on this one? He'd been up that trail plenty of times before. Besides, the idea of seeing his old chikee put a hollow feeling in his stomach, a strange ache he couldn't define.

It made him wonder about things. How the hell had he ended up like that, sick and filthy, in the hands of government strangers? People who put him beneath those stiff white sheets, talking and joking as if he wasn't there, giving him the same thorough attention they might give a sick dog.

"That chikee hut ain't my home no more, Buster. Why the hell you want to see it?"

He touched his boots to the horse and headed south. The Tamiami Trail, black as electrical conduit, cut through the saw grass and disappeared east and west. The water ditch on the north side of the road, created by the floating dredge that had made the roadbed, was littered with Styrofoam cups and beer cans. Joseph had to hunt to find a good place to cross to the highway. He took his time, waiting out traffic.

"I'm gonna tell you right now, Buster—watch out for cement trucks. Them bastards get paid by the load and don't give a shit for fine livestock."

The horse didn't seem to be listening. Probably looking for something to jump.

"Even you can't jump one of them things. They got a great big tank on the back that turns round and round."

The rain caught them on the Trail, a thunder burst of water and green sky, so he took shelter beneath the tin porch roof at Jimmy Tiger's Souvenirs. Jimmy Tiger and his family were Miccosukees; lived there, putting on alligator-wrestling shows and giving air-boat rides for the tourists. There were little Indian stops like that all along the Trail. Rubber tomahawks and birchbark toy canoes made in China.

Looking out through the rain, hearing it drum the roof above him, Joseph wondered what Chinamen thought of Indians. Sitting there in China sewing little pieces of birchbark together, putting rubber hatchet heads on painted sticks.

"Probably think we're little tiny midgets that eat plastic eggs." Talking to the horse, even though he knew Jimmy Tiger's grandkids were staring at him from the windows of their palmetto-roofed home. Jimmy Tiger, who was a young man when Joseph was a boy, was probably in there looking, too. But it wasn't polite to make eye contact—they weren't like white people. Joseph knew that, even though they treated him as if he were white, the Miccosukee and Seminole both. Always there to help if he really needed help, but keeping their distance, too, letting him know he wasn't a part of the tribe. Not that he blamed them, the way his grandfather had acted, always so uppity. Great-grandson of Chekika, the Indian who raided an island in the Keys, killed all the whites, and escaped up through the Ten Thousand Islands into the Glades. Known to the soldiers who hunted him as a Spanish Indian, though the Glades Indians knew better. Chekika wasn't Spanish. He wasn't Miccosukee or Seminole, either. He was the last, or one of the last, of the mound builders, the Calusa, physically huge and wild in a fight.

A little drunk or a lot drunk, his grandfather liked to say, "Our fathers was trading with the Mayas, building shell temples when them ones calls themselves Seminoles was running buck-ass-naked through the woods, howling at the moon."

Which didn't make him a favorite of the Jimmy Tiger clan, or the Buffalo Tiger clan, or the Joe Dan Bowlegs clan, or any of the others. Him being a snob like that. Which Joseph had recognized, even as a boy, but he still didn't like the way they'd treated his grandfather, or his mother, either—she was a Cuban Indian—and it had stuck with Joseph. They didn't accept him, he wouldn't accept them. He didn't mind being an outcast, though it bothered him sometimes to be treated like a white by the Indians and like an Indian by the whites. Except for Tuck, who treated all people the same—as if nobody had much sense but him. He was good to be around because of that. Joseph could relax around Tuck.

"Hear me, rider!" A voice was calling to him from the window, shouting because of the rain. Joseph glanced around just long enough to see that it was old Jimmy Tiger, long gray hair, wearing a bright rag-patch shirt.

Turned toward the window but staring at the ground, Joseph heard the old man say, "You have the look of Joseph, the grandson of Chekika's Son. That you, Joe?"

"Me, Jimmy."

"*Chee han tha mo!*"

Automatically, Joseph replied, "*Cha mo,*" talking in the old tongue. Didn't even have to think about it.

"You not dead? Someone's lied to me!" The happiness in old Jimmy's voice seemed genuine, and Joseph was touched by it.

"Not dead yet."

"We've got fish. Fish and beans. You can wait the rain inside."

Joseph had been invited into Miccosukee homes before, but this time there was no grudging formality about it. Jimmy had probably run out of men his age to talk to. "I promised to get back. Sure would like to another time."

"I was thinking of your grandfather, and there you were on a black horse when I looked out the window!"

Joseph turned to pat Buster on the neck and got another quick look at Jimmy Tiger—the man's eyes were cloudy blue white. Blind now, or nearly so. How the hell did he know the horse was black? Joseph did not speak.

"I heard the frog eaters took you to the government place."

Which was the old way of speaking of whites—because they ate frogs, which no Indian would eat unless he was on the trail and starving.

"Heard you musta died there, because your shack was empty. That was some nice calendar you had. Pretty women!"

"Didn't die," Joseph replied. The rain had slowed, and Joseph let the horse have his head. From the gravel parking lot, near the sign that read JIMMY TIGER'S FAMOUS REPTILE SHOW, he heard the old man's voice call to him: "Only the young have time for old differences! Good to see you, Joe!"

Joseph waved as Buster took him away in a smooth canter, heading to Mango the back way, across the pasture, where they jumped the gate, hoping Tuck was watching. But Tuck wasn't on the porch, where he usually was at that hour, a bottle of beer in his hand, spitting Red Man, looking at the smooth bay after the daily storm had sailed through, watching night come. And there was a blue Chevy pickup in the yard, the bed carrying buckets and a pair of rubber boots—Joseph could see in from the vantage point of the horse—and he knew it was Marion Ford's truck.

"See there, Buster? Tuck's got company. Nope, his mullet boat's gone, so he's out on the water someplace. Let's us go get a drink."

He turned the horse south toward the mangroves, then got off and walked him along the muddy trail. Then he stopped, squinting through the gloom. He said to the horse, "Somebody's just come through here. See the muddy water in the footprints?"

He walked for a while longer, then said, "It ain't Tuck. Tuck always wears boots." He stopped and looked once more. "It ain't Marion. He'd a stopped and looked at that big spider hanging in its web. At least, that's the way he always used to be. This person didn't stop, just walked on past."

They came out of the mangrove swamp and made their way through palmetto scrub, watching for snakes, and then the trees closed in above them as they headed up the mound, where Joseph slowed and whispered. "See, Buster? Just like I thought." Meaning the long-haired man, Tomlinson, sitting cross-legged on the ground beside the artesian well.

Tomlinson said, "That's weird, I knew it would be you," hardly moving his head to look, staring straight ahead, kind of glassy-eyed. Hippie-looking, with yellow hair down to his shoulders, a dark little beard that touched his chest, the way his chin was pulled in. Wearing some kind of baggy clothes, but hard to see what exactly because the light had faded. Sitting there, Tomlinson said, "For sure, this is one of those karmic deals, you and me meeting by chance on an Indian mound. The way the sky's been so strange lately. It's all a sign—I've got an eye for this kind of thing. You get to know me, you'll see."

Joseph took Buster's reins and threw a clove hitch around a gumbo-limbo limb, feeling his own butt bones creak, his back hurting him and his feet a little numb, too. All that riding. Thinking, Why'd the hippie have to be here? I wanted it to be just me and Buster.

He knelt by the spring—the ground was mushy around it—stirred the water with his hands, and took a drink, hearing Tomlinson say, "Mr. Gatrell wasn't home. So I just came on out here, hoping you wouldn't mind. Doc's back at his lab working. He let me borrow the truck."

Joseph thought, Oh, but didn't speak. Letting the hippie do all the talking, just as he had the other night.

"When you brought me out here before, I didn't have a chance to get a feel for the place. You know what I'm saying? Certain places have a feel? I wanted to zero in on it. Get a fix on the vibes." Tomlinson seemed to shake himself, coming out of his trance or whatever it was that made his eyes glassy. He rolled his head around on his shoulders, stretching, but stayed on the ground, looking now at Joseph. "And it is heavy. A very heavy feel to this mound. Like the air's thick; vibrations zapping all around. A power place, that's what the Indians call a spot like this—hey, but wait a minute, I'm telling you your business, man. Sorry."

Power place, like something his grandfather had once said. Joseph thought, These hippie people, they always talk so strange. Like years before, back in the sixties, he guessed, there had been a lot of them, hitchhiking on all the roads or driving rusty minibuses, always stopping him to ask odd questions. Was he on a vision quest? Did he know the Way of the Circle? Did he sell peyote buttons? Would he like to join them in a sweat lodge? But some of those hippie girls were pretty. Lively, too, if he could get them out of the sweatbox before the heat had drained all the energy from them.

Tomlinson said, "I've been sitting here trying to open all the receivers and I finally locked in. It was intense. There're a lot of souls here. I sat for about an hour, then opened my eyes. You know what I saw?"

Joseph looked around and up into the tree canopy. He could see a few faint stars glimmering, nothing else. A little bit of the bay. "Maybe you saw Tuck? He's gone in his boat."

"Hoo-hoo—perfect, man!" Tomlinson was chuckling. "Reality of the moment. Cut through all the bullshit, yeah. The perfect Zen reply. 'Tell me of the void,' the student asks. 'Shut up and let me eat my rice,' the master replies. You are a very wise man, Joseph."

Mentioning rice put a picture in Joseph's mind of the Chinamen who made Indian souvenirs. But then he thought, That's nice of the hippie, calling me wise, and he sat down on the ground as Tomlinson continued. "But I've had a little touch of enlightenment sitting here. Seriously, man. I know, I know, it's small potatoes probably to the training you've been through. The visions. The spiritual journeys. You can see a lot further than I can. Hell, the old indigenous ways, you probably lived them. What are you, about seventy-something?"

" 'Bout," Joseph replied. "But I don't see so good anymore. You get old, your eyes start getting bad." Let the hippie think him wise if he wanted, but Joseph wasn't going to lie about his eyesight.

"Wonderful!" Tomlinson was chuckling again. "Shift the metaphor and let humility shine through. Don't tell me that Eastern spirituality and the spirituality of Native Americans don't come from the same tree. Asia is the source of both, remember! Nonlinear spark of being. Oneness, man. Spontaneity of life. You hear what I'm saying?"

"Sure. It's just my eyes. I still hear good."

"*Exactly.* Nailed it right in the heart." Tomlinson was running his fingers through his hair, his enthusiasm showing. "I knew you were enlightened. The moment I saw you, I sensed it, felt it. But I'd like you to listen to something, man." His tone became sober, respectful. "I flashed on something here, a whole big scene. The molecules are probably a few hundred years old, but they're still floating around. You know, like light and sound never stop? They just keep right on happening after they can't be seen or heard? But this enlightened thing I experienced grabbed ahold. Put them right back in order, and I could see it all like it was on a movie screen. No, better than that. Like it was in three-D, all around me in stereo sound."

Joseph almost said something about the television he'd wanted to take from the rest home, but he didn't. Maybe the hippie wasn't really talking about movies. It was hard to tell.

Tomlinson said, "I saw the way this place used to be hundreds of years ago. Thousands—this is an old place. A million souls. More. All crowded in on this stretch of coast. The mound Mr. Gatrell's house is on. The other lower ones. Mounds all along the Gulf; a whole civilization of people; dugout canoes; kids running naked on the beach; thatched temples that would hold a thousand people; and shamans wearing wild wooden masks to frighten away evil. All right here, man, right where we're sitting. I saw it!"

Joseph was interested, following along.

Tomlinson said, "Listen and you can still hear their voices. Let your mind go—hey, try it!—open up to the old sounds. They're still vibrating in the shells, man. That's what I tuned in to. I mean, the shells *resonate*. That's what you meant when you said you could still hear just fine, isn't it?"

Intent on listening, Joseph didn't answer. He could hear the mangroves creaking in the evening sea breeze, and he could hear a bubbling, cackling sound, probably Rigaberto's chickens. No, wait—most of them had been moved to the rich horse ranch. The artesian well, that's what the noise was. Bubbling right there beside him. The only voice Joseph heard was Tomlinson's.

"I've been doing some reading, too," Tomlinson said. "Researching human history, ethnology, that's my work, man. I'm a professional. I haven't had time to do any original research yet, but I put together a few things. Ran a search through Compuserve, scoped out the local library. Found some pretty good translations of letters written by Jesuit priests sent by Spain to convert the people who built these mounds. From back in the seventeenth and eighteenth centuries. They were a great people—big and strong, those mound builders. Great fishermen and divers. The Calusa. They never needed agriculture, yet they were a highly complex society that ruled most of the tribes on the Florida peninsula, exacting tribute. Ass kickers, that comes through in the data."

Joseph thought, Now he's starting to sound like my grandfather again. He moved as if to get up, saying, "I just come up here for a drink—"

"Right, man. The past, the future. All in this moment."

"—since Tuck was gone. He doesn't want me drinking from the spring no more. He keeps big jars of water in the icebox, afraid somebody might follow us and know where we're getting it. He'd be mad, he knew I come."

"For sure. Understand entirely. My lips are sealed." Tomlinson twisted an invisible key and tossed it away. "But the point here is, Doc was telling me something about you."

"Marion?"

"Uh-huh. He said you've got a thing about not being mistaken for a member of one of the Glades tribes. And I was just wondering—"

"Marion and me, we used to have nice times, back when he was a boy. He didn't have to be talking all the time."

"Hah! The man says five words in a row, it's a speech. But about you, he mentioned this thing you've got; he said you may be re-lated to the people who built these mounds."

Standing, feeling uneasy but not minding this hippie so much anymore—he seemed strange but nice—Joseph said, "My great-great-grandfather was Chekika." He shrugged.

"My God!" Tomlinson got to his feet, fingers working at his hair again. "I know that name. Even before I started researching, I knew that name. I don't know exactly why—hey, maybe I heard it in a vision? You think that could be? A karmic message?"

Joseph said, "I'm going to take Buster on back. Tuck doesn't want people up here." He was untying the horse's reins. Maybe the next thing the hippie would say was that he'd seen Chekika riding in a Cadillac, another death message. Joseph didn't want to stick around for that.

"The point is"—Tomlinson was following him down the mound as Joseph took his time, leading the horse in the dark-ness—"I may have a way for you to keep possession of this mound. Hell, maybe all the mounds. Your people built them, right?"

Joseph didn't reply. The way the hippie jumped around from subject to subject was making his head hurt.

"The U.S. government never had a treaty with the Calusa—see what I'm saying? They've taken the land illegally, and if we can prove you're the last living heir . . . these mounds are your birth-right, that's what I'm saying."

Joseph said over his shoulder, "I don't have no birthright. I wasn't born in a hospital, so I don't got no papers at all."

"Birth . . . ah-h-h? Oh, you mean birth certificate! Doesn't mat-ter, man. Hell, it's probably better you don't. I might be able to do it, prove you're a descendant. Don't you see? That's why all those souls were talking to me. And man"—Tomlinson was looking up—"those clouds look like they're on fire. It's all a sign!"

Joseph kept walking.

"You're probably wondering how we can do that. Prove it, I mean. Hell, hardly anyone else would know. But I do. That's my point: exactly why they chose me! That's why they showed me the way this coast used to be; invited me to meet the family, so to speak. The karmic bond. I'm going to have to contact an archaeol-ogist who's worked in the area, then this old buddy of mine who's like the top dude in the field. Then I'll need some of your hair, Joseph. I hope we won't have to, but maybe a bone sample, too."

Joseph stopped, turned, looking at the hippie's dim shape beyond Buster's rump. "I need my bones! If you saw my grandfather in a Cadillac, he's lying!"

Tomlinson said, "Now, now. Just a little scraping, that's all. Won't hurt a bit." Then he said, "Have you ever heard of a thing called DNA testing?"

EIGHT

❦

After a month on the sailboat, Sally Carmel's little white and yellow cottage seemed huge, a clapboard and tin delight with enough room to dismantle her tough on-board schedule and replace it with a more luxurious routine that, along with maintenance, study, and gardening, allowed space for soapy baths, morning jogs, and, in the evening, dancing alone, barefooted on the oak-strip floors.

Sometimes at night, sitting in the living room with just a reading lamp on, her legs curled up and with Ansel, the white cat, vibrating on her lap, Geoff would slip into her mind, the heat and weight of him. Geoff, her ex-husband. The man sounds he made, the intensity of his presence, filling the house with him, him, him, so that there was hardly room for her.

Geoff was a spoiled ass. . . .

Still, it left a hollowness in the cottage—a hollowness in her, too. Not that she was still in love with him—well, maybe just a little—but losing a mate created a void that grew stronger in the lonely night hours and sucked at the foundations of the new life she told herself she was building.

You failed at marriage, and you'll probably fail at living alone, too. . . .

Which was the way she felt sometimes, like a failure, for her marriage was a task started but not completed. An indictment of her own judgment and maturity. Her intellect, too.

How could I have been so stupid! I knew what he was before I married him, but I wouldn't let myself admit it and I went ahead and did it, anyway.

All true. It was like being in a car that had lost its brakes, gaining speed, faster and faster, and she'd ridden it right into marriage and beyond, a crazy smile frozen on her face.

On the worst nights, she would think, And I knew what I was, too—so it was a failure from the start. I loved the idea of having a hand in the design of great buildings; could picture him asking my advice about form and fountains and balconies, depending on my eye for composition. And I liked the idea of the money. What girl who grew up poor wouldn't . . . ?

Feeling the chilly wave of depression move through her, letting the silence of the little cottage punish her. Sometimes it was intense, but it never lasted; came sneaking in at night, particularly just before her period. That's when her whole body seemed a bloom of raw nerve endings—her nipples sore, her mood cranky. The recriminations linked to her own body's cycle, like moon tides, flooded full then drawn dry. She could look out the window at a low tide, sea grass lying flat, the bay empty and exposed, and she could feel the draining of it in her own abdomen and breasts.

I've no more control of its effect on me than a damn oyster. . . .

That wasn't true, she knew. Just something she felt sometimes. So at night, when the mood was on her, she'd put down her book, put aside the cat, and lose herself in work. Go to the darkroom she'd built and soup film or experiment with printing. Or she'd work around the cottage, cleaning and neatening and arranging. She'd bought some old cherry-wood shadow boxes at a yard sale and refinished them, then hung them in the living room and kitchen to display the collection of cream pitchers her mother had given her. She liked brass, too. Around the house, over the fireplace mantel and on the window seals, there were brass unicorns, horses, cats, and brass candle holders. She collected more than two dozen candle holders over the years, all holding long green candles, a color she favored; felt the green candles implied warmth even without being lighted. On the porch, there were woven baskets with arrangements of dried wildflowers, and in the kitchen there were shelves holding Ball canning jars and country crockery.

She'd completely redone the little cottage, gave it a whole new feel, a fresh identity, scrubbing and painting and rearranging to rid the place of its history of Geoff and failed marriage. Even so, he came stomping back some nights. Not him, really, but the feel of him, his presence. Which was depressing enough, but with that mood came the emotional need and body longing that refused her contentment and mocked her independence.

It must be so easy to be a man. Everything is either superficial or disposable. . . .

That's the kind of bitterness that came over her sometimes, like the last few evenings, watching the new moon tilting westward above dusk's last light. Feeling it draw the water from her body, abrading the nerve endings. Damn it, she was tired of being alone in that cottage night after night. Not that she wanted a man—no way, not so soon. She just felt like doing something, going somewhere.

Which was the only reason she'd said yes to Tucker Gatrell. Old Mr. Tuck—she'd called him that as a girl. One of the fishermen who'd flirted with her mother—they all had, her mother was so handsome and strong-willed. Back then, he'd been just one more grinning face in the moving throng of adult faces, but now he was one of the last remnants of old times in Mango. Because Tucker had been a part of her childhood, there was added importance to his role in her life as an adult, so she rarely denied him anything he asked. Usually, it was breakfast. Sometimes dinner. Lately, though, the favors he'd asked had something to do with trying to stop the government from condemning much of old Mango to make a state park. Going to the library for him, getting copies of documents made. Like earlier that afternoon. He'd come sauntering up to the door in his jeans, cowboy hat in hands, saying, "Miz Sally, I got a big favor to ask. Has to do with that damn Peeping Tom nephew of mine. I want you to take him a bottle of the vitamin water, have him test it. I'd do it myself, only I got to go out in the boat."

Any other time, she would have said no. But now, with the dark mood threatening her, she agreed to go. It was something to do. Besides, the chance to see Marion Ford's uneasiness again appealed to a quirky, perverse streak in her. As a girl, Marion had made her uneasy often enough: the high school football star she'd tagged after. Once, when she was ten, she'd hidden in the shadows and watched him and a girl kissing in the old gray car he'd owned. It was one of the most exciting things she'd ever seen, but also one of the most hateful. Marion had always been so . . . mature, so neat—then to see him acting like such a fool.

She'd run off in tears.

It irritated her to think about that. Particularly now, driving her white Ford Bronco west on the Tamiami Trail, then north toward Sanibel Island, a Ball jar full of water beside her on the seat, headed for Ford's house.

Sally Carmel had her routine and Ford had his. Every morning, he was up at 6:30; didn't need an alarm clock, just woke up automatically. On the rare day he would have slept through, the noise the fishing guides made would have awakened him, anyway. Starting their boats, yelling in to Mack how much fuel and how many baits he should mark them down for, loading ice and drinks while they talked business across the docks, enjoying the private time and the morning coolness before their clients arrived.

Marinas were noisy in the morning—nice boat sounds to hear from a cool bed.

First thing Ford did was fit his glasses on his face, pull on shorts, then go outside to check his main fish tank. Made sure everything had lived through the night—no small drama, because more than once he'd found a soupy mess of decomposing specimens, the filter fouled or the raw-water intake plugged. Because Ford awoke to the fear of that every morning, his first ten paces of each new day were shaded with mild dread.

Usually, though, the tank was working just fine. The pumps were pumping raw water in, spilling overflow out. The hundred-gallon upper reservoir with its subsand filter cleared the water, then sprayed it in a mist into the main tank, where sea squirts and tunicates continued to filter until the water was too clear to support the weight of a human eye. Ford could look right through to the bottom. Even at morning dusk, the water seemed a brighter world: small snappers, sea anemones, swaying blades of turtle grass, sea horses, horseshoe crabs, whelk shells, the whole small world alive. Ford could see them all in a glance. Then his attention would focus, and he would pick out his favorite specimens, allowing his eyes to linger: three tiny tarpon stacked beneath the exhaust of the upper reservoir, as motionless as pale bars of chromium. Immature snook, too, heads turned into the artificial current. The half dozen reef squid were the hardest to find, because their chromatophores allowed them to blend with the sand bottom. Ford enjoyed looking for them. It was part of his morning ritual, and he always took his time, allowing the dread to fade with each small discovery.

Once he was certain his specimens were okay, he lighted the propane ship's stove and put coffee on to boil, then made his bed. If he was working on a project—and he almost always was—he made notes while he drank his coffee. He had a simple breakfast, English muffin or fruit, unless there was a female guest. If he hoped the lady would stay another day, he cooked with a flair: mango and onion omelets, or fish poached in lime juice and coconut water. If he was ready to have his house and lab to himself, he'd ask her to follow him to breakfast at the Lighthouse Café on Periwinkle Way and hope she'd take the hint.

But it had been a long time since he'd had company—a couple of months, maybe more. So these days, after coffee, he did a short morning workout. If the tide was up, he'd swim to the spoil islands east of the channel and back. If the tide was down and the water wasn't deep enough to swim comfortably, he'd do pull-ups on the crossbar that connected the rain cistern to the cottage, then go for a quick jog down Tarpon Bay Road to the beach. There, he'd stretch and swim in the Gulf.

Then it was work, and the work was always varied. Sometimes it was collecting specimens to fill orders. Sometimes it was dissecting in the lab, injecting dye into the veins of whatever animals that high schools and colleges around the country had requested to buy for their classes. That kept him busy because Ford was a perfectionist, and he had built a steady clientele of repeat business.

As the fishing guides often said, they lived on repeat business and partied on walk-ins. The biological supply business wasn't much different.

Ford liked the marina's guides; enjoyed hearing them discussing fish and fish habits. Which is why he joined them during their lunch breaks, sitting on the picnic tables in the shade, talking above the noise of the bait tanks. Took pleasure in the community feel of the small marina, listening to gossip about the live-aboards, arguing politics and boats until it was time to go back to his lab and more work. By five or so, though, he was usually finished, then he disciplined himself with a longer run and a tougher workout before joining the guides again on the docks, where he opened his first beer of the day while they washed down their boats.

That was Ford's daylight routine. The monotony of it pleased him; appealed to his sense of order, and he didn't like to vary it. Same with his after-dark routine. He'd fix his own supper—usually fish the guides had given him or that he'd caught himself—then he'd have another beer out on the porch, looking at the water. If it was a good clear night, particularly if Jupiter and its moons were high and bright, he'd look through his telescope. Or he'd listen to his shortwave radio, carefully logging any unfamiliar world-bands stations he happened to stumble across. Then, about nine, he'd hear Tomlinson's little skiff start, and Ford would go to the refrigerator and set out another beer, anticipating Tomlinson's nightly visit.

Ford looked forward to the visits, though he would have never said so—there was no reason to comment on such a thing. But Tomlinson was as brilliant as his interests were eclectic, and it was nice to sit in the cottage or on the porch and try to follow the man's assaults on conventional wisdom. It was a game they played. A subject would be selected, usually something commonplace, such as baseball, or sex, or the effects of television on society, and Tomlinson would accommodate the game by making an outlandish observation. "Celibacy is healthy! You shouldn't be complaining!" Then the two of them would argue the various byways and small branchings of thought on the subject until the subject itself sagged or burst into absurdity. "You mean *absence*. Absence makes the heart grow fonder. Not abstinence! Geeze!"

It was something to do, part of Ford's routine, part of the life he enjoyed living. Only lately, he hadn't been enjoying it that much. Things had changed around the place. Jeth was gone, off being feted in some Central American country—Ford still hadn't heard from him. And Tomlinson had changed. Gotten fatherly, which wasn't so surprising, since he had fathered a child. Tomlinson and a woman from his commune days, Dr. Musashi Rinmon. They had had a daughter, and Tomlinson was spending a lot of time in the air, flying back and forth to Boston to see his little girl. Now Tomlinson, who for years hadn't driven anything faster than a sailboat or more traffic-worthy then a beach bike, seemed to have embraced a faster world. He borrowed Ford's truck—a lot. He was always running errands, going places. He had even bought a pair of slacks. *Slacks.* And he had joined Ford in the habit of going to the marina to read the local newspaper each day. "Been out of touch for the last couple of decades," Tomlinson had explained to Ford. "After Nixon, I thought it was safe to kick back for a while."

And Tomlinson wasn't the only one who had changed around the marina. Mack, who owned and operated the place, suddenly seemed obsessed with modernizing the operation and expanding.

"Do you know how much money I lose because of these old docks?" he'd complain. "Do you have any idea how many more boats I could handle if I had one of those big aluminum storage barns? This place is so old and run-down the government might damn well come in and try to close us if I don't do something soon."

Well, it was in the air—change.

Not that Ford had anything against change; he just resented it interfering with the neat perimeter of his own life. It made him irritable, cranky. Worse, now Tucker was nipping at his heels, trying to maneuver him into one of his absurd schemes. The man was poison, had always been poison. Tomlinson wouldn't believe that. That afternoon, Ford had stood on the dock and told him, but Tomlinson wouldn't listen. Had to borrow his truck anyway and drive down to Mango.

"I've flashed on one of the all-time great ideas, man! Your uncle wants to keep his land, him and Joe, then I'm the man to do it. Seriously, Doc, I don't see why you won't kick in a little help."

"Because I don't want to help, that's why. And if you're as smart as I think you are, you'll see Tuck for what he is and stay the hell away."

Blinking at him, giving him his new fatherly expression, Tomlinson had said, "I've got to say something here. You're the best friend I've ever had. I love you, man, but you're dead wrong."

"Aw, Lord, spare me the analysis."

"I'm just saying that the price of hate is too high. I can feel it coming out of you, man. Like heat whenever I mention the old dude's name. Now, it may not be any of my business—"

Handing him the keys to the truck, Ford had said, "You're right. It's none of your business," and turned away.

Ford felt badly about it now, the way he had talked to Tomlinson. The guy was weird, a flake sometimes, but he was as sensitive as a child and there was nothing to be served in hurting him.

When he gets back with the truck, I'll say something to him. Apologize. Thinking that as he cleaned up his lab, scrubbing the dissecting table with Clorox and water, covering his microscope, checking to see that all the jars and vials and chemical bottles were in their proper places. Give him a couple of beers, he'll forget all about it.

Ford checked his watch: 6:00 P.M. He'd worked later than usual, cleaning and curing a two-hundred-gallon tank, then fitting in the Plexiglas shield that would divide it in half. Into the tank, he would pump raw turbid water from the bay. There would be only sand on the bottom of the control side of the tank. On the other side, he would introduce the floating mobilelike device upon which sponges, sea squirts, and tunicates were already growing. The strings of the sea mobile, with their clumps of sessile life, would serve as surrogates for natural sea grasses. The question was, how would the turbidity of the water be effected by the organisms—organisms that depended upon the grasses as bases for their own growth?

Ford hadn't made any further headway on the paper he wanted to write. Had decided to wait until he got the procedure down pat before he put anything on paper. Which gave him an excuse to spend all his time out collecting, or perfecting the procedure in his lab.

So he had worked later than usual and Tomlinson still wasn't back.

Probably drinking whiskey with Tuck, out wrecking my truck.

Thinking mean thoughts, Ford locked the door to his lab, crossed the roofed walkway between the living area and his lab, then knelt before the little refrigerator to take out two grouper fillets for supper. But then he thought, I'm not even hungry. Why bother?

He felt like doing something, getting out, going someplace.

If I had my truck, I could!

Ford stripped off his shirt, kicked off his shoes. He'd do a kick-butt workout, that's what. Be a good time to work out, get cooled down by the afternoon thunderstorm he could feel coming. Maybe that would wash the restlessness out of him. Run to the Sanibel Public Pool and back, nearly five miles; push himself, try to make it in thirty-five minutes, then dive right into the bay and swim out to the spoil islands. His own little biathlon. The same routine he'd once done with Dewey Nye, his tennis player friend. Only now she was a golfer, spending the summers up on Long Island . . . and just thinking about Dewey stirred the longing in him.

I'll call her tonight. Tell her I miss her.

Which was true. Missed feeling her arm over his shoulder, ragging him, the rough housing; missed having a woman to talk to as a confidante. They weren't lovers, just friends. Yet thinking of her fired his restlessness.

Maybe I'll fly up and see her. Take the weekend off—I'm not married to this place. Have Mack feed my animals, and just go. And if she's busy, I'll . . . fly to Central America, that's what. A week in the jungle, that's what I need. Head down to Masagua, go in illegally because of the State Department and see how General Rivera's doing. Speak a little Spanish and eat some decent beans. . . .

Ford was walking around the room, thinking restless thoughts, putting on his running shoes, depositing his sweaty work clothes in the wash bag kept outside the door. That's when something caught his attention out in the bay, an odd movement out toward the rim of mangroves. The bay was choppy, streaked with contrails of dark and light: the afternoon rainstorm blowing in.

Ford stood and looked, trying to define the dark shape he saw—something big thrashing around close to the sandbank that ringed the bay, or maybe on the sandbank. It was hard to tell at this distance, maybe a mile away. He ran inside, returning to the porch with his Steiner waterproof binoculars. With his glasses atop his head, he allowed his eyes to focus through the binoculars . . . then he knew what it was.

Bottle-nosed dolphin . . .

Something wrong with it, too, the way it was kicking around. No other dolphins near it, either. That was unusual. He watched the animal's fluke tail throw a bright fountain of water into the green squall sky. It was either panicked or in pain, the way it rolled onto its side, then smacked its head on the surface. The dolphin's behavior had the flavor of desperation. . . .

Ford swung into the house, put the binoculars on their hook, then swung right back out. His flats boat was tied to the stilt platform's north dock, and he was tilting the boat's big engine into the water when he heard, "Excuse me . . . excuse me?" A woman standing at the end of the boardwalk; red-haired woman wearing jeans on skinny hips and a cinnamon colored T-shirt. "I'm supposed to drop something off. Your uncle asked me."

He was so intent on getting to the dolphin, his mind had to scan around to connect the woman standing on the dock with a name: Sally Carmel. He called to her, "I can't talk now." The engine was in the water and he had the throttle's idle button in, ready to start the boat.

"I didn't come to talk. I came to—"

The engine fired in a haze of blue smoke, and Ford went to the stern, then to the bow, untying lines. "I may be gone a while."

"What?" She couldn't hear because of the motor.

"I MAY BE GONE A WHILE!"

"It'll take me fifteen seconds to give you the message your uncle wanted—"

Ford was already pulling away, but then suddenly he popped the boat into reverse. He yelled over the engine, "Get in!"

"What?"

"I said, get in. I may need some help. We have to hurry."

"Help doing what?"

"GET IN! YOU'RE WASTING TIME!"

Sally Carmel put the jar of water on the deck and got in the boat.

The storm was pushing from the north, accelerating and expanding. It became a smoky veil around the bay. Ford could see the rain: a silver haze with abrupt boundaries, as if sprayed from a nozzle; the sky a comberent gray with tentacles that drifted across the sea, absorbing light, blurring the horizon. Before he could get them away from the dock, the squall wind hit: a wall of air, cold and volatile, that ripped at his clothes and tried to lift the boat airborne before charging into the shoreward mangrove bank. Ford yelled, "Hang on!" as he punched the throttle. The bow of the boat jumped so high that, for a wild moment, he thought they might flip. But then the chines of the eighteen-foot skiff found purchase, the boat settled itself on plane, and Ford touched the trim-tab toggle to adjust the boat's pitch as he hunkered down behind the little console, Sally Carmel holding on beside him. Running into the wind, it seemed they were going a hundred miles per hour.

"WHY ARE WE DOING THIS?" The woman had to yell over the noise of the storm and the engine.

Ford glanced at her just long enough to imprint the image of wild red hair and facial features contorted by the wind stream; got the impression that she not only wasn't afraid but was enjoying it. "You see that out there?" Ford pointed. "Keep your eye on it. The rain's going to be on it soon."

"But why—"

"It's a dolphin. I think it's hurt. In some kind of trouble."

"I can see something splashing."

"That's it. Don't lose it." .

The rain caught them midway to the dolphin—fat drops smacking at their faces, then a stinging waterfall. Ford backed the throttle, slowing, then cupped fingers over his eyes to provide a shield, trying to protect his glasses and his eyes. The drifting partition of rain became a unit of movement and weight, a silver body that ingested them, then reduced their world to a circlet of breaking waves and tarnished light.

Z-Z-Z-clack-VOOM.

With the storm pod over them, the lightning blasts seemed to suck air out of the bay, replacing it with an odor of ozone so penetrating that it might have been the fluttering debris of an explosion.

"That was close!"

"Yeah."

"Oh damn. . . ." The woman was looking down at herself, as if she'd spilled something.

"What's wrong?"

"Um . . . lightning scares the hell out of me." Ford's quick look was a question, so she added quickly, "Not that I want to go in. I was just saying it scares me."

"You still see it?"

Sally had her face pushed forward. "No-o-o-o."

"Keep looking."

"Slow down." She was making a hushing motion with one hand, holding the other up to protect her face. "It can't be far."

Ford pulled the boat off plane to fast idle speed, stepping up onto the boat's gunwale to get a higher vantage point. The rain was so heavy now, he couldn't even see the hedge of mangrove trees that formed the boundaries of the bay. Plus, his glasses were a smeared mess. He took them off, squinting. "Lost it."

"Hey—" Ford could feel the woman pulling at his T-shirt. "What's that?"

Ford turned the boat, looking. The tide was so low, he tilted the engine to keep it from kicking up bottom, going slow, searching. "Where? I don't—"

"I've got it. I've got it." Sally put her hand on the wheel, steering the boat in the direction her finger pointed. "You see it now?"

Ford did: a dark shape isolated by the scrim of rain, moving. He shook the water from his glasses and put them on again. There it was, a large gray dolphin probably seven or eight feet long, twisting, thrashing in water so shallow that a silt bloom grew from beneath it as the animal's tail slapped up mud. He gave the engine gas, then switched off the key, coasting to get closer, knowing the propeller would spook the animal.

The woman said, "It's sick or something. Or maybe it's like when whales beach themselves."

Ford thought, Ear parasites, but said nothing as the boat drifted toward it. He moved up to the bow to get a better look. "I don't see any obvious injuries . . . but its color is strange. Kind of spotted? You see what I'm saying?"

"Yes. Like the chicken pox or something, you mean?"

Ford said, "The anchor's in the dunnage box. I'm going to see how close it'll let me get."

He swung his legs over the gunwale and was already knee-deep in water before he remembered he had his good running shoes on, almost new Nikes. Saturated with muck, they'd stink for a month. He balanced himself on the boat, pulled the shoes off, and tossed them onto the deck, noting that the woman was getting the anchor set, no problem.

The rain had settled into a steady downpour, the wind gone, probably busting out over the Gulf now, racing ahead of the storm front. But there was still lightning, great clicking bursts that touched the distant mangroves. When the lightning struck close, Ford could feel the dissipating voltage move up through his legs toward his heart, and he thought, I haven't done anything this stupid for a while. . . .

The bay water felt warmer than his own body temperature, or maybe it was just that the rain was so cold. Mud that sucked at his feet was hot, a mushy compact of accumulated heat. The dolphin was ten yards or so away now.

"E-e-easy . . . e-e-easy. Not going to hurt you. . . ." Talking in soothing tones as he got closer. The animal knew he was there; had probably known long before, tracking the boat, then Ford's own body with a steady series of clicks and pings. Into Ford's mind popped a memory of sitting in the Triton Hotel, downtown

Havana, watching a rerun of the old television series "Flipper" dubbed in Spanish but with Russian subtitles. That's what the noise the dolphin was making sounded like: Flipper trying to warn Bud and Sandy about something. But along with the squeals and squeaks, there was a sound Ford had never heard a dolphin make before, a moist *whoop-whoop-whoop*. It sounded like pain, that noise.

"E-e-easy . . . just want to find out what's wrong. . . ."

Even through the splattered glasses and with his bad eyes, Ford was close enough to see the animal fairly clearly now. Big blunt-nosed animal that looked as if it were made from wet clay. White splotches all over its body—he'd never seen anything like that before. But the splotches didn't appear to be ulcerated, didn't have the look of disease.

He took a few steps closer, wanting to get a better look . . . but the dolphin spun toward him, rolling its dark eyes, then sprinted away with a thrust of its tail. Didn't keep going, though . . . rolled to its side after only twenty yards and opened its mouth in wild chattering.

"She's pregnant!" The woman was yelling to him through the rain. "There's a tail sticking out of her back end. Did you see it? A little tail?" Now Sally was out of the boat, wading toward the dolphin. Pushing through the water at a pretty good clip. "It must be some kind of breech birth. Does that happen?"

Ford couldn't see what she was talking about. "I don't know. I don't know much about dolphins."

"I bet that's it. I bet her baby's stuck. She can't get it out; that's why she's rubbing herself in this shallow water."

Ford had read somewhere that when a dolphin gave birth, there was always at least one other female dolphin in attendance. The attendant dolphin was called something . . . auntie dolphin? . . . midwife dolphin? Something anthropomorphic, which had irritated Ford. And probably why he hadn't anchored it in his memory. But this animal was alone.

"You sure you saw a tail?"

"I don't see how you could have missed it. It was sticking right out. See . . . there, when she rolls, I just saw it again!"

"She's not going to let us get close. I think we ought to leave her alone. I know some dolphin people. We could give them a call, maybe—"

"She might sense that I'm a woman. That I'm trying to help—"

"What?"

"Maybe she wouldn't let you get close because you're a man. Male. Maybe she senses that."

Ford thought, *Right.* . . .

"See? She's looking at me. . . ."

Ford watched Sally Carmel drop to her knees in the shallow water, then to her stomach, pulling herself over the bottom, closer and closer to the dolphin. Ford kept waiting for the animal to bolt. It didn't. He stood motionless as the woman reached out and touched the animal . . . touched it again after it shied. Then she was stroking the dolphin's back, making a cooing noise Ford could barely hear above the squeaks and clicks the animal made. He saw Sally stroking her way toward the dolphin's big tail.

"You've got a little baby in there. . . . Come on out, little baby. . . ." Talking steadily in low tones, the emotion registering in an alto huskiness as Sally lifted her head high to reach beneath the animal's belly.

"My God!"

The dolphin was gone in an instant: a blur of moving water and great fanning fluke tail.

"I've got it. I've got it. I've got your baby!" Sally Carmel was sitting in the water, a small dark form cradled in her lap, yelling, "Don't go away!" as Ford ran to her, calling, "Keep its head out of the water. Keep it on the surface. . . ." Both of them were watching as the mother dolphin turned and cruised back into the shallows, pinging and clicking.

Sally looked at Ford, her expression a combination of shock and wonder. "It's alive!"

Ford was close enough to see now. A small gray calf, maybe three feet long, pale birth bands on its sides and white splotches already showing on its skin.

Ford said, "It's not a bottle-nosed dolphin; it's a different species. That's what confused me. The spots are natural."

Sally said, "It's so warm! Look how its little porthole opens and closes! All I did was grab his tail."

Ford said, "The female must have come in from offshore. That's what happened. Having trouble."

"I almost fainted when she took off so fast, and there it was, right in my hands. I just held on. . . . Oh-h-h, you're hungry." She was talking to the calf now. "Look at you move your little tail."

Ford said, "To break the umbilical cord, that's why she took off so fast. Spotted dolphin? I think there's a species called that. I'll look it up."

The woman got to her feet, holding the calf on the water, then gave it a gentle push. "There's your mother. Go on now . . . swim!"

The calf kicked toward the mother, its head slapping on the surface crazily. When the woman took a step to go after it, Ford touched her elbow. "It's okay. They're supposed to act like that. Getting used to breathing on the surface, I think."

The mother dolphin circled the calf, then nudged it several times, steering it toward the mouth of the bay and deeper water. Ford was watching but turned when he heard a high mewing noise: the woman standing there beside him, face in her hands, red hair hanging sodden in the rain, clothes plastered to her body, crying. "Hey," he said, "hey . . . the calf's fine. They're both okay." When he put his hand on her arm, Sally leaned against him, then buried her face against his chest. He said, "You did a great job. I'm amazed she let you get that close."

Sally was sobbing now, her whole body shaking. "I told you she knew. She did; she did . . . on the way out, my period started. She knew!"

Ford cleared his throat. Jesus, why did she have to tell him that? Still holding her, he said, "Let's get out of the rain."

Awkward now, standing in his own house with Sally Carmel, making it a point not to look at the way her wet T-shirt showed her body, trying not to sound strained and formal, which caused him to sound very strained, very formal. Saying, "Here's a towel. If you need to use the head . . . ah, the toilet . . . ah, the facilities. To dry off, I mean. Not to—" Ford wiped water off his face. It was just getting worse and worse. "Make yourself at home. I'll put some tea on."

It was nearly dark. The lamp beside the reading chair was on. Through the window that faced the bay, the night sky was descending upon a band of fading pearl. Lighting the propane stove, Ford could see the woman wiping her arms and neck with the towel. Watched her swing her head down so that her hair draped her face. She took handfuls of hair and scrubbed at it in sections. Pretty hair. Darker because it was wet, a deep amber color. Curlier, too. Bright ringlets above her ears.

Ford said, "It's outside—the facility. It's like an outhouse, just to your left as you go out the screen door, but there's a chemical toilet inside. Like for a boat."

Sally threw her hair back and began to dry her face. "We used to have an outhouse when I was a little girl. In Mango? Do you remember that?"

"Electricity but no plumbing. Sure. A lot of people had outhouses. I didn't mind it."

"I remember something about you getting in trouble because you threw firecrackers into one. I remember being afraid to use ours at night, afraid you'd be out there with a firecracker."

Ford thought, That goddamn uncle of mine, but said, "Nope, I never did that."

"Sometimes," Sally said, "I think about that, being a little girl. It seems like another lifetime, I've changed so much."

One minute she was sobbing, the next she was being nostalgic, talking to him like nothing had happened. How could women be that way?

Ford put water in the kettle and set it over the fire.

She said, "I remember feeling so jealous of the girls in town, they had such nice bathrooms. Of course, they weren't—not compared to now. And televisions, garbage disposals. Things like that. I remember feeling ashamed when they'd come over. I tried to work it so we'd be so busy, they didn't have time to drink."

Ford said, "Huh?"

"So they wouldn't have to pee."

"Oh!" Ford was searching the condiment shelf to the right of the stove. "What kind of tea do you want? Tomlinson brings them over. All kinds here—"

Sally Carmel said, "I *like* him. He has such wonderful eyes. Like . . . poet's eyes. I've seen them in some of the very old image work by Matthew Brady, eyes like his."

Ford was saying, "Green tea, orange pekoe, Morning Thunder, Red Zinger . . ."

"I met him in Mango, up at your uncle's? I think he'd be a good friend to have."

"He keeps things interesting." Ford held one of the tea boxes up. "What kind?"

"Whatever kind you like. I only talked to him for a moment. Your uncle introduced us, and he was so . . . different-looking, that I thought at first . . . well, he just struck me as being very kind. Real nice."

Ford didn't like any tea except the kind that came with ice and lemon, but he said, "Orange pekoe?"

"That has caffeine in it, and it's getting late."

"Oh."

"Tell you the truth, it's so sticky after it rains, I'd love a cold beer."

Ford turned off the fire. "There's an idea." Hearing that was like a little bit of Christmas. Maybe tonight he'd drink four beers. To hell with his rules.

She was folding the towel. "I keep thinking about the baby dolphin. That was one of the most . . . touching experiences of my life. . . ."

Ford saw her looking around for a place to put the towel; watched her eyes stop on the red telescope standing by the window. Before her expression changed, Ford said, "I want to say something about that."

Her voice softer, she said, "You don't need to say a word. It's okay."

"No, I want you to know this—"

"Let's don't talk about it, please. I saw you with that dolphin, talking to it, out there in the water, with lightning everywhere—"

"I'm going to finish, whether you want me to or not. About me spying on you through my telescope—"

"That's ancient history, Marion. Hey . . . do you want me to call you Marion or Doc?" Smiling wryly at him, trying to change the subject.

Ford pressed on, anyway. "I watched you only once. While you were swimming. Getting ready to swim. You know . . . late afternoon—"

Sally was looking at the window. The lights of the marina were white streaks emanating from the boat docks. "I like the way the water feels on me. It's no big deal."

Ford said, "But that's the only time I looked."

"At that time of day," she amended.

"Yeah, of course. That time of day. I use the telescope a lot, but not then I didn't. Because you were there, and I didn't want to . . . look then."

He was uncomfortable and she knew it, which was probably why she was still smiling. She said, "That's what I remember most about you. When you lived down the road from us? You being so stern and so shy all at once. I could never tell which one you'd be, stern or shy." Then she said, "Wait a minute. . . ." Thinking about it. "That's not much of a compliment. Looking once but not looking again."

Well, he had explained it as concisely as he could, and there was no pleasing her. He said, "It's Coors Light," handing the beer, already poured into a big coffee mug, to her.

She put the mug on the table, then wiped at her jeans as if that would dry them. "Gee, I'm a mess."

"I have dry clothes. They'll be too big, but—"

"That's not what I mean."

"Ah . . . oh. Then you'll need to—"

"I have to go to my car and get my purse first." Then pushing open the screen door, Sally said, "Your outhouse is to the right, you say?"

It was nearly midnight, the two of them sitting on the porch looking at the water, looking at the sky.

"All those stars . . ." She had said that several times. "Another meteorite!"

That made seven.

After the rain, the air was so clear, they could look right through to outer space. Orion, the Big Dipper, Andromeda with its unseen quasars, Cassiopeia, looking like a drunken M. To Ford, the constellations were familiar shapes; the Milky Way a glittering mist that refused definition to the eye or to the mind.

"This is one of the things I like best about sailing. Lying on the deck at night." Speaking softly, her voice was deeper, more relaxed.

But they weren't lying on the deck, though Ford had imagined that more than once. They were sitting on wooden chairs, close enough so that her elbow sometimes touched him when she gestured.

"That's probably the most disappointing thing about photography."

She'd been talking about that, photography. Talking about working her way through classes in design and journalism at the University of Florida, about working as an intern at the *Miami Herald*, about going free-lance when she married, because she had inherited the house from her mother, plus her husband wanted to live on Florida's west coast. About how tough it was to break into national magazines, particularly the natural history magazines. But now Ford had either lost the thread or what she said made no sense.

"Huh?"

"I said, trying to photograph the sky is probably the most disappointing thing in photography."

"Ah."

"Anything else, the lens will give precise values. The lens captures exactly what the photographer sees. What the artist sees. That's the way I think of it—an art."

Ford said, "Sure." He held up his Coors bottle to see how much was left. His fourth. A big night, breaking his own tough rules. But he still didn't feel as sinful as he hoped to feel. "You ready for another?"

The nice outline of the woman's face blurred when she turned toward him. "I'd like to, but I can't. Two's my limit, and I have a long drive."

"Oh yeah, that's right." As if he'd forgotten.

Sally said, "Like an autumn moon. When it's full, like it'll be in a couple of weeks. It comes up huge. You know, this giant ball of soft light. Orange light, kind of rusty. But if you photograph it, it prints up as a pinhole on a black field. To really get it, you have to shoot through a telescope, then sandwich the negative with a landscape shot. Even then, the color values aren't authentic. You have to really filter it down."

Ford said, "I didn't realize that," enjoying the fact that she knew her business, that she could articulate it and make it understandable. The whole evening had been like that, the two of them sitting around talking.

She said, "All those stars, the moon. The lens can't handle it. Maybe our eyes can't, either. It takes our minds to amplify the light and give it depth of field. It's the only thing—the only reality?—that has to be interpreted. No . . . there are probably others. . . ."

Ford didn't say anything. Was comfortable just sitting there listening.

Tomlinson had returned earlier, made an appearance, then disappeared when he correctly read Ford's expression. Tomlinson had said, "I've been down visiting your uncle. Joseph, too."

Ford had said, "I know."

Sally had said, "I saw you. Remember?"

In the long silence that followed, Tomlinson had raised his eyebrows and said, "Love to stick around and talk, but I can't. Let's do lunch—tomorrow?" Smiling, handing Ford the truck keys, then climbing into his dingy to putter back to *No Mas*, his sailboat.

Ford had given her dry clothes. A pair of running shorts and a T-shirt, both so big and baggy that her body moved around inside them. He couldn't help noticing, then he didn't try to keep from noticing. He'd cooked dinner: the grouper fillets steamed in coconut water and lime juice, fresh mango slices and garlic toast. They'd gone for a walk around the docks, talked to some of the live-aboards. Ford had showed her his lab; had explained his fish tank to her; had appreciated the way she o-o-ohed and ah-h-hed over his favorite specimens. A couple of times, she'd mentioned the jar of water she'd brought for Ford to test, but he had shifted topics so abruptly that he knew she sensed his reluctance. But she didn't push it, just let it slide. Same thing when she tried to talk about old times in Mango. Same thing when she asked what he'd been doing in the years after high school. How could he tell her about that? Not now, not yet. Sometime, maybe. . . .

They talked a lot about the dolphins.

"I had its tail in my hands . . . next thing I knew, there it was! So warm, kicking around . . ."

Spotted dolphin, Ford had been right about that. They'd gone through his research library until they found it. Nice sitting there looking over her shoulder as she leafed through books. Could smell the shampoo she'd used in his rainwater shower. Prell, which smelled a lot better on her. She was beginning to look different, too. Not her body, but her face. It was a curious phenomenon Ford had noticed before in his life. See a friend unexpectedly in a crowd and, in the seconds before recognition, the friend's features would be as foreign as those of a stranger. The friend would appear older, taller, fatter, skinnier, younger, smaller, larger, always less important. But then recognition would modify the features, factor in personality, and the physical form would be transformed in the mind's eye. The mind amplified the retinal impression and made additions. Like Sally had said: It saw things the camera did not.

Same with Sally. Through the telescope, her face had appeared the way he had hoped it would appear: an idealized face for an idealized body. But the day he'd tried to introduce himself, it had seemed narrower, pinched by her anger. A happy disappointment. But now, after only a few hours, her face was different again. It wasn't pinched or narrow; it was angular and interesting. She had large dark eyes, brown, with copper flecks and black, black pupils—eyes that moved around, taking things in, looking out from beneath sun-bleached lashes and heavy brow like the eyes of a small, calm creature peering out from beneath a ledge. Her hair had changed, too. It was no longer dark red. It was black amber or gold-streaked, depending how she moved her head to the light—which changed the color of her skin, in turn, from pale Irish white to burnished brown. She was an interesting-looking woman, that's what Ford decided. He liked her face. It changed aspects in light and shadow. It kept the beholder on his toes. Plus, he couldn't disconnect it from the face of the freckled child he had once known. That seemed to add depth and history. It was a good face to look at; Ford decided that, too. Better than the idealized model's face he had imagined. There were things to discover in a face like Sally Carmel's.

"Hey, Dr. Ford, are you listening to me?"

Well, he was and he wasn't, but he said, "Every word. You have a very nice voice." He sat up straighter in his chair. "I'm serious. You sound like a woman who could sing jazz. That kind of voice, but not as raspy. Probably because you don't smoke . . . at least I've seen no signs—"

"No. I don't." She was sitting up now, too, and he could tell by her movements she was about to leave. "You always do that when I mention your uncle. You change the subject."

She had been talking about Tucker Gatrell? Then he hadn't been listening. Sitting there thinking about the way she looked and smelled. Ford said, "What about him?" expecting her to mention the water again.

Instead, she said, "Maybe it's none of my business. I shouldn't have asked, but I was wondering how you happened to end up living with him."

"Tuck? I didn't end up living with him. I ended up living here."

"See? It's none of my business."

Ford said quickly, "I lived with him two years, then off and on before I went into the navy. My last year in high school, though, I had my own place. A little groundskeeper's cottage off West Gulf Drive. Here on Sanibel. I did work for the rent."

"I guess I was asking about your parents, why you weren't with them."

Ford said, "Oh." He sat for a while looking at the water before he spoke again. "My parents were killed when I was about the age I remember you being in Mango."

He felt her hand on his arm. "I'm so sorry, Doc."

"Nothing to be sorry about."

"Here I am pushing you to talk about . . . to think back about something that . . . well, that's going to upset you, and it's been such a great night."

"Upset me?" Ford put his hand on hers. "Why would something that happened twenty-five years ago upset me?"

"It's just . . . sad, you know? A child that age being orphaned. You, I mean. I don't blame you for not wanting to talk about it."

"There's no reason to talk about it, but I don't mind talking about it." Ford thought, Why's she being so emotional about this? He said, "They were killed in a boating accident. They were in a boat that had an inboard gas engine and it blew up. Gas fumes, you know how they can collect in the bilge? They were going on a cruise down in the islands because it was their . . . anniversary?" Ford had to think about that a moment, it had been such a long time. "Yes, anniversary. Wedding anniversary. It would have been their eleventh, I think."

She was squeezing his hand so hard; Ford liked the feeling of that, the heat and intensity of her coming through.

"That's why you didn't want to come back to Mango. That's where it was."

"The accident? Well, yeah, they left for the islands from Mango, but—"

"No, where you lived. When you were little."

"Before my parents . . . ? Yes . . . right on the big curve as you turn along the bay. There was a big white house there. Well, maybe it wasn't big. And there was a brown boathouse built out—" Ford stopped. It had been years since he'd remembered that.

Sally finished for him. "Built on pilings over the water. I remember. Before the fish house my mother ran was closed down, when they banned commercial fishing in the national park. The little house built on stilts. I used to play in it, and she'd get so mad because there were holes in the dock. Before your uncle tore it all down. You know what, Doc?" Ford waited, then listened as she said in her soft voice, "That's what I thought about when I sailed into this bay and saw this house. The two are alike. Old icehouses that had been converted into something else."

Ford released her hand. "Believe me, that has nothing to do with me living here. It never crossed my mind."

"Your uncle kept coming over, talking to me, saying he couldn't get you to come down to visit him. To help, but he never told me why. Just that you two didn't get along, but I don't think the poor old guy ever made the connection."

"There's no connection to make."

"I'm so sorry, Doc."

Why did she keep saying that? "Look," he said, "Sally . . . you're attaching emotional values to this that just don't exist. You're talking about . . . one thing, and I'm talking about Tucker Gatrell. Connections? Tuck makes all kinds of connections that most people don't suspect. Unfortunately, he just doesn't do it very effectively. Don't let him fool you."

"You're still angry at him."

"Why would I be angry at him?"

"That's what I'm wondering. If you'd like to tell me—"

"I don't feel anything toward him. I was making an observation, a reasonable assessment of his behavior." She had to keep talking about it. Ford could feel the evening's good mood slipping away.

"I'm sorry. So damn sorry." Her hand was still on his arm, patting him.

"Now wait a minute." He turned to look at her, wanting to find a way to seal the subject. "I'm touched by . . . what you're feeling right now, I honestly am. But you have it all wrong. Look at it this way—why did Tuck say he wanted me to test the water? This

146

whole scheme of his, finding an artesian well with some kind of magic healing properties. Has he explained it to you?"

Sally said, "I don't see it as a scheme. He found what he found—he really believes the water makes him feel better. Maybe it does. . . . If you could see Tuck and old Mr. Egret romping around down there, riding their horses."

"Yes, but that's not the point."

"I don't see that it's so much to ask. He told me that you're a biologist, and that if you tested the water, it might carry some weight. I mean, all he wants to do is market the water and make some money so he can buy his property back."

Ford was shaking his head. "I've been all through that with Tuck, I don't know how many—wait." He wanted to explain it to her, make it as clear as he could. "Okay. For one thing, I don't have the knowledge or the facilities to do the kind of test he needs. I've told him that. But did he tell you that? No. Another thing, you just don't fill a Ball jar with water and take it to a lab. The bottle has to be specially prepared, depending on what you're testing for. See, Tuck needs a certified report that lists all elements contained in the water—minerals, chemicals, salts, that sort of thing. To prove it's safe to drink and market. The state lab in Tallahassee can do that, and there are some private labs around, too. But I can't."

"But he wants you involved. Is that so hard to understand?"

"You're saying that he wants me to help him stop the state from taking Mango and making it into a park. That's what you believe?"

Sally said, "What's wrong with that? I like parks . . . I know the land has to be protected. But I think the state has taken enough from people like your uncle. Besides, who are they to say he's not protecting the land? Or me, either, for that matter. My house is there. They may try to take it, too. In fact, your uncle says they will. What gives them the right?"

Taking Tucker Gatrell's side, no doubt about it. Ford would have sighed, but he didn't want to show his frustration. He said, "You're a trusting person; that's a wonderful personality trait. I'm not criticizing—"

"You think it's silly, don't you?" That's what she said, but her tone told Ford she thought he was being an asshole, not wanting to help.

"No, not silly. It's nice, it really is. I admire you for trying to give him a hand. But Tuck sent up some copies of papers for me to look at, data about his property, some copies of newspaper articles—"

"I did that, most of that research for him. All the copying." Her voice was beginning to sound a little chilly. "I got everything I could find on water. The makeup of it, the state's regulations regarding water. He had a stack of books and papers this high." She held her hands far apart, then put them in her lap. No more touching his arm now.

"That's a lot of work. I know. I hope he appreciates it." Ford was thinking, There's no way I can save this. Why am I trying? But he said, "Then you're familiar with the chronology. Do you mind listening while I go through it?"

"If you want. I don't see why—it's getting so late." Looking at her watch.

Ford said quickly, "Wait . . . late last year, the state announced it wanted to build a park adjacent to Everglades National Park, and that it was beginning the preliminary studies. Early this year, Tuck sold off a hundred acres of his property. Why would he do that?"

"Because of taxes," she said. "The state assesses all waterfront property higher. Pricewise, even if you've lived on it for a hundred years. It doesn't matter if you're a poor fisherman. That's put a lot of people out of business. Tuck couldn't afford it."

Ford said, "Okay. That makes sense. But what did he do with the money?"

"Money? . . . Oh, the money he received—"

"The money he got from selling a hundred acres. It had to be a lot of money, right? Even in an undeveloped place like Mango. Hundreds of thousands of dollars. But now Tuck claims to be flat broke. From the papers he gave me, he sold it to some kind of conglomerate. Kamikaze Enterprises, which sounds Japanese—"

"Yes, he told me that. A big Japanese company. When he came down to tell me, he seemed angry about it. He said something like, the Japanese have bought the rest of the country, they might as well have his land, too. I remember that."

Ford leaned forward, sensing he was finally getting somewhere. "That's my first point. Tuck despises the Japanese. He was in the South Pacific during World War Two. It was a favorite topic, the sins of the Japanese. The Bataan Death March, using American prisoners of war for scientific experiments, using Dutch women as sex slaves. Mention the Nazis, he had a whole speech about how the Japanese were just as bad. Tuck would never have sold his land to a Japanese company. No way. Besides, why would an overseas company buy land the state planned to take, anyway?"

That got her thinking. "You're saying he sold the land to someone else?"

Ford said, "I'm saying I doubt if he sold his land at all. He may have had that good old boy lawyer buddy of his, Lemar Flowers, set up some kind of dummy corporation as a front—"

"But why?"

"Tuck's tricky, that's why. It's his nature. Tuck never does things the . . . normal way. He never has and he never will. Hell, look at his house! Everything is jury-rigged, thrown together. That's the way he's lived his life. Anything conventional or orderly offends him."

"A lot of people, old-time people who live out in the country, that's the way they are. Junk in the yard, patched walls. He's no different."

"But Tuck is different . . . *on purpose*. He sees himself as an inventor, smarter than everybody else, but in fact he's just contrary. Give him the simplest problem and he'll take the most absurd route to solve it. The stranger the better. Tuck confuses convolution with brilliance. He always has. He likes being different because that's the only thing he's ever been successful at." Ford stopped, realizing his voice had risen. In a calmer voice, he said, "I'm trying to get you to see the other side of the man."

Sally said, "I'm starting to understand," in a way that could have meant something else.

Ford started to react to her tone, the knowing sound in her voice, but then decided to let it go. Maybe she'd drop it after she heard the rest. He said, "Why would anyone do that? Sell land to a dummy corporation, I mean. To most people, it's nuts, but Tuck would see all kinds of reasons. For the state to exercise its powers of eminent domain, it first has to do the standard title searches. Find out precisely who owns what land. Selling off to a dummy corporation would murk things up. That's the way Tuck might see it. Particularly a company with a Japanese name. Those people are very tough negotiators, and the state might just throw up its hands and say to hell with it. Scare them off that way. He's trying to buy time."

Another way to buy time was to kill or shanghai a couple of state employees, but Ford didn't say that.

Sally said, "You two are just so different." There was nothing chilly in her voice now. Instead, she sounded troubled. A little hurt, too. Ford found that unsettling, as if he'd explained to someone why there was no Santa Claus. She said, "Then what about the artesian well? He seems so sincere."

"That's one thing Tuck's good at, sounding sincere. But consider this: Even if he sold his land to a dummy corporation, he still had to pay sales tax and capital gains. On a hundred acres, it probably cleaned him out. He's probably telling the truth about being flat broke. He needs the money." Ford could see that hurt her, too, so he added, "Understand, I'm just guessing at all this. I have no proof."

"Yeah, I know but . . ." She was thinking about it.

Ford said, "But here's what I suspect is his real motive. The spring he says he found? Let's say he convinces a bunch of people that water from the spring really is beneficial. That there really are some health benefits. Let's say the water has all the necessary minerals—whatever it is people look for in bottled water. And he proves that by having the water tested. Okay, that makes his property even more valuable. If he can prove the water is a marketable, inexhaustible resource, the state will have to pay him ten, maybe twenty times the current accessed worth of his property. Do you understand?"

"Yes, of course. . . . Well, no, but it makes sense. The way you say it."

"I just want you to see why I don't want to get involved with Tuck. One of his schemes. That it had nothing to do with . . . what you were talking about."

Sally stood, putting her hand on Ford's shoulder as he stood to face her. "I think it does."

He could look down right into her eyes, her face softer in the darkness. He put his hand on her waist, not even thinking about it. "You're leaving?"

"I have to. It's late."

"But you're not mad."

As she shook her head, her hair made a wind sound, brushing against her shoulders. "No. Just confused. And sleepy."

Ford wanted to say, "Then why not stay over?" but the words couldn't get past his own reserve. Instead, he said, "I'll wash your clothes and dry them. You can pick them up next time you're here." Looking at her face to see how that was accepted.

Sally touched her finger to his cheek. "You really are a nice man. I wonder if you believe that." Studying his eyes with hers.

"Or I could drive down to Mango tomorrow. Drop them off. If Tomlinson will let me use my truck."

Using his shoulder as a brace, standing on her toes, she leaned slowly, slowly, and pressed her lips to his, eyes open . . . then closed as Ford pulled her to him, feeling the weight of her breasts flatten against him. Then, talking into his chest, she said, "I've wanted to do that for a long, long time, Marion. Kiss you."

Ford didn't know what to say to that, so he said nothing, just held her.

She said, "Maybe I could make dinner for you tomorrow night. At my place."

Ford whispered, "While I'm there, I can take some samples, have the water tested? I'll have to call someone, find out the proper procedures."

She kissed him again, then said, "I'd like that. But I'd make dinner for you, anyway."

NINE

As Charles Herbott, the thirty-year-old environmental consultant, paused to stretch his back, to rest his arms, he said to Chuck Fleet, the thirty-five-year-old surveyor, "I've finally figured out why you keep lying about what day it is. You're trying to manipulate me, make it seem like it's not as bad as it is."

"What?"

"That's right. So I won't take care of you-know-who." Herbott motioned with his head toward the old man sitting in the shade of a ficus tree, shotgun in his lap. "Because you're so afraid. That's why."

Chuck Fleet didn't bother to look. He was hunched over, holding stalks of sugarcane with his left hand, cutting the stalks with his right. He'd cut for three or four steps, then bundle up the cane in his arms and carry it to the bamboo sled. When the sled was heaped high, he would harness himself into the rope and drag the sled to the old cane press on the other side of the mound. That's where the Captain kept the fire going, a huge black pot suspended over the buttonwood coals, boiling the cane water into syrup. Ten gallons of cane water made one gallon of syrup, after a lot of skimming, stirring, and more skimming to make the syrup clear.

Charles Herbott said, "It's Wednesday, not Monday. You're lying about that. I'll been on this goddamn island two weeks tomorrow. I've been keeping track. I know."

Chuck Fleet said, "Okay, it's Wednesday, not Monday. Whatever you say." Thinking, First Bambridge goes crazy, now Herbott. The difference is, Bambridge isn't dangerous. Herbott is potentially homicidal. . . .

Herbott returned to cutting, hacking at the stalks with the rusty machete the old man issued him each day, then collected each evening. Cut-cut step, cut-cut step. Cut the base of the stalk, then lop off the top. Stalk after stalk after stalk. Christ, he was beginning to feel like an animal, his clothes rotten from sweat, his hair and face caked with the black sand. All the work he'd done, everything by hand. "The way I know you're scared is, you won't even listen to my plans anymore."

Fleet said, "Keep your voice down. The Captain's old, but he's not deaf."

"And quit telling me what to do!"

From the direction of the ficus came the old man's voice. "Yew boys got a job a work to do! Fuss on yer own time."

"Sorry, Captain!"

They chopped in silence for a while before Herbott said, "You're getting bad as Bambridge, the way you kiss that crazy bastard's ass. 'Least Bambridge gets something for it. Living up there in the old man's shack, cooking the meals. That fat asshole's happy as a clam now, acting like he's one of the guards instead of one of the prisoners. But you, hell . . . he's going to work you to death. Which I don't mind, only you're going to take me down with you!"

Fleet started to respond, but then thought, What's the use? He gathered two cane stalks into his left hand, then cut them at the base with a single swipe of the machete.

"We run off right now, at least we've got the knives. That's what we ought to do, just scatter. Catch him dozing in the shade."

Fleet shook his head, "These old-timers, crackers, they aren't like people today. They say they're going to do something, they do it."

"So?"

"So he'd shoot us. At least one of us. He'd have time for that, to get both barrels off."

"But he's never threatened to shoot us—you're the one who keeps saying that!"

"I know, but he means for us to do this work. He'll do whatever it takes. I think he'd get at least one of us with the gun."

"No way, man. We just dive for the brush, then we've got the whole island. We'd be free."

Chuck Fleet said, "I'm going to say it one more time: Then what? Huh? Then what? We're free on the island. Big deal. Even if we could find our boats, they're broken down. What are we going to do, walk across the water?"

"Couple of nights ago, I heard a powerboat you did, too. We could flag somebody down. Couple of times, I've heard a boat."

"Twice, maybe three times in almost two weeks. Nobody

comes back in here. It's so shallow, nobody in their right mind, anyway. Only novice idiots like us."

"I know, I know, it's shallow enough, we could walk. We could walk a lot of it—"

"Twenty miles back to Barron Creek Marina? All of it mangrove and muck. Just keep on walking and have a nice dinner at the Marco Island Inn. Might as well do that while we're at it. Get serious, Charles."

Herbott said, "We take his boat, I've already said that. Take his rowboat, use the mast and sail. He had it rolled up in there on the deck. I saw it. Or you could create a diversion while I've got the knife, and I could—"

"Yeah, yeah, I know. Murder him. Cut his throat." They'd been through this a hundred times. Every night, sitting in the pit with the mosquitoes clouding around them. Herbott talking about different ways to ambush the old man, saying just leave the rough stuff to him. Getting wilder and wilder, the way he talked. The heat, the bugs, the fear rendering what sensibilities the man had into a bedrock hatred that now scared even Fleet.

Herbott said, "You keep using that word, but I'm talking self-defense. It's not murder."

"What is he, eighty, maybe ninety years old? That's murder."

"You think what you want. But I've got enough connections in Tallahassee, they won't touch me."

Fleet had heard a lot about that, too—Herbott's connections. Out of college, Herbott had worked as a biologist for the state long enough to learn the system. Testified in suits against outlaw developers and provided input in the writing of some of the state's environmental-protection laws. But then Herbott had gone where the money was, set up his own consulting firm. That way, the outlaw developers could hire Herbott to circumvent the very laws he'd helped write. Environmental audits, water testing, permitting—his small company could take a development project from conception to ribbon cutting. Called himself an environmentalist, but what he was was a developer. Not that all developers were bad—it just irritated Fleet the way some of the new environmental consultant companies pretended to be one thing but in fact were something else.

"You're going to tell me about your buddy the governor again."

Herbott said, "That's right, a personal friend. I got permits for a condo project—almost all on wetlands—nobody else could push through. For his cousin. Why you think the state still hires me? For the tough projects, that's why. The Captain there puts a gun on me, nobody's going to say a word. No matter what I do."

"Just kill him. That'll solve everything."

"I'm getting a little goddamn tired of your attitude."

Chuck Fleet stood with a bundle of cane in his arms and yelled, "New load ready, Captain!" Then in a lower voice, he said to Herbott, "We get his cane in and make his syrup, he's going to let us go. He salvaged our boats; we owe him. That's the way he sees it. If you talked less and worked harder, we could be done in a week. Maybe less."

Herbott took a wide swing with his machete, lopping the cane he was holding but also just missing Fleet's leg. Looking up at him, Herbott said, "Don't try to manipulate me! And when the time comes for me to take the old man down, don't you get in my way!"

The surveyor walked carefully away and dropped his armload of cane onto the bamboo sled. His heart was pounding; pounding from the work and the heat, but mostly from adrenaline, knowing how close Herbott had come with the knife. The man was nuts.

"Yew there! Tall'un." That's what the old man called him: Tall'un. Never used his name. He was Tall'un; Herbott was Short'un; Bambridge had been Fat'un before he'd gone to work inside and became the Cook.

"Captain?"

"Yew let Short'un take a turn on that there sled."

"Yes sir, Captain!"

"You can go to hell!" Herbott was suddenly standing, looking up toward the old man on the shell ridge. Holding the machete out like he meant to use it. "You can call me by my name, or you can drag the goddamn stuff yourself."

Fleet called out, "I'll pull it, Captain. I don't mind," as the old man got slowly to his feet, feeling around for his straw hat on the ground beside him, not taking his eyes off Herbott.

The old man said, "Mister man, you raise a knife to me on my island again, it'll be the last time," lifting the shotgun, pulling the two hammers back with his thumb but holding the barrel toward the ground. To Fleet's ears, the noise the hammers made, *ka-*

latch, ka-latch, deepened the island's silence and turned the constant whine of mosquitoes into a long, steady scream.

Herbott's voice had a new unsteadiness: "You have no reason to call me . . . by anything other than my name."

"Yew workin' for me, I'll call you what ah want!"

"But it's not . . . fair! It's not fair, and it's not right."

The barest twitch of expression came to the old man's face. A smile? "Life ain't fair—that why yew short, boy! But the way I works my crews, that's fair 'cause I don't let one man do all the draggin'. Now get yo'self pullin' that sled!"

Fleet didn't want to look at Herbott. Didn't want to see the anger drained from his face, replaced by fear. Didn't want the burden of seeing Herbott's humiliation. The man was dangerous enough without sharing that.

"No more your sass! Move!"

Behind him, Fleet heard the metal sound of a machete dropped onto shell, and Herbott brushed by, headed for the sled, whispering as he passed, "I am going to kill him. . . ."

Because morning was his favorite time, Tucker Gatrell was up before everybody. All his life, it had been that way. Now he was up before Joseph—or so he thought. Tuck put coffee to fire and added a handful of chicory for body. Outside, birds made their tentative first twitterings from the hush of jasmine and poinciana, and in the autumnal darkness the wind was freshening from off the bay, smelling of open sea and far islands. When the coffee was ready, he carried his mug to the porch, propped his boots on the railing, scratched Gator's ears to make sure he was there, then settled himself in that quiet time to watch the landscape change.

In the east, there was no sun, but an orange corona boiled over the horizon, throwing shards of westwarding light. The sky was a fragile lemon-blue, translucent as a pearl, and clouds over the Gulf absorbed the light in towering peaks, fiery, like snow glaciers above a dark sea. Birds flying . . . Tuck could see their gray shapes closing. A formation of ibis—curlew, he thought of them—glided across the bay and were briefly illuminated, combusting into brilliant plumes that produced an ethereal white light. Then the birds banked into shadow, silent as falling stars, and were gone.

Tucker watched them, feeling a strange sense of loss and a curious ache, like nostalgia.

Used to be thousands of them birds. Millions. Me an' a lot of other dumb butts chewed up this land pretty good. . . .

From the mangroves arose the catlike buzz of raccoons fighting—or mating. Across the road, tail-slapping their way across the bay, a carousel of bottlenosed dolphins—porpoise, Tuck called them—foraged the grass flats, exhaling moistly while a pileated woodpecker thudded like a drum on the dead palm that leaned toward the junk pile near the barn.

He paused to consider the junk pile. In the dusty light, the rusted fenders and coils of wire, the sections of wood and discarded fencing, the broken bottles and rotted pilings and the tilted fly bridge of the wooden boat became a single unit, all grown over with vines—a single strange shape, like a sculpture—or a monument.

Every screwup in my life ended up in that junk heap. Surprised it's not bigger than the barn by now. Bigger than all the islands. Makes me tired just lookin' at the gawldang thing. . . .

That's the way Tuck felt, tired. Not sleepy, just weary. All the running around he'd done in the last few weeks, all the planning, all the phone calls, all the reading, all the . . . thinking

Used to feel like I was flyin', like them curlew. Now it's like gravity's got a hook in my butt, cranking me toward the ground.

That was the problem: gravity. Tuck crossed one boot over another and sipped at his coffee, musing. Gravity wasn't just a problem; it was the biggest problem. Tuck gave it some thought:

Moment you come outta your mama's belly, gravity's right there and the fight starts. A baby spends a year wrestlin' with it before that baby can finally get up on his legs. After that, he just keeps gettin' stronger and stronger until he thinks the fight's over, gravity can't do nothin' to him ever more—but it's a lie. Get old, and gravity starts draggin' your shoulders down. Then it stoops your back. Then your brain starts gettin' heavy, like lead, 'cause the damn stuff's always there tryin' to pull you back into the dirt. Gravity don't like a man walkin' upright.

The novelty of the thought pleased Tucker. He still had the ache in his stomach, that nostalgic feeling, but thinking about gravity helped focus the feeling, made it something he could deal with.

If a problem ain't been solved, it's 'cause nobody's give it enough thought.

Same thing he'd told Ike the time Eisenhower'd come down to fish, out of the Rod & Gun Club in Everglades.

Tuck had liked Ike. Liked him better than Truman, the little man with the hat and the goggles, though it seemed to interest people more when he told them about Truman.

Course, Harry fished with me more'n Ike, too. . . .

He caught himself—his mind was drifting. . . . Which was nothing new, but it seemed to be getting worse and worse ever since he'd had what the doctor up to Fort Myers called a "little stroke."

"It's called old age," the doctor had said. "Do you understand what I mean by that?"

"You can kiss my ass," Tucker had replied with heat. "You understand what I mean by *that!*" Filled with anger—not at the doctor but at the damn circumstances. The feeling that his brain was a traitor, of having no control.

Now Tucker concentrated, forced his mind back to the topic and turned his full attention to gravity; thought about ways to neutralize it. Helium, that was an idea. Like the gas they put into balloons to make them float around—he'd seen how that worked at the fair in Miami.

Maybe take everybody when they were born and give them a squirt of it . . . ? No . . . people would just burp it out, kids especially. Kids loved to fart and burp. So . . . maybe put the helium in a sack, a plastic sack, and have doctors sew it in.

Tuck pictured all the sack makers and the helium makers getting rich. The doctors, too. Nope, he wasn't going to give away any more great ideas. He'd done that enough.

Problem is, I'm thinkin' about this the way everybody else thinks about it. . . .

There it was! The answer wasn't to neutralize gravity; the answer was to get rid of it altogether. Go to the source!

But what the hell causes gravity . . . ?

Tuck didn't know. He could send Sally to the library, have her look it up. But he'd been doing enough of that lately. Some kind of magnet in the earth, it had to be something like that. Yep, he'd read that somewheres. Big ball of metal in the center of the earth, boiling metal or some damn stuff, that's what made a compass work. So all you had to do was drill down and pump the stuff out. Pump it . . . where? Pump it . . . into spaceships, yeah, and send them off. Only thing was, you wouldn't want to pump all the gravity out 'cause then people would just float away. Pump out just enough to make things easier, so a man didn't have to fight so hard when he got old.

If we could dig a roadbed across the Everglades, diggin' a deep hole and settin' up pumps ain't nothin'. And hell, the spaceship place is just over on the other coast. Ain't far at all. Cape Canaveral.

Tucker sat up a little and pushed his cowboy hat back, pleased with himself.

All a man has to do is think big and advertise, that's all. Don't know why I've been so worried about this water business goin' right. . . .

He finished his coffee, then leaned to get at the foil pouch of Red Man in his back pocket as morning spread itself into gradated light, from dusk to pearl to pale green-blue.

"Don't that air smell sweet!" Talking aloud, though no one was around to hear but the dog.

It did smell good. To him, nothing smelled so good as a cattle ranch on the sea. All those nice smells mixed together: brackish-water bay, cow pasture, big wet jungle leaves, hay in the loft, the shady smell of a wooden porch, mangroves, horses.

There had been only a couple other places in the world where those odors could be found in combination. Central America . . . Cuba. Always on the coasts, always with jungle growing right up to the pastures. Tucker had loved Cuba. Had almost gotten married there to that little black-eyed girl, Mariaelana, that sweet child with the soft brown breasts and the small blue tattoo on her hand, a sea horse. The only person he'd ever met in his life who was so kind and good that he felt gentler just being with her.

His mind was drifting again. He knew it, but the thoughts and the smells were so pleasant that he just let it go, let the memories take him. . . .

Beside him, Gator lifted his big head and growled softly, looking toward the barn.

Tucker jumped slightly, startled. "I know what's wrong with you—you can't figure out why them damn chickens ain't been crowin' all morning."

The dog stood, looking at the barn, still growling . . . until Joseph exited through the open sliding doors, walking toward the porch.

159

To the dog, Tuck said, "Just ol' Joe. You ought to know by now them Injuns smell different!" Then in a louder voice, he said, "Thought you was still in the sack. Hell . . ." Studying the approaching figure. "You're soakin' wet. You been swimmin'?"

Joseph stopped at the steps and put his big hands on the railing. "Buster's got spots all over his butt!"

Tucker lowered his head, laughing. "That's what you're in such a sweat about?"

"No . . . I been running. What about them spots? White ones— and his mane's cut off, too!"

"Some woman's husband chasing you, that's the only reason an old fart like you'd be running. Been thimblin' the neighbor ladies again."

Joseph stood there glaring, waiting for an answer. Finally, Tucker said, "Damn right I painted that horse up. Turned him into an Appaloosa and give him four white stockings, too. While you was sleepin' last night, I was out there working my tail off. But don't bother thankin' me—"

"Buster don't like it and I don't, neither. He looks like a . . . like some circus clown owns him."

"Then that's good."

Joseph put a foot on the step, getting angry. "You got no right to mess with a man's horse. I liked him just the way he was."

"You like the idea of that Cypress Gate horse owner recognizing that horse on the television and having us thrown in jail?" Tucker leaned forward and spit over the porch railing to punctuate his point. "It ain't like that man ain't gonna have time to look. With them chickens around, he'll be up watching the television all night long."

"What're you talking about? I ain't being on no television. Buster ain't, either."

Tucker stood and stretched. "We'll see about that." He looked at Joseph's soggy T-shirt. "Hope you didn't run yourself outta energy. We got a long ride today. Next day, too, and the next day after that. Hey—" Joseph felt Tuck squinting at him. "What the hell happened to your hair? A big chunk missing . . . ?"

Joseph let his breath out, some of the anger going with it. "The hippie come down, Marion's friend. He cut some of it with a knife. Pulled a couple out by the roots, too. It hurt."

"Jesus H. Christ, and you let him?"

"He don't make no sense when he talks, but he's . . . nice. Sure. He didn't take much."

"Probably using your hair to make a voodoo doll right this minute, sticking pins in it. Or rolling it in paper to smoke like marywanna. Don't you be givin' away your body parts to no hippie."

Joseph didn't reply. He was thinking about Buster, how silly he looked with those spots painted on his rump. But Tuck was right—there was no denying it was a smart idea to disguise the horse just in case the owner came looking around. He said, "Every day, I been walking up to the main road, then running back. Well, kinda joggin' back. I can't run too fast no more. Sally loaned me a watch. I been timin' myself."

"That's all I need—for you to die on me now." Tucker snorted, disgusted. "All the problems I got."

"You don't seem too worried to me."

"Hah! You ain't paying attention, that's why. I got a stolen horse, a couple thousand stolen milk jugs up in the loft—"

"You got the bottles?"

"No thanks to you." Tuck spit again and turned toward the screen door. "I got a woman cop snoopin' around askin' questions, callin' me on the phone. I got them state park people breathin' down my neck, helicopters flyin' all round like I robbed a bank. My tallywhacker ain't been hard since the night I fell asleep against the icebox, and Ervin T. Rouse was expectin' us *yesterday*. Now you're out trottin' around in the heat, seein' if you can get a heart attack. My schedule's too tight for funerals, Joe."

"I run my fastest time. Ran almost the whole way. It's because of the water."

Tucker said, "When the television people ask you, you tell 'em just that. Sell that water. Now you go saddle up the horses."

Agent Angela Walker, now driving one of the department's white Dodge Aries to save miles on her new Acura, slowed for the turnoff to Mango, scanning the narrow road ahead for passing cars or crazy drunks. This road across the Everglades had seen its share of carnage, and she had no intention of becoming one of its statistics. All along the way, there had been vultures on the wires, redfaced or black-hooded, as if they were just waiting for an accident to happen. Sitting on the PORT OF THE ISLANDS signs, the WOOTEN

AIRBOAT RIDE billboards. Gave her the shivers, seeing those evil-looking birds.

The turn was clear . . . the pitted macadam road to Mango empty, glittering in the morning heat as it curved into the mangroves and disappeared. But ahead, on the main road, she could see something—cars pulled off to the side . . . blue lights flashing . . . looked like a couple of figures on horseback, too. If it was a wreck, she didn't want to see it—not that it would have bothered her. At least not that she would have shown any emotion. She'd been through emergency driving school and the combat driving school in Pennsylvania, and they had shown the bloody films of highway accidents, complete with sound. She knew how a professional was supposed to react in those situations. But the Florida Department of Criminal Law didn't work accidents.

Still, her instincts told her to go have a look . . . something about those people on horseback.

She checked the rearview mirror to make certain some fool wasn't passing her at the last minute, then accelerated back to highway speed, past the turnoff to Mango.

The car with the flashing lights was FHP, Florida Highway Patrol, black and gold—they drove Fords—and there were other cars pulled off into the shade of a little roadside picnic area. A couple of vans with television logos on the doors. Three or four cheap compacts with PRESS plates.

Something must have happened—all these journalists, and no free booze.

No bottles she could see on the picnic tables, anyway, set beneath cypress trees beside a creek that had white flowers floating in it. Some kind of lilies, maybe—she didn't know. But there he was, right in the thick of it: the old man, Tucker Gatrell, sitting on a horse, with people standing around him, some of them holding cameras, looking up at him and talking. Another man beside him on a horse . . . an Indian-looking man wearing a cowboy hat that was even dirtier than the saggy felt mess Gatrell wore. And a sleepy-looking cow with horns, too, packs tied to its back. The Indian had the cow on a lead rope.

Crazy old crackers . . . probably drunk. And me with questions to ask . . .

Trying to access some of the cop cynicism she was trying to cultivate, but it didn't last. There was something about Gatrell that she liked, something that amused her at least. Then she realized what it was: He reminded her of her grandfather. Wild old man—Popee, she'd called him. Said a lot with his eyes but not much with his mouth. The relative she most favored, her father had observed more than once—always said it like a criticism, too.

Well, that was it, the thing that had been tickling at the back of her mind every time she saw Gatrell. He was a little bit like a southern Popee, with those narrow eyes and see-everything smile.

Not that it would influence the way she handled the investigation.

Walker parked in the shade and pulled on her blue blazer before getting out, touching the pocket to make sure her ID wallet was there.

She could see the state trooper: a short black man, very thick shoulders, and with a belly pushing against his gray uniform. The straw patrolman's hat he wore made him look taller, but not much. He was standing to the rear of the small group of people that circled the old man's horse, shaking his head about something. Some kind of dialogue going on between the trooper and the old man. Or maybe he was just listening—yeah, that's what the trooper was doing, because when he saw her approach, he stepped away and said, "You might as well keep on moving, miss. I'm breaking this up right now. Show's over."

Seeing the look of acknowledgment in his eyes—one black person meeting another in this isolated southern place. That look, a brief softening of the facial features, was not so welcoming as some probably thought. Sometimes there was suspicion in the exchange, sometimes animosity. An "I know what I'm doing here—but what are you doing here?" look that Walker ignored.

"I didn't come to see a show." She took out her ID and flipped it open. "I stopped to see if you needed any help, Officer Cribbs." He had the silver name badge over his pocket, black lettering.

The trooper leaned to read. "Flor-dah Department—" Then he looked up at her, a little startled. "Florida Department of Criminal Law? What, you people driving around, checking up on the FHP?" as if he was joking, but he wasn't—she could read that in his expression. He looked guarded.

"No, just on my way to an interview and saw your flashers, these guys on horses. Thought I'd see if I could offer any assistance."

"Howdy there, Miz Walker! You lookin' particularly pretty this morning." Tucker Gatrell was calling to her over the heads of people. Grinned at her, teeth missing, then took his hat off in a respectful old-time way. "Don't she look pretty, though, Joe? That's Miz Walker." Tucker turned to the other man, the Indian-looking man, but the Indian hardly moved to stare. Just sat on his horse, glum-eyed, miserable, as if he hated being the center of attention.

Walker smiled, nodded.

Gatrell hollered, "Be with you soon's I'm done getting interviewed," while the trooper said, "You *know* these men?" Incredulous.

"The one, I do. I've met him. It had something to do with a case."

Trooper Cribbs said, "Running dope, I bet. These old guys down here that know the islands, I've worked a couple of those calls with the DEA. They call us in sometimes."

"No, not drugs," letting him know with her tone she wasn't going to say anything more about it. "What's going on here?"

"You tell me, if you know the guy. I got a call to check it out. Some motorists were complaining about men on horses backing up traffic. I came out of Marco Island and found them about five minutes later, 'bout one klick down the road. These two guys towing that steer. Not right out on the road, but close enough on the shoulder to slow things down."

The trooper's gun belt creaked when he leaned his weight on it—probably a Vietnam vet, Walker guessed, from his age and the way he said *klick*. Kilometer.

"That's why all these newspeople are here?"

"Wait, I was just telling you," Cribbs said. "The one guy there, the white, the Caucasian guy, he won't pull over when I tell him to stop. Can you see me? Driving along with my window open, about two miles an hour, and this old dude won't pull over." He was chuckling, looking at her to see how informal he could tell it. "I mean, what am I gonna do, run him off the road? Him and his horse. He says, 'I've got an appointment at the picnic place,' pointing up here. He says, 'Us cattlemen got a right to move our livestock, road or no road. Check the law books; they never took out the part about open range.' The old guy just chattering away, me listening, with the window down."

"Where does he say he's going?" Walker was listening to Cribbs

164

but looking at Gatrell, who was still sitting on his horse, talking nonstop and gesturing with his hands to the men and women looking up at him.

"That's what he's been telling them about," Cribbs said. "Next thing I know, these news cars start pulling in. They're looking for some kind of protest cattle drive someone's called them about, and they are slightly piss—not too happy about finding only two guys on horses and one cow. But they stuck around and listened anyway, took a few shots. Figured since they were already here, I guess. One of them tried to get some quotes out of me, but we've got a no-comment policy; everything has to be cleared. Same at the FDLC?"

Walker said, "Yes, that's the same."

Cribbs didn't say anything for a moment, just stood there puffed out in his uniform, leather creaking. Then said, "You going to be around a while, maybe we could get some coffee together. I've got a call in now, checking on that law thing, the legal aspects, I mean, of them riding horses and having that cow on the road. I've got some time, once I get this squared away."

Walker knew he had looked at her left hand, the bare ring finger, but she had pretended not to notice. This middle-aged guy hitting on her already, and she'd hardly said two words.

"I'd like to, but I'm in kind of a hurry—"

"Hey," Cribbs said, "that's the dispatcher calling now," walking toward his car. "Don't run off."

Walker stepped into the shade, closer to the horses. The mosquitoes were thick, buzzing around her head, covering her legs. Swat them and she'd have blood splotches all over her panty hose, so she shifted from one leg to another, trying to spook them away.

That's what the two horses were doing—the cow, too—moving their legs, swatting with their tails. She heard Tucker Gatrell say, "I don't want to tell you your business, but you television people want, you can follow us the whole way. Ervin T. Rouse, he won't mind. He's used to being famous."

One of the newspeople said, "I've never heard of that guy. The song 'Orange Blossom' what?"

"You tellin' me you never hearda the greatest bluegrass song ever been written?" There was something touching in the way the old man said that, genuinely taken aback. And Walker guessed from the look on his face, things weren't going too well. Whatever it was the old man wanted, he wasn't getting it. He said, " 'Special,' the 'Orange Blossom Special.' That's its name. I suppose you ain't never hearda Johnny Cash, neither."

"These goddamn bugs!" The newspeople were dancing around, too, flapping with their hands.

"What I was sayin', you television people can follow us right along. Meet Ervin T. Rouse, get him playin' the song on his fiddle. And I brought plenty of Glades Springwater along. Jugs of it on Millie there."

He must have meant the cow, Millie—as if he was introducing the thing.

But the newspeople were talking at the same time, no longer pretending they were listening. She could hear them.

"Christ, this is a publicity gag. Cure all your aches and pains."

"We could do a bit, like it's an old-time medicine show."

"I do journalism, not advertising."

"I've had it, man—"

"What we ought to do is a piece on all these goddamn mosquitoes! Why they should make the whole place a park, leave it to the bugs."

Swatting as they moved away, leaving Gatrell and the Indian standing there. Most of them jog-walking, slamming the doors of their vans and their cars, acting as if it had just begun to rain.

"Have you ever heard so much bullshit?"

"Got us out of the office, anyway."

"Sure, but we've still got to come up with two minutes and an intro. Maybe stop at Marco, do something on pelicans?"

"The *National Enquirer*, he should have tipped them. Weirdo stuff like this, they love it."

Walker heard a woman's voice, not very loud, say, "That's right, we do." Mousy little woman in a strange velvet jacket with lace facing and a little feathered box hat, as if she bought her clothes from one of those secondhand boutiques. She was the only one still standing there listening to Gatrell. Writing in a notebook and holding a tape recorder under her arm. Stepping back to take some photographs as Gatrell swung off his horse for a moment to point at his horse's underside.

"There they are," she heard Gatrell say. "Both of 'em. Get a picture if you want. Roscoe, he ain't shy."

Walker wondered why that made her feel good, seeing the old man poised and smiling.

She heard the old man say, "That's fine, but you move to the other side now, you'll get my good side. And make sure you got Chief Joseph in the background. He's an Injun, you know. . . ."

Walker had spoken with Marion Ford a couple of times on the telephone, and he had that same quality, always holding something back, just like his uncle. Why did she find that attractive?

The old man talked a lot, but he said only what he wanted her to hear, never what was on his mind. Which would have been offensive, coming from most people. But with the old man, it was more like a game. He knew that she knew that he knew. . . .

Dr. Ford hardly said a word, but there was an intensity in the way he did it. His way of holding back.

Walker's own grandfather had been like that; he'd had that reserve. A blue-eyed Belgian who didn't speak the language well enough to understand it was wrong to marry the woman he married, so he just went ahead and did it, anyway.

To Ford, on the phone, Walker had said, "I see what you mean about if all three boats looked alike. Somebody could have been laying for them and taken Bambridge by mistake. Or taken the two state guys by mistake. But Bambridge's boat was different. A flats boat? Says here a Hewe's Redfisher. So the whole thing falls apart. The state guys, Herbott and Fleet, they were in state-owned Boston Whalers."

Telling him a little bit so that he might tell her more in return. What she wanted to know about was his uncle.

Ford had said, "That's assuming one, two, or all of the disappearances aren't accidental."

"Of course—"

"It doesn't necessarily follow that if you find one, you find them all."

"I know. But what are the odds of at least two of the three being connected? Probably all three."

"Then you're talking about abduction. Isn't that an FBI matter? The infrared surveillance hasn't turned up anything? That's what surprises me."

Not asking her whether the Coast Guard helicopters had been

using their infrared tracking system, or even inventing a reason why he knew about the systems.

So she had replied, "A couple dozen small brushfires or camp fires, a few boats fishing the park illegally and one cocaine bust, a sailboat crossing from Cancún. What, it would take the systems eighty-seven consecutive working nights to graph the whole area? That's what they told me, the Glades and those islands. It's the biggest single uninhabited and roadless landmass in the United States. That's the stat that really surprised me. I always thought of south Florida as crowded. Two choppers working different grids six hours a night still couldn't check it all." Being frank with him.

National Security Agency field-service people were familiar with the options. Same thing: She knew that Ford knew that she knew that he knew. . . .

The second time she'd spoken with him, she'd said, "When they were doing the coordinated searches—" The logged searches had been called after seven days, which was policy. "—they did those searches going just about everywhere their boats could go. I think they should have looked where their boats couldn't go."

Ford had answered, "Everywhere they could go south of Mango."

"Well, of course. The boundary of Everglades National Park is south of Mango, and that's where Fleet and Herbott were both headed. They wouldn't drive their boats north to reach a place that was south, for God's sake."

"Of course," Ford had replied. "Why would they turn north to go south? I guess I haven't checked a chart of the Ten Thousand Islands lately."

Something about the way he said that.

But she had pressed on: "Maybe that's what I should do. Try south and look at places where boats can't go."

She could picture Ford with the phone to his ear, standing in his wobbly house with all the books and vials and those pretty fish in the tank outside. She had left the observation vague enough so that he was a little confused. "What are you saying? That you plan to get hold of an airboat?"

"No, I plan to talk to your uncle again." Said that just as frankly. Then added, "You know, I'd hate to see him get into trouble. There's something about him . . . he's just got this likable way about him."

To which Dr. Ford had said, "Yes, but you can't allow that to interfere with your work."

Walker was thinking about the way Ford had said it, a CIA kind of flatness in his voice, maybe telling her he didn't care about his uncle, or maybe telling her that she couldn't sweet talk her way into his confidence. Replaying it as she stood in the mosquitoes watching the strange-looking woman waddle back to her car with its Lantana plates.

Lantana on Florida's east coast, that's where the *National Enquirer* was?

Behind her, she heard trooper Cribbs creaking toward her. Heard him say, "Just like I thought. We can't touch him." Like he'd known all along.

Walker said, "You mean the stuff about open range, the old man was right?"

"No. Well, I don't think so. The lieutenant, he agreed with me. Looked it up, and all it says is horses and things. Bikes and wagons, that sort of transportation? They have to go by the same laws cars and trucks do." Cribbs tried to say something with his expression, one of those macho beer-commercial smiles. "So I just warn the old dude it'll probably be horse versus semi, he keeps it up. Then maybe I can follow you along to where ever you're going and buy you lunch. Professional courtesy."

Walker said, "Next time, maybe," walking toward the horses, where Gatrell was waiting for her, watching her with his hat off, smile fixed, calling out, "You got more questions for me, Miz Walker?"

She did, but Cribbs was at her elbow, listening. So she just said, "No, I happened to be passing by. Quite a coincidence." Playing it cool.

"Surely is at that. Wouldn't you say so, Joe?"

The other man was standing beside the cow now, messing with the ropes that held the packs it carried. As if she wasn't even there, the Indian man said, "Steers ain't made for this, but you wouldn't listen to me. We shoulda took two horses—" Then he seemed to notice her and abruptly stopped talking.

"You must be going on a trip."

Gatrell said, "We both was, but only one of us might make it," giving the Indian man an odd look. Then he said, "But if you need to talk, you can find us down off the Loop Road—'bout forty miles

169

east of here?—or we'll be back home in 'bout three, four days. We
got a friend down there, Ervin T. Rouse."

Walker thought, If Cribbs wasn't here, I'd ask him right now.
Just come out and say it, see how he reacts. The old man likes
games so much. Look him right in the eyes and say, *"Where are
they?"*

But instead, she said, "The trooper here says you're absolutely
right. Riding horses on the highway, there's nothing he can do—"

"It's not very smart. I need to advise these gentlemen that."
Cribbs had to throw that in. Show everyone he was the one in
control.

Gatrell gave her that innocent grin, said, "One thing about
being my age. You remember all kinds of old laws."

Walker said, "I bet you do . . . I bet you do. I'll keep that in
mind." Then got in her car, out of the bugs, and sat watching until
Gatrell and the Indian rode away.

TEN

In 1938, Ervin T. Rouse and his lyric-writing collaborator, Earl, took a train all the way to New York City and recorded a song Ervin'd written, the "Orange Blossom Special," for RCA records. They'd stayed in a hotel that had menus in French and a drinking fountain in the bathroom that Earl liked but Ervin never trusted.

"I might get down'n my knees to drink whiskey, but not water," Ervin had told Earl. "Lord knows, somethin' ain't natural 'bout that."

Staying in the hotel was a big deal because, since childhood, they'd been traveling with a flimflam preacher, playing music at minstrel shows, playing at tobacco warehouses and country bars, going by a variety of names. The Three White Ducks, The Redhot Smokin' Tarheels. The names changed as often as their numbers did, but it was always Ervin on fiddle, Earl on the single snare drum. They collected money in a hat. They slept in many a barn.

But in 1937, riding around Lake Okeechobee in an open white roadster, sobering up on beer after a long night of whiskey, Ervin came up with the tune and lyrics (Earl had passed out) of a song he would later say "just kept bangin' around in my head till it come out whole." That song was the "Orange Blossom Special," a fast fiddle piece so haunting, so demanding of the artist, it has been called the greatest train song in the history of bluegrass music.

Looky yonder comin', coming down the railroad track
It's the Orange Blossom Special, bringin' my baby back. . . .

At the time, though, Ervin didn't think the song was anything unusual. He and Earl had written hundreds of the damn things and nothing had ever come of any of them. But one afternoon, playing the song outside a Kissimmee barbershop, passing the hat, an Atlanta musical agent heard them, and the next thing they knew, they were on a train for New York, a recording session at RCA, and a stay at the hotel that had menus they couldn't read and a drinking fountain that Ervin, at least, refused to use.

They made the record, Ervin signed some papers, Earl pocketed a check for three hundred dollars, and it was mostly all downhill after that.

In the decades that followed, Ervin heard his song played on every late-night talk show by nearly every American country band. He heard it played on the radio. In bars, he heard it played on the jukebox. Once he turned on the public television station and a big orchestra was playing it, up there in that goddamn city, New York. The sheet music was easy to find, too. All the music stores in Miami carried it, and that meant every music store in the country probably had it. Miami was such a modern place.

Whenever Ervin got the chance, he would thumb through the bins of sheet music, or flip open the books until he found it: the "Orange Blossom Special"; music and lyrics, Ervin T. Rouse."

His name was always right up there at the top, plain to read. Trouble was, nobody in the music stores believed it was him when he tried to tell them. Same with the country-music stars when he wrote them letters, putting on plenty of postage so the envelopes would make it clear to Nashville. Same with the country radio stations when he'd call the special phone-in lines.

"You want to request the "Orange Blossom Special'?"

"Nope, I wrote it. Just wanted you to know."

"Sure you did, partner, sure. That song's been around forever," they'd always say.

And Ervin would reply, "Man, I started young! What was I, seventeen, eighteen when I did it?" But they'd hang up before he had a chance to play the song for them over the phone. By the time he got the phone cradled so he could mount his fiddle under his chin and raise the bow, he'd hear *click*.

That song was just so famous, nobody'd believe it was him that wrote it. But if they'd heard him play it, they'd've known. Nobody could play the "Orange Blossom Special" like Ervin T. Rouse.

It was his old white liquor–making buddy, Tucker Gatrell, who pointed out that not being famous was the least of Ervin's worries. "You supposed to be getting paid, you dumb shit. Every time some big star makes a record of your song, you supposed to get a little somethin'."

Well, Ervin knew that. In fact, had always felt the three hundred dollars he had been paid was a little thin to cover a song that had become so popular. But it took Tuck, who didn't lack for gall or

rains, to go to Miami and convince a fancy Coconut Grove law-
er to look into the matter. A few months later, Ervin received a
Manhattan check for one thousand dollars. On the phone, the law-
er told him, "You don't need to thank me, Mr. Rouse. You just
gn some papers, turn the royalties over to me. I'll make sure you
t a nice check once, maybe twice a year."

He got those checks, too—sometimes for as much as five hun-
ed dollars.

Ervin used the money to buy a piece of land in Pinecrest, a little
mber and gator-poaching settlement south of the Tamiami
rail, way back in the Glades, about midway between Miami and
aples. Him and Earl built a plywood shack up on blocks because
the rainy season, trucked in a stove and a generator, and lived
etty well. Pinecrest had a store that sold dry beans and canned
ods, and there was a bar there, too. The Gatorhook, where ev-
yone believed Ervin wrote the song because they heard him play
so often.

The one person who didn't care whether he'd written a famous
ng or not was the woman he married. His best friend, that's the
ay Ervin thought of her. A woman so smart and funny and
wdy that he could say any stupid thing that came into his head
d she'd make sense of it. Got so he hated being in the house if
e wasn't around. Hated coming around the corner, fearing her
uck wouldn't be there because she was out shopping or doing
me damn thing. When she left the house, it was as if she took
e air with her and he couldn't breathe right until she returned.
at's how much life that woman had in her.

But one day she left and didn't come back, and Ervin waited and
aited, until he finally went looking, and he found her beyond the
nce at the little Midway Airport, where she worked. Her truck
as still running, but her heart wasn't.

That woman had a heart too big for just one person—that's what
vin always said. But even it couldn't handle the strain of all that
ring.

He wrote a song about that. He wrote a lot of songs for his wife.
When she left, she took his life with her, and then Earl died, and
vin figured his career as a songwriter was finished, too—he
dn't been doing much with it anyway, what with so much time
ent drinking and mourning and reading the Bible. But then
cker Gatrell said he wanted to give it a try, become his new

collaborator. If Ervin could make so much money on a single song, they ought to make a whole bunch more, Tuck said, once he got involved.

Tuck was always like that, real bossy. He wouldn't put up with anyone moping around when there was work to be done.

Tuck had spent a week with him in Pinecrest—too long by the standards of peace-loving Gatorhook patrons—and the two of them turned out seventeen songs, music and lyrics. A few of the songs were pretty good, Ervin thought. "If Jesus Rode the Range I'd Saddle My Horse Right Now." "Hog Dogs Got My Girl by the Ear!" "Redfish Ain't Roses to My Darlin'." They'd have written more, too, if one night Ervin hadn't fallen off the roof of the shack and landed on his Jim Beam bottle wrong. He almost bled to death by the time Tuck sobered up enough to drive him to the hospital in Miami.

But when those songs didn't do anything, Tucker lost interest—the man didn't have a long attention span. And that left Ervin T. Rouse to live with the knowledge that, for him, there would be only the "Orange Blossom Special"—a song that dominated him, dwarfed him, and now had a life of its own.

This tragic knowledge might have driven lesser men into deadly or debilitating extremes: strong drink, religious fanaticism, depraved excesses. But fortunately for Ervin, his early lifestyle had hardened him. He had always liked strong drink, and his early years with the flimflam preacher left him cold on organized religion. There were no interesting alternatives left, so he contented himself with living alone in the Glades, hunting and fishing, and sometimes flying around stone lonely in his wife's beat-up old plane.

And almost every Saturday night, Ervin T. Rouse would stagger with great dignity to The Gatorhook, where he would play fiddle in return for free drinks, sawing out the "Orange Blossom Special" until the tears streamed down his face.

The day after leaving Mango, late in the afternoon, Tuck and Joe rode into Monroe Station, an old mess camp back in the late twenties when the Tamiami Trail was being built, but which was now a diner and fuel stop. Monroe Station was a solitary place with its two gas pumps and hand-painted signs: WILD HOG SANDWICHES. That stiff white house sitting alone on the highway, like an island set among cypress trees at the edge of the asphalt and a whole horizon of saw-grass prairie beyond.

Tuck reigned to a stop in front of the station and looked up at one of the upstairs windows. As a boy, he'd bunked in that room a couple of nights, traveling with the crews as the dredge pumped its way through the swamp. Later, the house had been used as an outpost for state troopers. Then it became a little bar and dance place, a place Tuck liked.

He pointed to the window and said to Joseph, "Remember what happened up there that one night?"

Joseph grinned for the first time all day. "Yep, I sure do 'member that."

Thirty years past, but Joseph could still look at the window glass and see the images of him and Tuck, both young men then, moving back and forth across the blank frame, dancing with the same friendly lady.

"Guess the restaurant's already closed. The gawldang television people was probably waiting on us but left."

Joseph patted Buster and looked away. Tuck had been talking about the television people all day. They had camped just east of Ochopee, and Tuck said the reporters would surely find them there, but they hadn't. Then he said the entrance to Collier-Seminole State Park was the place, but again no cameras.

By noon, Tuck was fuming. "I just don't understand it. Best news story in the state and not a sign of them muck thumpers. Maybe they got lost—I bet that's it."

Joseph thought, Lost on eighty miles of two-lane highway? But he didn't say anything. Back at the picnic place, if Tuck had only closed his mouth for a moment, he would have heard the reporters laughing at him. But he hadn't. Never noticed the looks they gave him—the kind of swervy-eyed look people gave drunks. There would be no more reporters. Joseph was pretty sure of that.

"Hey, I know what." Tuck couldn't stop thinking about it. "I bet they went straight to Ervin's place."

Joseph said, "Maybe so."

"You notice how some of them pretended not to know 'bout the song, like they'd never heard it? That was their way of bein' sneaky, trying to throw the others off the track."

"You'd know about that."

"Wanting to get to Ervin first."

Joseph shrugged.

Tuck said, "They'll show up, don't you worry."

"They do, I'll tell them about the water, just like you said." Trying to make Tucker feel better.

"There you go. Now you're using your noggin, Joe."

Monroe Station looked abandoned. At least, no one seemed to be around, so they found a spigot out back, where all the swamp buggies and airboats were kept fenced. They watered their horses.

"I was gonna have me a roast pork sandwich and a beer once we got here."

Joseph said, "Yeah, and some Vienna sausages. I like to drink the juice."

"Well, it's a hell of a disappointment."

"I don't care, just long as we don't have to ride on the highway no more. Them fast trucks gives me the spooks."

They remounted and set off down the Loop Road, Roscoe's and Buster's hooves clip-clopping on the dirt road. The trees moved in, forming a cool tunnel above them. Some had butterfly orchids growing in the shade. Within an hour, they came to the first of Pinecrest's few houses: simple one-story places, none built close to the other.

"Where'd The Gatorhook go?" Joseph was looking around, trying to remember the place. He hadn't been to Pinecrest in ten, fifteen years.

"Burned down a little while back. Maybe two months ago. The state people won't let 'em rebuild it, neither."

That was a surprise. Joseph didn't know how to react to news like that. Why would anyone stay in Pinecrest with The Gatorhook gone?

Tucker said, "Best thing that coulda happened. Only way to get Ervin to put down his fiddle and give up whiskey long enough to get any work done. Him and me went for a little airplane ride a while back. In that crop duster his wife flew, the two-wing job? Never woulda got him up there if The Gatorhook was still around."

Joseph had flown with Ervin once, and shivered at the thought of it. "I ain't goin' up in no plane with Ervin. You got that on your mind, you better tell me right now. He don't even have a license."

Tuck was peering ahead—it was dusky now, with thunderheads showing themselves over the trees, way east toward Miami. "He don't have a license to drive a car, neither. Or to fish and hunt gators, but that never slowed him. He does okay in that plane. Gets lost, he just flies around until he finds a water tower. Cities paint their names on water towers, and Ervin can read just fine. Say—" He was looking through the trees toward what Joseph remembered as Ervin's shack. "What is that, some kind of big tire? Leaning out backa the house."

Joseph knew what it was, one of those new antennas for a television. But before he could say anything, Tucker said, "I'll be damned, a satellite dish." He got Roscoe walking again. "Ervin musta got another check."

Sitting there with a cigar in his teeth, his flat Celtic face alight in the television's glow, Ervin T. Rouse said, "I'd come with you, but I got this now. It keeps me pretty busy."

Meaning the television: a nice one with a great big screen, like the kind Joseph had seen in the store windows at the Cypress Gate shopping mall the time he'd stopped to buy beer.

"Ervin, you promised me." Tucker was sitting in the rocker looking at him but not getting much response. Ervin had a glass of whiskey in his hand, a baseball cap on his head—it read FLORIDA MARLINS—and he was wearing an old Seminole jacket, all colors of rag ends tied into it—red, green, yellow, lots of blue. "You said you'd come along with us to Mango, help us get some publicity. You're the only famous person I know that's not already dead."

"You got a television?"

"Got a radio."

Ervin hooted. "Hell, I threw my radio out the window the day I got this. Heard my song played one too many times and just gave her a toss." He held the remote-control unit out, pointing it like a pistol. Talking to Joseph, Ervin said, "Watch this," and began to flick the channels, stopping only to explain them. "See this one? This here's Cable News Network. Goes all over the world. People in India probably watching it right now. Can't get that with an antenna! And looky here—hear those people talking? That's a foreign language. Could be Jewish folks, for all I know. Maybe French. Their cameras take a picture and radio it up to outer space. Then the satellite radios it back down here to the Glades. Hits my dish on the button, every time."

"You promised me, Ervin," Tucker pressed. "When we was flyin' back in the plane, that's just what you said. 'I promise.'"

"What I promised was, we'd probably get back alive. That's what I was talking about. Us being in the plane." Ervin sunk down in his chair, irritated. "Them ailerons creaking, the horizontal stabilizers corroded from being parked in the barn so long. Hell, I didn't mean nothing by it. I just thought it'd bring us luck." He began to flick channels again. "Besides, that was right after The Gatorhook burned down. I wasn't in my right mind."

"You give your song more publicity, you'll just make that much more money. Hey," said Tucker, "you could buy a bigger dish. And they'd want to buy the songs you and me wrote. Now those are some good songs. 'The Mango Tango'? That's a song people'd buy just to dance to."

Ervin said, "Uh-huh, I notice all the reporters crawling around here. What, they out hiding in the bushes?"

That was the wrong thing to say to Tucker. Joseph knew it and saw Tuck's expression change. "We missed our connections, that's all. But I guess a rich man like you don't need any more money." Not trying to hide his sarcasm or his anger; Tuck had a way of making his voice sound sharp, like a blade. "Sure was lucky, you having a friend smart enough to hook you up with that lawyer so you could get them royalty checks. Not that I mind doing favors—"

"Favors, hah!" Ervin turned his glass up and took a gulp. "Seems to me, I was the last one to do you a favor." He looked at Joseph, knowing Joseph would understand. "No radio, bugs in the cockpit, coulda been arrested for a hundred different reasons, and I can't even swim. 'Want to take a little trip,' he says!"

"How many years you been getting checks now? One little ride in the plane takes care of all that?"

"If it galls you me getting checks, you can breathe easy, because I'm not getting them no more. That's what this here is. An entertainment system, that's what it's called, and I signed a paper giving that Miami lawyer all the rights in trade."

"For a television?"

"Nicest one they had. Felt bad about all the money the lawyer had to pay for it, but you got to be tough when it comes to business."

178

"I'll be damned. Why didn't you just give him your house while you was at it?"

"I don't see that it has anything to do with you, Tucker Gatrell. Turns out that lawyer owned mosta the song, anyway—don't ask me how that happened. Figured giving him the rest for something nice as this was a pretty smart deal."

Tuck started to say something else, but Ervin cut him off. "Can't you close that trap of yours for two seconds? Joseph and me are trying to watch a show." Then to Joseph, he added, "Wait till you see the kind of Western pictures they make now. The women take their clothes off and the Indians almost always win."

Tucker stood abruptly. "If you can't get your mind off that television long enough to talk about this, I guess I can find a way to do it." Going out onto the stoop, letting the screen door bang closed behind him.

"Let him go," Joseph said. He was watching the screen now, hoping Ervin would flip the channel. He wanted to see one of those new Westerns.

Ervin yelled toward the door, "Don't you touch that dish!"

"Ain't gonna touch it. I'm gonna shoot it!"

Ervin got slowly to his feet—he weighed more than two hundred pounds—then went toward the door in a hurry. Looking through the screening, he said to Joseph, "He's going through the packs y'all brought. He got a gun in there?" Then he hollered, "I'll call the law on you! Lordy, Lordy"—he was talking to Joseph again—"he doesn't mean it, does he? He's not going to hurt my dish?"

Joseph said, "The way I put it together, he mighta been the one who burnt down The Gatorhook."

"*No.*"

"Seems he's pretty serious about this."

From outside came Tucker's voice. "I heard that! I heard that! I never did it! I'd never burned down The Gatorhook!"

Ervin said, "Damn if he doesn't still have that white-handled pistol of his. Uh-oh, he's gonna do it—"

Joseph got up quickly and put his hand on Ervin's shoulder, trying to get him away from the door. "Let's get down behind the couch. He could hit the house, the truck, anything. Maybe us, the way he shoots." That made Joseph think of something. He turned his face toward the screen and hollered, "Tuck, you hit Buster, I'll . . . I'll cut your head off and hide it!"

"No sir, by God, I'm not going to let him!" Ervin pulled away from Joseph, pushed open the door, and stood looking at Tucker, who had the cylinder of his revolver open, putting in cartridges. In a quiet voice, but deadly serious, Ervin said, "Tuck, I believe you've finally gone around the bend. I believe your brain's finally gone crazy."

Tucker looked up at him and said just as quietly, "That may be, Ervin T. It may be my brain ain't as healthy as it used to be. But by God, you promised."

Ervin T. Rouse stood in the silence for a while. Finally, he said, "I never pictured you in the water-sellin' business. That flimflam preacher used to take me around, he did a little of that. Called it medicine. I just figured never to go back to it. What he did to us boys . . ." The way his voice trailed off, he sounded sad to Joseph. Far away and sad. The only other time he'd heard Ervin sound like that was when his wife died.

"I ain't that preacher, Ervin T."

"True enough. Reckon if you was, I'd kill you. Shoulda done it back then."

Tucker said, "And you ain't no boy no more."

"Nope. I'm sure not no boy." Ervin cleared his throat and put his hands in his pockets, looking around. "Welp, if you're that set on it."

"I am. I plan to get this thing done."

"I see that . . . I see that." Then after a long time, as if he was listening to the crickets and the owls, Ervin finally said, "I'll go. But I'll drive my wife's truck, you don't mind. I don't have a horse, and I'm sure not riding that steer."

It took Ervin a few days messing around Pinecrest to get ready. "I've got affairs to put in order," he said. What he meant was, his fiddle was broken and he had to wait to pick it up at the repair shop in Miami.

That was okay with Tucker and Joseph. Tuck had things to do, and Joseph finally got to watch one of the new Westerns Ervin had described. The women didn't take their clothes off, but the Indians did win, and that was almost as good.

The only thing Tucker wanted to watch was the news. He kept

calling the stations from Ervin's wall telephone, but no one wanted to talk to him.

"I don't get it," Tuck kept saying. "They know who I am."

Joseph thought, Yeah, that's the problem, but he kept his mouth shut.

Mostly, Tucker used Ervin's truck and drove different places. "Getting ready," he explained. "I know what we've been doing wrong now."

They never did see themselves on the television.

On a Sunday morning, the first of November, they finally got going. Tuck had Ervin's truck fixed so that there was a flashing orange light on the roof ("Make it easier for the cement trucks to find Buster," he had chided Joseph), and he bolted a big hand-painted sign to the truck's bed. The sign read:

> GLADES SPRINGWATER
>
> MANGO FLORIDA
>
> FEEL FLORIDA FRESH

Ervin didn't like it. "That's my wife's truck," he kept saying, talking as if she'd be mad if she found out. But he didn't press the point. Tuck had already confessed that he might be crazy. And he was wearing his pearl-handled pistol right out in the open now. Kept it in a holster belted low on his hip.

With Ervin following in the truck, light flashing, they rode the Loop Road back to Monroe Station, then turned west onto the Tamiami Trail. With the truck to carry the packs, they didn't need Millie anymore, but Tuck had insisted on that, too—taking Millie. "How you going to have a cattle drive without cattle?" he wanted to know.

Joseph just kept quiet and towed the steer, hating the way those cars whistled by. There was always a lot of traffic on the highway, but Sunday was the worst. Even in early November, hurricane season. Once was, the tourists only came to Florida in the winter. But now, judging from the license plates—Ohio, Michigan, New York, Iowa—there was no slow season. All those cars flashing past, throwing a hot wind wake. Some honked. A few cussed them out the window because they had to hang back until it was safe to pass. Most, though, slowed to gawk and take pictures.

People in the cars yelled things, too.

"Hope that water tastes better than the Everglades smell!"

"I bet I know where that water comes from!" Pointing at the steer.

Tucker didn't seem to mind when the drivers said stuff like that. He just grinned. "Advertising," he yelled back to Ervin. "Doesn't matter what they say about you. Just 'long as they say somethin'."

But Joseph cared. He didn't like strangers looking at him. He especially didn't like them taking his picture. He had heard somewhere—maybe his grandfather had told him—that it took a little piece of a man's spirit, having his picture made. His grandfather had been wrong about almost everything else he'd ever said, but the cameras the people used made sharp clicking noises, like the sound of scissors snipping away.

It made Joseph uneasy. He didn't like that sound, and he didn't like all those people staring. He wondered what they thought, seeing them riding along the edge of the road. Probably thought they were old crazy men.

But they didn't. Most didn't, anyway. For the tourists in their station wagons and Toyota vans, seeing men on horseback was a welcome break from the saw-grass monotony of the Everglades. A pleasant diversion from the pressured arguments about routes and vacation schedules. Something to point out to the kids: two old riders wearing western garb—hats and neckerchiefs, even a gun, and that one looked a little bit like an Indian. See how they tipped their hats? See how slowly they went? See how peaceful their smiles were out there beyond the air conditioning, the FM noise, the wrinkled road maps, and the sour cups of 7-Eleven coffee? An orthopedic surgeon from Grand Rapids who, only moments before, had snapped at her husband for some small error in navigation, suddenly turned to him and smiled sheepishly. "I'm sorry," she said. "For a moment there, I forgot we're on vacation." Her husband watched the riders momentarily and felt the same strange, sweet longing. He smiled back and said, "I wonder where Mango is?" A man from New Jersey who drove as if every car on the road was his private enemy actually slowed and let a Greyhound bus pass him, and a bank president from Omaha gave his road-weary, bedraggled wife a playful pinch on the breast and said, "Ya know, I can't think of a single reason why we have to make it to Disney World tonight. Check the map for that place, Mango. We'll stop and see if there's a motel."

Hundreds of cars passed them; thousands of people saw them, but Joseph got no sense of well-being from it. Which was why he didn't protest when Tuck reigned up at an access road with a sign that read:

PALM VALLEY RANCH
A PLANNED MODULAR COMMUNITY
AFFORDABLE LISTINGS!

Tucker considered the sign for a moment, then said, "This might be a good place to stop, rest the horses for a while. What is it, 'bout noon? I bet they got some beans cooking, too. From here, we can go backcountry through the Glades."

Joseph studied the sign for a moment, then said, "It ain't that kinda ranch." He looked back at Ervin, who was getting out of the truck, probably wondering what the holdup was. Joseph called to him, "You ever been in here? What is this, some kind of golf course place?"

Tuck said, "Hell no, it's a ranch. Says so right on the sign." To Ervin, he yelled, "Let's head in here, get some food."

Ervin was nodding his head, unsure of what they were discussing. "A restaurant? Yeah, they probably got a place in there. It's big enough."

Tuck said to Joseph, "See there? A ranch so big, it's got its own restaurant." He touched his heels to Roscoe, talking to the horse. "You're the only one don't argue with me every two minutes. Guess that's 'cause you know me so well. . . ."

The access road wound through a forest of shabby gray melaleuca trees on one side and a massive mown weed field on the other. After half a mile or so, they rounded a bend and saw a whole city of trailers: row after row after row of mobile homes, lined up like cartons that gleamed in the November heat. Each trailer had a neat patch of lawn, a white cement drive, a couple of dwarf palm trees, a citrus tree or two, and a carport. Narrow roads branched off the main road, and all the roads led to a massive circular commons area where there was a swimming pool and a big red aluminum building shaped like a barn. The barn was gated by two rearing plaster horses.

Montana Circle, Nevada Circle, Gold Rush Lane: The streets all had names like that.

"Jesus," said Joseph, "I didn't know there was this many trailers on earth."

Tuck was oddly quiet, riding along, slouched in his saddle. After a while, he said, "I thought it was going to be a goddamn ranch! I mean—I mean, I feel just a little bit stupid. Kinda *dumb*. What the hell kinda world is this when they can tell lies on a big sign that's right out in public?"

Joseph said, "There's some people over there. We can ask them about a restaurant." He motioned with his head, taking no joy in Tucker being proven wrong. It happened so often.

To the right of the aluminum barn, a cluster of people stood near a block of green runways—shuffleboard courts—watching as the riders and the slow truck approached. Retirement-aged men in shorts and sports shirts, their hair combed. Holding long sticks, though they didn't seem to be using them. No one seemed to be playing shuffleboard; the men just standing there talking to three or four ladies who sat on chairs in the shade. A couple of the ladies were pretty good-looking, Joseph noticed. Had button-up blouses and nice skin.

Tuck steered Roscoe toward the group, tipping his hat as he did. Smiling when one of the women said, "You're a day late for Halloween!"

"Miz?"

"Halloween—that was yesterday. We all dressed up like cowboys yesterday. You could have come to the party." The people laughed in a friendly sort of way, as if they were glad for the company. Then the lady said, "You know, you look very familiar somehow. . . . I've seen you. . . . Have you ever been here before?" Touching her chin, thinking about it as she studied them, then lifting her head a little to look at Ervin just getting out of the truck. "Not him, but I've seen you two somewhere. . . ."

Joseph sat up straight on Buster, trying to look his best. He liked the woman's face. Her bright green eyes and whitish hair piled up on her head, everything nice and neat, like she took good care of herself. Probably had a nice neat trailer, too.

The woman said, "I bet I know where!" Her eyes widened a little. "I'm sure of it. . . . Say, wait right here." Then she jumped up and walked quickly toward a row of trailers.

One of the men said, "What in the world got into Thelma?" The whole group was watching her, interested. The man stood and held out his hand to Tuck, saying, "I'm John Dunn. Is there something we can help you with . . . ?"

"Tuck Gatrell."

"Mr. Gatrell."

Another of the ladies said, "You know, that *does* sound familiar." Now she was searching their faces, thinking about it.

Tucker said, "My friends and me, we just stopped to get a bite to eat and rest our horses. See what kind of ranch you folks had here." Chuckling a little as he said that, as if he'd known all along it wasn't a ranch.

John Dunn said, "If you're interested in a lot . . . or maybe a complete unit?"

"Naw," Tucker said, "a place this nice, we couldn't never afford to live here. Could we, Joe? We got ourselves a run-down little place called Mango. A shack on the water, that's us."

"You might be surprised at how affordable it is," Dunn said. "And the facilities . . . well, they're just great. Aren't they?"

Behind Dunn, heads were nodding up and down. "Just great," the people repeated, but Joseph didn't hear much enthusiasm in their voices.

Tucker said, "We got all the time in the world. Why don't you tell us a little." But Joseph knew he was trying to get them friendly, maybe get some free food.

"About prices? I can take you over and introduce you to—"

"No, 'bout the way things are here. What you do. There're things to keep you busy enough here?"

Dunn said, "Oh, plenty. Here at the ranch? Why, everyone's got a full schedule. The whole thing's planned out. We've got the pool, the clubhouse, parties, shuffleboard, crafts. You name it. Lawn maintenance? They do that, too. And a weekly schedule printed up, so you know what to do and when to do it."

"It goes by streets," one of the ladies said. "People on the same street, we're like a family. This is our shuffleboard time."

"Yeah," said one of the men, a stubby guy with glasses, "we get two hours to play, even if you hate the goddamn game. Which we do." Laughing like it was a joke, only he wasn't joking. Tuck found that interesting. Joseph knew by the look on Tucker's face—a mild expression, but kind of sly, like his brain was going real fast.

"But the other stuff," Tucker said, "I bet you sure love the other stuff."

Joseph thought, Just so long as he doesn't keep them talking too long. I'm hungry, as the others responded, "Of course we do. It's great."

But another man said, "Except for those damn crafts."

"Lloyd, you don't have to do crafts if you don't want."

"What the hell else is there to do?"

Tucker looked at Joseph, then at Ervin, showing that same mild expression. As if to say, "Forget about lunch. Let's listen to them squabble."

"You know what I don't like?" The stubby man was talking again. "I don't like not being able to plant more trees. Two palms, two citrus—what the hell kind of rule is that?"

"You have to have some control—"

"No, I agree with Bill on that one. We should be allowed to plant trees on our own property if we want."

"That's the thing. It's not our property. Sure, we bought our lots, but the Association retains all rights so that—"

"Let people plant trees, next thing you know, they'll be planting tomatoes."

"What's wrong with tomatoes?"

"Nothing's wrong with tomatoes, that's not the point."

"I wanted to build a little place for my orchids, but they told me no."

Another lady said, "You know what I miss? I miss having a cat. I've always loved cats, and just having one nice little cat doesn't seem like it would bother anyone."

"Cats?" Tucker said it so loud, people jumped. "Ma'am, you ever want a cat, you just come on down to Mango. We got about a jillion cats roamin' around. Well, the ones the chickens didn't run off, anyway." To the stubby man, he explained, "The tarpon come onto the flats. By my shack in Mango? They come in and purely tear up the mullet. What the tarpon don't eat washes up on the beach, so cats have an easy time of it. Yes ma'am"—he was speaking to the lady again—"you ever want a cat, just come on down and help yourself. I'll have my dog catch a couple for you."

"No, they'll never let me have a cat. I tried."

"One person has a cat, the next thing you know, someone will want a kennel."

But most of the men were focused on Tuck now. "You say the tarpon feed right by your house?"

"Only in the spring and summer. This time of year, it's the snook, isn't it, Joe? Gets so noisy at night, it's kinda hard to sleep. All that splashing."

"That's why I like redfish," Ervin said, giving Tuck a look, showing him that he was in on whatever joke Tuck was playing. "They're quieter. Let's you hear the owls at night, so you can go out and look at the orchids growing wild."

Joseph thought, Put two frog eaters together, and they'll fight over who can tell the biggest lie. Back at Mango, all Tuck did was complain about how the fish had disappeared.

John Dunn said, "It sounds awfully nice. I don't think I've ever heard of the place. Mango?"

"Just a run-down old fish camp, most the places abandoned—"

"It took me awhile, but I found it!" The nice-looking woman, Thelma, was hurrying toward them, holding up some kind of paper in her hand. Tuck seemed irritated by the interruption, but he waited politely as she came closer, listening to her say, "I bought it at the supermarket this morning, but Jenny wanted to borrow it, and she loaned it to Mrs. Butler over on Nevada. But here it is! Now I know where I saw you." She was beaming at Tuck. "There's a whole story about you here. The *National Enquirer*."

Tucker said, "The *National* what?"

The lady who had been studying them said, *"That's* where I heard the name."

Thelma held the paper out to him. "You mean you haven't seen it? It just came out. It's brand-new, every Sunday—"

Tucker flipped the pulp magazine open, holding it out at arm's length so that he could see. "Say, now . . . say! Looka that there headline!" He was reading to himself, moving his lips a little. "This paper—many people buy it?"

"Of course, millions. All over the nation. Everyone I know reads it." Thelma was beside Tuck's horse, the others crowded around behind her, trying to get a look at the paper. "You're a celebrity, Mr. Gatrell. And we're not going to let you get away without having some lunch and telling us if it's really true or not. I've always wondered about those stories! Lloyd, don't we have some sandwiches left over from the party yesterday?"

John Dunn said, "I don't care what the story's about, I want to hear more about those fish."

Joseph thought, I could eat three or four sandwiches, and I bet they won't charge us a cent. Tuck swung down off his saddle and held the paper up for Joseph to see. "What you think, Joe. Is that the best damn picture of me and Roscoe you ever seen? And you look pretty good yourself."

In the photo, Tucker stood grinning beneath his cowboy hat, pointing at Roscoe's withers while Joseph, on Buster, looked on. Buster looked nice, Joseph thought. Real handsome, except for the cut mane—and those crazy spots on his butt.

Beneath the photo, there was a line that read: "Native Floridian Tucker Gatrell has proven that an artesian well found on his ranch has amazing regenerative powers."

While Joseph read, he heard Ervin, behind him, say, "Hang on, let me park the truck. Say—you folks like fiddle music?"

ELEVEN

Ford said to Sally Carmel, "You mean you buy this kind of newspaper? Or, what is it—a magazine?"

They had the new issue of the *National Enquirer* spread out on the table, opened to the full-page story about Tucker Gatrell.

The headline went across the top of the page: FLORIDA'S FOUNTAIN OF YOUTH DISCOVERED!

Standing beside Ford, her arm folded over his shoulder, Sally said, "No, it was like I told you. I was standing in line at the grocery—at Bailey's Store?—and I happened to pick it up and leaf through because there were people ahead of me, everybody writing checks. And there it was. I just started laughing when I saw the picture."

All around Ford's living quarters were sacks of groceries—stalks of celery sticking out, the tops of two wine bottles, Asti Spumante. There was a twelve-pack of Coors Light with condensation beads showing on the cardboard as the ceiling fan whirled overhead. Sally had been in such a hurry to show him the story that she and Ford hadn't taken time to put the groceries away yet.

"I can't believe he'd pull a stunt like this. No, I take that back. Of course I believe it. Vitamin water, that was hard enough to believe. Now it's the Fountain of Youth."

Sally touched a finger to the paper, reading. She said, "Maybe he didn't tell them that. You know how these papers exaggerate. Maybe he said vitamin water, and they just blew it up to make a better story."

The story read:

> Why is native Floridian Tucker Gatrell smiling?
> Because he has discovered the long-sought and legendary Fountain of Youth, that's why. Gatrell is a Florida cowboy and he and his best pal—his horse, Roscoe!—found the little artesian well bub-

bling on a forgotten corner of his own cattle ranch in the bayside village of Mango on Florida's southwest Gulf Coast.

According to Gatrell, he and his best pal, along with several other of Gatrell's friends, started drinking the water months ago. All of them have noticed amazing changes in their health.

"I know what it's like to be young again," Gatrell told the *Enquirer*. "Not only that, but I had Roscoe gelded years ago. Now his reproductive organs have grown back. You would have to be a man to understand what news like that would mean to someone my age!"

Sally said, "See? That's not the way Tuck talks. He'd never say something like that. 'Reproductive organs?' Come on."

"No, I see what you're saying. But that's Tuck. This is exactly the sort of thing he'd do. Do you remember me saying how tricky he was? That's why I didn't want to have any part of it." Ford stepped away from the table and began to put away groceries while Sally continued to read.

"Don't be mad at him, Doc. The old guy's trying so hard."

"Uh-huh, that much is true." He looked over at her briefly. Pretty woman in her go-to-the-grocery jade blouse and Land's End slacks that were pleated, belted up around her lean waist. Brown toes sticking out of her sandals, and that hair of hers, bright as liquid copper, swinging in the light as she bent over the table to read. It made him smile, looking at her. Knowing he could go over to her if he wanted and put his arms around her and hold her, touch her if he wanted, and that it would be okay . . . and it also made him a little uneasy, knowing they had become much more intimate than he had planned, far faster than he had hoped. Ford told her, "I'm not saying I would change anything."

She looked at him, a soft expression on her face, her eyes moving to his eyes. "Thanks, Doc. Me, neither."

That's the way it had been. For four days? Five days? No, it was Wednesday, so it had been more than a week now. Since . . . the night after he'd driven to Mango and she'd fixed dinner. Nice dinner, with a candle on the middle of the tablecloth, her face and hair flickering in the shadows, sitting across from him. Moving her food around but not eating much, holding the fork in her long fingers. Ford had had no appetite, either. Being that close to her, alone in the same room. They had talked but didn't say much, because of that feeling. Like something pressing on his abdomen every time he tried to breathe. Then they were standing over the sink, washing the dishes, talking about something, and the next thing Ford knew, his hand was on her's, then she was in his arms, soapy or sweaty—he didn't know or care—and then they were kissing, their faces wet.

It had almost happened that night, but not quite. Sally had said she wasn't ready yet, because of the marriage. The divorce, she meant. But then they were holding and kissing again, touching, yet it still didn't happen because of something she said they had to talk about.

"I don't know how to . . . what I'm trying to say is . . . we should talk about our backgrounds. It's so terrible even to have to worry about it. . . . Do you understand what I mean?"

Ford had understood. He and Tomlinson had spent enough time talking about it. "The Modern Specter," Tomlinson had called it. "The Dark Gift. Because of it," Tomlinson had said, "the human race will never again know total spontaneity. Never again will we know a moment free of the knowledge of our own vulnerability. Or our own mortality. The last retreat has been taken from us."

Which, Ford had thought at the time, was just more spiritual wailing in the face of a serious biological anomaly: a fatal virus, sexually transmitted. But in that instant, in Sally's arms, Ford realized that Tomlinson was close to being right.

So they had talked. Talked all night, nearly. Coyness couldn't be tolerated; discretion became a necessary casualty—one more ghost of romance that had to be abandoned to hard reality. In ways, that kind of complete disclosure seemed to Ford as demeaning as being marched naked through a crowded laboratory. To betray so many past confidences . . . to impose upon the privacy of other women he had known. Even though their names were never mentioned, it seemed an intrusion upon the essential privacy of whatever time they had shared, and Ford felt diminished by it. Even so, there was also something oddly sensual in that kind of total honesty. It demanded a complete letting down of facades that at once mocked their frailties but also brought them very close in a very short span of hours.

The next night, after a sunset boat ride at Ford's place, it had happened. The next morning, too. And the late morning. Then again in the early afternoon, the late afternoon, and most of the next night. Once they started, it had seemed, they couldn't stop.

Their first joinings had been enthusiastic but wary, a little self-conscious, and slightly mechanical—he and the woman trying to do everything just right. But then their couplings escalated into a strange kind of binge behavior. They couldn't get enough of each other. The touching, the exploring, the freedom of being naked and alone, just the two of them, free to please the other in any way at any time. Lying spent, sweating, all Ford had to do was look for a moment at her breathing form, the slow lift of abdomen, the pale blue veins of her breasts, the slow pulse of color in her nipples, her deep-set eyes holding him . . . and his body stirred, ready again.

"You're going to think terrible things about me. The insatiable woman. The way I'm acting."

"No. Never that."

"I'm not like this. I'm really not. I just . . . feel like I've known you for such a long time—"

"You have."

"And now. To finally let go. I don't know what it is. . . ."

Ford had thought, *Lust is what it is*, but at odd moments he too had wondered about their behavior. It had, he thought, the flavor of revolt. A kind of wild insubordination in the face of the Dark Gift. Like captives who flipped hand signs through the bars at their captors, the two of them had lunged around, bare-skinned, in an insurrection against the latex shield that ultimately separated them. And it always did. It was always there, the subject of many bawdy jokes that unfailingly brought laughter because the only alternative was to weep—or so Sally had said. The blood and bones make-up of their own bodies could not be trusted. No human's body could ever be completely trusted again.

"We should both get blood tests. I mean . . . if you think . . . or would like the relationship to continue."

Ford had almost said something about already driving vials of water to Tampa for testing (he had; a buddy of his would drop the results back in a couple of days) and now she was asking for blood. But he didn't. The subject was too serious. He had answered, "Of course. It's something we should think about," because any less evasive answer would, to him, have seemed like a commitment.

And he wasn't ready for that . . . and he hoped to hell she wasn't either.

They had split their time together, staying at Ford's place, then at Sally's, then back at Ford's again. On Sunday, though, she had arrived with a flight duffel of clothes and her big camera-equipment bag, telling Ford that she had arranged for her neighbor Mrs. Taylor to feed her cat. And Mr. Rigaberto had agreed to take care of Tucker's dog and cattle. Having sold most of his chickens, he had little else to do.

"If you don't mind," she had said. "This way, we can both get some work done."

Ford had thought, She already wants to live together? but he had said, "Great, stay as long as you want," convincing himself that it would be a mistake not to at least give it a try. She was an attractive woman; he enjoyed her company . . . and hadn't he spent the last few months damning his own loneliness and wallowing in self-pity?

So, for the last three nights, she had stayed with him. She used his skiff to probe the rookery islands in Pine Island Sound, shooting rolls of film. He worked in the lab, shipping off specimens and doing research for his paper on the effects of turbidity and nutrient pollution on sea grasses. Every other day, he checked his sea mobiles, weighing the dripping mass of growing sponges, tunicates, and sea squirts.

They made love. They talked a lot. Each morning he made breakfast for her. Eggs with mango slices. Fish poached in coconut water.

Yesterday, though, Tuesday, she had made a comment that, Ford suspected, foreshadowed an inevitable conflict. He had entered his lab to find her photography equipment, cameras and lenses and filters, spread out on all the tables while she cleaned them. It wasn't unexpected. He had offered her the use of the room, any time. But looking up at him, she had smiled softly and said, "I'm in your way."

"Nope. There're other things I can do."

"We don't have a lot of room here, do we?"

"It's like living on a boat." He had almost added, "That's why I like it," but he didn't.

Last night she had disappeared, and he had walked out to find her sitting on the deck, looking at the water. He had touched his hand to her shoulder, and she had taken it, without looking at him, and held it to her lips. "A lot has happened very fast, huh?"

"Yeah, it has. Are you getting homesick?" Ford hoped he hadn't sounded as wistful as he felt.

"No. Well, I miss my cat. But being with you, that's what I want now."

"It's . . . been fun."

"But you know. I was sitting here thinking"—she had turned to him, still holding his hand—"I was wondering. Those things you read . . . about the way people act after a divorce?"

"I've never read them."

"Oh."

"You think we're going too fast?"

"Maybe. I don't know." She had made a fluttering sound with her lips. Frustration. "I don't know what to think. I know I've felt good, being here."

On the rebound? That's what she was thinking about—Ford could almost feel her cerebral electrodes zapping the possibility back and forth. She had loved her husband. She had already told him that. So the conflict was understandable, though Ford could have never brought himself to push the subject. That was Sally's life, her private realm, and small caches of private experience were becoming rare these days.

But there was something he could talk about, something else, he suspected, that had motivated her brief withdrawal.

"Staying here, having to use a rainwater shower and an outhouse. I've been thinking that that must be hard on you. You probably got enough of this when you were a girl?"

Ford had been surprised at her surprise, at the wide-eyed look she'd given him. "How do you do that?"

"What?"

"Break in on my thoughts like that? That is exactly what I was thinking, the instant you said it. And you did it yesterday, too. About the camera mount. How? How do you do that?"

Yesterday, he had seen her looking at his telescope. Then she'd gone over to check the calendar, and he had said, "If you need a camera adapter to get shots of the full moon, there's a photo supply on the island."

But standing alone with her on the deck, Ford had said, "Just a guess."

"I was hoping it was something more. The Spanish have a word for it. *Simpático.*"

Ford had said, "I'm familiar with the word," but offered nothing more.

A while later, breaking the silence, Sally said, "You love this house, don't you?"

"It's a good place to work."

She had stood then and kissed him. "Then it's where you should be."

That brief uneasiness was gone Wednesday morning, and Sally had dressed to go grocery shopping while Ford worked on the two big glass tanks he was building to do the procedure with his filtering sea mobiles.

Then she had returned with the new issue of the *National Enquirer*, still reading it now as Ford moved around putting groceries away. He heard her say, "Uh-oh, you're not going to like this."

He stopped. Now what? He leaned against her to read over her shoulder. She was pointing to a bottom section of paragraphs, which Ford skimmed. The state was trying to take Tucker Gatrell's property to make a park. But how could the state set a price on something as valuable as the artesian well Gatrell had found? Were they willing to pay him what it was worth? Not that he wanted to get rich off it, no; Mr. Gatrell was a simple man. Just a regular working guy. He wanted to share the water with anyone willing to come to Mango to get it. Naturally, he would have to charge a small price—bottles, handling, that sort of thing. He had to make a living, after all. But he was going to sell the water cheap. Help people, that's what Mr. Gatrell wanted to do, the story said. Help people feel young again.

Then the story quoted Tuck: "A number of scientists are already studying the composition of the water. A Florida biologist, Dr. Marion Ford, has already assured me that the water contains unusual properties."

That wasn't Tuck talking; it was the reporter. But Tuck had used Ford's name. How else would the reporter have gotten it?

Ford said, "Damn him. He's gone too far."

"He's trying to get you involved, Doc."

"Of course. But to have my name associated with something like this!"

"I know. He's wrong, he is. But I think he's desperate."

"All the years he's owned that land and done nothing but make a junk heap out of it. Suddenly he's desperate to keep it?"

"I don't think that's the reason he's desperate. I think it has something to do with you." Sally leaned back so that her head pressed against Ford's stomach, a warm physical prompt, asking whether he wanted to talk about it.

Ford kissed her on top of the head. "I'll put the last of these groceries away."

"He's not a bad man. And you certainly aren't."

"Yes, but only one of us is crazy. No, make that two. It must be catching, because now Tomlinson's got it. I have to hunt through some more papers on his sailboat and Federal Express them this afternoon."

Tomlinson had been in Boston since Friday. "Might as well, man," he had told Ford privately. "I can't even stop over at your place for a beer anymore, the musk is so thick. I'm afraid it'll peel my tan off."

Right. What he really wanted was an excuse to go and see his daughter, Nichola, and use a research facility he knew about near Cambridge. "They've got the new Genesis machine for DNA testing, and the head honcho owes me a favor. An automated sequencer that pops everything up on the computer screen, no fuss, no muss. Du Pont makes it. Same folks who gave us napalm. This world, it just keeps getting wackier and wackier."

Even so, Tomlinson had called Ford nearly every day he had been gone. Sounded oddly troubled, too. Sort of deflated, as if running on low batteries. Not at all like Tomlinson, but Ford wasn't the type to press for explanations. Tomlinson told him what books and papers he wanted, and Ford said okay. He was getting to be pretty good friends with the Fedex lady.

Now Ford folded the last of the grocery bags, saying, "I have to find the papers and get them off by three, or they won't make Boston's morning delivery. The way Tomlinson keeps his boat, they could be anywhere."

"Hey . . . hey." Sally had him by the hand, turning him toward her. "You're upset."

"Nope. I'm not."

"You're tense. I can feel it in your shoulders." She was kneading his neck with her strong fingers, looking up at him, the two of them standing so close, and Ford recognized the gradual transformation of her mood, her body: knees bent, breathing more shallowly, the sleepy sag of her eyelids.

"Seriously. I told Tomlinson I'd do it. I don't know why, but I told him, so—"

She pressed her lips to his, sliding them back and forth, back and forth, her tongue moving to lubricate his lips as her right hand slowly moved to her own chest for a time before she began to unbutton the jade blouse, pulling it open to show him the translucent cotton bra full to bursting, stretched taut, holding her. "I can't let you go off like this," she said.

Ford hesitated—he really had promised Tomlinson—but then his hand found the little coupling at the front of the bra. It was automatic now; didn't even have to stop to think about how the tricky thing worked. Then, as he stooped to kiss her, he felt her hands on his belt, sliding down to grip him, and he didn't think about Tomlinson or Tuck or anything else for quite a while.

TWELVE

❦

The reason the package didn't make the Thursday Fedex delivery, Tomlinson decided, was because Doc had probably gotten caught up in his work, forgot all about the time. Tomlinson could picture the man hunched over his microscope or peering through his thick glasses at some vial, doing—what was it now?—yeah, research on nutrient pollution in water. The projects changed, but Doc's intensity didn't. Ford was compulsive about work. Probably sat there in his lab and forgot all about the clock. Tomlinson could just see him, down there on Florida's Gulf Coast in the autumn heat and tropical squalls, oblivious to the world. All the man's sentient energies being poured into linear problem solving, which wasn't healthy. Really murked up the aura. Made it opaque as used dishwater, like this Boston weather. . . .

Now it was Friday, and Tomlinson was walking along the north bank of the Charles River on the bike path from Watertown to west Cambridge, and he glanced up at the sky. There was no sun, just a pale smear without borders—a cold pale light in a gray meld of smog and haze. Simon and Garfunkel kind of day, that's the way he had once thought of it. Everything gray and black: oaks and maples, mossy wet, twisting in a November wind that swirled down the Charles. In the high trees, a few remaining leaves fluttered, their glow of first frost weeks gone, solitary as brown flags.

Cold, man. Should have stopped in at Musashi's to give Nichola a quick kiss and borrow a coat. Can't be more than thirty-five, forty degrees. Should have just walked right up and pressed the doorbell, let Musashi know I can be assertive, too. Musashi may be the girl's mother, but I'm the father, and fathers have rights, too.

Tomlinson walked along, thinking about what he should have done, carrying the Federal Express envelope under his arm. His hair was pulled back into a ponytail and he wore old frayed jeans and a black oiled wool sweater a friend had brought him long ago from Northern Ireland. Made a present of the sweater to him back in the days when there was so much energy in this town that an outsider could touch the grass on Harvard Commons or stick a toe into the Charles and he would feel a sort of electrical shock. Nothing negative, just a wild kenetic energy that flowed through the whole scene, Cambridge and Boston, even the MIT campus—a kind of kick-butt tribal power created by the coming together of thousands of young souls fired by Beatles music, first-rate intellects, social consciousness, the outrage of Vietnam, and some damn fine drugs. A truly inspiring venue for experimentation and social revolution that grew and fermented, getting stranger and more wonderful until about . . . what, 1970 or '71? . . . until the killings at Kent State seemed to stick a pin in their beautiful balloon and reversed the momentum. That was peak tide, and the ebb had been running ever since.

A few nights before, roaming the old section of Harvard's campus, distraught, depressed, nearly loony with Musashi's combative behavior, Tomlinson had fallen into the grips of nostalgic despair, and it seemed he could see the high-water mark of his generation's youth: a faded paisley stain at limb level on trees beneath which he had once made speeches and made love.

I'm the outsider now. Students, they seem all of a type. Snobby and full of themselves, but without grace or tolerance. All they care about is What Bo Knows. Pricey cross-training shoes, MTV, Walkmans, and paying lip service to causes—usually the Environment, capital E—to which they bring anger without understanding. They're all style, man. Style without substance.

He had said essentially the same thing to Musashi, and her cutting reply had hurt and confused him: "Were we any different, Tomlinson? Do you really believe that we were? That we had understanding without anger? That we were substantive and graceful and tolerant? Think back and tell me then if you really believe that."

He had said to her, "But at least we had an honest cause. Vietnam. Vietnam as an issue wasn't substantive?"

And her reply to that had been shocking. "I remember anger. That's what I remember. I remember being angry as hell, absolutely sure that we were right. But now, when I think about it—and I try not to think about it—but, when I do, I have a very difficult time reconciling our self-righteousness with the fact that four or five million Vietnamese and Cambodians were slaughtered when we finally got our way. When we finally made them bring the troops home. It's hard for me to feel righteous about that."

"My God, you're not saying we were wrong to protest—"

"No, of course not! I'm saying that now I see clearly enough to know that the world does not tolerate clarity. That, in those days, maybe we had a lot more anger in us than understanding. Simple answers require the simplicity of youth. We despised complexities—don't you remember? So we took all the hated unknowns and cloaked them with our certainty. We were children, Tomlinson. We were no different."

Replaying the conversation over and over in his head as he walked, Tomlinson caught himself. He was getting hung up in a flow of negative vibes. A whole negative, destructive trip that seemed to be sweeping him along, and Musashi was right at the heart of it. The woman who had asked him to father her child but who now seemed intent on squeezing him out of her life and worse, their child's life. How could motherhood have changed her so much? Or perhaps she had changed gradually in the years prior to their joining to make the child, but he had been too enamored of their past to recognize her new reality. But one thing was certain: Each trip he made to Boston, Musashi seemed to get a little colder. A little more abrupt. And more obvious that he was no welcome.

She was going by the name her parents had given her at birth now, refusing to answer when Tomlinson slipped up and called her one of the names she had chosen from the old commune days "Moontree," that had been his favorite. But she couldn't abide i now. Gave him a boiling look when he used it. It was one mor way, he thought, for her to cut away the strings of their relation ship.

He had hoped it would be different this trip. Instead, it wa worse. Started on Friday night when he had called from the air port.

"You expect me to drop everything, open my home to you, jus because you arrive on a whim to see Nichola?"

Two days' advance notice was a whim? He had called from th marina on Wednesday and left a message on her answering ma chine that he was flying in.

"No, two days is not enough notice! Two weeks, perhaps. Tw

months would be better. Yet you take it for granted that your wishes have first priority. Not everyone lives on a boat, Tomlinson. More to the point, not everyone lives in the past! Some of us have jobs. I have classes to teach. Nichola has her own schedule at the nursery and the day-care center. And the election is only four days away!"

That was the main thing. For now, anyway—the election. Musashi was campaigning for a friend of hers, a man named Niigata, one of her professor buddies who was running for the state assembly. Because of the baby, Musashi didn't have time to be Niigata's campaign manager, but she was one of his first lieutenants. Perhaps the man's lover, too. At least that's what Tomlinson was beginning to suspect. The way Musashi tensed up whenever he mentioned the guy's name. Got so nervous when Tomlinson suggested that he and Niigata meet. Something was going on, and Tomlinson wondered why she didn't come right out and say it. He felt no jealousy—well, not much. But as he had told Musashi, "Because we created one flesh doesn't mean we can't live separate lives."

To which Musahi had said, "I know, I know: Saints don't marry. And please don't be confused. I'm not asking you."

"Bitch!" The word slipped out as he walked, and the nastiness of it stopped him. Tomlinson glanced around. Bare trees, wind, people jogging, people roller-blading, people hurrying through the late-afternoon gloom toward dinner or a late class, or the dorms. If anyone had heard, they made no sign. He might have been invisible, a rut in the bike path to be swerved around. Tomlinson pushed his hands into his pockets, hunched his neck into the weater, and continued on. Never in his life had he used that word in reference to a woman. Well, not a woman whom he knew, anyway. That word wasn't an oath or an assessment; it was a short cut, a way of avoiding difficult realities. To say it was a piggish tupidity.

Tomlinson thought, Somehow, I've gotten railroaded into destructive currents. I feel as gray as the weather. Feel like my cell walls have sharp edges, cutting me a little every time I move.

A few blocks later, just across the street from the modern marble and steel two-story office complex that was Massachusetts Research Labs, Tomlinson thought, What I've got to do is get my work done, try to help Joseph and Doc's uncle. We've all been

karmically linked, and it's bad luck to ignore such things. I'll ge
my work done, kiss my daughter as much as I can, then get back t
Florida on the first flight out. There's something growing in me
Maybe sunlight can cure it.

Tomlinson's friend at Mass Labs—that's what they calle
it—was Ken Kern, a buddy from the old days, one of the univer
sity's founders of Students for a Democratic Society, SDS. Bac
then, Kern had had hair to the middle of his back, wore a silve
cross of infinity along with the Star of David, and smoked unfil
tereds. Now, Kern was nearly bald, wore a Freudian black bear
and a white smock. He was the lab's senior geneticist, and Tom
linson's daily visits were beginning to make him uneasy. Tomlin
son could tell. The way Kern tapped his fingers at the securit
desk, waiting for Tomlinson to get his own smock buttoned an
clip the visitor's pass to the pocket. Kern's habit of saying, whe
they were alone together, "You know, I'm going out on a helluv
limb for you." The way he checked his watch when Tomlinso
was around, using body language to say he didn't have a lot of tim
to spend on private projects. A project they had been working o
after hours, four or five hours a night for the last week. A projec
that could go on for another two weeks, or even a month. That
what Kern was worried about.

Tomlinson never reacted to Kern's uneasiness. Always ju
smiled kindly—Kern had been one of his closest confidants in co
lege; a great man with a great brain, but always worried abou
something. The nervous type, so he and Tomlinson had balance
nicely through five years of weirdness and revolution. What Ker
probably remembered as clearly as anything was that Tomlinso
had willingly taken the rap on twenty-two counts of possession c
illegal substances: fifteen blotters of acid and seven dime bags c
truly fine Jamaican ganja the campus cops had found in their dor
room. All Kern's. But as Tomlinson had said at the time, "N
sense involving you, Kenny. This is the seventh time I've bee
arrested, and seven's my lucky number."

Now the two men were walking down the hall toward La
Room C—the tile and stainless-steel room where they had bee
working. That's where the PCR machine was kept—PCR fc
Polymerase chain reaction, the key apparatus used for amplifyin

202

specific units of DNA, deoxyribonucleic acid. A second machine, an ABI 4800, automatically sequenced the base pairs.

From his reading, Tomlinson already knew the basic procedures and objectives. But, talking on the phone before Tomlinson left for Boston, Kern had put it even more simply: "All living organisms derive from a single unit that generates complexity. That unit is DNA. From a single strand of DNA—the way its base chemical pairs are sequenced—the researcher can, theoretically at least, determine not only an individual's sex and race, but what that person looked like, how he sounded, and, to a degree, how that person behaved. Take a strand of DNA two to three centimeters long, and it's all there, little dots and dashes. Like a fingerprint, only more telling. Life is nothing more than an expression of the DNA instructions encoded in the genes." Kern had chuckled after he said that, knowing that Tomlinson still saw all things as spiritually fired, constructive or destructive. Kern had said, "Remember that freeze-dried food we took the time we went looking for mushrooms? In those tinfoil packages? It's kind of like that. To create life, you just add water."

Which Tomlinson didn't believe, not for a moment. Though Ford would like it—and would probably accept it—when he told him.

To create life, just add water.

But what interested Tomlinson most was that Kern said it was possible to take the root of one of Joseph Egret's hairs and to isolate a cell that contained strands of DNA. He had also said that if Tomlinson could come up with at least thirty separate specimens of bones from Calusa burial mounds, he might be able to find a DNA sequencing pattern—flags, he called them—found only in that race of people.

"We don't need much," Kern had told him. "Maybe a gram or two from each bone, but they have to be good bone from the femur. If we don't get that, we might end up isolating the DNA of the archaeologist who dug them up and put them in the sack. The outside part could be contaminated by the archaeologist's hands."

So, prior to leaving for Boston, Tomlinson had spent five full days going to Florida's universities and museums, calling in favors from old friends, humoring scientists he'd never met, collecting little nubs of bone—something archaeologists didn't part with easily. Sometimes he nearly had to beg: "Only a gram. Only this much—" Holding his thumb and index finger a quarter inch apart, "And I'll send you all the data we produce."

Even so, it was tough going. Tomlinson had even considered driving back to the mounds at Mango to do a little digging himself. But just the thought of that outraged his personal standards of the human ethic. Defile the sacred artifacts of fellow human beings? It made no difference that they had lived and died hundreds of years before him. They were still people. People who had walked and wept and worried and laughed, people who had scratched their butts and hugged their babies and made love in the same subtropical milieu he called home—Florida. Only scum would impose upon the dead. Someone with a black hole for a conscience.

In the end, Tomlinson gathered nineteen specimens of Calus bone. Not enough for an ideal survey population, Kern told him, but it would have to do.

"If you had a hundred specimens, we probably wouldn't find anything, anyway," he had said. "Like that saying: Everyone knows what race is, but no one can define what race is. They're always so mixed. The most Irish Irishman in Boston is probably at least twenty-five percent ethnic something. Spanish or Italian or Swede, or any mix in between. The blackest black in Harlem averages about twenty-five percent Anglo-Saxon. A thousand years ago, or today—people mix. That's one thing that makes race supremicists so laughable. We're not the same people our great-great-great-grandfathers were, genetically or otherwise. Our species is in a constant state of flux. Historically, when strangers of the same sex meet, they make war. When strangers of the opposite sex meet, they make the creature with two backs."

But Kern's enthusiasm for the project had faded as the repetitious nightly work continued. He said his wife was badgering him to get home earlier. He said if they continued to work after hours on the project, it was just a matter of time before the lab's management found out. Kern said that, with just nineteen specimens, there wasn't much hope, anyway.

In reply, Tomlinson only smiled.

Now, on this Friday night, Tomlinson and Kern put on surgical booties, gloves, and masks before unlocking Room C. Kern switched on the lights and said, "Well, the crapshoot continues."

The light in the room was cold white, as sterile as the tile floors and walls.

In the far corner of the windowless room was the PCR machine—Genesis II, it was called. Genesis was a little high-tech box not much bigger than a stereo turntable, at the center of which were fifty uniform holes punched into aluminum stock to hold bullet-sized test tubes. There were wires and plastic programming keys. Cables connected the machine to computer monitors.

Kern found another key and knelt before the stainless specimen locker. "I'll get the samples out and you can set them in the machine. I think you know the procedure well enough."

Tomlinson said, "Sure, man. In fact, you want to go home to your wife, I think I can manage the whole thing. Except for maybe identifying the anomalous gene markers right off—"

"No kidding," Kern broke in dryly. "It only took me—what?—three or four years to get the hang of that."

"Hey, no doubt. It's a complicated gig. I'm not saying I don't need you, Kenny."

Kern took a rack containing twenty test tubes from the locker, stood, and said, "I know . . . I know. Same old Tomlinson. It gets to me, that's all."

"Like preparing the samples," Tomlinson said. "I didn't have a damn clue about that. Drilling to the bone cortex before taking samples. Doing all those little steps so neatly. Purifying, separating, all that stuff. Taking the strands and making them soluble in a water-based buffer. Like you said: Just add water, huh? Even from reading the books, I didn't know about any of that."

"The way you catch on to things so easily," Kern said. "That's what I mean." He was carrying the rack of test tubes across the room so carefully that the tubes might have been filled with hot tea. "It used to bother me. It did."

"Naw . . ."

"I don't mind being honest about it now. It's not a big deal anymore. Back in college, the way you always just cruised, but I had to work my ass off to keep up."

Tomlinson was surprised to hear that; a little saddened by it, too. "You were brilliant, man! Come on. Everybody said so."

"No, I'm gifted. And I'm a worker. At least, I was when I wasn't hanging out with you eating drugs." Kern was positioning test tubes in the Genesis machine as he talked, thinking in

fragments as he did: Why am I telling this man these things? W
were students together; now we're strangers. . . . And mayb
that's why. . . .

Kern said, "But you, it was like you were born with a trillio
bits of data and just needed your memory refreshed every now an
then. Like writing all those papers for the journals when yo
were—what?—just a sophomore? Hell, I've got colleagues no\
who hold dinner parties when they're lucky enough to get pul
lished."

Tomlinson had the main computer on, checking the hardwar
before punching in the program they'd be using. "You think bacl
Kenny, you'll remember there was no cable television in thos
days. Sometimes a guy wakes up at three A.M. and just doesn't fee
like watching static. And you always had that typewriter ready t
go by the window. No shit, if we'd had 'Gilligan's Island' rerur
back then, it woulda been a whole different story. The Skippe
Maryanne?" Hunched over the keyboard, Tomlinson snorte
through his gauze mask. "My left hand pretended to be Maryann
so often that—when I hear the theme song?—the damn thing sti
jumps around like a cat. You shouldn't feel bad about tha
Kenny."

"I don't. That's what I'm telling you. I look at what we ended u
doing, the way we turned out. My life compared to your life." A
the words left his mouth, Kern thought to himself, That's a dam
cruel thing to say. Where is all this bitterness coming from? Th
pressure of running this damn department . . . the pressure of be
ging funds and grants every year . . . the strangeness of living wit
a woman I no longer even know. . . . And he instantly felt miser
ble, wishing he could take it back. Wishing he could take back s
many, many things.

But Tomlinson was nodding his head, dark goat's beard bobbir
up and down as he threw an arm over Kern's shoulder and sai
"Don't you be jealous about that, Kenny. You want to live on
sailboat, you should do it. This little bay where I'm anchore
Dinkin's Bay, there's plenty of room. I could introduce yo
around. Every day, when the fishing guides get back, we sit arour
the docks and drink beer. Me and this friend of mine . . . you'd lil
him. A dude named Ford. He's got a little lab, and he'd probably l
you use it when you got the urge."

Kern touched the power button of the Genesis machine, and

began the slow work of cycling temperature up, then down, in preface to decoding the basic life structure of nineteen ancient lives. As he sat himself in the chair, Kern smiled a little and said softly, "Same old Tomlinson."

Four hours later, Tomlinson was taking a break. Sitting on the floor outside Room C, going through the papers he'd received from Ford that afternoon. Among the papers was the memoir of Do. d' Escalante Fontaneda, copied in the original archaic Spanish. In 1545, at the age of thirteen, Fontaneda had been shipwrecked off the southwest Florida coast and captured by the indigenous peoples—*indios*, or *yndios*, Fontaneda called them, though they later became known as the Calusa, or Caloosa, for they were dominated by a warrior chief the Spaniards called King Carlos. These were the people who had built the mounds.

Fontaneda lived among Carlos's people for seventeen years before he was finally rescued. Returned to Spain, he had produced the thin monograph from which Tomlinson's copy had been transcribed.

Through other reading, Tomlinson knew that Fontaneda had spent time on the mounds near what was now Mango—if not Mango itself, for it was possible that Mango had been that ancient nation's small capital, and home to Carlos. What Tomlinson wanted to determine was the approximate population of the Calusa in the year's Fontaneda had lived among them. Kern had hammered at the problem of crossbreeding, how it muddled up the genetic flags. Tomlinson hoped to present him with evidence that, year to year, the population of the Calusa was small, probably not more than a few thousand. Which meant there had to be a lot of inbreeding, generation after generation. To a geneticist, that would be good news. Maybe it would help renew Kern's interest in the project—the man seemed so irritable lately.

Legs crossed on the floor, Tomlinson translated as he read, going very, very slowly, sometimes checking other reference books to help him transcribe a line or a single unfamiliar word. Fontaneda had been a bright man, but he'd had little formal education because of the shipwreck, and, worse, he didn't have a writer's sense of sentence. The memoir was convoluted, a bear to read. So far, there had been no estimate of the population, only long lists of the food the Calusa ate (they were hunters and fishermen and divers, not farmers) and descriptions of the thatched common houses built atop the mounds—houses with woven walls upon which were hung the bizarre-looking masks of Calusa demons. It made Tomlinson smile, thinking that atop one mound a thatched house decorated with demons had been replaced by Tucker Gatrell's little ranch house with its rickety porch, brass spitoons, and empty beer bottles. Where the only demons on the wall were a few old photographs—one, a photograph of Marion Ford as a high school football player.

But then Tomlinson's attention vectored as he came to a surprising part in the memoir. The archaic Spanish began: *"El Rio jordan que dizen Es bucion de los yndios . . ."* Tomlinson translated the poor spelling as he read: "The River Jordan [the River of Life?] is a superstition of the Indians of Cuba, which they embrace because it is holy. Ponce de León, giving credence to the tale, went to Florida in search of that holy river so that he might earn greater fame and wealth . . . or so that he might become young from bathing in such a river. [Many kings and chiefs, Tomlinson guessed] sought the river which did this work, the turning of old men and women back to their youth. To this day they persist in seeking the water. . . ."

Tomlinson stopped reading, amused. Every school child knew that Juan Ponce de León had been mortally wounded by the indigenous people of Florida. Probably by the Calusa, for the attack had occurred on the southwest coast. Sitting on the floor, Tomlinson imagined the pompous little Spaniard, his armor glinting, being rowed to shore, only to be confronted by the physically huge Calusa (not all accounts agreed, but at least some Franciscan priests took time from their religious diatribes to note the unusual size of the Calusa people). Maybe Juan Ponce had tried to land at what was now Mango. Wherever it was, the explorer who had helped destroy the lives of thousands of native people found death on that shore, not life.

Most interesting to Tomlinson was that Fontaneda, who had lived with the Calusa, said plainly that the belief in the River of Life had originated with indigenous peoples. Tomlinson had always assumed the story was one more assault by Hollywood on American history. Or had been invented by some superstitious Spaniard. But not this time. Fontaneda had lived it; he would know.

Tomlinson continued to read. There was more about the River of Life, so he made notes. He had just translated a portion of script that read: ". . . many people sought this place in the province of Carlos, so they formed a settlement. . . ." when Kern gave a muted call from inside Room C. "Tomlinson? Hey? Get your ass in here!"

Tomlinson swung the door open, to see Kern's face bright in the glow of the computer screen, his attention fixed. The man didn't even glance at him when he ordered, "Get your mask on; there's something I want to show you."

"You find something?"

"Get in here!"

Tomlinson returned, still tying on the gauze mask as he bent over Kern's shoulder. "What you got?"

Kern touched a gloved finger to the screen. "Take a look at this."

The fluorescent green pixels formed a scrolling line of vertical letters that read: TT-AA-TG-CT-TG-TA-GG-AC-AT-AA. . . .

Kern highlighted the letters. "This sequence," he said. "The double *T*, double *A*, *TG-CT-TG* sequence. We're looking at a mitochondrion D loop. Do you know what that means?"

Tomlinson started to answer that he did know, but caught himself. He said, "Nope. What the hell is it?"

"Its characteristics are passed on only through female lines, and those characteristics vary rapidly from generation to generation. But ten of the last eleven specimens have had this exact sequence. There was a similarly unique sequencing in the HLA genes—which are passed on by both female and male. They might be the flags we're looking for. The genetic marker." Kern returned his attention to the screen. "These people must have been inbred all to hell, I'm telling you."

"It didn't help Juan Ponce de León."

"What?"

Tomlinson was following the scrolling screen. "I said, you know, the explorer. Ponce de León? All that inbreeding didn't help him. The people we have mushed up in the test tubes, they could have been the ones who killed him." That's the way Tomlinson thought of the specimens, as people. Tiny somnolent lives suspended in time but indifferent to the drops of water that had temporarily freed them. "And you found the same pattern in Joseph?"

Which was how they refered to the strands of DNA Kern had isolated from Joseph Egret's hair: Joseph. A test tube with a name, for it contained all the codes and biological keys that had choreographed the man's living form.

Kern said, "I haven't got to that yet. Joseph's still waiting." He turned to look at the lone test tube remaining in the rack, then looked at the digital clock on the desk. "That'll take another two, three hours. And I've still got to do the remaining eight unknown specimens. We don't have a large-enough population as it is; we can't skip any."

Letting his enthusiasm hide his disappointment, Tomlinson said, "Oh yeah, for sure. We've got to do it right. And it is getting late. Let's go. I'll buy you a beer or two, then hit it again tomorrow afternoon. Oh . . . hey, wait—"

"Lab's closed," Kern said. "Tomorrow's Saturday."

"Exactly. That's just what I was going to say."

"Sunday, too. I'd have to explain why I wanted in."

"Whenever you can get to it, Kenny. I'll plan around you, and glad to do it, too."

Kern sat silently for a moment, looking at the clock but no longer thinking about the time. "You were hoping to be back in Florida by Monday, weren't you?"

"I booked the red-eye out for early Monday morning, just in case. But no big deal. I've already said that. There's this meeting I'd like to go to—I tell you about that? Yeah. But you can't hold discovery to a schedule. And you need to get home to your wife."

Kern tapped his fingers on the desk, looked at the screen again, then looked at the clock. Then he looked into Tomlinson's eyes, and he was reminded of something he had once pondered in college: How can such a happy man have such sad, sad blue eyes? Kenny Kern started to agree. It was much too late to continue. But then the words slipped out: "Hey, man. When's the last time we pulled an all-nighter together?"

Had he said that? Yes, undoubtedly. Kern recognized an old and almost forgotten energy in his own voice.

"You mean it?" Tomlinson had his hands on Kern's shoulders, shaking him a little, excited.

"Hell yes I mean it. But you know what we need?"

"Damn right, man." Tomlinson was almost shouting now. "Mescaline! Just a couple of blotters to add some nice backlighting. Keep us interested. Hey—" He stopped for a moment, scratching his head. "I don't even know where to buy that kind of stuff anymore. But beer—I know where to buy beer! They sell it almost everywhere!"

Kern had a high, dry laugh, as if he was having trouble getting air. He had almost forgotten what that sounded like, too. "No. No beer. Not in the lab, anyway. I need coffee. That's what I meant. You go get us some coffee. A lot of it. We've got eight or nine more hours of work to do."

Two nights later, Sunday night, Tomlinson found himself sitting in his rental car outside Musashi Rinmon's neat brownstone apartment. Dr. Musashi Rinmon, respected professor, the woman to whom he had once written poetry during their on-the-road hitchhiking and back-to-the-earth commune days. The woman who had popped in on him out of the blue decades later, and who was now the single working mother of their child—Nichola, a daughter. That's the way Musashi described herself: single-working-mother, saying it as if it was a one word declaration of pride, but tinged a little with anger, too.

Tomlinson sat at the wheel exhausted, bleary-eyed. The radio was on, AM, the tail end of a jazz program. He sat listening to the final set, trying to decide whether he should go up and see Musashi and Nichola. Say good-bye. Risk one last scene before he caught the early-morning flight back to Florida. Since Friday morning, he'd had—what?—maybe three hours' sleep. Which would have been okay if he'd had time to do his meditation, let his brain cells settle down and catch a whiff of universal energy. But he and Kenny Kern had been too hard at it for even that. All night Friday, then right into Saturday, and finally finishing late that afternoon. Kern broke only to call his wife, then again to hop into Tomlinson's rental car to track down food or a few beers for breakfast. The two of them sitting in the parking lot of a Circle K, the one just across from Joey's Used Car sales at the corner of Kennedy and Beacon. Little paper bags around their sixteen-ounce tall boys, giggling like kids and talking about old times. Then back to the lab and more work. "I lied about not being able to come in on Saturday," Kern had admitted. "You know, it's weird. I never used to lie much at all, back when I was a bum and not respectable. Now that I'm important, I find myself doing it all the time.

Hell, if I couldn't work on Saturdays and Sundays, I'd have no excuse for getting out of the damn house."

A lot of pain in the man, Tomlinson could hear it. A spirit as flawed and gray as the sky, which made him feel unwell, for, to Tomlinson, the pain of others was palpable as vapor and contagious as a virus. It seeped into his brain, then his soul. He didn't just empathize; he absorbed and shared. Tomlinson loved people for their faults—not because there was comfort in weakness but because flaws were the conduits of humanity.

"Kenny," Tomlinson had said, "I'm not being judgmental here—hell, you know me, man—but if you're unhappy with your wife . . . I mean . . . if you don't like her—"

"But I do like her," Kern had cut in. "See, that's the thing. I like her; I admire her; I respect the hell out of her. She's a good human being. I think I'm a good human being. But we don't . . . we just don't . . . it's like all the years and secrets we've shared have made us strangers. When you come to know the blood and bones of a person, there are no illusions left? Something like that. I can't explain it. Things just . . . changed."

"Check me if I'm wrong here, Kenny, but I get the feeling you're telling me you've called it quits. Given up. You can't be afraid of change, man—"

"Me? Hah, that's a laugh." Sitting beside him in the rental car, Kern had drained his beer, then crushed the can. "Look at yourself, Tomlinson. I mean it. Go look in the mirror. At least I hung in there and tried to change. I'm still trying in some ways. But you still look like you did in 1969. Just older, that's all. And you wonder why you're having trouble relating to Musashi?"

That had stuck with Tomlinson all day, even when they were working, even as they finally got Joseph's DNA sequencing up on the computer screen. *You still look like you did in 1969. And you wonder why you're having trouble relating to Musashi?*

Back in his motel room, Tomlinson had stood naked in front of the mirror, taking an interest in his own appearance for the first time in . . . how long? Since back in high school, maybe. He couldn't remember. He had touched his own long hair, holding a length of it out in front of his eyes to see. Golden hair sunbleached blond, and the cells at the very tips of the hair could be ten, fifteen years old. He rarely even trimmed it. Not like his beard, which he kept neat. Well, sort of neat . . . oh, hell, his beard was a mess, too, and Tomlinson wondered why he had grown the thing in the first place.

Well, maybe Kenny had been right. . . .

Tomlinson had stepped out of the motel bathroom to check the clock by the bed—he didn't own a watch—and saw that it was half past eight. In a city this size, even on a Sunday, there should be a clothing store open somewhere. He stood and thought for a moment, then said aloud, "I wonder if they still sell Nehru jackets?" Then, in a rush, he had dressed and driven to the nearest shopping center—Walden Mall—where a salesman persuaded Tomlinson that a gray silk Brooks Brothers was better suited to both his dignity and the current decade.

Tomlinson was a little disappointed. He had always wanted a Nehru jacket.

Later, he shopped for a hairstylist. But the only thing he found open was a little place in Boston's industrial section called Benny's Quick Cut. There, a startled man in a blue smock studied Tomlinson's scraggly hair and beard for a moment, grinned as he recovered his composure, and said, "I'd do this one for free, buddy!" And he waved him into the old Koken barber's chair.

Now it was nearing midnight, and Tomlinson sat outside Musashi's apartment building, wondering whether he should go in and say good-bye.

He would, of course. That's why he'd done the shopping. But he wanted to gather his spiritual reserves first. Didn't want to face the woman while negative vibes still controlled his spirit. Finally, he stepped out of the car and walked up the steps to the door, where he took a deep breath, straightened his tie, touched the doorbell, and waited.

No answer.

He was about to touch the button again when he remembered that the bell didn't work. So he tapped on the door, three soft raps, then knocked a little harder when no one answered.

The door swung open on its own.

Tomlinson stepped into the apartment, worried that something was wrong. But then he saw the empty champagne bottles on the counter, the two empty wineglasses, the ELECT JOHN NIIGATA signs in a stack on the floor, the CONGRATULATIONS JOHN! banner tacked to the wall, and Tomlinson knew it was okay. Musashi had had a little party and forgot to lock the door. Probably a private

213

celebration—her man had won last Tuesday. Tomlinson already knew that.

He felt uneasy standing in her apartment. Japanese pen drawings on the walls; screens made of rice paper; shelves with rows of books. It was Musashi's private space, and it was wrong to invade that space without invitation. But then he began to wonder whether she was home. It was so quiet. There was a light on over the sink and a night-light in the bathroom. That was all. Even Nichola's little room, down the hall to the left, looked dark.

She's my daughter, Tomlinson thought. If she's here, I should check on her.

He crossed the carpet to the hall, past the master bedroom . . . then stopped. Through the wedge of open doorway, he could see the outline of Musashi's sleeping face. Beside her was a man, a black-haired man with a neat black beard.

Tomlinson touched his own bare face, now so smooth after his visit to the barber.

Damn it. I shaved for nothing!

In his abdomen, deep within, he felt a growing spasm of jealousy. It was so abrupt and strong, he stepped away from the door in an attempt to dull the feeling. He stood in the dark hallway, breathing slowly, rhythmically, wanting the hurt to fade, wanting to access the calm that was at the very core of him.

I have no right to be angry. I've been wrong all along. Kern could have been describing Musashi instead of his own wife: She's a good human being. All she has been trying to tell me is that I have no claims on her life.

Quietly, very quietly, Tomlinson reached out and pulled the bedroom door closed, then entered Nichola's room. His daughter lay beneath soft blankets, asleep. There was a night-light plugged into the wall—a plastic bird in flight—and just seeing the infant's small form, asleep, at peace, caused Tomlinson to sag a little at the weight of the love he felt.

"Little daughter, my dearest child . . ." He whispered the words as he bent to kiss her: tiny warm creature, butt hunched up beneath the covers, blond curls, with little wrinkled hands that grasped and held his big fingers reflexively. "Somehow, we will work this out. I promise."

He turned quickly then and fixed the lock on the open apartment door, pausing briefly when he thought he heard the whispered words "Good-bye, Tomlinson." He hesitated, looking toward Musashi's bedroom. Had he imagined her voice, or had the words been muted by plasterboard and dry-wall?

He choked out a reply: "My loves . . . good-bye," then stood motionless in a silence too repellent to endure.

Quickly, he stepped out onto the stairway and closed the door behind him.

Outside, the city night was as cold as the leaf-strewn concrete. Above the haze of sodium lights, scudding clouds gave the illusion of a few frail stars adrift in a wind that, to Tomlinson, seemed to blow right through him.

He started the car and drove numbly toward the airport, his small suitcase on the backseat, the sheath of lab results in a manila envelope on the seat beside him. Musashi's apartment was miles behind before he realized the radio was still on. The jazz program had been replaced by a talk show, the volume turned so low that it could not pierce the roar of Tomlinson's own thoughts. He reached to touch the radio's scan button, but then something that was familiar about one of the voices caused him to pause.

Oh, it was Larry King, the interviewer. Tomlinson turned the volume up and sat back to listen. If he no longer had the power to still his own thoughts, perhaps he could divert them.

King was saying, ". . . who claims to have made a startling discovery, is our guest this hour on the Mutual Broadcasting Network. He's controversial, eclectic—you may have seen him on CNN a few nights ago with newswoman Margaret Lowery. We have him on the phone, live from his home. Before the break, you were talking about some of the famous people you have known—"

The next voice Tomlinson heard was even more familiar: "Yep, I knew 'em all. Well, most of 'em that come to fish this coast of Florida. I was telling you about the fat one, the rich man from Hollywood."

Tomlinson leaned forward and whispered, "Good God, that's . . . Tucker Gatrell!"

"I'll remember his name in a minute—"

"Samuel Goldwyn? Louis B. Mayer?" Larry King was always so helpful.

"That's it! He's the one! Mr. King, he says to me, he says, 'Boy, go fetch me a cup of water.' That's just what he said, Mr. Louie B.

Mayer, the moviemaking man. 'Boy'—called me that on my own boat. So I says to him, 'Boy? *Boy?* I hope to hell you said *Roy.*' Hah! Then I says, 'How'd you like to go home and tell Clark Gable some boy just whupped your fat butt to a frazzle? After that, he didn't want to use me in the movies no more."

Tomlinson began to smile . . . then he began to laugh . . . laughed until the tears came and he was no longer certain whether he was laughing or crying.

On the radio, Tucker was saying to Larry King, ". . . what you ought to do is come on down. Hell, I got plenty a room at my ranch. Sleep in my bed, if you want—I slept in barns before, by God, and liked her fine. See for yourself this little town of mine ain't so little no more. Fact, thanks to nice people like you, Mango's getting bigger by the minute. . . ."

THIRTEEN

❧

When the Captain told William Bambridge that he'd be taking him and the two Chucks back to the mainland day after tomorrow, Bambridge thought, Damn! I was going to make ceviche. . . .

The Captain told him, "Tall 'n' Short got most my cane in. Debt's paid. And you a fair damn cook. All them dishes I never had before. But I promised a man to deliver a load of goods on the ninth. Even gave me a calendar so I'd know the days. And I ain't the sort to break a promise."

"That's the truth, Captain. No one's going to argue with you there!"

When he got the news, Bambridge was sweeping the shack with a broom he'd made with his own two hands. Cut a green bamboo handle and lashed a bundle of dried reeds to it, trimmed neat. Every morning at first light, he swept the shack. Tied open the bamboo shutters to let the air and fresh sunlight in, then went to work on the packed dirt floor. For more than two weeks, that had been part of his routine. Truth was, he'd come to enjoy the routine; didn't realize how much until the Captain told him he'd be leaving.

I've got so much to write down. I've got to make more notes! What I really need is a couple more hours just listening to the Captain talk.

Every day, the first thing Bambridge did when he got up was get the stove going. Not a stove, really—a metal bucket with holes punched in it and openings at both sides for draft. Then he'd put coffee on and sweep the shack while the water boiled. He liked to sweep; liked the way his broom made neat swirls in the dirt, and each morning, he decorated the floor with new patterns. He'd fold the two bed pallets, both stuffed with moss and leaves, then he'd get breakfast going.

The cooking, that's what he liked best.

The first day, the Captain had told him, "Grits and mullet. That's all I got; that's what you'll cook. Boil 'em both, 'cause springwater's the onliest thing we got plenty of."

Which explained to Bambridge why he hadn't been able to eat much, the food was so bad. So that first afternoon, with the Captain down overseeing the two Chucks, Bambridge decided to scout out the place. He took one of the machetes and cut his way through the jungle that canopied the island's low mounds. Escape had been on his mind, but he got too hot and tired, so he sat down to rest—and there, by his feet, saw that the ground was littered with little yellow limes.

"Spanish limes," the Captain would tell him later, though Bambridge guessed they were really called key limes.

The limes smelled wonderful—like sweet flowers—and so did the leaves of the tree that bore them. Bambridge had collected the limes in a pile, then set off to explore some more.

Two hours later, he returned to the shack using his shirt as a makeshift bag. He had the limes, plus ten ripe avocado pears, a bunch of guavas, a green papaya, several big knobby oranges that were too sour to eat (but would be fine for making drinks), lime leaves for seasoning, and a half dozen eggs from the nest of some kind of bird—pelicans, maybe. Bambridge didn't know.

The old man had eyed him narrowly as Bambridge came into the clearing. "Thought yew'd hightailed it."

"No sir, Captain." Bambridge had smiled, trying to ingratiate himself—God, he'd die if he had to go back to the pit! "I was out doing some shopping."

The old man had studied the fruit and eggs, shrugged, and said, "I knowed such truck was out there, just seemed too fancy to spend time huntin' it. You don't mind pickaninny work, he'p yourself."

Cooking became fun after that.

Now, for breakfast, they might have an egg or two with grits cakes soaked in cane syrup. For dinner, they might have mullet baked beneath orange peels, guava sauce, and avocado slices marinated in lime juice.

Every day, Bambridge tried to come up with something different.

After the first week, Bambridge had said to the old man, "Captain, what we could really use is a different kind of fish."

"Mullet's the onliest kinda fish I catch in my throw net. Mullet and a sand bream sometimes."

"Yes, I know, and the men love it—I think I can speak for them. But I want to do a poached fish dish, use the lime leaves and this kind of peppery plant I've found. And mullet is just a little too greasy and strong for the sort of thing I have in mind."

The old man had a way scrunching his face, an expression of sour bemusement. Without a word, he had dropped a coiled fishing line into Bambridge's lap, then walked off.

So that gave Bambridge freedom of the whole island, not just the thick interior. Not that there was a beach. Nothing like it. Mangroves grew right down to the water; trees so dense that the old man had had to carve out a little tunnel beneath the limbs just to have a place to keep the boats. But Bambridge could still wade out and collect oysters and clams; even found a couple of big mahogany-colored shells he thought might be conchs. Beneath the rocks, at low tide, there were all kinds of crabs. A few small shrimp, too.

That night, the old man had sniffed the steaming pot. "Fish soup?" he asked.

"Bouillabaisse," Bambridge corrected, feeling pretty good about himself. "Perhaps the finest I've ever made. And that, sir, is saying something."

Foraging for food became Bambridge's passion. When breakfast was made and the shack was neat, he headed out. The mosquitoes didn't bother him so much anymore. His body had been covered with welts, but the welts disappeared, though the damn bugs continued to bite. So he walked and swatted, waded and gathered and swatted some more.

Surprising, but Bambridge had to admit it: He had even come to like the old man. The Captain kept his distance; couldn't easily be drawn into conversation. But sometimes, after a good dinner, he'd start telling stories, extraordinary stories of Florida's pioneer days. Of the things he'd done, of what it took to survive. And Bambridge would sit making careful mental notes, not saying a word for fear that to speak would remind the old man that someone was there listening.

The old man didn't like to be interrupted, and he didn't like to answer questions.

Early on, while cleaning the shack, Bambridge had found a pretty flower-print dress folded in the corner. Without thinking, he had held it up and said, "Captain? Do you have a daughter?" The old man had given him a surly look and said, "Man's got time fer questions ain't got enough work to do. Maybe you need to get back at that cane."

Bambridge didn't ask any more questions after that, just listened.

Something else he didn't do anymore was go down and visit the two Chucks—not socially, anyway. Just to carry food, if the Captain made him. Or to dip them a bucket of water from the spring. Even then, Bambridge didn't take the trouble to offer them advice. Not after the way they'd acted those first few times when he'd tried to share what he'd heard from the old man. "I'll tell you what makes the Captain mad," he had told them. "The way you two stand around in the shade and he has to remind you the break's over, time to get back to cutting. He says grown men shouldn't have to be reminded—and I agree. Remember, the quicker you two get done, the quicker we all get to go home."

Just a little pep talk, that's all it was. But Chuck Fleet had stood to freeze him with a chilly look, and Charles Herbott had screamed and thrown a big whelk shell at him. "You fat son of a bitch, you used to cry like a baby when you had to work in the field! You big fat-assed son of a bitch! You ever hear of a thing called the Stockholm syndrome? You're no better than him now!"

Well, if that's the way they wanted to behave, he'd leave them alone. Calling him fat! When he wasn't. Not now. He had to tie his pants up with a rope after nearly a month on the island; had lost forty, maybe fifty pounds, and he felt great! And that business about the Stockholm syndrome—suggesting that he, Bambridge, had begun to sympathize with his kidnapper. That was almost laughable, but what could you expect from a cretin like Herbott? The Captain wasn't a kidnapper; he was just a lonely old man with turn-of-the-century principles. They were in the Captain's debt, and the old man's sense of fairness required that the debt be paid. What was wrong with that?

Herbott—environmentalist indeed! The man was a gutter-mouthed savage who belonged in a pit. Why, Herbott himself had proven it just a few days ago.

Bambridge had heard the old man calling him: "Fat 'un! Fat'un! Get yo-self down here—and bring a rope!"

And there, by the cane press, had stood Charles Herbott, as still as a feral dog, his eyes wild, his whole body trembling, threatening the old man with his machete.

But the Captain had his shotgun up, the two men facing one another. Later, Bambridge would remember an odd stink in the air, a strange, musky acidity that, forever after, he would associate with human rage.

In the silence, the Captain spoke softly. "This scattergun knows her work, boy. She's done it before. Now yew drop that'er knife. Let Fat'un tie your arms till you cool off."

Herbott had dropped the machete . . . but then threw himself on the ground, pounding his own face with his fists while he screamed and cursed. Over the noise, Chuck Fleet had yelled, "His brain's snapped, Captain! Couldn't you take him back to the mainland before he hurts himself—or one of us? I'll finish the damn cane by myself!"

But the old man wouldn't do that. He had to keep Herbott tied now, when he wasn't in the pit; it was the principle of the thing. And the old man was right. Bambridge had told him so later. "Captain, you give Short One an inch, he'll try to take a mile. I know his type."

On the morning the old man came in and told him, "I'll be takin' you three back to the mainland day after tomorrow," William Bambridge finished his sweeping, poured the Captain's coffee, then walked down to the pit to tell the two Chucks.

On the way back, he decided he'd stop at a tamarind tree he'd found. The pulp inside the tamarind's seedpods made a wonderfully sweet drink, and its red-striped flowers were delicious, perfect in a hearts-of-palm salad.

Get a really good meal into the old man, and maybe he'd tell a few more stories before they had to go. Use the pencil he'd found to make more notes on the grocery bags he used for paper.

Bambridge stopped at the screened opening of the pit and kicked the roof frame. "Hey, you two awake yet? The sun's almost up!"

Looking down into the gloom was like peering into a cave, and he could see the two dim figures getting slowly to their feet. "What the hell you want, lard ass? Go away!"

Herbott: not so wild now, but still crazy with meanness.

"I'm not talking to you. I'm talking to Chuck. And if you don't stop being so profane, I might not tell either one of you the news."

"What news is that, Bambridge?" At least Chuck Fleet could be civil.

"This news: We're going home."

"We're going—"

Bambridge repeated, "We're going home."

"*What?*"

"That's right. Just like he said he would. The Captain's taking us back to the mainland. He told me not ten minutes ago."

"Jesus Christ, you mean it! He's really—"

"If you get your work done! You finish up with the syrup, do a good job, he'll take us back day after tomorrow. But if you don't, no deal."

Bambridge just threw that in; knew you had to use leverage on men like this.

"I'll be damned. . . . You really think he means it?"

"He means it. He has to deliver a load of syrup and stuff to a man who lives in Mango, and he's going to take us back with him. I told him he could tow our boats in later. He gave his word."

"His word, my ass!" Herbott mouthing off again. "Here or back on the mainland, it doesn't matter a bit! You tell that skinny old nigger it's too late!"

"Don't you call him that!"

"And I'll take care of you, too!"

"He's got a name! Use it!"

Bambridge had told them both the Captain's name. It was Henry Short.

FOURTEEN

❦

Tuck told Joseph, "Looky how things is working out. You don't think God's dropped everything else to sign on for this drive? Got us free food, free beds, 'bout twenty secretaries, and my own command post. The marines messed up when they made me a private, Joe. That's what I'm telling you. I was naturally meant to be an admiral or a major. Something like that."

The two of them were leading the horses around, letting them graze on the green sod pastures of Palm Valley Ranch. They'd been there three days, and the horses and Millie had to eat something besides the bran muffins and apples the women kept sneaking them.

Driving range was what it was. Golf balls all over the place. Only Tuck called it the north pasture—he still wouldn't let go of the idea the place was a real ranch. A long, open field the maintenance crew didn't keep mowed, so there was grass for the horses, and a little bulldozed pond, too, only Tuck wouldn't let the horses drink there.

To Joseph, he had explained, "If you knew what I know about water, you wouldn't stick your pinkie in that mess. The way they squirt around their fertilizer and their bug dope. Nope, we pour them a jug of spring-water back at the command post, like always."

Meaning the red aluminum building shaped like a barn, where there was a phone so he could do interviews, and a little podium so he could stand and give speeches to the four or five journalists who'd hunted him down. Acting like he was talking to a big crowd, even if there was just one in the room.

When one of the journalists would ask, "You got a phone number, if I need to get back in touch with you, Mr. Gatrell?" Tuck would say, "Check with one of my secretaries. They know my schedule." Just so the women—Mrs. Butler or Jenny or Thelma or one of the others—would smile at him, feeling important.

Not that he ignored the men. That first night, Tuck had talked up Mango so much that a couple of them, John and Bill and Lloyd, decided they couldn't wait to see the place, so Tuck volunteered Ervin T.'s truck and drove them there. Mango was a long day on horseback, but only forty minutes by car, yet they didn't make it back until after midnight, smelling of beer and the three men raving about what they called "The most beautiful little place in Florida."

It irked Ervin T., being left out like that. "Hell's fire, the old fart leaves me here with nothing to drink but tea and buttermilk, and stays gone in my truck! And they don't got no satellite dish here, neither."

But it didn't bother Joseph at all. Anyplace that Tuck wasn't seemed quiet in comparison, and it was a relief after so many days with him on the road. Besides, that nice woman, Thelma, had invited him back to her trailer for dinner, saying, "I'm a very good cook." Which may have been true, though Joseph never found out. But she sure did have smooth skin.

The next day, John and Lloyd and Bill, along with a few others, wanted another look at Mango. So many they had to take a couple of cars, and Ervin decided he'd just go along and not come back. Let Tuck and Joe finish the ride on their own, while he remained in Mango to keep an eye on things. That night, Jenny said she felt sorry for Joseph, him left at Palm Valley all alone, so she invited him to her trailer for dinner. Same thing happened—Jenny never got around to cooking, and Joseph got out just in time to listen to all the beery men tell him what a nice place Mango was.

Now, leading the horses back toward the aluminum barn, Tucker said to Joseph, "The trailer park men want to have a meeting with me this morning." He let Joseph see his sly smile. "Wonder what it could be about. Yes indeedy . . . I just wonder."

Joseph said nothing, just walked along, feeling Buster's warm muzzle rubbing at his arm, his back.

Tuck said, "Should be able to pull out right after lunch, if things go right. At the meeting, I mean. Ride back to Mango."

Joseph said, "None too soon for me. If we didn't, I'd have to eat dinner with Miz Butler tonight. Edith? I think that's her name."

"I know, I know"—Tuck was making a conciliatory gesture with his hands—"you're kinda pissed off about me leaving you alone so much. But you have to admit, these here are nice people.

The way the women keep taking you in, stuffing you full of food. Hell, I musta had four women come up to me at breakfast, ask me if you was free for dinner. Couple more days of this, you'd be too fat to move."

Joseph nodded his head soberly. "Another couple of days, I'd have trouble moving. That much is true. You know"—he looked over at Tuck—"I think them women are gossips."

Tuck started to say something, but then he jerked up on his horse's lead rope and wagged his finger at him. "Gawldamn it, Roscoe! You eat one more of them golf balls, you'll be shittin' rubber bands for a week!" He pursed his lips at Joseph. "And they call this place a ranch."

A whole group of the trailer park people were waiting for them in the barn, sitting around a table that had coasters for the glasses of iced tea and little doily place mats probably made in one of the craft classes. Tucker picked up one of the place mats and said, "Hoo-ee, now ain't these pretty?" as he swung himself into a chair, moving his head around so he could beam at everybody at once. "You keep this place neat as a preacher's sock drawer. No wonder you love it, folks."

Sitting at the far end of the table, John Dunn cleared his throat. "We appreciate that, Mr. Gatrell—"

"Tuck! You got to learn not to be so formal. You folks ain't livin' up north no more."

Dunn chuckled along with the others. "Exactly right—Tuck." He glanced around the table as if to say, "See? He's gone right to the point of the matter." "In a way," he added, "that's what we want to talk to you about. Where we live. Where we want to live. That's why we wanted to meet with you."

"No place nicer than this," Tuck said. He turned to Joseph and gave a little wink. "Three days here makes me ashamed of that old shack of mine."

"See, that's where we disagree, Tuck. We've been talking about it—" Dunn took another look around the table, gathering support. "Everyone you see here, we've visited Mango. You took us around, then we went back on our own. Hope you don't mind, but we did. Just walked around looking and thinking and talking. This morning, we went back again just to be sure."

"Be sure of what?" Tuck asked.

"To be sure, well . . ." Dunn hesitated. "This is awkward for me, and if you're not interested, just come right out and say it. There'll be no hard feelings. But we've been talking about it, and everyone here feels the same. We'd like to try and work out a deal with you—"

"About buying Everglades Springwater? No problem. You can have all you want." Tuck thought for a moment before adding, "At a discount, too."

"It's not the water," one of the other men said. "It's those little houses of yours you said you used to rent. Down by the bay? That's what we're talking about. Tell him, John."

Dunn said, "That's exactly right. We're offering to rent those houses. Or perhaps buy them, if you're willing. We want to live in Mango."

Joseph watched Tuck take his hat off; saw the familiar look of stage surprise on the man's face. Thought to himself, They can't see through this flim-flam old fool? as Tuck said, "Them old shacks of mine? That's what you're talking about? Why hell, folks, they ain't fit for animals to live in."

"We'd fix them up," said one of the women. "It would give us something to do besides sitting around here playing shuffleboard, listening to our veins harden."

The man named Bill said, "I spent forty years in the construction business, Tuck. John put in about the same amount of time as an engineer."

"Electrical engineer," Dunn said. "That's what I was getting around to. If you would rent those places to us at a reasonable fee, we'd do the work, take the cost of the materials out of the rent, and within a year we'd have Mango looking like a postcard. Here—" He reached out to hand Tuck a rolled sheet of bluish-looking paper. "We sat around last night, Bill and I, and drew up these designs. The way the houses would look once we were done. They're just quick sketches, of course. If there's anything you don't like . . ."

Tuck rolled the paper out on the table, scratching his head. "Little dots and dashes . . ." He glanced up. "These are my shacks?"

Bill came around to stand behind him, pointing to show him what was what. How they'd rip out such and such beams, put pilings in where, how they'd re-tin the roofs and pour cement for new foundations, where the flower gardens would be planted, what the porches would look like. "A couple of us want to keep our units here, sort of commute," Bill said. "But most of us are willing to move in, go to work right away."

"It would be like camping out," one of the women—Jenny— said. "An adventure, like in the pioneer days."

Tuck said, "Just so you can be near the spring?" Enjoying it, letting all these people convince him.

"No," said Dunn, "the spring has nothing to do with it—no offense, understand. We don't question your claims—"

Thelma said, "I certainly don't," smiling at Joseph, watching him sigh and look at the ground. "I'll be drinking that water! I have a feeling I'll need the extra energy."

Dunn said, "That's up to each and every individual. What I'm saying is, Tuck, we'll support your claims when it comes time for you to talk to the park people. That'll be part of the agreement. We'll be your neighbors, and neighbors help neighbors—that's the way I see it. My own reasons for wanting to move to Mango are . . ." He smiled softly, looking from face to face. "My personal reason is, I see it as a chance to do something constructive, something different. Personally, I'm damn tired of being old."

Riding the horses, still leading the steer, Tucker and Joseph followed a winding ridge known, in the old days, as Fahkahatchee Trace. The Trace crossed the saw-grass prairie, east to west, and sometimes swooped far enough south so that they could hear the piercing vibrato of truck tires on the Tamiami Trail. It was an odd noise to hear amid all that silence; sounded like a prolonged animal cry, fading and rising on a gusting wind that diffused the heat, then propelled it in drifting, oily pools across the Everglades. Joseph on Buster lead the way, though every so often Roscoe would lunge ahead and try to nip Buster on the rump, only to be yanked down by Tucker, who would hiss, "You dumb bunny! You want to get paint-poisoned?"

Not that Tucker really minded. The horse had spirit, and Tuck was feeling pretty good about himself. True, his back and butt hurt a little and, if he sneezed or coughed, he could feel that tender vessel up in his head throb, reminding him that his own flesh and blood body was still a traitor. But he was used to that; didn't let it bother him much anymore. Hated to give the damn thing credence by worrying about it. Otherwise, he felt okay; full of ginger, as a matter of fact.

As he rode, Tuck let his brain drift around, grazing on those topics near and dear to him. He pictured the Monday-afternoon meeting with the park people from Tallahassee. He'd have a table set up outside so the mosquitoes would feed on them; see if those shitheels could survive a couple of hours without air conditioning! The folks from the trailer park would be there, too—but they'd be too busy cheering for his speech and getting interviewed by reporters to pay much attention to the bugs. Tuck imagined that pretty lady, Thelma, smiling at him, telling him how smart he was. Now there was a woman with potential. Any woman with enough heart to feed a worn-out old Indian like Joseph had to have some spirit, as well. True, she wasn't as pretty as his old Cuban love, Mariaelana, but that didn't mean Thelma wouldn't know what it took to make a man happy.

Tuck imagined the way Mango would look. The trailer park folks would have only a few days' work under their belts, but they were energetic as bees. The women had been ordering supplies when he and Joseph left, while the men assembled their tools. That would be a nice shot for the TV cameras and the newspaper photographers: men on ladders hammering, hauling off trash, setting pilings. Give Mango the look of a young town, too full of life to be killed by them Tallahassee shitheels. Of course, Marion would be there. Henry Short, too! And that girl policeman, Miz Walker, if Tuck could arrange it. She was so smart and pretty, it would make him feel good to give her career a boost.

Tuck imagined the look on Duke's face as he listened to old Lemar Flowers give them government people what for. Lemar with his white hair and old-timey black suit, while him and Duke stood there listening.

That was a nice thought, him and Marion on the same side, for once, two grown men standing shoulder-to-shoulder, blood relatives.

Tuck allowed the image to linger, musing on it, getting the taste of it, feeling what it would be like to beat those shitheels, using the same water he'd been drinking for more than seventy years to make 'em cry uncle.

Sell water! Get the whole country's attention, everybody wanting to buy the stuff.

Maybe those French people with their little green bottles weren't so dumb, after all. . . .

On his saddle, Tucker jolted abruptly, then hollered out to Roscoe, "Whoa, gawldamn it! You run up that big black's ass, you'll get us both kicked!"

Ahead, Joseph had stopped. Stopped at the edge of a myrtle flat and little cypress head. From the trees, egrets and ibis flushed white as ice shards, swirling out of the hot swamp gloom.

Tuck took his hat off, used a red neckerchief to wipe his face. "Joe, sometimes I think the onliest thing that separates the Glades from the equator is a sick palm tree and a Key West whore. Ain't it hot?"

Joseph had dismounted. He said over his shoulder, "Find some shade. I want to take a look around."

"Why you stopping?"

"Just am."

Tuck let his eyes roam, getting his bearings. "Hey—ain't this one of your old hunting camps? Didn't we use this little hummock as a gator base once?"

Joseph said, "I won't be long," walking toward the woods, hoping Tuck wouldn't follow—but knowing he would, the man was so nosy.

Joseph stepped into the shadows of the cypress dome, and the temperature instantly dropped ten, fifteen degrees. The ground was soft as sponge, all those cypress needles, and the roots of the trees poked up out of the black-water pond, orderly as headstones in a cemetery. Joseph found the old path that circled the pond to the back of the cypress head, and there, beneath silver limbs, was his shack. What was left of it, anyway.

Joseph stood staring, hands on hips, feeling as if there was a weight on his chest.

The door had been ripped off its rope hinges, and part of the palmetto thatching had imploded. He ducked under the doorway and stood inside, waiting for his eyes to adjust to the darkness. Someone had a made a mess of the place. Beer cans and cigarette butts all over the ground, and the bed tick he'd filled with egret skins had been kicked open, gray feathers everywhere. The shelf that had once held the few tin plates and cups he owned had been ripped down, too. Joseph stooped to retrieve a cast-iron fry skillet, noted the rust on it, then tossed it into the corner by the wooden

229

bed frame near the *Playboy* calendar that was still tacked to the timber post there.

Behind him, he heard Tuck's voice. "This was where you was living? Nice place. No wonder they figured you was crazy and took you to the rest home."

Joseph said, "I don't 'member asking your opinion."

Tuck stepped inside. "Sure is a pretty picture on the wall, though. I always was partial to redheads. Grab her and let's get going. I want to make Mango before sundown."

"You're in such a hurry, go on ahead. Me and Buster don't mind riding alone." Joseph had picked up the bed frame and was swinging it out of the way; paused to say, "Smells like somebody crapped in here." He was down on his knees, digging with his bare hands.

"What you looking for?"

Joseph didn't answer, just kept digging. After a few minutes, he said, "At least they didn't find this," and held a canning jar up for Tuck to see.

"Who didn't find what?"

"The bastards who tore my place apart. I had money buried here, all my life savings." Joseph was trying to get the rusted lid off, then took his knife out of its sheath and began to pry.

"No kidding, how much we got?" Tuck was thinking, A partnership is a partnership; shouldn't be too hard to convince Joseph of that.

Joseph said, "Forty-three dollars, I think. Maybe more—it's hard to remember." He had the jar open and was counting the soggy money.

"Forty-three dollars? That ain't a life savings; that's one weekend at The Gatorhook. If it hadn't burned down." No longer paying much attention, Tuck was looking out the door toward the horses, eager to get going.

"Couple of silver dollars my grandfather left me, plus a brass medal from the old days when soldiers was down here in the Glades." Joseph was still counting. "Thirty-four, thirty-five . . thirty-seven, counting the silver. I musta spent some when I was sick. Don't remember that." Standing, he put the money in his pocket and brushed off his pants.

"No wonder the treasure hunters was back here," Tuck said. "Looking to get rich on your life savings."

Joseph either missed the sarcasm or ignored it. "Probably was. They're always looking for Indian places, treasure hunters. Hike in looking for mounds to dig up—" He stopped in midsentence. "Hey, that's probably just who it was. Treasure hunters. I didn't think of that." He pushed past Tuck outside, suddenly in a hurry.

"Where you going now?"

"I want to see about something."

Tuck snorted, irritable. "Any chance of getting out of here while I still got hair on my head?" He watched Joseph duck under limbs and disappear into the brush at the back side of the cypress hummock. He called after him, "I'll give you ten minutes, then I'm leaving!"

After about five minutes of impatient waiting, though, Tuck decided to follow along and find out just what in hell the fool Indian was doing now. He wasn't easy to follow—the ground was too springy to hold tracks. But after casting back and forth through the trees, moving toward the saw grass while calling Joseph's name, Tuck finally heard: "You don't give up, do you?"

He saw Joseph through the trees, kneeling on a low earthen ridge. Looked like someone had been digging there, the way the dirt was piled up. Joseph was studying something, holding it in his hands, and he didn't reply when Tuck said, "You find some more money? Hell, you're bad as a squirrel."

Tuck drew closer. Saw that Joseph was holding what appeared to be a length of bone, using his shirt to polish the dirt off it. Tuck said, "If you buried you a side of beef, too, that was bad planning. What the hell is that?"

Joseph turned toward him briefly. "Just what I thought it was." As if that explained everything.

"Ah."

"They didn't know what they was looking for, just started digging. See there . . . and there? More holes. Thinking they might be Indian graves and they'd find some beads, maybe. Or some pots. Stuff like that, so they could take it home, put it on their shelves."

"Dead Injuns, huh? Them beads worth anything?" Tuck was momentarily interested.

Joseph shrugged. "Doesn't matter, 'cause the only thing in this hole was my grandfather."

"You buried him?"

"How else you think he got here? Shoulda known back then it wasn't safe, somebody'd come looking with shovels."

Tuck took the bone, considering it. "Looks skinny enough to be the old fool. Hum. Damn if he ain't scattered all over the place. Probably good for him, up here getting some air."

Joseph was assembling the bones in a pile.

"You want to push him back in and cover him up?"

"What I ought to do is bury him someplace else. Here, they'd just find him again. Maybe I'll come back with a sack."

Tucker liked the sound of that. "Come back later, you mean. Another day."

Joseph was placing the bone shards in the hole, covering them with sand. "No offense, but it's something I'd like to do in private. So, yeah. Come back another day." Joseph stood, dusting his hands off. "Besides, he ain't in no hurry now."

Relieved, Tuck added, "Well, we are."

FIFTEEN

Just when Ford was beginning to feel claustrophobic—his stilt house was simply too small for two people—Sally Carmel told him she had to get back to Mango for a few days, check on her cat, the phone messages, and mail.

Ford had said, "I'll try to stay busy with work," hoping he didn't show the private undercurrent of relief he felt.

Then she said, "Well, maybe we both need a little time away from each other to see how we . . . feel about all this." Letting him know that she was a little relieved, too.

Not that Ford was worried about that. People always built a little distance into good-byes when they knew they weren't going to be apart long.

She said, "I'll call you from home."

That was Saturday afternoon, but by Sunday evening, he still hadn't heard from her.

He had both hundred-gallon tanks nearly finished for his demonstration on the effects of filtering species on turbid water, and that's what he worked on all afternoon and right into dusk. The only interruption was when his friend from Tampa delivered an envelope-size package: the test results from water samples Ford had taken from Tucker Gatrell's artesian well.

Ford scanned the results quickly, then sat down and read them again. When he was finished, he folded them, shaking his head. "Jesus Christ," he whispered. "That poor old fool."

Then he got back to work.

Everytime he passed by the phone, though, he couldn't help looking at it. Even when he tried to ignore it, his eyes drifted to the damn thing and wouldn't let go. Maybe half a dozen times, he picked the phone up to make sure it was still working.

He thought, This is silly. I'll call her. But then he reminded himself, She has a right to her privacy, her time alone. Hell, I was glad to see her go! She'll call when she wants.

233

After a late supper, he filled both tanks with murky bay water, placed a single biofouling assembly in only one of them—the ropes were loaded with sea squirts and tunicates by now—and set the timer. If the filtering animals cleared the water, how long would it take? He decided he would check the tanks every three hours; sleep off and on through the night. So he searched around for something else to do while he waited.

The house didn't need cleaning again, and Tomlinson wasn't back from Boston yet, so he decided to read. Listen to some nice Gregorian chants on the stereo and kick back with John D. MacDonald. But he found himself staring at the wall instead of the book he held, so he finally picked up the phone and dialed.

Sally Carmel said, "I was just about to call you," when she answered. "I tried a couple of times yesterday, but you weren't there."

Ford said, "I was out late on the trawl boat, getting specimens. Don't worry about it."

"Me, too—I've been busy. Running around like crazy trying to get caught up, get these slides mounted and mailed, but every time I got some momentum, somebody knocked on the door."

Ford said, "What?"

"Asking for directions, or where there was a restaurant. Once it they could use my toilet. All day long, it's been like that."

"In Mango?"

"Of course, that's what I'm saying. The people down here," she said. "You wouldn't believe the people. Cars driving up and down the road, all the traffic. A family had a picnic on my lawn! I walked right into a circus; that's just what it's like. All because of your uncle, the publicity he's getting."

Ford said, "Tourists looking for the Fountain of Youth." He was thinking about the test results.

"When they're not looking for a toilet or for food, yeah." She said, "Wait a minute—you'd get a kick out of this. . . . There are three campers. I can see them through the window right now. Those Winnebago kind of vans, parked out on the road. And there are more down toward your uncle's place. Hey"—her phone clacked against something, a window seal, maybe—"he's got a bonfire built down by his house, your uncle does. And I can hear fiddle music, like they're having a party. Can you hear it?"

Ford listened, then he said, "No," thinking that maybe he

wouldn't call Tuck and tell him about the test results. Not tonight. Why spoil the party?

Sally said, "It sounds familiar, the tune. The 'Orange Blossom Special'? Bluegrass kind of music. Doc, you've got to come down and see this for yourself."

He wondered whether that was an invitation. But before he could feel her out, she said, "Look, Doc, something's come up. It's no big deal, but there was a letter waiting for me here, and maybe we should talk about a couple of things."

"Letter?"

"But I hate to tell you over the phone."

"I'd drive down, but I just started this procedure."

"Not even for an hour or so? I'd like you to be here when I tell you about it." Putting a little pressure on him. It was his turn to go to her place, no question about that.

He thought about the sea mobile in its tank of murky water, the care he'd taken in recording the weight of the assembly, everything noted and dated, times set. He'd have to go through the whole process over again.

"Maybe you could tell me a little bit about it now, then we can talk more later."

She said, "Okay, if that's the way it has to be."

"It's one of those procedures where I have to stay close, make notes, that sort of thing." Ford thought, Why am I feeling guilty? This is my work; she should understand that.

There was a silence, then she said, "First off, I think it's pretty good news," with a manufactured heartiness in her voice, and it took Ford a moment to realize that she was already telling him about it. "I got a letter today from Geoff. I mean, it was here and I opened it when I got back."

Geoff was her ex-husband; Ford knew that. He said, "Oh."

"Nothing personal, it was more in the way of a business letter. That's the good news."

"Oh."

"Don't sound so concerned." Being facetious.

"Something to do with the divorce? He wants to give you more money or something?"

Ford had no idea what the terms of her divorce were.

Sally said, "It was from his office. Miami still isn't all the way back after the hurricane, there's a ton of rebuilding going on, and

they've been contracted to design and build a professional biocer
ter. His company has. Geoff's."

"A what?"

"A twelve-story office building on its own grounds, plus an ou
door mall. It was a job offer, the letter. His group wants to hire m
as a consultant. To help on visual continuity. It would pay a lo
only I'd have to live there three, maybe four months. In Miam
It's too far to commute."

Ford listened to her describe the biocenter, what her dutie
would include; knew she had already discussed it with her ex
husband—too many details for a letter. As he listened, For
stretched the phone cord out enough so that he could see throug
the screen door into the lab where the paneled tanks sat on th
dissecting table.

Squinting to see the tanks, Ford said, "What? I didn't unde
stand the last part."

Sally said, "They want floral diversity, but an architectural con
tinuity—the fountains, the mini–rain forest, the themes of th
shops. And they need someone to coordinate, give them an ove
view."

Ford was still squinting at the water in the tanks; removed h
glasses to get a more accurate look. "But you're a photographer
he said.

"Yes, which is another way of saying I'm a visual compose
That's what they need. I've done work like this before." Her voi
wasn't stern, but a little cool, as if she wanted to deflect any fu
ther challenging of her credentials. Then she said, "I was real
surprised to hear from him," meaning Geoff.

Ford said, "I know this: You'll be good at anything you choo
to do. And if you've already accepted . . ."

One of the tanks appeared to be empty, the one with the s
mobile hanging in it. Christ, the tank was leaking—the water w
gone.

Sally was talking again. "Not officially, I haven't. I wanted
hear how you felt about it."

"I feel . . . well . . ." Ford pulled away from the phone for
moment, staring at the tank. "Sounds like a good opportunit
Miami? I get over there occasionally."

It was a while before he realized she wasn't talking at all no
Just silence. He said, "Sally?"

She said, "That's how you feel about it? A good opportunity?"

"Isn't that what you said? More money, right? And if it's work ou like doing—"

"It is. I guess it's what I've always wanted to do."

Ford wondered whether her tone had changed or if he was just misreading her. Then he heard her say, "They want me to drive ver tomorrow, spend a couple of days sitting in on planning discussions. I think it's because they want to hear my ideas before ey make it official."

"Of course. That makes sense."

"So I'll have to miss the public hearing. The park thing, tomorw. I haven't talked to Tucker yet, but I'm worried he'll be disappinted if I'm not—"

"He's going to be disappointed, but it won't be because of you."

"Huh?"

Ford expected to see water seeping under the door any second. he public hearing. I said don't worry about it. I received the test sults today. They're not going to let Tuck sell his springwater. d, if they did let him, no one would buy it. That's what I ean—he'll be disappointed, anyway."

"What are you talking about?"

"The water's contaminated. The water I collected and sent to e lab? Pesticides . . . herbicides, benzene from gas—contamied. Everything. Maybe the worst I've ever seen. The moment e state park people see it, Tuck's lost his leverage. Any worse, d it would be poison. . . . Hey? Sally?"

"The water they've been drinking."

"Yes . . . look there's something going here I need to check —"

"Then you can't let the park people see the report. It's that sim-. You can't do that to your own uncle. You're not going to show o them, are you?"

"They'll have their own test results. If not now, they eventually ll." Ford had the phone cord stretched as far as it would go. ally, listen for a minute. Something's happened here. Can I call a back?"

"You're not hurt?"

"No. It's in the lab. I think I've got a tank leaking. I'll call you ht back."

ord opened the screen door, stepped into the lab, and stood

237

searching the floor—dry. He glanced at the control tank: T
water was still murky green. Then he looked at the hundred-g.
lon tank within which was mounted the living, filtering sea m
bile; had to step closer to be sure. The tank hadn't leaked; tl
water was still there. But unlike the control tank, the water w
now window-clear, a flat transparent body that did not hind
light.

He whispered, "That can't be," as he checked the timer.

The transformation had taken less than fifteen minutes.

When Sally Carmel stepped away from the phone, she stood f
a moment glowering at the couch, then picked up a cushion a
threw it. "Goddamn men!" Didn't yell it, just said it loud
enough for her own ears to test the emotion behind it. Then s
picked up the cushion and replaced it tidily on the couch befc
going to her bedroom to pack.

If he doesn't care if I go to Miami, then I'll go to Miami.

That's what she was thinking. But on a deeper, private lev
there was a little hum of absolution. She didn't have to make t
decision; Ford's indifference had made it for her. She felt relieve
Her anger was like a wedge bar, providing insulation between t
desire to take the job and whatever pain the rest of her felt.

The chance to build something: to take form, color, and spa
then transform it into something big and modern and solid. I
what she had always wanted to do. Well, to play a part in it. To p
a little piece of herself into something that would last. Plus, the
was the money. More money in a few months than she had ma
in the last two years.

Geoff had said, "Miami's floating in it. The insurance comp
nies and the government disaster people keep throwing it at
Hell, my crews can't wait for the *next* hurricane. We wrote a
sign coordinator into the contract and they didn't even blink
eye. Just said, 'How much?' The job's yours, if you want it."

That was Geoff being Geoff, cool and smooth, the confide
businessman. But Sally knew that he was just trying to do it aga
prove to himself that he could still manipulate her if he want
He was like a kid. If he had it, he didn't want it. If he didn't have
he wanted it.

"This is strictly business," he kept saying. "You're the best m
for the job."

The New Age male proving there were no hard feelings, that divorce was just one more negotiation, nothing personal.

Well, this time, she was going to turn the tables. He wasn't going to use her. She was going to use him. She was going to use this job as a springboard. Make a nice portfolio and carry it on to bigger and better things. And if he tried to lay a hand on her, she'd just smile and say, "Really, Geoff. Don't you know the government has laws against that sort of thing?"

Use the word *government* so he'd remember who was paying for the biocenter.

She zipped the bag, swung it onto the bed, and took another from the closet. She had so damn much to do! There were plenty of people around Mango now. It wouldn't be hard to find someone to take care of her cat. And the sailboat, she'd have to have it hauled. The electric, she'd leave on so she could spend the weekends at home. And she'd have to find an apartment in Miami—Coconut Grove, maybe. Something small but plush, with a functional kitchen and a great big bathtub. She deserved it, and she'd be able to afford it, with the new job.

For some reason, that made her think of Ford. She stopped packing and wondered for a moment.

Oh, the bathroom . . .

She could see herself trying to live in Ford's little house. Taking outdoor showers, using a chemical toilet. An outhouse, really; just like when she was a little girl. Well, she'd worked too hard for that, and Doc would just have to understand. . . .

Then . . . unexpectedly, Sally found herself oddly close to tears, overcome by a profound sense of being untethered. All that passion, getting so close in such a short time. Why? And for what? It had been like an explosion, all mixed together with nostalgia and loneliness, what she was as a child, what she was now . . . that plus the wildness of her own body, which almost no one knew about but her.

Well, Ford knew now. And it wasn't as if they couldn't still see each other on weekends. This was just a job, for God's sake.

So why had he been so damn distracted and impersonal on the phone?

Then she remembered: He had yet to call back!

She checked the clock on the reading table beside her bed. It had been more than an hour. She stood to pick up the phone, make certain that she hadn't left it off the hook in the kitchen.

Nope. Doc was just too busy to call.

Sally threw the second case on her bed, yelling, "Goddamn men!" and was instantly worried that she had spoken so loudly, because, in the same instant, she heard someone tapping at the front door.

There stood Tucker Gatrell's old friend, the tall Indian with the long hair and the wide, slumped shoulders. She wiped her face, hoping he wouldn't see that she had been crying, as he said, "I'm real sorry to bother you, Miz Sally, but there's something I'm needin' to find."

Sally showed him a big smile. "Why aren't you up at the party, Joseph?"

"There's too many people there for me, Miz Sally. Ever'body asking me questions, wanting to talk. Figured it was a good time to ask you. What I need is a nice sack. A pillowcase, maybe. Somethin' real plain."

Behind Joseph, from the shadows, the voice of a mature woman called, "I told him I had pillowcases, but he insisted on coming to you."

She could see the shadowed form of a woman there, and Sally's smile broadened. "Why, Joseph! You shouldn't leave your new friend standing out there in the dark."

The big man sighed, his face forlorn. "If I asked all my new friends to come in, there wouldn't be no room for us. Besides"— his soft voice became even softer—"their pillowcases all got little flowers and stuff on 'em. What I need is something a man wouldn't mind."

Sally found a pillowcase for him—refused money for it when he took out a soggy roll of bills, then watched him ramble away, the smaller outline of the woman trailing after him.

Remembering about the public hearing, Sally called to him, "Oh, Joseph? Could you please tell Tuck that I won't be at the meeting tomorrow? I have to go out of town on business. I'm really sorry."

Heard Joseph's reply: "Don't blame you. I ain't going to be there, either."

Then the woman's voice: "Oh yes he will be there!"

Closing the screen door, Sally thought, That's the way it is. The way it is and always will be, men and women at odds. Out of synch on a mutual path. The only question was, who would lead and who would follow?

Sally thought of her mother—Loretta Carmel was no follower! She had been a damn smart, tough, and independent woman. And if it was good enough for her mother . . .

Sally worked around the house, packing, doing bills, getting ready for the drive to Miami, telling herself that she didn't care one way or another whether Ford called, but thinking that he probably would, any minute.

He never did.

By midnight, Ford had repeated the procedure a half-dozen times. It was always the same. Take murky bay water, drop in the strings of sponges and tunicates, and within fifteen minutes, the water was transformed.

Ford noted on a yellow legal: "Turbidity zero."

According to anecdotal accounts, the bays of southwest Florida had been tannin-stained but clear up until the turn of the century, when a powerful consortium—the Army Corps of Engineers and the state government, plus land-boom developers—began its assault on the swamps, dredging, filling, building roads, straightening rivers. It was generally accepted that the wholesale loss of root structure had murked the water system. Erosion. It was also generally accepted that, because most of the dredging had been stopped in the 1970s, the bays would gradually heal themselves.

On the notepad, Ford wrote: "The initial loss of root structure undoubtedly created a sudden increase in turbidity. Did that turbidity interrupt the life cycle and range of filtering species?"

The question implied a startling concept, and Ford was pleased with himself.

If murk caused by the early dredging had killed a significant area of grass habitat, then the filtering species may never have had a chance to reestablish themselves. To remain clear, water required filtering species. Sea-grass meadows required clear water. Filtering species required sea-grass meadows. One was constantly dependent on the other. Remove one symbiotic element from the system—even if for only a few years—and the whole system was sentenced to gradual, inevitable doom.

That was the premise.

Halt the dredging, replant all the thousands of acres of lost mangroves, but if the estuaries continued to be fouled by fresh water carrying nitrates and phosphates, it wouldn't make much difference.

The bays would never heal themselves unless a way was found to provide surrogate bases for a massive reintroduction of filtering animals.

Sea mobiles . . .

Ford stepped away from the dissecting table, excited. He had the blood and bones of the paper he wanted to write. But there was so much more research he wanted to do.

He leaned to jot something on the legal pad: "Do filtering animals also remove invisible contaminants? Contact labs; get price for long-term test series."

That caused him to think of Tuck, the tests he'd had done. Ford had the brief mental picture of dropping a sea mobile into the old man's artesian well, instantly decontaminating the thing—which was absurd. Exactly the kind of idea Tuck would come up with. But tunicates and sponges couldn't survive in fresh water. Particularly Tuck's springwater, judging from the long list of pollutants it contained.

Ford returned his attention to the legal pad, made a few more notes, then hurried across the roofed walkway to get a chart that included Dinkin's Bay. He wanted to calculate the approximate amount of water in the bay so he could get a rough estimate of how many biofouling units it would take to effect the turbidity. Perhaps it wasn't practical. Obviously, water flushed in and out with the tides, but he still wanted to try and set up some kind of proportional model.

He set to work converting the bay's circumference into rectangles, keeping careful track on the chart as he did the math.

From the other room, he heard the phone ring. He ignored it at first, then carried the chart across the roofed walk, still calculating as he went.

A bay roughly 10,250 feet long by 4,400 feet wide . . . with a median depth of, say, four feet. But the average depth would be more because of the channel, all the potholes. . . .

He picked up the phone and said, "Sanibel Biological Supply."

He heard Sally Carmel's voice but didn't hear all of what she said.

242

Hunched over the chart, he said, "Sally? Hey look, I'm right in the middle of something here. Can I call you back in an hour?"

Ford heard Sally say, "That's what you said three hours ago. I was worried. . . ." as he wrote, "Average depth, 5 feet+−.," and then began to do the math.

Sally said, "I'm leaving for Miami in the morning, and I don't know which hotel I'll be staying in, so—"

"First thing, then. I'll call you when I get up." Ford was writing: "10,250 × 4,400 × 5 = 225,500,000.

More than 200 million cubic feet of water! Or perhaps he should set up the model in pounds: pounds of water to pounds of filtering animals it would take to have an impact on the bay's turbidity. Base the model on that.

"I thought we ought to at least say good-bye!"

"You're absolutely right," Ford said. "Oh—wait until you see what I've been doing here. It's amazing. That's what I want to tell you about."

"If you can find the time."

"First thing in the morning."

"Good-bye, then!"

Ford said, "Thanks for understanding," then hung up the phone, still writing as he walked back to the lab.

Four A.M., and Ford thought, Well, I ought to try and get a little sleep before I do any more. I'm starting to make mistakes.

The lab was a litter of papers and books lying open, places marked with clips. Everything Ford had on water, salt and fresh; everything he could find in his own little library. Scientific journals, university bulletins, government publications on water assessment and environmental law—by guessing lag time, scientific interest in water pollution could be traced through legislation passed to protect it. Plus, he would certainly have to apply for special permits to plant sea mobiles on any expanded bases. The regulations were something he would have to know about.

So he had spent the night reading and making notes. Took time out to do the tank procedure one more time—the precision of it, the inexorable efficiency, delighted him.

Tomlinson would appreciate this. When the hell's he getting back!

In one of the journals, Ford had read: "In the South Florida aquifer, from which water streams sometimes percolate upward, under pressure, to create artesian wells, groundwater attains ages of hundreds to thousands of years. Research by Hanshaw and Back suggest that an armoring of the limestone surface by inorganic ionic species, or by organic substances, may produce a state of pseudoequilibrium between crystal surfaces and solution."

Which was of no interest in his own work, but it was exactly that kind of datum bit that Tomlinson could take and weave into a whole monologue on the timelessness of time, the elemental symmetry of life. Water held in the veins of the earth, existing through eons in its own dark space, until sumped skyward by nature or the ingenuity of man.

And what about the man-made additions, such as benzene and pesticides?

Tomlinson would probably make that fit neatly into his own example of the unceasing harmony of existence. Ford could just hear him: "We manufacture, then cast off emotional pollutants every day, man! That doesn't mean we're flawed!"

Ford smiled, then considered his lab one last time before flicking off the lights. He hated to leave the place in such a mess—but he'd get back to work right after his morning run, so it was almost the same as working right through. Even so, the disorderliness of the lab created an uneasiness in him, which he stood taking in for long seconds . . . then he decided that it was less trouble to neaten up than to worry about it, so it was nearly 5:00 A.M. when he finally lay down on his cot.

More than four hours later, Ford awoke with a start, aware that on some level of dream or consciousness, his brain had arrived at a solution to something . . . what?

He sat up groggily and threw the sheet back.

Sunlight glared through the windows. Overhead, the ceiling fan labored, making a whispered *whap-whap-whap*.

What the hell had he been dreaming about? Something to do with his work . . . something about water. His subconscious had been wrestling with some problem, exploring ways to best some obstacle . . . and finally had succeeded. Nothing else could account for the sense of triumph that had awakened him. But a solution to what?

Ford stood, preoccupied, scanning the memory tracers, willing the data to return. He made the cot up military fashion, stretching the gray-and-blue-banded navy-issue blanket tight enough to bounce a quarter on.

"Something to do with water," he said aloud.

Beside the cot was the brass alarm clock. He checked the time against his own watch, startled that he had slept so late. Which caused him to think of his promise to Sally Carmel, and he immediately went to the phone and dialed.

No answer.

"She's probably already left for Miami. The job interview." Talking to himself.

So she'd be back late that night. No . . . she had mentioned a hotel, so she'd be back the next day, Tuesday. Or would she? Had she said?

Ford thought, Well, she'll call. Or I can leave a note at her house when I go to Mango for the public hearing. . . .

Which was when he remembered that it was now Monday; the meeting would start in—what?—less than two hours.

Christ!

Ford began to hustle around, making coffee, collecting his papers . . . then stopped, transfixed. It was all coming back to him, the dreamy workings of his own subconscious. It had nothing to do with his own work, but it was about water. Fresh water. Artesian wells. Contaminants. And the solution . . .

It was both a revelation and a disappointment. In that instant, Ford knew how to prevent the state from taking Tucker Gatrell's property.

SIXTEEN

❦

Monday just before noon, Tuck gave the three representatives of the Florida Park Acquisitions Board their choice. "I got your table and chairs out there, all set up. But you want to sit in the sun? Or the shade of that big mango tree?"

Tuck stood on his porch and let them make their own decision, smiling at the two women and the man, but talking to the man because he was the one acting as if he was running the show. Introduced himself as "Mr. Londecker," as if he and Tuck would never be on a first-name basis, so there was no reason for Tuck to know any more. Snooty-acting kid, maybe thirty years old, already looking hot and put out in his blue suit and black shoes when he stepped out of the van that had probably brought them from the airport. White state-owned van with yellow plates and the Great Seal of Florida stenciled on the door.

The kid said, "In the shade, of course. As long as we have to be outside." Businesslike, but with a tone to his voice probably meant to put Tuck right in his place.

Tuck said, "The shade. You sure?"

"Sit in the heat, or sit in the shade—that's not much of a decision for most people. What I don't understand is, why is everything here so sandy?"

Meaning the film of cinnamon-colored dust that, in just the last day, had settled upon trees, trucks, houses, and boats, as if it had descended, like rain, from the sky. It reminded Tuck of back in the early 1960s when, for the first time, they got what the Glade farmers called yellow rain. Killed the crops and burned the feet of insects, it was that potent.

But all Tuck said was, "Must be all the traffic, people coming to buy water. You ever seen so many outta state license plates?"

Londecker gave the woman beside him a look; rolled his eyes a little, but made sure Tuck saw it, too. What Tuck mostly noticed was that he had been wrong about Londecker. Londecker wasn't the one in charge; the oldest of the two women was. The kid's kissy-butt attitude told him that, and the way the woman remained expressionless, showing she was important, letting everything come to her, then judging it.

Tuck grinned, displaying his missing teeth. "Shade it is!" But he was thinking, Which is exactly what you deserve, letting this sorry little shitheel do your thinking for you. . . .

He waited until they had gone back to their air-conditioned van—Londecker and the two women hadn't shut the engine off since they'd arrived. Just sat there in the coolness with a couple of other people, secretaries, probably, waiting for the hearing to start. Then Tuck found a piece of rope and led Gator outside, talking to the dog as they walked down the mound toward the road: "Them ones in the van, you can bite them anytime. Just not today, that's all. They ever come back, though, I want you on your toes. Hey!" Tuck jerked at the leash. "You listening to me?"

The dog's pink tongue was lolled out, all slobber-faced. He looked up at Tuck, panting affectionately.

"That's better. Now . . . you know the trailer park people. Leave them alone. They gonna be living here now, specially the women. Don't be biting them. The one's making me sweet and sour pork tonight, and you can have what I don't eat. The rest of these people"—Tuck looked up and down the road—"they're tourists. I stand to make a fair piece of money off 'em, so just leave 'em be. I don't care if all two or three thousand come over and try to take your picture, scratch your ears, whatever. Don't bite 'em."

Which was how many people Tuck guessed were in Mango this late Monday morning. A thousand, maybe more. The road was packed with cars and strolling people, and it seemed to Tuck he couldn't go ten feet without some stranger stopping him, pumping his hand, saying she'd heard him on the radio or saw his picture someplace.

They'd say, "Mr. Gatrell, you're a celebrity!"

And Tuck would just grin and answer, "Yes, ma'am, I am. High time, too!" Trying not to act too uppity.

They'd say, "Does that water of yours really work?"

And Tuck would reply, "All I can tell you is, I ain't never felt better in my life."

Which was pretty much the truth, things were going so smooth. The trailer park people had been working like fools, pounding, pouring, hauling trash, and the whole place was already starting to look like something. Ervin T. and his fiddle had pulled in more publicity than even Tuck had hoped for, and now the musical agents were beginning to call, talking about recording this, documenting that—why, Ervin was up to the house playing for a man from Nashville right now. Tuck could hear the music above the ruckus of all the milling people, and he stopped for a moment, concentrating. Ervin was playing the . . . the . . . "Mango Tango."

Enthused, Tuck popped the rope to get Gator's attention. "You wonder why that song's prettier than the 'Orange Blossom Special'? 'Cause I wrote it. Me."

The dog sniffed a tree, then, with great ceremony, hiked his leg.

"Hey—I did, too," Tuck insisted. "The words, anyway. That's what I wrote. Which that dumb bunny ought to be singing, if he really wants to sell it."

Stiff-shouldered, Gator dug around in the sand, then pissed again.

Tucker frowned. "Believe what you want. I ain't tellin' you nothing no more."

Not that everything was perfect. Joseph had saddled Buster and ridden off at first light, telling Tuck, "You don't need me around to make a fool of yourself. You always managed that fine on your own."

Smart-alecky Indian; don't know when a person's trying to do something good for him.

And Henry Short still hadn't arrived. Which wasn't so surprising, Henry being old and crazy both. But what the hell was he going to tell Miz Walker if he didn't show up at all?

She'd walked up to him first thing and said, "Mr. Gatrell, I had other work planned for today, so you better have a very good reason for insisting that I be here this morning." That's what she told him, talking formally, but a little peeved, with that cop look in her eye.

She hadn't much let him out of her sight since. She was always somewhere close by, with her pretty face and gray skirt and jacket.

Tuck stopped as if to pet the dog, but really to take a look behind him, see if she was there.

She wasn't. At least not that he could tell.

That woman acts like she don't trust me!

Otherwise, things were going like he wanted. The trailer park people were ready for the meeting. Lemar Flowers was, too, looking more like a judge than a lawyer with his black suit and leather briefcase. The only big disappointment Tuck had had all morning was that Marion hadn't arrived yet.

Lemar had told him, "If that nephew of yours ain't here by noon, just go ahead without him. I never saw the point in the first place. It's not like it's an imperative."

To which Tuck had replied, "You just do the thinkin', Lemar. That's what you're good at. But leave the planning to someone who knows how. He'll be here—I know that boy. We got the same blood, and he's almost as smart as me."

But now it seemed as if Lemar might be right. Still no sign of Marion and, to Tuck, it was the biggest disappointment of the day.

To the dog, he said, "Duke'll be here. You just wait and see," and tugged at the rope, telling the dog to follow.

A couple of smart businessmen had brought little trailers that opened up into hamburger stands, and they had the flaps up, selling burgers and hot dogs and Coke. As he walked along the road, Tuck could smell the meat frying; made him think of the old county fairs that he'd loved as a boy but never got to go to much. His people were so poor.

Tuck told the dog, "That's maybe what we'll do next. Open us up a restaurant. Potatoes and tomato gravy, and some Chinese food, too. When we get all this other stuff squared away."

Near one of the hamburger stands, down by the bay, a television remote truck was parked. It had a strange corkscrew antenna sticking out of the top and cables strung all over the place. Tuck stopped and tapped on the side of the truck. When a man poked his head out the back, Tuck told him, "They want to start in about a half hour. You boys ready?"

The man seemed a little miffed. "Perhaps I didn't make myself clear, Mr. Gatrell. You're not the producer here. I am. The meeting's not important to the piece we're shooting—"

"I thought you wanted to interview Ervin T. Rouse."

"We do. That's the point—"

"Get him on camera, playin' and tellin' stories?"

"Yes—"

"Then the point is, Ervin'll be a lot more willing to give you the interview if you got your cameras set up for the hearing. I'm his manager, and you got my word on that." Tuck smiled sweetly at the man's angry expression, then turned away.

In front of old Rigaberto's gas station, Tuck had built a nice stand so they could sell jugs of water. Well, he'd had the trailer park people build it, but it was nice just the same. Real simple, but right on the road, so it was the first thing people saw when they came around the sharp curve. Nothing fancy, just a plywood table, a chair, and a couple hundred milk bottles filled with springwater stacked behind. And a hand-painted sign tacked to the table that read:

WHILE IT LASTS!
GLADES SPRINGWATER
$10

Figured he'd start the price high, just to see how it went. They could always paint another sign. But these tourist people never even flinched, just took their wallets out and stood in line.

Lloyd was sitting at the stand now, a couple of the Palm Valley women helping him. But there were only a half dozen people or so waiting to buy, so Tuck wagged his finger at Lloyd, called him over for a private talk.

Tuck said, "Looks like business is starting to fall off a little, Lloyd. You been here all morning?"

"I was over helping Dunn at the junk pile, so just the last hour or so. But it's been steady." Lloyd glanced over his shoulder. "You know how much we've made just since I've been here? Like four or five hundred dollars. Which makes it something like three or four thousand, total, just from yesterday and this morning. That's a lot of money."

Thinking, *We'd better make it while we can,* Tuck said, "Sure, but we need more, a lot more. To get this place fixed up right, we need all we can get. Big Sky Ranch Fund, that's what I'm calling it. My lawyer's got the papers all fixed, making it legal. Takes money for lumber and paint, and to pay truckers to haul stuff. Say"— Tuck motioned Lloyd closer—"you been handing everybody one of them fliers Thelma typed, ain't you?"

The flier, a single mimeographed page, began: "If you don't want the state to steal our springwater and all of Mango to boot, then make yourself noisy at the public hearing today. . . ."

Lloyd nodded. "Handing them out here and on the street, too."

250

"You notice anybody coming back to buy more water once they used it?"

"This is only the second day we've been open—"

"After they tasted it, I mean."

Lloyd was momentarily uneasy. "That's the thing. It tastes so sulphury. Like medicine, maybe that's what people will think. If it's good for them, they won't mind—"

Tucker was saying, "Uh-huh, uh-huh, but I got this idea about using cherry flavor. I got a gallon of it up to the house. Just don't say nothing to the Indian about it—"

"Joseph."

"Yeah, he's real sensitive."

Lloyd was nodding his head, agreeing with him. "You know, that's exactly what the women say about him. My wife, that's what she said. I guess Mr. Egret spent an hour last night showing her the barn, the horses, telling her stories. They sure like him. My wife seemed so cheerful after her tour."

Tuck's eyes narrowed, reviewing what Lloyd had just said, matching that up with what he knew about Joseph's cow-hunter morality. But then he said, "Naw-w-w-w . . . ."

"Naw?"

Tuck started to say, "Those ladies are too respectable," but then he remembered who he was talking with. "I mean, naw-w-w, 'cause they're such good women and they feel sorry for him, that's all. The poor old fool. But about that cherry flavor—"

"Just between you and me," Lloyd said.

Tuck said, "Mums the word," as he started to amble away, but then he stopped. "Oh, and there's one more thing. Them state park people want their table in the shade. The mango tree down by the water? You and the ladies get a minute—"

"In the shade? The mosquitoes will eat them alive. That's where the bugs stay during the heat of the day. Even I know that."

Taking his hat off to scratch his head, Tuck said, "Mosquitoes? Well, I guess that's true," like he hadn't even thought about it.

He found John Dunn near the barn with some other men, sorting piles of trash in the junkyard. When Dunn saw Tuck stop and pull out his pocket watch at the crest of the mound, he called to him, "I know, I know, we've got to get cleaned up for the hearing. But while you're here, let me ask you about something."

Tuck stepped through the fence into the pasture, listening to Dunn talk but not looking at him. He had his eyes on the bay, scanning the water, thinking, That damn Henry Short, I shoulda gone and brought him in myself!

Dunn said something else, and Tuck said, "Huh?"

"The way we're sorting this stuff," Dunn repeated. "You told me the things that would float or leak gunk, we'd pay to have that carried out by truck, right?"

Tuck said, "We got the money for it. I was just down talking to Lloyd. A couple thousand bucks already, so we can get a crane in here and yank out the big pieces, yeah. Plus money left over." He was looking at the fly bridge of the ruined boat; the vines had all been cut away.

Dunn said, "And you want to make a reef out of the things that sink, so we're making a whole separate pile. But what about stuff like this?" Tuck had followed Dunn to the heap he'd created, watching him stoop to touch a twenty-foot length of rusty cable. The cable was an inch thick, freshly crusted with tiny barnacles, as if it had recently been pulled from the water. Clamped to each end of the cable were heavy grappling hooks. Tuck muttered, "Gawldamn!" as Dunn continued: "Something like this could tear the propeller right off a boat, couldn't it? Or ruin the underwater part of an engine? If a boat hit this, we'd be in a lot of trouble. Not to mention the people in the boat—"

Tuck already had one of the grappling hooks and was starting to coil the cable. "Where the hell you get this?" He looked over his shoulder, hoping not to find that Angela Walker was still following him around, spying.

"Inside that old boiler. It was filled with stuff, and I just . . . did I do something wrong?"

"Hell, yes! I mean . . . hell, no." Tuck had the cable up, lugging it back toward the boiler. "What I mean is, you boys are working too hard at this. You don't have to be pulling stuff apart, looking at everything. I was talking generally; about the reef, I mean. Find us a good piece of deep bay water to dump this junk, give you folks a nice easy place to catch groupers and snappers. Plus save us the expense of trucking it out." Tuck dropped the cable into the boiler, thought for a moment, then piled more trash on top before slamming the iron door closed. "Just leave things as they is. I mean, the job ain't got to be perfect." Tuck's eyes surveyed the area again: barn, house, shade trees, people milling on the road, Lloyd and the women carrying the long table toward the mango tree, the state park people still sitting in their air-conditioned van. No sign of Miz Walker . . . but there was Marion, just pulling up in his truck, his blond hair all wind-scattered, wearing those thick glasses. Getting out with a manila folder under his arm.

Tuck let his breath out, relaxed a little bit. To Dunn, he said, "You boys best get cleaned up now. When you talk to them park people, I want you looking like somebody."

SEVENTEEN

❦

Ford was thinking, What the hell are you trying to pull, old man? He was looking into Tucker Gatrell's wild blue eyes. Stood there a minute or two listening to Tuck patronize him before finally cutting him off, saying, "The only thing I need to hear from you is the truth. Do you really want to keep your land, or are you trying to leverage the state into paying double what it's worth?"

Ford didn't respond to Tuck's indignant reaction, but he almost smiled a little when Tuck said, "Your brain sure does come up with some strange ideas sometimes! Must get it from your daddy's side of the family."

Ford said, "I need an answer."

"Hell, it ain't even my land anymore. Most of it, anyway. Just a measly twenty-five acres. What leverage I got?"

He sensed the slyness in the old man's voice; pointedly ignored the irritation it generated in him. Ford said, "I got the tests back you wanted me to do. The results can help you, or they can ruin you. That's why I'm asking. It all depends on what you want—"

"Ruin me!" Tuck was laughing now. "Hell, boy, I been ruined 'bout a hundred times over. I'm an expert at ruin, which means I'm damn near fearless. So I hope you're not trying to scare me—'

"I'm trying to get you to answer a simple question."

Tuck patted Ford on the shoulder; took a look around. The waterfront was rimmed with people, some standing, others sitting on makeshift benches, all facing the table at which members of the Park Acquisition Board were now seating themselves. Tuck said, "Meeting's getting ready to start," and held an index finger to his lips.

"You're not going to level with me, are you?"

Tuck was silent for a moment, then turned to Ford. "I'll tell you this, boy. I'd rather fall down dead than see those shitheels take land that's always been mine." Tucker winked at him. "That right there is straighter'n I shoot."

When Angela Walker spotted Ford standing off from the crowd's perimeter, listening to the Park Acquisition's staff introduce themselves, she thought, He's part of this? She watched him for a moment, standing there in his wrinkled khaki slacks and gray shirt, looking as if he'd just gotten off a boat. Maybe he had. Maybe he'd driven that fast jade-colored boat of his down all the way from Sanibel, then just stepped off onto the mud beach. Nice way to travel. No traffic, no stoplights. Just drive along looking at the birds and the dolphins until you got to where you were going. Easy, if you were good with boats and knew what you were doing. Scary if you didn't.

Walker knew about that now.

Each of the last three mornings, she'd rented a skiff from Barron Creek Marina, then headed out alone, going from island to island, looking for some sign of the missing men. Her plan was to follow the unlikely routes to the boundary of Everglades National Park. Start at the channel that led out from Barron Creek (Sandfly Channel, it said on the map), then head south. Trouble was, there weren't that many unlikely routes because a labyrinth of mangroves and shoals fingered out from the mainland, east to west, with no cut-through spots. Not that the map showed, anyway. To get around them, you had to drive a boat almost eight miles toward the Gulf, then turn left. Worse, it all looked so different when she was actually out there. Her boat, which had seemed sizable at the marina, shrunk down to almost nothing when the few channel markers ended, leaving her alone with all that water and sky and all those mangrove islands crowding in. There was something creepy about the look of mangrove trees. Their roots hunched up out of the muck like an old man's fingers, with a tangle of trees balanced on top. As if whole islands could crawl around if they wanted; could get up on those root fingers and walk. Like giant crabs.

The second day, though, she had started to feel a little more comfortable about it. And yesterday, the third day, she'd actually enjoyed herself. She'd run aground a couple of times, but she still liked the feeling of driving a boat, being able to go anywhere she wanted. But she hadn't found a sign of the three men or the three missing boats. Not a thing. There was just too much area to cover, and too few routes to the park boundry.

Plus, she kept reminding herself, almost all of it had already been searched. By boat or by air, most of the thousands of acres below Sandfly Channel.

Which was when Walker remembered something Ford had said to her earlier, some innocent-sounding phrase that kept banging around in the back of her brain until, last night, lying in bed, she had finally isolated it. It had sat her straight upright, legs swinging out from beneath the covers, running to find the map. That quick, she knew where she would search; would have been out in the rental boat right now if Tucker Gatrell hadn't called her, saying, "You want a big boost for your career, show up in Mango for the hearing."

Well, he was trying to use her; she knew it. But she figured, give Gatrell enough rope, he'd hang himself. Not that she wanted that—strangely, she didn't. Still, the law was the law, and it was fascinating to play give-and-take with the old man, trying to guess just what he was up to, and why. And now to see Ford here . . .

She stood looking at Ford; noted how miserable the park staff appeared beyond him, one man and four women at the table, all of them fanning at the peppered haze of mosquitoes that had formed around their faces. The man, who introduced himself as Alex Londecker, had thus far done all the talking, but he kept interrupting himself to slap at the bugs, so his sentences had a staccato rhythm, ruining whatever authority over the meeting he wanted to establish.

Walker stood watching for a few minutes, then walked to her car and returned with a map of the Ten Thousand Islands folded in her hand. She tapped Ford on the shoulder, smiling at his expression of surprise as she said, "Somehow, I don't see you as the kind of involved citizen who attends public hearings."

Ford smiled a little in return; actually seemed kind of pleased to see her. "I'll let you know in a minute if I'll be sticking around." But what he was thinking was, All the dogs are closing on Tuck at once.

"You're trying to help your uncle. That's why you're here?"

"I'm not sure it's possible to help him."

"But you'd like to. I mean, you're related. You'd like to help him if you could?" Ford was so hard to talk to!

Ford listened to Londecker laying out the rules of the meeting, saying that citizens who were pro-park would speak first; the people against, second. Listened to Londecker say, "I'd like to stress again that wild claims about the beneficial qualities of . . . [slap] . . . water found on the land in question are a . . . [slap] . . . nonissue unless the speaker has legitimate scientific evidence to back up the claims." Then Ford turned to look at Walker and said to her, "You've met Gatrell. He's not an easy man to help."

"I've got one way." She was unfolding the map.

"A way to help you, you mean. Find the three men."

"I know he's involved. You know it, too." She could see Tucker Gatrell over near the table, standing beside a white-haired man who, in his dark suit, looked like an old-time preacher.

Ford said, "No, you're wrong. I don't know that." He was thinking, But I assumed it from the beginning.

"Look at this." She handed him the map. "There was something you said to me a week or so ago. It was the way you said it, talking about the missing boaters. 'Why would they turn north to go south? Maybe you should look at a map.' Something like that. It kept bothering me."

Ford had taken the chart; was unfolding it to see the familiar swirls and hedgerows of beige-green on blue. All those islands. "Oh?" he said.

"The thing that bothered me was, you grew up here. Or so your uncle told me. Why would you need a map?"

"Some people live here ten years, they still need a chart."

"Not someone like you. So I just kept going over it in my mind. Why would someone turn north to go south? Last night, I figured it out." She touched a ginger-colored index finger to the chart. "See here? About a mile out of Sandfly Channel, you turn north . . . curve in and out through these little islands. What's that, about five miles? Almost due north. Then turn back east about two miles until you come to this tiny little cut-through here."

Ford considered the woman's nails as she tapped the chart: trimmed short, carefully clear-glossed; a fastidious woman who used her hands for more than decoration.

She said, "That cut, it's not much wider than a pin on the map. That's what I'm still not sure about. Could a boat fit through?"

Ford knew the place; he didn't need to look at the chart. His uncle had always called it the Auger Hole.

He was still looking at the woman's hands. "Judging from this," he said, "it's maybe ten, fifteen feet wide. So sure. Plenty of room for a small boat. What you're saying is—"

"I'm saying they could have passed through that cut, then followed it to this series of creeks and bays south, clear to Everglades City and the national park boundaries." She slapped the chart for emphasis. "It's probably a little shorter, plus maybe faster, too, because they wouldn't have to drive clear to the Gulf first. They went north, not south! Only no one would think of that, even looking at the map, so no one bothered to search north of Sandfly Channel."

Ford smiled. He had turned his attention to Londecker once more. "So get a boat, Agent Walker. Go find your men."

"That's what I'm talking to you about. Did you drive your boat down here? You know the water—"

"I came by land. My truck, the blue one parked up there."

Londecker was saying, "Even though this is an informal hearing, all speakers must first introduce themselves, because Ms. [*slap*] Cullum or Ms. Ibach will be making notes, and this will all become part of official public record. . . ."

"Then maybe we could rent a boat. It's not far to Barron Creek Marina. You help me now, Dr. Ford, I'll promise you that it'll reflect favorably on your uncle—"

"If he was involved."

"Yes. If he was involved."

Ford had folded the chart and now handed it back to Angela Walker. "Maybe. I'll think about it—but after the meeting."

"So you are staying."

"I just decided, yeah. Just this second."

EIGHTEEN

❧

The trouble is, Alex Londecker was thinking, the woman doesn't realize how much work I've put into this, how much thinking and planning, plus a hell of a lot of business savvy, too. If she knew . . . hell, she probably wouldn't appreciate it, anyway.

He wasn't even listening to the steady file of people who came forward to speak in favor of annexing Mango for a park, people from groups he'd contacted in advance. The Save Our Everglades Coalition, the Naples chapter of the Florida Environmental Watchdogs, and a half dozen similar groups, plus several key state biologists. Londecker knew what they were going to say in advance, so he didn't have to listen. All these knee-jerk environmentalists with their impassioned pleas to save the earth, going on and on while they struck the noble pose of martyrs. They were all of a type. But they were useful, always just a phone call away. He had sat with them and their kindred through hundreds of similar meetings (though always indoors), so he knew the precise tilt of head, the exact squint of eye required to project the impression of rapt attention. Which allowed him to ruminate about his boss, how hard it was to impress her.

Meaning Margaret Faillo, the woman who sat soundlessly beside him, her expression pleasant and professional but her eyes stony cool whenever she turned to him. Which wasn't often; once when he'd sucked down a mosquito and started coughing during his opening remarks. Turned her olive-pit eyes on him for just a moment, letting him know she wasn't impressed, that she didn't appreciate the situation he had placed her in; stoic as she tried to ignore the swarming bugs, but that Latin temper of hers simmering through.

Sitting there beside her, with the gavel at the middle of the table, he could still feel her disapproval. A smart, tough Cuban who'd worked her way up to Director of Park Acquisitions, and she didn't put up with any bullshit from subordinates. Which Londecker knew, and which was why he'd worked so hard putting this project together. Even though his official title was Assistant Director of Park Acquisitions, it was the first project Faillo had let him do all on his own. Almost as if it was some kind of test, because his coworker, Connie Dirosa, had already been allowed to head up two acquisitions and a land recovery project, even though he was Dirosa's senior by more than a year. Now, the word was, Faillo was about to be promoted still higher up the government pyramid; maybe even a cabinet position—female Hispanics were the preferred currency of a minority-hungry bureaucracy, and her job would be open soon, no matter what. Which meant that either he or Connie Dirosa would be the natural choice to fill Faillo's spot.

Trouble was, Faillo favored Dirosa. Londecker knew that. They were both women, both Hispanics, and though it would have been professional suicide even to suggest that a rising star like Margaret Faillo could be influenced by race and gender, Londecker suspected that it was true. Hell, it was standard operating procedure in government—though it was taboo to talk about it. Even so, a month ago, Londecker had sent a confidential memo to the head of the Florida's Office of Equality and Compliance in Hiring, apprising them of his suspicions. Down the road, he figured, it might come in handy to have something on the record if Dirosa got the job. Just in case he wanted to file a complaint.

But Londecker hadn't given up yet. He had sweated blood over this project. It was his one chance to show Faillo just how competent he was, so he had worked nine-, ten-hour days to make sure the acquisition went through without a problem. But, goddamn it, he'd had nothing but problems. First, two of the men he'd hired to do the groundwork had gone out in boats and disappeared. So the project was still way behind schedule as far as the all-important environmental survey. Then, during the title searches, they'd discovered that one of the main landowners, Tucker Gatrell, had sold off a hundred prime acres to some blind land trust, so now the state was having to go through the courts just to find out who the principals were. Which was putting them even further behind schedule—all the while having to negotiate with Gatrell's shrewd, bullheaded attorney. And just when Londecker thought it couldn't get any worse, he had turned on CNN, to see that dis gusting old cracker, Gatrell, telling a pretty blond reporter that he had found the Fountain of Youth on his property.

Outrageous! But the fools in the media loved it.

The key to success in government service included one unspoken rule: Avoid publicity. Now he was getting a dozen calls a day from newspapers, television stations—big-time national reporters who were damn disrespectful when he tried to sidestep them.

All Faillo had said to him was, "Are you up to speed with the Mango project?" As if she had no idea of what was going on.

She knew, though. But that goddamn steel maiden was too smart to let him involve her now in a project that was threatening to turn sour. Not this late in the game. For the last week, he'd felt like a leper; Faillo wouldn't have allowed him to discuss the problems with her if he had tried.

But three days ago, Friday, Londecker had finally gotten a break. Connie Dirosa, of all people, had come into his office and dropped a manila envelope on his desk. All she said was, "I was thumbing through some in-load over at Environmental and just happened to come across this." Then she'd stood there watching as he took out a sheath of papers and began to read.

They were water analysis results from a private lab in Tampa that, by law, had to notify the state when they found contaminants in water that grossly exceeded state DER standards. Dirosa had said, "The water samples came from your buddy's property, the old lunatic who's been giving you trouble down in Mango. It was a hell of a stroke of luck, me finding them."

Londecker had felt like kissing her—but was then instantly suspicious. Why did Dirosa want to help him?

"Look," she had explained, "let's put the knives away for a second, Alex. The way I see it, no matter who gets Margaret's job, we're still going to be working together. We're the senior staff of the department, so you help me, I'll help you." She had stuck out her meaty hand. "Deal?"

No, they didn't have a deal, though he took her hand, anyway.

He had said, "As long as I can memo Ms. Faillo, giving you full credit," watching Dirosa's expression for some trace of duplicity. Could just imagine her bragging to Faillo: "Londecker was in a mess till I saved his bacon."

But all Dirosa had said was, "Nope, Alex. It's your project; you

take the credit. Leave me out of it entirely. Just promise tha
you'll do the same for me when I get in a jam."

So he had his ace in the hole! And maybe a new friend, too–
Connie Dirosa. Who wasn't a bad-looking woman, except for he
weight. He'd caught her staring at him lately, too—he knew tha
look. And if Connie did get Faillo's job, a little romantic involve
ment wouldn't hurt his career a bit.

Now, sitting at the table, fanning his hand at the bugs, Lor
decker jumped slightly when Margaret Faillo nudged him, the
slid a note in front of him: "I'm going to take a break in the vai
Speed this up!"

Londecker nodded without looking at her. The two stenogra
phers were already trading off, taking turns sitting in the air cond
tioning, out of the bugs, so he wasn't surprised. Just so long a
Faillo was present when the water tests were read into the recore
as Londecker prayed they would be. He couldn't do it—this was
public hearing. And to wait until his department finally finishe
and published its own tests wouldn't have nearly the impact. Th
television cameras and the reporters were here *now*. The peopl
who were whining about the state imposing on Tucker Gatrell
rights were here *now*. The pathetic lunatic fringe who believe
Gatrell's claims about the water were sitting out there in the hea
waiting their turn to rail at him. Now was the perfect time fc
them all to hear the truth about Gatrell and his scam, the idea
time for Margaret Faillo to see how neatly he could cut the leg
out from under park opposition.

But Londecker couldn't do any of that himself; had to just s
patiently, hoping that somewhere in that crowd, probably amor
the group of droaning environmentalists, was the woman or ma
who had commissioned those tests—someone named Dr. Mario
Ford.

Lemar Flowers leaned over a chair piled with a briefcase, p.
pers, and two volumes of *Florida Statutes* so that he could whi
per, "Goddamn it, Tuck, go sit in the house for a while, find son
shade! You're sweating like a chain-gang coolie, but your face is a
white as a baby's butt. I'll come get you when it's our turn 1
speak."

Tuck, who had his hat off, mopping his head with a red ba
danna, glanced irritably at Flowers. "Judge, I hope you're not goii

262

to charge me for that advice. Say—" Tuck's face crinkled into a wicked smile. "You know the difference 'tween a catfish and a lawyer? One's a low-life, shit-eatin' bottom feeder, and the other's a fish!"

"You trying to hurt my feelings," Flowers said blandly, "you gonna have to get a lot more personal than that. I'm just sayin' it won't help none, you having a stroke in front of these vultures. They'll pick your bones clean—"

"Quit worrying about me and worry about the job I'm paying you to do!"

"I have to remind you again, Mr. Gatrell? I took this case on contingency. You haven't paid me a cent yet."

"Christ oh frogs, you got ways of making a man mad!"

"That's my job. Now sit down and cool yourself." Flowers took up a volume of the *Florida Statutes* and began to peruse it nonchalantly.

Tucker said, "Well, it ain't like I ain't got a reason"—meaning a reason for being mad.

He did have reason, too. Lemar hadn't said a word about people showing up to speak in favor of the park. Hell, Tuck had just thought they were more tourists, all these smart-acting people in their bird-watcher's clothes. Where was that damn Joseph when he needed him? Joseph didn't have any love for bird-watchers, but now he was out somewheres riding that big black instead of being here where he belonged, maybe scaring a few of these busybody gull-humpers with his mean Injun looks.

Worst thing, there was so many of them. And they all talked so long. The reporters and television people would probably get tired of it, just pack their things and leave before Tuck and his people got a chance to speak. That's what he was really worried about.

To Flowers, Tuck whispered, "I've heard funeral preachers more cheerful than these yardbirds. What I might do is bring Ervin T. down, have him start sawing on the fiddle. That'll change the mood!"

Flowers kept turning pages. "You'll do no such thing. Sit there and relax till it's our turn. Have yourself a chew of tobacco."

"I don't want a chew. I don't want to relax." Tuck stood momentarily and scanned the bay. No sign of Henry Short's boat. "Gawldamn it, things ain't going right! And don't get me started on that old idiot Henry. I tried to tell you, a nigger's got no more

263

sense of time than a rabbit. Say"—Tuck pulled out his pocket watch—"what time is it, anyway?"

"You and Henry have been friends for fifty years. Who'd he come to for help when he was sick, living out there all alone on that island? He'll be here."

"Yeah, if he didn't fall down dead. That'd be just like him, too." Tuck flipped the watch closed. Almost 2:00 P.M. Up at the table that man Londecker looked as if he was about to wilt. He was mostly alone now, with the women coming and going from the van. The heat and the bugs—well, good. Let them get a taste of what it was like for the people who near worked themselves to death trying to scratch out a living in these islands.

Flowers said to him, "For the next ten, fifteen minutes, I don't want you to say nothing. Just sit there and calm yourself. Like these young lawyers tell me: Think nice thoughts."

Tuck tried. Let his mind slip around, looking for something pleasant to settle on. Remembered that time Marion hit his first home run up there at the old Pirates spring-training park. That was nice. Big blond-haired boy with the same blue eyes Tuck still saw every morning in the mirror. Which caused him to think of the boy's mother, Melinda. Prettiest little snow-haired baby he'd ever seen, so young and tiny . . . but, no, he didn't want to think much further about that. But the old times, it was still nice to think about them, and Tuck began to try to recall what the Glade and the islands were like when he was still young—all the place names that were familiar in those days but now were lost, not to be found on maps. There was Devil's Garden, that shady place with all the wild orchids just north of Charlie Buster's Marsh. Hadn't some fancy-minded nudists tried to set up house there? Tried to breed what they called their own "superrace"?

That made Tuck smile.

The bugs had chased them out in less than a month, and now these were probably their grandkids, sitting here in their bird watchers' clothes, running off at the mouth!

There was Ocaloachoochee Slough that flowed right through the Big Cypress Swamp. Before the damn government had straightened the rivers and diked Lake Okeechobee, you could canoe right up the thing, from Everglades City clear to La Belle. And there was Charlie Tommie's Hog Camp and Rock Island and Grover Doctor Split and Charlie Tigertail's Casino, all just little camps, places for a man to sleep or buy a little food from the Seminoles when he was hunting or working cattle, but they were the same as towns in those days.

And what about Deep Lake? A small lake set way back in, probably thirty miles from the Gulf, but every spring tarpon would show up there. Those wild mirror-bright fish would appear like magic, hobbyhorsing on the surface, no one knew why or from where, then disappear again, come fall.

One night, discussing Deep Lake around the campfire—this was back in the thirties—Tuck had said to Joseph, "The reason no one figured it out but me is because they think of Florida as if it's land. But she's not. Florida's more like a boat. Or like that thing in Babylon, a floating garden. There's fish probably swimmin' around beneath us right now. In tunnels! That's where those tarpon come from, and them tunnel walls is like an anchor. Keeps Florida from drifting off."

Deep Lake and the rest, it was pretty to think about, all those past places, all those old times. Florida had been so big and wild, jungle and oak flats clear to the sea.

Remembering it made Tucker feel good . . . then it began to cause him to feel bad. What the hell had happened?

Tamiami Trail was one thing. Sucked the soul out of the land as fast as it funneled new people in.

Me! I'm the one who caused that!

Another was all them big developers, come down from out of state, building their "wham-bam, thank you, ma'am" condos and corporation towns, then hightailing it with their pockets full of money.

Who's the one showed them around! Told them the best places!

And all the theme parks!

Give Dick Pope the idea, not even knowing I was cuttin' my own throat.

And then the government coming in, taking control, screwing up one thing after another. Them yahoos needed guidelines just to find their tallywhackers. But that didn't stop them from messin' with the way land and water worked.

Shit always flows downhill—Florida proves it. I shoulda told Harry, he wants to build a park so bad, start with Hiroshima.

"Gawldamn it now, I've heard just about enough!" Tuck was on his feet, not even realizing it; was surprised as anyone at the public hearing to hear his own loud voice.

At the table, Londecker was so startled that he sat up straight. "Excuse me?"

"I said these people have talked long enough! When you gonna give my side a chance?" Lemar Flowers was tugging at Tuck's shirt, trying to get him to sit down, but Tuck pulled away.

"You're out of order, Mr. Gatrell—"

"Mister, you whack that gavel at me one more time, I'll show you what being out of order is like!"

"Tucker!" Flowers was trying to get him back in his seat, but behind him, the trailer park people and some of the others were starting to yell, too, demanding that they be heard. The whole crowd getting noisier and noisier, grumpy from the heat and the droaning boredom, while Londecker kept banging away with the gavel.

"Quiet, please! You'll have to wait your turn."

"My turn's come and gone, Londecker. That's what this whole business is about!"

"I said, QUIET!"

" 'Fraid you might learn somethin'?" Tuck spit ferociously. Didn't none of them understand? He felt like jumping up on his chair and shouting, *Dumb shits! Don't tell me. I'm the one lived it!* Instead, he noticed Ford at the far edge of the crowd, and called out, "Marion! Hey, Marion! Now you see what I'm up against?" before he suddenly felt so woozy that he had to quick sit down. Otherwise, he'd've collapsed right there in the grass.

Marion?

Londecker heard the crazy old cracker yell the name once, twice, before he picked out the man Gatrell was calling to: big blond-haired man with wire glasses, standing off by himself. Dressed more like a fishing guide than a scientist, but how many people named Marion could there be?

"I'll adjourn this meeting right now and leave the record as stands! Order!"

Holding his anger in check, hoping the television cameras and the reporters recorded how professionally he was behaving despite all the noise. Londecker took a nervous glance toward the van. Margaret Faillo was still inside it, staying cool, but Connie Diroso

266

was right there beside him, neutral, showing no emotion, watching to see whether he could regain control of the meeting.

He had to do something, and do it quick.

That goddamn old man! I'll turn his house into a staff bungalow, and I'll spend the holidays there myself!

Londecker rapped the table three more times, then stood. "Mr. Gatrell has made a very good point. I'm saying—I agree with him."

There, that got their attention.

Londecker waited, then said it again. "I agree! I think we've heard enough from the proponents." He fixed an expression on his face that he imagined to be a kindly smile, allowing the silence around him to build. "We're all hot. Maybe a little irritable. And some of the testimony about why this land should be protected has been repetitive—though very compelling, I think."

"You can kiss my butt on the county square, Londecker!"

Tucker Gatrell yelling from his chair.

Londecker forced himself to laugh along with the others, a dry little chuckle, before he replied, "I'm not sure I'll have the energy, Mr. Gatrell, the way these mosquitoes are draining me."

Which got an even bigger laugh.

Londecker caught Connie Dirosa's eyes, felt new confidence when she nodded her approval.

That quick, Londecker was back in control. He decided to continue the exchange with the old man; let people see just how kind and fair he could be. "How about this, Mr. Gatrell? How about we allow one more speaker. With a time limit—say ten minutes, ups. Then we take a short break, and the rest of the afternoon is ours. All the time you want."

Couldn't help but take pleasure in the way the old man fidgeted his seat.

I've got you now, you bastard.

In front of Connie was a blank notepad. Londecker picked it up and pretended to read it. "Is there a Marion Ford here? A Dr. Marion Ford?"

Which won him another nod of approval from the chunky little than She mouthed the word smart as she patted his leg under the table—well, he'd give her a chance to do that and more after the hearing.

Still pretending to read, Londecker said, "I have a note here that says Dr. Ford would like to speak. Dr. Ford? Ah!" He waited until the big man made his way through the crowd before adding, " don't think we've ever met before, have we?"

The man had a soft baritone voice, not shy, but talked in a way that forced people to listen. "I'm certain we haven't."

"Are you with one of the groups here? Political-action group such as the Save Our Everglades—"

"No. I'm here independently."

"Would you mind reading your credentials into the record? Then Londecker sat back to listen, wondering mildly why an American would take a masters at the University of San Marcos in Lima and a doctorate at the University of Durban in South Africa. Mostly, though, Londecker tried to ferret out the connection between Gatrell and a marine biologist—

Marion! Now you see what I'm up against!

—and hit upon a scenario. Gatrell had sold property to a land trust, and the land trust had probably hired its own environmental census team; would probably try to work out its own deal with the state. Donate X number of acres of property to the park in return for permits to build on abutting property. Property on a park boundary would double, maybe quadruple in value. That was it! wouldn't be the first time a developer helped the state ramrod through a park project. Gatrell was being duped!

Londecker said, "You have ten minutes, Dr. Ford." Then, as the man began to speak, Londecker jotted a note to Connie Dirosa: " don't want Margaret to miss this!"

"My name is Marion Ford, and I'd like to read into the record a report from Tampa Environmental Laboratories Incorporated. . . ."

NINETEEN

❦

Bonnie Dirosa gave it some time. Sat there patiently while
Rex Londecker, the sneaky little brownnoser, nudged her, tap-
ing repeatedly at the note he had scribbled. Folded her hands
calmly on the table and listened to the man, Dr. Ford, speak in a
scholarly monotone: ". . . water samples were taken from property
owned, or formerly owned, by Mr. Tucker Gatrell—the legal de-
scription's in the report, which I'll leave with the panel."

Tried not to smile when Londecker, in his pompous, official
way, interrupted. "These water samples—the water tested, I
mean. Are you indicating that it is the same water Mr. Gatrell is
selling as a sort of magic elixir?" Only to have the old man's attorney leap to his feet, calling, "I object to that, Mr. Londecker. The
phrase 'magic elixir' is not only prejudicial, it is wildly inaccu-
rate."

Heard Londecker backpedal: "I would remind Judge Flowers
that this is a public hearing, not a court hearing. But because the
state wants to be absolutely fair, I'll ask Mrs. Ibach to strike my
remark from the record."

The man, Dr. Ford, stood quietly until the two were finished
before continuing. "Even so, it's the same water. Samples were
taken from the artesian well, and also from a sump-pump site near
the barn"—Ford pointed, and people craned their necks to see,
all listening to him—"in a procedure that is noted in the report,
which, as I said, I will leave with you."

"Tampa Labs is state-accredited," Londecker said helpfully.
"We've used them ourselves. I certainly don't question their procedures."

Dirosa decided to wait and make sure that the man was actually
going to read from the report.

"The analyses indicate that the water is normal in terms of
mineral content—that is, normal in terms of water found in the
Floridan aquifer. It is significantly supersaturated with calcite,

dolomite, and contains, as well, other chemicals, such as pota
sium and magnesium, all of which are necessary to normal huma
biological functioning. In fact, as electrolytes used by the brai
such trace minerals are essential."

Londecker said, "Huh—?" as Gatrell also stood and yelled, "S
how healthy it is? And only ten bucks a bottle!"

Dirosa wondered, What's this guy trying to pull?

But then Ford said, "Of particular interest, though, are the r
sults of EPA test two fifty-four, EPA test two fifty-five and EP
test six twenty-four. Tests for specific contaminants," and Diro
began to relax again.

"The results show that the water sampled drastically and da
gerously exceeds state and federal standards of five parts per b
lion when tested for benzene, toluene, dieldrin. A variety of pes
cides, herbicides, and petroleum contaminants exceeded twen
parts per billion. . . ."

As the man actually began to read the test results, Conn
Dirosa gave Londecker a sharp nudge of her own, then left t
table. She walked slowly, taking her time, heading toward t
state van.

Margaret Faillo was inside, using her briefcase as a table, doi
office work, when Dirosa tapped on the window. Fallio folded h
bifocals, stepped out, and closed the door behind her so the oth
secretary, Mrs. Cullum, could not hear.

Dirosa said, "Just what we were hoping for."

Even when she was pleased, Faillo had a tough, abrupt quali
"Londecker found somebody to read the tests?"

"It's going on right now. The guy who paid for them. But I ca
figure out his angle."

As Faillo got her briefcase out of the van, she said, "Does it ma
ter?"

Margaret Faillo was thinking, A long way to come just for th
but it's worth it.

All Connie's idea, too. The girl was quick on her feet—she
make a great department head.

Back at the table, Faillo stared blankly at Londecker's ingrati
ing "I've got something to tell you" grin and took the seat besi

him, wanting to hear a little herself before she finally pulled the plug.

Listened to the speaker conclude the reading of what she already knew was a long list of toxins—Connie had showed the report to her before giving it to Londecker—then listened as Dr. Ford suggested, quite reasonably, that the contaminants may have been introduced into the Mango water system as a result of dredging for Cypress Gate Estates, plus the fertilization-extermination cycles of the region's scores of golf courses and tens of thousands of lawns.

"An additional source," the man said, "may be posions used in the state's own melaleuca extermination program. As you may know, the state imported the melaleuca tree back in—"

Faillo didn't like the direction of that, so she cut him off. "Excuse me, I was unable to hear the beginning of your statement."

Beside her, Londecker could hardly contain himself. "The water Mr. Gatrell is selling? Dr. Ford just read a report from a state-accredited lab certifying that the water is contaminated. Dangerously high levels of—"

"You let him read that into the record?"

Faillo could see Londecker puzzling over the tone in her voice. "Well, of course. I felt Mr. Gatrell was seeking an advantage, trying to inflate the price of his land—"

Even when Lemar Flowers yelled, "That's supposition and hearsay!" Faillo kept her eyes locked on Londecker. She said, "Do you realize what you've done?"

The man standing before the table was still speaking: "In view of these test results, I would like—as a concerned citizen—to make certain that your department already has funds set aside to restore the water to its original uncontaminated state . . . as it must do, by law, when condemning or annexing private property."

Londecker said, *"What?"*

Behind Ford, Gatrell was on his feet, poking at his attorney, yelling, "I told you he was almost smart as me! Didn't I tell you? Hot damn, Duke, kick him right in the ass!"

Faillo stood and said loudly, "I'd like to call a five-minute recess while I discuss a few things with Mr. Londecker."

*   *   *

Alex Londecker felt a little dizzy listening to Faillo. So dry, he couldn't make spit form in his mouth. He told her, "I know what the law is. We've done projects before where we had to clean up water."

"Ah! So you've already budgeted for it?"

"No, I'm just saying—"

"You're talking a hundred thousand dollars. Maybe a quarter million. For a project this small? Do you want to try to justify that before the legislature? I don't think they'll want to listen to you, Alex. Not after they watch tonight's news."

"But we could just plug the spring. Cement it in—"

"Like that little Dade County project? Or Warm Mineral Springs? We had the money allocated in advance. Plus, we did it quietly. Here, we'd get national headlines: 'Fountain of Youth Asphalted!' Jesus Christ, Alex!"

He had never heard Faillo swear before. "The way you say it . . . you're making it sound like—"

"Oh, quit stammering. You went into this thing blind. You didn't have your environmental census finished—"

"The crew disappeared!"

"Then you should have postponed the meeting! Then to allow that report to be read publicly, my God. Who do you think issued the permits for Cypress Gate Estates? The state! You didn't see the television cameras?"

"Now wait a minute! Using the water analysis was Connie's idea—"

Dirosa hadn't said a word until then; just stood their smirking. But now she jumped right in. "Hold it, Londecker. This is your project. You get all the credit. Remember?"

"I don't think I received a single memo advising me of Connie's participation, Alex." Faillo at him again.

"But she did!"

In a deadly cold voice, Faillo said, "Maybe if you had spent more time keeping me informed, and less time writing letters to my friends at Equality and Compliance, you wouldn't be in the mess your in."

Oh, God. That explained it.

In a small voice, Londecker said, "I'm sorry, Ms. Faillo. I mean it. I wasn't thinking at the time."

"You're going to be sorrier, Alex. You know what that old man did to you? Gatrell? He got you looking so hard in one direction that you never realized he was coming from the other. He blindsided you, Alex. He pulled a switch—a *switch*, you dumb ass. And you fell for it. With this on your record, I don't think I'll have any problem from Equality and Compliance in Hiring. Or the personnel department, for that matter." Faillo closed her briefcase firmly, a knuckle-cracking sound. "I'll make it official when we get back to Tallahasse, Mr. Londecker, but be advised that you have two weeks' notice. You're terminated. Now"—she straightened her jacket and brushed her black hair back—"I have to go make a statement to those people. Tell them the state is withdrawing from the project." She smiled at Connie Dirosa just a little before adding, "For a year or two, anyway."

TWENTY

❦

William Bambridge said to Chuck Fleet, "Why are all thos‹
people standing on shore? You think they're expecting us?"

Fleet sat on a plank at the stern of the old man's sloop-rigge‹
pulling boat, one hand on the tiller, the other on the daggerboard
hoping he could steer this final reach into Mango without runnin‹
aground yet again, ripping the daggerboard out of its lashing. "I
the Captain awake? He had that delivery to make. Maybe he tol‹
the whole town."

From the windy bay, the village of Mango was a pale break i‹
the darker rim of mangrove islands: coconut palms, a few houses
a brown rind of beach. People lined the water, milling on wha
must have been a road. There were tables and chairs set up, an‹
lots of cars. Like some kind of meeting.

Bambridge had torn his shirt into rags—there wasn't much lef
of it, anyway—and now he reached outboard to soak a piece, the‹
used it as a compress. Henry Short lay with his head in Bam
bridge's lap, eyes closed, brown skin looking gray in the sunligh‹
a deep gash on his forehead, more cuts on his hands, his arms, an
a bad one in his side. For the last four hours, he had been bleedin‹
through his rag bandages; now the water in the lapstrake bilge wa
iron red.

"Captain? Can you hear me, Captain? We're almost there! Han‹
on for a few more minutes. We'll get help."

The old man moaned softly, his breathing quick and shallow
The first part of the trip, Henry Short had been able to rall‹
enough energy to rise up and point out the route to Fleet; describ‹
to him the cuts he had to make, the oyster bars and sandbars t‹
avoid. But in the last hour, he had lapsed into a kind of concen
trated silence, as if he needed to focus all his energy on just stayin‹
alive.

To Fleet, Bambridge mouthed the words *I think he's dying.*

A voice from the bilge: "Good. I hope he does die. It'll be easi‹

for all of us. Like when a burglar breaks into your house, you're better off killing him."

Charles Herbott talking. He lay with his belly flat against the ribs of the boat, hands and feet wrapped with rope, then pulled tightly together, so he resembled a man less than he did cargo, all soiled and blood-streaked, packed for lifting. "You guys need to come around to my way of thinking. It's not too late."

"Damn you, I told you to SHUT UP!" Bambridge looked down into Herbott's dark, feral eyes. Forcing back the urge to kick the man in the face was like fighting the need to vomit. "Not another word!"

Fleet said, "Easy, Bill, easy. Just ignore him." After the insanity of the morning, then having to fight fifteen miles of shoal water, Fleet was so emotionally drained that he had lapsed into a shell of stoicism. Endurance mode, that's the way he thought of it.

A hundred yards at a time. We'll make it. A hundred yards at a time . . .

"But he'll scare the Captain, talking like that. We should have gagged him, too."

"Forget about him. We're almost there. Only about seven or eight hundred more yards."

Bambridge touched the old man's head tenderly—his hair had the texture of rough cotton. He said, "Hear that, Captain? Mango's just ahead. Smells a little like a horse farm. Or cattle? And someone's cooking food, too. But I bet they don't cook as well as I do, huh?" Bambridge sniffed and turned his head away, trying not to cry. For the last several hours, he'd wanted to. Just wanted to break down and let it all out. But he hadn't. It might upset the Captain, plus he didn't want to give Herbott the satisfaction.

Earlier that morning, Herbott had said to Henry Short, "Old man, why don't we let bygones be bygones. I don't want to ride back to civilization with my hands tied, and you three need help loading jugs and getting our boats rigged right so we can tow 'em."

Not jugs of cane syrup as Bambridge had expected, but jugs of water from the spring back in near the shack at the base of the Indian mound. In explanation, all the Captain had told him was, 'There's an ol' boy in Mango, he got a taste for this water 'bout six months ago. Nothin' you need to be nosy about." Bambridge had been so busy puzzling over that, plus trying to get his notes together, that he hadn't paid much attention to Herbott. Took just

275

enough time to whisper to Short, "Don't trust Herbott, Captain," then went ahead with his work.

About two minutes later, he'd heard a guttural shriek; a finger-nails-on-chalkboard sound that stunned him so completely that he was already running toward the source before he realized what he was doing.

They had been in the mangroves, near the tunnel that hid the boats. Herbott was bent over the Captain, hacking at him with a machete.

The roots and trees were so thick that the knife had hit mostly limbs, but each time it struck flesh, Bambridge knew, because it made a distinctive sound—a butcher shop sound, like a cleaver piecing chicken.

"Charles, stop it! You're killing him!"

Shouting as he ran, Bambridge had kept on running until he tackled Herbott from behind, then Fleet was mixed up in it, trying to wrestle the machete out of Herbott's hand.

"Goddamn it, Charles—you're *insane.*"

Bambridge had kept punching and scratching and screaming at the man until he'd heard Herbott yell, "Okay! Enough," all three of them wheezing, spent and winded in the muck.

But the instant he and Fleet had loosened their grips, Herbott had bolted away, trying to escape, and they had had to do the same thing all over again.

"Hit him over the head with something! Find a limb! Kill him!"

Had he, Dr. William Bambridge, really said that?

Yes, and he had meant it. But instead of a tree limb, Fleet had found a coil of rope, and the first thing they had done was pull noose around Herbott's neck so they could control him. They' tied his hands and feet tightly, then tumbled him over the side into the Captain's antique boat. He and Fleet both so loaded on adrenaline that they'd walked and talked with the exaggerate control of drunks.

"We have to stay calm, Bambridge."

"Yes, calm. Exactly right."

"He left us only one option."

"Our actions are entirely justified. That *son of a bitch!*"

After that, things were a blur. Bambridge had tended to the old man while Fleet rushed around trying the portable VHF radio each of them had stored in their skiffs, just on the chance they was another boat in range. But the batteries were dead. So he had cut their own boats free and waded the sailboat away from the mangroves far enough to get the raw wood mast stepped and the sail up.

The whole time, Herbott had been yelling, "Let's think about his. We can make a deal here. Cut me loose and we'll talk about t. I have connections!"

Calm despite his wounds, Henry Short had sat on the bow, directing them through the first narrow cuts toward Mango, his shirt and pants sopped with blood. To Charles Herbott, all he had said was, "Short'un, you had no call to throw my side-by-side into the bay. I'm gonna miss that gun."

Which had caused Herbott to laugh hysterically. "You know he funny thing, boys? The gun! That fucking gun! It wasn't loaded!"

What got Angela Walker's attention was someone down by the water yelling, "Call an ambulance! A doctor! This is an emergency!"

She turned and saw a decrepit-looking boat with a peeling gray hull and a leaf brown sail moving slowly, slowly toward shore.

She had noticed it earlier, farther off, but had dismissed it as just another sailboat.

The man doing the yelling had matted hair, a scraggly beard, and his shorts were belted with a rope. He looked like a shipwreck victim . . . and that's when it dawned on her.

My God . . . it's them.

She had been hunting around for Tucker Gatrell; wanted to congratulate him before she pinned him to the wall and made him admit that he had wasted her whole day just to demonstrate how clever he could be.

As if she didn't already know that.

Maybe confront Ford, too—find out whether he had been helping his uncle from the start. But hoped he hadn't been. For some reason, she kept imagining herself in that jade-colored boat of his, learning how to water-ski.

But then she heard the man yelling, and she fell in with a group of people jogging toward the boat.

"Someone find a doctor. We need an ambulance!"

The scraggily man kept repeating that, even as he jumped into the shallows and pulled the boat ashore. "Somebody get to a phone and call the police!"

Walker pushed her way through the crowd, hesitated at the water, then slogged through the mud to the boat, saying, "I am the police," as she started asking questions, trying to place the two men who stood there gaunt as scarecrows, looking at her.

The one at the back of the boat was Chuck Fleet, the surveyor. He was burned copper by the sun, and had a reddish beard, but it was him. She could tell from the photographs she had studied every night—for how many nights?

But when the shirtless man said he was William Bambridge, she couldn't believe it. The Bambridge she knew from the files had pork-chop face and a professorial smugness. This man was hollow-cheeked and wild-eyed. The skin flopped around on his bone as he continued to swing his arms, shouting orders. "We can't stand around talking. The Captain's hurt bad! Someone get his legs. We'll carry him to land."

Walker knew she had to assume control, and she did. She caught Bambridge by the elbow, swung him around, saying, "This woman says she's an off-duty paramedic." She motioned toward woman who was already leaning over the injured man. "So you let her take care of things while we talk, okay?"

"But he's my friend—"

"He's a kidnapper!" Some unknown voice calling from what seemed to be the bottom of the boat.

The paramedic called to Walker, "This guy's lost a lot of blood. We need air rescue, a chopper."

To the crowd, Walker said, "Someone go find a telephone. Say Special Agent Walker is requesting a helicopter. Now!" as she leaned to look into the boat for the first time.

What in the hell was going on here?

A wiry old man—with his parchment brown skin, he could have been a hundred years old—lay unconscious, bleeding, bandaged in an assortment of rags. On the floor beneath him was the thin missing man, Charles Herbott. Herbott was roped up tightly, belted to the deck, but he could still look up at Walker by arching his neck. Actually managed to smile at her as he said, "You really are a cop? Great. Then arrest these three men. The old man for kidnapping. The other two as accessories. Now, get a knife and cut me loose!''

"Why is Mr. Herbott tied?" She was looking at Fleet, who hadn't said a word so far. Just stood there with a mild look of relief on his face, stretching his arms and neck as if he was very tired.

"Because he attacked Captain Short with a machete, that's why. So we had to restrain him, tie him up like that. Self-defense. He'd've done the same to us. I think he needs some psychiatric help."

"That's a lie!"

The way Herbott screamed out the words made Walker think that Fleet was probably right about the last part.

"But the old man, he did kidnap you?"

"No. Absolutely not." Bambridge talking again—she couldn't get over how skinny he was.

Fleet said, "It's complicated, but, no, he didn't kidnap us."

"No one hijacked your boats? The old man? No one else?"

"They broke down, all three. Captain Short helped us."

"Then why did Herbott attack him with a machete?"

"That's complicated, too. But the attack was unprovoked—"

From the boat: "They're out to get me, I tell you. He's lying!"

"No, I'm not lying. I saw the whole thing from the bushes. The entire chain of events. If anything, you should arrest Herbott for attempted murder."

"Talk to the governor, lady, and see how far you get with that. Hah!"

To Walker, Herbott was sounding crazier and crazier.

Walker said, "Okay, one at a time, one at a time. I'm not arresting anybody. No one's going anywhere till I hear the whole story. Mr. Fleet, first you. Privately. Dr. Bambridge, you just stand there on the beach. Wait until we're done."

Herbott from the boat: "Goddamn it, untie me! You're detaining me illegally."

"I'm not detaining you, Mr. Herbott. I just don't have time to set you free. Be patient."

Walker listened to Fleet, then to Bambridge; felt sorry for the men—they were so exhausted, they were weaving. Once she had to interrupt Fleet, tell people in the crowd to step back, stay away from the boat. Another time to point Tucker Gatrell to the injured man as Gatrell came splashing up, demanding, " 'Scuse my language, Miz Walker, but what the deuce is goin' on in my bay?"

She paused long enough to watch Gatrell kneel over the man; heard him say, "Gawldamn, Henry, you back down every bad actor in these islands, only to let one of these pencilheads get the drop on you?"

Every now and then, Walker would think to herself, *I found them.*

By the time it was Herbott's turn, the helicopter was dropping down, scattering sand and throwing water as it landed on the beach. The thing was going *whap-whap-whap,* and Walker had to hold her skirt down as she ducked beneath the blades. She identified herself to the pilot; asked him to radio the Sheriff's Department and have them send a detective unit to help her get this mess sorted out. From her purse, she took one of her cards, and wrote on the back, "I've got the three missing boaters."

But when she got back to the sailboat, she realized that was wrong.

A man was standing there, one of the gawkers, a sheepish expression on his face. "The man in here?" he said to her. "When I untied him, he just shoved me out of the way and ran off. No thanks or nothing. That's him—see him up there? The one running up the road toward that white van."

TWENTY-ONE

❧

When the paramedic told Tuck, "The IV's kicked Mr. Short's blood pressure right back up—things are looking pretty good," he thanked the man, turned to tip his hat to Agent Walker, then walked back toward his ranch house, shaking hands along the way.

People would say to him, "Glad the state ain't taking your land, but too bad about the water."

Tuck would say, "Well, maybe it kills germs, being poisoned the way it is. One way or the other, it's keepin' me young."

He wanted to sit in his chair on the porch, just look at the view, enjoy the feeling of the land being his. Let Lemar Flowers handle things when Miz Walker stopped to ask more questions, as he knew she would. Just sit there smiling, watching her face as Lemar explained the facts of life when it came to old maritime law.

"As it so happens," Lemar would say, "I am also Mr. Short's legal counsel. And I hope you don't waste the court's time by trying to involve him in some frivolous charges."

Old Lemar, he knew how to weave words together. Like that land trust business. Lemar had said, "You want to sell your nephew seventy-five acres without him knowing it? Then you put it down on paper at appraised value, but only pay yourself a buck; do it all through a set-up corporate front. Name it Development Unlimited and Key Enterprises. Let the state try to figure out what it is. That's what you call him, isn't it? D-u-k-e?"

Tuck had liked that. Only he'd changed Key to Kamikaze— thought it had more flair. And Marion wouldn't know a thing about it.

"Until you die," Lemar had pointed out. "Then he gets it, free of inheritance tax."

Lemar had sounded kind of eager when he said that. After all, he had the same deal—only Lemar just got twenty-five acres.

Tuck already had plans for who got the rest.

Which made him think of Joseph.

That damn Injun. First time a plan of mine's ever worked right, and he's not around to see it. Maybe I'll call that Cypress Gate man, have him return the chickens and give back his horse in trade. Kinda miss the noisy little bastards, plus, it would keep Joe at home.

At the road, Tuck stopped to check for traffic—couldn't wait until all these damn tourists lost interest and headed home. First time in his life he could remember having to look for cars before crossing.

That morning, before saddling his horse, Joseph had told him, "What you done was make Mango just like the rest of Florida. That's saving it?"

But like Lemar said, "You got to break a few eggs to make an omelet."

From where he stood, Tuck could look beyond the sharp curve that led up Mango Road to the Tamiami Trail. A few cars were headed away, not many. People were too busy gawking at Henry Short down by the water. Even some of the state park people, standing there as if they might be able to help, but really just fascinated by the blood.

People don't get to see blood no more unless it's on TV or in a hospital. Like they're surprised we're made of it, blood and dust.

Tuck started to cross but then paused to watch the helicopter flap off. That took a minute or so, and the next time he glanced up the road, there was Joseph! That big black horse, Buster, had been quarter-gaiting in close to the mangroves, which is why Tuck hadn't seen him in the first place. It was always something Tuck took pleasure in, watching Joseph ride—though he would never have admitted it. The big man could sit a horse. Held himself on the saddle so that he flowed right along with the animal, no effort at all. Like he was doing now: Joe holding the reins in his left hand, wearing jeans and a pretty blue shirt one of the trailer park women had made for him. Had something in a white bag tied to the saddle horn, and . . . something else that was different, too, but Tuck couldn't figure it at first. But then he realized, Joseph wasn't wearing his roper's hat. Joe almost always wore his hat, especially when he was riding, but now he was bare-headed, except for a bright red ribbon of rag he had tied around his forehead so that the ribbon snapped in the wind.

Gawldamn, now he's even startin' to dress like an Injun.

Joseph looked up and waved, a look of amusement on his face. Tuck waved back, then stood there figuring how he'd work it. Joseph would ride up and say, "How'd the meeting go?" But Tuck decided he wouldn't answer right off. He'd say, "You want to know so bad, whyn't you stay here, see for yourself?"

Let Joseph stew a while, then just let the story slip out kind of matter-of-fact, like he'd expected to beat the park people all along, no problem.

Tuck grinned. Yep, that's just what he'd do. Make Joseph pull the story out of him; let the man see for himself just what a smart partner he'd had for all these years.

But then Tuck heard a woman yell, "Somebody stop that man!" and he stopped thinking about Joseph.

It was Miz Walker's voice, Tuck realized, and he whirled around to see that pretty woman sprinting away from the beach, pushing people aside as she ran toward the road.

A couple hundred yards ahead of her, someone else was running, too. A man, short little guy with muscles, that Tuck remembered from the marina, the day he'd used the chart to convince him that, by boat, the best way to Everglades National Park was through a narrow little cut. The Auger Hole, which was only about three or four miles from old Henry's island.

Herbott, that was the guy's name. Tuck had gotten another quick look at him, hog-tied in the bottom of Henry's boat.

Some cop. I deliver her four men and she's already lost two of 'em.

"I am ordering you to stop!"

Gad, now she had a gun out. Little black pistol—*that* made people scatter!

Tuck watched the man hesitate at the road, as if unsure which way to go. Walker was closing on him. That woman could run, even in a skirt! Then Herbott seemed to notice the white van—the engine was still running, keeping it cool inside. That quick, the man had the door open, jumped inside, and spun the tires, peeling out fast.

Tuck shook his head, chuckling to himself . . . but then he abruptly sobered, feeling a chill as if from a sharp wind. His eyes found Joseph, who was riding out on the road now, just east of where the blind curve swooped south. Then his eyes found the van again, accelerating fast from the south, with Herbott hunched over the wheel, no intention of slowing for the curve or anything else.

Then Tuck was running, too. Running hard toward Joseph, waving his arms at him, calling, "Get over, get over. Move that horse over, you gawldang fool!"

He was still yelling and waving when the van skidded around the curve, and then everything seemed to happen at once, but in terrible slow motion. Tuck could see surprise widen Joseph's eyes . . . the shock of being confronted by an out-of-control truck coming too fast to avoid hitting him . . . then a different kind of surprise—a kind of joyous bewilderment as his horse, Buster, exploded into one quick galloping stride and then jumped higher than any horse Tuck had ever seen jump before. . . .

As Joseph Egret approached the last sharp curve into Mango, he saw the expression on Tuck's face, and he thought, I'll be damned, the old pirate won.

He could tell by Tuck's smirk, the way he had his hat tilted at a jaunty angle, thumbs in his belt loops, bowed legs and boots set firmly on the ground, like it was his forever, the land, the bay, the livestock, and everything else either one of them had ever cared much about.

It was Tuck's "you don't have to thank me now" pose.

Sure enough, he won, but he won't tell me about it. Not right off. He'll make me spend the whole night pullin' it out of him. Then I won't be able to get him to shut up about it for the next ten years.

That made Joseph smile, and he let Tuck see the smile as he waved back, talking to Buster as he did. "Know what this means, Buster? Means Tuck'll let me wash these spots off your butt. No more crazy business. For a while, anyway. Tuck always likes to take a little vacation after something big like this. 'Bout six months, maybe."

Joseph had been talking along to Buster all day. Talked to him as they crossed the Tamiami Trail and followed Fakahatchee Trace back to his old palmetto shack. Talked to him as he dug up the bones of his grandfather and set them in the shade in a neat pile, all the earth brushed away, before placing them in the white pillowcase Sally Carmel had given him.

"He never amounted to much, but he wasn't a bad granddaddy, Buster. Took me all over the islands, campin' and fishin', and told me all them stories." Joseph had looked up at the horse briefly. "He did a lot of fightin', too, but it was all inside. That's what took his energy. But a man don't have to make something of his life to be worth somethin', huh?"

Later, Joseph told Buster what he was gonna do was rebury his grandfather down in the islands, maybe Henry Short's place. "Tuck says it's got a couple of nice mounds there, and flowin' water. And the mosquitoes is so bad, the treasure hunters won't come lookin'."

Before he left his old shack, Joseph took the *Playboy* calendar off the wall, then tied the door back on its hinges. It made the place look more respectable, Joseph felt.

Two hours later, he stopped at Jimmy Tiger's Famous Reptile Show, where he tapped shyly at the door and gave the calendar to Jimmy Tiger as a present.

"Joseph, you sure you don't need it?" Jimmy Tiger had shuffled him inside, brushing aside crawling great-grandchildren, then found a place by an oil lamp where, by holding the calendar right to his nose, Joseph knew the old man could see the calendar, because he described the photographs in detail.

"Look at that one! Ooh, and looka this one!"

While Jimmy's pretty granddaughter, Maria, fried fish for lunch, Jimmy asked him, "Joseph, you had any white women?"

Taken by surprise, Joseph had answered, "Today, you mean? It's still pretty early."

The last thing Joseph did before he left Jimmy Tiger's was give his black roper's hat to Maria. He could tell by the way she asked about where he'd bought it that she liked it. "Havana," he told her. "Nineteen fifty-eight."

"The price?" she had asked.

"Uh . . . no, the year. But me, I'm feelin' younger every day."

In return, she had tied a red scarf around his head. "A wind ribbon," she had told him. Then, standing back to look at him, said, "Oh—aren't you handsome!"

The whole way back to Mango, Joseph had wondered about the

285

way she'd said that. Maria was a big, healthy girl—and such nice skin.

Before he rode off, Jimmy Tiger had told him, "When the signs is right to bury your grandfather, Joe, let me know. We'll do it in the old way. Get the drums out and maybe have some whiskey. Chekika's Son would like that."

Joseph had thought about that, too. He had felt good, sitting in Jimmy Tiger's chikee, with kids running around and the smell of food cooking over a wood fire. It would be nice to spend more time there. But Joseph wondered what kind of signs the old man meant. The sky still had its fiery look at night, only not so bright—but maybe that was because the moon was now full. There was still a strange red haze at sunrise and sunset, but now the haze touched the earth, drifting down in the form of fine brown sand.

Well, maybe that was a sign in itself.

Frustrated with himself, Joseph had told Buster, "Damn it, you'd think that was somethin' I'd be naturally good at. Knowin' what a sign is and what it ain't."

He had been puzzling over that—and thinking about Maria, too—as he approached the curve. But when he saw Tuck, he reigned the horse out into the road so he could cross at the curve . . . but then Tuck started making an odd swinging motion with his arms; had a strange pinched expression on his face, too.

"What the hell's Tuck runnin' toward us for, Buster—"

Joseph didn't finish the sentence . . . or it was drowned out by the squeal of tires as the white van careened around the curve, still accelerating.

Joseph sat numbly in the saddle—not frightened, just numb seeing nothing but the glare of the vehicle's windshield and grill, it was on them so fast, and he felt his body relax, his mind calming because the collision was inevitable and there was no escape.

Beneath him, though, the horse was not calm. Buster seemed to buck once, lunged right at the van, and then, Joseph realized, they were both airborne, flying. Looking down, Joseph watched the horse's hooves clear the vehicle's hood by a good six inches as they sailed across the road, and then he had time to catch Tuck's eye among the blur of faces, feeling very high and proud . . . until Buster jolted, untouched, back to earth and Joseph lost a stirrup.

The last thing Joseph thought before impacting with the asphalt was, *What kind of a sign is this!* . . .

The only time Ford had ever heard the same mixture of horror and hurt in his uncle's voice was long, long ago on a night that had been lost along with his own childhood.

"Duke! Get over here—make these vultures back off. He's hurt real bad!"

Tucker Gatrell shouting to him over the heads of a massing crowd and a hundred yards of mangrove beach.

Hearing that voice, that tone, again gave Ford chills. Made him want to walk the other way and just keep walking.

But he didn't. Instead, he began to jog toward his uncle.

Christ, now what? . . .

Ford hadn't seen any of it. Hadn't seen Walker chasing Charles Herbott, didn't see Herbott speed off in the van. He'd been down by the water, off alone, testing himself to see how he felt about being used by Tuck one more time.

That bastard knew all along about the water. Probably had the analysis done in Georgia or someplace, one of his redneck buddies up there, but needed an outsider to introduce the data. Me, the outsider.

Well, that sounded just about right.

Ford had been going through all the possible scenarios in his careful, obsessive way. Didn't want to think about it, but he couldn't help it. Tried to shift his attention to Sally Carmel, but that didn't last; even allowed himself to consider Agent Walker in a less than professional way—the woman had impressed him.

But then he saw something out in the bay that did focus his attention: a jade green flats skiff, poling platform like a roof over the outboard, hunched down and throwing a rooster tail as it planed toward Mango.

"That's *my* boat."

It was, too. No mistaking it as it drew nearer. He could read the stenciled name on the side: SANIBEL BIOLOGICAL SUPPLY.

Ford began to walk quickly toward the dock, squinting at the figure above the wheel. He didn't recognize the man . . . still didn't recognize him as the man tied off and stepped out of the skiff, though there was something familiar about the way he moved: tall, gangly guy with a military haircut and carrying a briefcase—which was right in keeping with the wrinkled gray suit he wore.

As the man strode toward him, beaming, Ford said softly, "Tomlinson?"

"Hey, Doc!" Same childlike grin, but it seemed broader because his face was shaved smooth. "Man, am I glad to see you—no shit, compadre! Sorry I'm late, but my flight got delayed, just one damn thing after another. So I borrowed your boat."

"Tomlinson?" Ford stood nonplussed as the man wrapped him in a bear hug, pounding his back.

"I know what you're going to say. In fact, consider it understood. I'll never do it again, use your skiff without permission. Even if you do go off in our truck without leaving me a note."

Ford wrestled himself free and stepped back. "What *happened* to you?"

Tomlinson said, "What? Oh—my hair! So you noticed."

"And a suit?"

"Strictly temporary. A one-trick deal. I took a flier in the real world. Sheer desperation, understand. But the vibes, man, it was like pissing in a Vegematic. I didn't have a single comfortable moment. But that can wait"—Tomlinson held up the briefcase—"because I've got something important here."

Ford was about to tell him the meeting was over, but that's when the screaming of tires drew their attention . . . and that sound was followed by a sustained tumult, crashing metal and shattering glass, the noise of an automobile rolling through mangroves.

"What the hell was that?"

The abrupt silence that followed was broken by the low, slow wail of a woman crying out, then the gabble of people running.

An instant later: "Duke! Get over here—make these vultures back off, he's hurt real bad!"

Fifteen minutes later, the off-duty paramedic looked up, a little teary-eyed herself, and said, "I think he's gone. I think his neck's broken."

Tucker Gatrell was on his knees beside her, his composure regained, dabbing water on Joseph's face, trying to force a little down him. "Don't you stop that mouth-to-mouth business till the helicopter gets here! Keep working on him. We'll bring him back yet."

"But Mr. Gatrell, the man in the van, he's hurt pretty badly, too—"

When Herbott had swerved to miss the horse, the van had plowed into the mangroves and flipped.

Tuck smacked the water jug down to emphasize his point. "Lady, you lift a finger to help that peckerwood, I'll get my gun and shoot him dead myself. Keep breathin'! Joe just ain't got the hang of it yet."

Joseph Egret lay on his back on the asphalt, eyes closed, a mild smile fixed on his face. Except for the blood, he might have been asleep and dreaming.

Buster grazed patiently near by, as if waiting.

Every now and then, Ervin T. Rouse would pat Tuck on the shoulder, begin to say something, then turn and walk away. Finally, Rouse returned to the ranch house, sat on the porch with his fiddle, and began to play and sing very softly:

"I'm a goin' down to Flor-dah, get some sand in my shoes . . . I'm goin' down to Flor-ee-dah, get some sand in my shoes. I'll ride the Orange Blossom Special, and shake these New York blues. . . ."

Just before the helicopter returned and the paramedics agreed, privately, that Joseph was dead, Tomlinson held up the sheath of research data he still carried, and he said to Ford, "All these people staring at him, but not a one of them realizes what he represents . . . not a one of them understands who this man was—" then his voice faded to a croak, and he couldn't say any more.

Much later, very drunk, Tuck would say, "Who doesn't understand? You know what it was? You know what it was that man invented?"

EPILOGUE

❧

During the first week of November in that year, from the high regions of the Earth's atmosphere, a great volume of polar air, ascending because of its own density, caught the jet-stream push of what meteorologists call the five-hundred-millibar surface, and it began to drift southward toward the 26th parallel. By the evening of November 9, the polar edge had gathered sufficient momentum to gravitate toward and then displace the warmer, lighter air of the tropics, and it arrived in south Florida as a blustering cold front driven by a wind that seemed to howl down out of the full moon.

Dust particles, a month ago transported by the Sahara High and still lingering in the stratosphere, were swept away.

On the morning of November 14, a Friday, the gale was still blowing when they buried Joseph Egret in the shell mound near the spring on Tucker Gatrell's land. Jimmy Tiger, who beat a skin drum throughout the ceremony, felt the wind rip the thumping notes from his hands and shoot them skyward.

Same thing when they placed the bones of Chekika's Son in the hole beside Joseph.

Later, over tumblers of whiskey, Jimmy would confide to Tomlinson, "I don't expect a frog eater to understand—but that strong wind, it was a very good sign."

The few days between Joseph's death and Joseph's funeral had been neither peaceful nor easy—a circumstance that privately pleased Tucker Gatrell. The first problem was, the State of Florida refused to allow them to bury Joseph on Big Sky Ranch. It was private property.

But Lemar Flowers went to work and got that settled. In a conversation with one bureaucrat, Flowers, genuinely vexed, had said, "You people still don't realize the kinda men you're dealin with, do you?"

The next problem was that archaeologists employed by the state petitioned the governor to block the burial because, as the petition read, "Digging in or excavating what may be a pre-Columbian burial mound is an outrage against basic human rights, as well as history."

Presumably they meant it was an outrage against basic human rights and history when done by anyone but themselves.

Using his connections, and data gathered during his work in Boston, Tomlinson swayed enough people to have the petition withdrawn, but for more than a year, a splinter group of amateur archaeologists would continue to fight through the courts, seeking to have the bodies exhumed and moved.

As Ervin T. Rouse would tell an audience during the first of several appearances on David Letterman's show, "Me and my partners, Henry and Tuck, we're kind'a glad about it. Come summer, it gets so hot and sweaty down in those Glades, a man's 'fraid to scratch his cheek for fear he'll slip and poke his eye out. But with them curs yapping at our heels, we'll be too busy to think about the heat."

Otherwise, the funeral went smoothly. The lone uncommon feature was the disproportionate number of female mourners compared to male. In chorus beneath a winter sky, the muffled sobbing of women is an icy sound, and when Angela Walker remarked upon it, Tucker Gatrell replied cryptically, "Ma'am, if their husbands just knew Joe a little better, you'd hear men crying, too."

By the evening of the first of December, though, the gale had blown itself out; the cold front had dissipated. South Florida was itself again, which is to say that it was a humid, muggy night when Marion Ford returned to Mango for the first time since Joseph's burial. In his old truck, he drove around the curve of the bay, elbow resting on the open window, feeling heat radiate out of the mangroves, taking pleasure in the familiar odors.

At Sally Carmel's house, he slowed—the lights were off, no car in the driveway—and he thought to himself, She must be enjoying Miami.

He hadn't heard from her, not once. And Miami information had no listing for her.

Probably staying in a hotel, enjoying indoor plumbing.

A thought that Ford neither explored nor allowed to linger. The catty cruelty of it didn't match his mood, or the way he felt about Sally.

She's been through a lot. And I know what it's like to try and break away from this place. She'll call when she's ready.

He drove on.

Along the bay road, moon-globe streetlights bloomed citreous yellow, casting their reflections into the water. By their pale light Ford could see that a great change had come over Mango. The fish houses were no longer falling; the stilt shacks were no longer dilapidated. Each had been rebuilt with raw wood; some were already painted white, or pastel blue, or conch shell pink.

There were flower boxes on all the porches.

The only house that looked the same was Tuck's, though there were signs of change there, too. As Ford pulled up the drive, he could see, in the sweep of his truck's headlights, that there were ladders up against the barn—probably putting on a new roof. And the fence near Tuck's yard had been ripped down to make way for a flatbed semi. The truck had been backed into the pasture, and it was now loaded with junk—among it, the superstructure of the boat that had been abandoned there.

Ford sat for a time, studying the boat, finally finding some sense of order, if not peace, by confronting it. In his mind, he replayed what he had said to Angela Walker the night of Joseph's funeral after she surprised him standing by the junkyard:

"Two people were killed when this boat exploded, but the local sheriff's department couldn't figure out how it happened. I was only ten at the time, but I spent the next two years going through it inch by inch. You know what I discovered? In the fuel line someone had replaced the brass shut-off valve with a plastic butterfly plate, then moved it above deck."

Walker had asked him, "Was that a dumb thing to do? I still don't know anything about boats."

Speaking very softly, Ford had said, "For a long time, I thought it was idiotic. But it was actually pretty smart—in theory, at least. Being above deck, the fuel line would be easier to maintain, and the butterfly plate was damn clever. It automatically filtered out sediment. The trouble was, plastic was pretty new to the person who designed it, and he didn't realize that gas would gradually dissolve it, then drain into the bilge by the engine."

"You were only ten?"

"Twelve by the time I narrowed it down to what had happened and who had done it—redesigned the fuel line, I mean. I had to use weezers and a magnifying glass to reassemble the burned parts."

"And no one else figured it out?"

"No one who would admit it, anyway. Right."

Now, when Ford punched the truck lights off, the boat vanished momentarily while his eyes adjusted. He stepped out into the yard and whistled for Gator, only to hear his uncle's voice calling from the beach: "That you, Ervin T.? Get your butt down here and help!"

Without answering, Ford walked down the mound, where he found Tucker and Henry Short bending into Henry's boat, placing jugs on the dock.

When Tuck saw who it was, he stood up quickly, wiping his hands on his jeans. "Gawldamn, Duke, I thought you was Ervin back from New York. Not that I ain't glad to see you, no sir! Just wasn't expectin' you, that's all."

There was something odd about the way the man was behaving. . . . Henry, too, shifting around on the deck, fingering the lone gauze bandage on his face. They seemed uneasy, as if caught doing something they shouldn't be doing.

Ford said, "Tomlinson wanted me to bring you these." From his pocket, he produced a Ziploc bag filled with nubs of bone—the specimens from the DNA lab. "He wants to know if you'll bury them. In the mound with Joseph, when you get time."

Tuck hesitated for a moment, then continued off-loading the jugs. "You know, I'm gettin' to kinda like that hippie. Surprised he didn't tag after you down here. If you want—" Tucker stepped into the boat to get a better lifting angle—"you can drive on home to Sanibel, get him, and we'll have a little party. Tonight, I mean. Give me and Henry time to get cleaned up."

Ford wondered about that for a moment before he said, "No, Tomlinson's busy packing. We're leaving on a trip tomorrow, Central America. A friend of ours is—" Ford started to say a friend was sending a government plane to fly them south, then assigning them a government Jeep to drive them anywhere they wanted; two weeks of jungle and beach and cold beer, trading stories with Rith Nicholes, on the Caribbean, while Ford's new sea mobiles grew in Dinkin's Bay. Instead, Ford finished, "A friend of ours down there is expecting us."

"Just you and the hippie?"

Yes, although there probably could have been a third in their

party. At the Florida Department of Criminal Law, agents r
ceived special leave as a reward for promotion. Angela Walker ha
called and, after telling him the good news, added, "I've alway
wanted to see Central America." An inducement that Ford ha
gently deflected by promising to take her skiing when he returne

Now Ford said, "Yep, just Tomlinson and me," as he picked u
one of the jugs and popped the lid. Then he said, "Water? Why a
you and Henry boating in water?"

He watched Tuck turn to Henry, saw Henry look down at th
deck again. Tuck said, "Well . . . you remember that Bambridg
fellow? The professor guy on TV? He wants to write a book abo
me. Well, actually, he wants to write it 'bout Henry, he ju
doesn't know it'll end up bein' about me. That's what we w
doin' out on Henry's island. Huh, Henry?"

Henry Short said gruffly, "You're the one with all the word
Tucker."

Tuck said, "See? That's what we was doin'. Makin' notes f
this guy Bambridge."

Ford smiled. What was going on here? "I was asking about th
water, why you're going to all the trouble of—"

But before he could finish, the sound of a woman's voice inte
rupted him; a nice Spanish voice speaking broken English, getti
closer and closer as her silhouette moved toward them on t
dock. "Tucker? Oh, Tucker? The dinner, I have it ready like y
say. The Chino food, not from a box."

The woman stood illuminated by a streetlight now: a pret
woman with olive skin, blue-black hair and young brown ey
Her eyes moved shyly from Tuck to Henry, then back to Tu
while Ford looked on, amused, at first, but then with a dawni
fascination—his mind scanning through remnants of all the c
stories his uncle had told him about Cuba—as he watched t
woman reach to brush hair from her face, her smooth ha
marked by the tattoo of a small blue sea horse. . . .